PATTERN of VIOLENCE
C. HYYTINEN

For Jan
You are a sweetheart.
Thanks for your help
during our salon.
C. Hyyt—
Bouchercon,
2006

Echelon Press

PATTERN of VIOLENCE

A novel by

C. HYYTINEN

Echelon Edge

Echelon Press

Crowley, Texas

Echelon Press
P.O. Box 1084
Crowley, TX 76036

Echelon Edge
First paperback printing: October 2003

Trade paperback ISBN 1-59080-278-0

www.echelonpress.com

DEDICATION

A special 'thanks' to all those who've helped me reach this plateau--Clay and the boys (Nick and Troy), my family, friends, and K.L.

PROLOGUE

There'd be Hell to pay when he got home tonight, and she was terrified. Her husband had turned violent more than once in the past week, consumed with a rage no one could possibly understand. She'd discovered there was no match against his brutal strength, fueled by drugs.

After calling the construction site, she found out he'd been fired late in the afternoon.

It was 8:15. He should have been home hours ago.

The young woman laid the baby down, kissing the child on top of her soft, downy head, then walked into the tiny kitchen to brew a pot of tea—more to keep busy than actually drink it.

She was just sitting down at the kitchen table when his old, worn-out pickup rumbled up the gravel drive.

The man stumbled through the back door, malice in every step, his hair damp with sweat and dirt; his bruised face streaked with dried blood and grime. The torn sleeve of his work shirt and bloodied knuckles gave testament to the fact he'd been in a fight.

As he approached, she backed into the far corner of the small kitchen. That was her first mistake—she knew from experience—but couldn't control her fear of him.

He sensed her terror and thrived on it. Closing the distance between them, he grabbed her, crushing her unwilling body to his massive chest and kissed her hard on the mouth.

He smiled at the blood that appeared on her lips.

"Don't...please," she begged.

"Shut up," he hissed, his breath reeking of cigarettes and alcohol.

"You'll wake the baby."

Laughing, he pushed her away, making her stumble and catch her hip on the edge of the counter.

Tears sprang to her eyes as she staggered to keep her balance.

"The baby? Not *my* baby, you stupid bitch," he growled, glassy eyed and crazed from the drugs and alcohol. "I knew from the minute that little bastard was born she wasn't mine. And I'm glad. Do you hear? *Glad*! I hate her as much as I hate her slut of a mother. Why do you think I do this?" He thrust his arm in her face.

She gazed at the needle tracks trailing up his arm and shuddered with disgust as well as fear. The broken veins showed an angry red against flesh bruised from the drugs he injected daily.

"'Cause I hate your fuckin' guts, *both* of you," he screamed, spraying her with spittle. He drew back his hand and swung, connecting with her jaw, sending her crashing against the kitchen wall.

Advancing toward her crumpled body, he pulled out the hunting knife strapped to his belt, promising over and over in his own crazy, whispered litany, to teach her a lesson she'd never forget.

From the other side of the room came the voice of a small child, timid and frightened. "Mommy? Daddy?" As the little girl looked at her mother lying on the floor, blood trickling down one side of her mouth, then at her father, knife in hand and murder in his eyes, she began to wail. Running to her father, she pummeled his leg with her tiny fists, crying. "Stop, stop! Mommy hurts!"

The man turned on the child, ready to kill. He raised the knife, hatred for them both burning in his insane eyes.

The woman looked up. Getting to her knees and shaking her head to clear it, she *knew* her child was in grave danger. Struggling to her feet, she lost her balance, but soon recovered, scanning the kitchen for a weapon of some kind. Grabbing the teakettle from atop the stove, she lurched toward the man holding her child. With all the strength left in her battered body, she swung the kettle in a high arc, landing it on his head with a loud *thwack*.

He fell backward, banging his head on the kitchen table as his immense frame crashed to the floor—then lay still.

"He must be dead," she muttered, cradling the sobbing child in her arms. Kneeling by her husband—a man she no longer knew at all—and placing her hand to his mouth, she felt the warmth of his breath against her palm.

He was still alive.

"Come on, honey. We have to hurry," she whispered. Clutching the child to her bosom, she ran out the back door to the old pickup truck that would get them to a safe haven.

"Oh, no. Damn!" The keys to the truck were in the kitchen, hanging on a nail above the sink.

Setting the child in the pickup, she was prepared to go back inside when she glimpsed the sparkle of something shiny reflecting in the sinking, golden summer sun. Miraculously, the keys dangled from the ignition. "Thank you, God," she muttered to the heavens. Kissing the child's tear-streaked face, she locked the door and climbed in the driver's side.

Never again would she come back here. She should have fled with her baby long ago, but feared it would have been their death if she did. Now, time was running out, and he'd almost killed them anyway—and still would when he regained consciousness.

Turning the key, her stomach lurched at the sound of the engine turning over and over again. "Please, God. Please," she chanted, glancing furtively at the back door, expecting her husband to come stumbling out at any minute with the shotgun that lay under their bed. She cursed herself for not remembering to grab it before leaving.

Taking a deep breath and holding it, she tried again. Still nothing but the incessant cranking.

"Damn! Maybe it's flooded," she told herself, looking at her beautiful little girl who was on the verge of sleep, despite all the anxiety her mother struggled with. Pressing the gas pedal all the way to the floor, she said a silent prayer and tried once more.

The old truck roared to life, black smoke billowing out the rear. Then it coughed, sputtered, and almost died.

Gunning the motor to keep it running, she slammed the pickup into gear and tore out of the driveway, gravel flying in all directions, never looking back.

They would stay with her brother, Carlos, in Chicago—a place she'd called home not so long ago. They would be safe there—for a while anyway. With pure determination, she sped down the endless black highway, homeward bound.

She'd been with her brother one week when she received the news from the police—her husband had been killed in a car crash. He'd hit a tree while driving on a country road late at night, going in excess of eighty miles per hour. The impact caused the gas tank to explode. A farmer plowing his fields discovered the charred remains of both car and driver the following morning.

1

A shrill, insistent ringing interrupted Maria's deep, dreamless sleep. She reached for the alarm clock, pushing the snooze button for an extra fifteen minutes of sleep, but the ringing continued. Realizing it must be the telephone, she groped with one hand, fumbling for the phone and almost knocking it to the floor. "Damn. Sanchez," she whispered in a sleep-induced croak. Her eyes snapped open and every muscle in her body tightened as she carefully listened to the facts concerning the most recent victim.

She hung up the phone and laid her head back on the pillow, closing her eyes. "Oh, God. Not another one," she whispered to no one in the darkness. "When is this nightmare going to end?"

Detective Maria Sanchez looked at the clock on her bedside table. 3:25 AM. Two teenagers going for a late night swim in the river had discovered the body at approximately 3:10 AM. She'd just gotten off the phone with the chief.

After starting the coffee maker, she took a quick hot shower, feeling some of the tension leave her tired, aching muscles. With only three hours of sleep, she felt surprisingly wide-awake, even though looking in the mirror, her blood-shot eyes betrayed her.

Applying minimal makeup and running a comb through her wet hair, she dressed quickly and poured a large thermos mug of coffee for the road.

Only the light of an occasional street lamp held back the darkness of the ghost-like streets.

The riverbank glowed in bright artificial light as technicians meticulously processed the crime scene.

"We ready to bag her?" the medical examiner inquired.

"Yeah, go ahead." Maria crouched next to the victim, watching as they untied the naked body of the young girl from the raft so the body bag could be slipped over her.

The victim's pale skin glistened a sickly green in the unnatural light, and her dark eyes stared empty at the starry night sky.

"Same as the others, right," Maria stated more than asked, feeling her heart sink at the sadness.

"Exactly," the M.E. said. "The River Rat strikes again. Look at this." He pointed to a necklace of dark bruises around the girl's throat. "Windpipe's crushed." Closing the bag, he added, "She's missing her right thumb, too." He stood up, removing the plastic gloves he wore, and smiled winningly. "Maybe you'd care to join me for the autopsy. I do my best work with an audience, especially one as lovely as you."

"Thanks, but no thanks," she said, amazed that he had the audacity to hit on her no matter what the circumstances.

Maria walked to where the two teenagers sat, off to the side of the crime scene. One hung his head between his knees, a puddle of vomit pooling at his feet, while the other was passed out cold.

"Where's the chief?" Maria asked the officer who was one of the first on the scene and keeping an eye on the two boys.

"Here and gone already—in a helluva mood, too," the young cop said.

"Yeah, I'll bet. You might as well take these two home," she said, nodding toward the two kids. "I'll talk to them later when they sober up."

"Yeah, okay. I just hope they don't puke in our squad. My partner will have a fit. And I just might join them," he confessed, glancing uncomfortably at the body bag being loaded onto a gurney for transport to the morgue.

It was 5:30 in the morning when her shoes echoed across the empty corridors of City Hall. She took the elevator to the third floor and walked down to the last door on the right, marked HOMICIDE. The place was deserted and dark except for a single bar of light visible under Chief McCollough's door.

Maria flipped on the overhead florescent lights and sat down at her desk. Pulling the files on the two previous victims from the bottom drawer, she tried to prepare herself for the sick feeling she got in the pit of her stomach every time she went through them.

Each file held two photographs. The first picture was given to Missing Persons at the time of disappearance, and the second photograph was taken at the crime scene when the body was discovered. To look at the difference between the two pictures—one of a smiling, happy child, and the other depicting the abuse of this madman—made her bile rise.

Maria studied the files again, looking for something, anything she might have missed. She reviewed what little information she'd previously entered into the computer:

> *Murders committed approximately two weeks apart.*
>
> *Victims: male-age 10, female-age 9—both reside in Minneapolis.*

*Pornographic video on male victim
discovered on West Coast (in FBI custody).*

*Bodies tied to rafts, found in Mississippi
River (Hennepin County).*

*Cause of death: Strangulation—both victims
beaten/raped repeatedly prior to death.*

*Two different seminal fluids found in
female—due to mixture of the two, semen
analysis inconclusive. No seminal fluids found
in male, though sodomy did occur.*

*Both victims sustained lacerations,
contusions on abdomen/upper torso, and one
or more fingers severed.*

*Internal bleeding and organ damage noted on
autopsy reports—attached.*

"These poor innocent kids," Maria said, running her hands through her short, dark hair and letting out a heavy sigh. "Now there's one more to add to the list." In the past six weeks this maniac had wasted three young lives. She went through the autopsy and crime lab reports several more times, but there just wasn't anything useful. No hair fibers other than the victims' were found. No skin under the fingernails. No distinguishable fingerprints were detected on the makeshift rafts either. All of which was undoubtedly due to the victims being immersed in river water for several hours before discovery. Imprint evidence was non-existent—recent summer storms and the high humidity had made the riverbanks a virtual quagmire.

The FBI initially became involved when a pornographic video containing footage of the first victim surfaced on the West Coast more than a month ago, before the case was even categorized as a serial murder. The video was one of many discovered by an undercover agent who'd infiltrated the underground. It revealed nothing of the assailants, but focused primarily on the boy, his fear and pain indescribable. Since then, the Behavioral Science Unit had created a psychological profile on the killer by studying the autopsy reports and pictures from the crime scene, which were faxed to them as soon as the homicide department received them. They'd cross-referenced databases nationwide, searching for similar crimes and offenders.

The Bureau of Criminal Apprehension was working closely with the Minneapolis Police Department as well. Agents from the BCA were in top form, following leads from the moment of abduction to the untimely demise of the young victims.

But they still had nothing substantial—no concrete evidence that would help them catch the killer.

Maria was still going through the files and mumbling to herself when Joe Morgan sauntered in around 6:30, looking as disheveled as usual.

He took one look at her and stopped in his tracks. "What the—"

"I was going to call, but knew you needed your sleep." He'd gone home sick yesterday with a bad case of the stomach flu—it was busy making its rounds through the entire department. Joe was the fifth this week to be disabled by it, and with only eighteen detectives in Homicide, the shortage was sorely felt.

"Another body was found this morning," Maria informed her partner. "This makes three. Damnit, Joe...*three!*"

"Son of a bitch!" Joe shook his shaggy gray head. "Same M.O.?"

Maria nodded. "Remember the missing-persons report

that came in on the eight-year-old girl about a week ago?"

"Cheryl Roe?" Joe recalled all too well the picture of the dark-eyed little girl the department had been searching for night and day.

"Yeah. Her parents were down to the morgue a couple of hours ago to ID the body. We'll have to wait until the autopsy and lab work is done before we have all the details. Her body was tied to a raft, floating in the Mississippi. Sound familiar?"

Joe sat his huge 6'4" frame down with a thud on the chair by her desk. "Yeah, too familiar. That's his pattern, all right, goddamn River Rat. Have you talked to the chief yet?"

"No, not since around 3:00 AM when he interrupted my beauty sleep. He's been behind locked doors, no doubt contending with the mayor who is mad as hell about the press coverage this latest victim is going to bring in." Maria looked at her watch. "The M.E. should be finishing up on that autopsy, probably within the hour."

The autopsy was being performed at Hennepin County Medical Center. After tissue samples were taken and analyzed, and the lab work was completed, the M.E. would then compile the data for the report. The latter part was done in the privacy of his office, which took up half a wing in the lower level of HCMC.

"I'll cruise over to the crime lab first, then catch the medical examiner on the way back. That way I won't have to wait around," she said, taking a gulp of her cold coffee and grimacing.

Joe laughed, knowing the morgue wasn't one of Maria's favorite places, but for reasons other than the obvious. It wasn't so much the dead bodies that bothered her as it was their keeper, the good doctor.

"By the way, how are you feeling?" Maria asked,

concerned.

"Better. I managed to keep down my breakfast, anyway."

"Good. You sure looked terrible yesterday. I was surprised you made it till afternoon."

"You and me both."

"I thought you could go comb the banks where we found the victim's body this morning, if you think you're up to it. Forensic technicians have already searched the riverbanks, but it was dark, and maybe they missed something. They'll be back out there again, now that it's daylight, and one of us should be there to call the shots and keep things running smoothly."

"Sure thing, kid," Joe said with a wink.

"I'll join you when I get done."

Some men might resent taking orders from a woman, especially one as young and beautiful as Maria, but Joe and everyone in the department knew she was one tough cop. She'd proven herself competent many times over the years. First as a rookie street cop, and then as one of the best homicide detectives in the Minneapolis area, receiving commendations for her exceptional work. She had the reputation of knowing when and how to fight dirty if necessary, and had moved up the ladder quickly.

Then there was a time several years ago when Joe didn't think he could make it through another day—after his wife, Laura, died of cancer. If it hadn't been for Maria taking care of him and helping him get through his loss, it surely would have been the end of his career as a cop. So, Maria was his friend as well as partner. And he loved that kid of hers like his own.

Maria had joined the force about five years ago. Back then he was the veteran and she the rookie. She learned quickly and after about a year of working side by side, they became known as the 'Dynamic Duo'. A couple of years ago they started spending time together outside of work and soon became close friends.

Joe supposed that was when he started falling in love with Maria Sanchez and around that same time grew close to Theresa, Maria's daughter. She needed a father figure in her life, and Joe was more than happy to be that role model. Tess was a miniature version of her mother with her rich chocolate-brown hair and smooth olive skin, and the same enormous dark eyes as Maria. She already had the same tall, lanky build, too.

As if reading his thoughts Maria said, "God, I miss Tess. I can't believe she's only been at summer camp for two days. It feels more like two weeks."

"Only natural," Joe said, "considering this is her first time away from home. When is she due back?"

"August twenty-third—eight more days. Then it's back to school already, a little more than a week after she's home. Oh, well, looks like I'll be swamped, both day and night, working on this case, anyway."

The chief buzzed Maria's intercom, requesting to see them promptly in his office.

"First things first," Maria muttered to Joe. "I guess the crime lab and M.E. will have to wait." She grabbed a notepad and pencil, and with Joe following close behind, knocked twice on Chief McCollough's door and entered.

Chief Frank McCollough was a large, ruddy-faced Irishman with a quick temper and a good sense of humor when he had a few beers in him. His down-home phrases and readiness to say the first thing that came to mind rubbed some people the wrong way, but Maria had learned from experience that he was a good man with a good heart—it was only his mouth that needed a makeover.

He looked mad as hell now, his face red and sweating, his eyeballs close to bursting from their sockets. He resembled an angry bull, ready to charge at the least provocation.

Needless to say, he was stone cold sober.

Purple veins stood out in cords on his thick neck as he bellowed, "We have thirty days to get this low-life, sleazy son of a bitch. And if *we* can't do it, the honorable mayor himself is sending in a special investigations team to take over and kick our butts outta here! We'll look like a bunch of goddamn college kids with our fingers up our asses. As it stands now, we already have the Feds, not to mention the BCA working with us. If you ask me, too many cooks in the goddamn kitchen already. We'll be lucky if *we* aren't the ones tossed to the wolves—the proverbial sacrificial lamb."

He leaned back in his swivel chair, his gut a majestic mountain, and blew air out of puffed cheeks. After deflating himself, he appeared somewhat calmer. Then looking at Maria through hooded lids, he said with a slight smile, "Now, I know you can do it, but the big question is can you do it in thirty days? Ten extra officers have been put out on the streets in Minneapolis and additional officers will be patrolling the surrounding Hennepin County area. I've been informed that the city of St. Paul is putting out extra officers as well." He paused. "I need you both to focus all your efforts on this case and nothing else. I've already reassigned your other cases to Detectives Liebert and Mackelroy. The same goes for anything else that comes in and doesn't have anything to do with this case. We gotta get this creep. *Now! Today! Yesterday! Top priority!*" The chief leaned forward in his seat.

"This is all making the mayor very uptight. Our kids are being slaughtered like hogs at the market and the whole fuckin' city is in a panic. Not too good for re-election. I'm on your side, but when the mayor pulls my strings, I gotta dance to his tune. Tomorrow morning at 9:00 AM, the mayor's office is holding a press conference at the Government Center. Plan on being there and looking your best. If you two do your job, we'll have some kind of lead by then."

Maria nodded.

"Visit the dead girl's parents. They've already been down to the morgue to ID the body. The mother got so hysterical she had to be sedated, but see if you can glean any useful information from them. The two teenagers who found the victim's body were informed last night that you'd be stopping by to chat with them sometime this morning as well."

"I doubt if they'll remember. They were pretty out of it," Maria said.

"Yeah, I know. I was there. Here's their address," he grumbled, sliding a piece of paper to Maria.

As they got up to leave, the chief shouted, "Hey!"

They both turned, prepared to be screamed at some more.

"Remember, you two are my best and we're all counting on you," he softly added.

Maria decided to leave her car parked at City Hall and took a squad car over to see the teenagers. It was a seedy dump of an apartment in the run-down section of the city, where a lot of violence and gang-related crimes took place in the early morning hours. It wasn't very long ago she'd walked this beat as a street cop. She climbed the rickety, broken-down stairs that led to their apartment. On the second floor landing, she almost tripped over a bum sleeping in the corner, a bottle of booze tucked protectively under one arm.

She knocked on apartment 210 and waited impatiently, hearing movement on the other side of the door. She was just lifting her hand to give the door another hard rap when it flew open. A dirty looking kid, about seventeen, with long, black greasy hair—the one who'd been out cold last night—opened the door.

"Detective Sanchez with Homicide," Maria said flashing her badge. "I'd like to ask you and your friend a few questions."

"Sure, lady," he said, looking her up and down, his eyes coming to rest on her Glock nine-millimeter. "Come on in."

"Freddie!" he shouted. "We got company!"

Maria could tell they had been smoking pot recently. The dope smoke still hung thick in the air. The place stunk like cat piss or strong BO, she wasn't sure which.

The other kid appeared in the bedroom doorway. He looked considerably cleaner, and slightly older than the first; his red hair cut short.

"Hope you're feeling better this morning," Maria said, smiling.

"Uh, yeah, sure," he said nervously, looking around the apartment, wondering where he left his bag of dope...

"What time was it when you boys first discovered the body floating in the river?" Maria pulled a notebook out of her handbag and flipped it open.

The red-haired kid, Freddie, stuffed his hands in his pockets and looked thoughtfully at the ceiling. "I guess it was around 3:00 AM, 3:15 maybe. We already talked to the cops last night."

"Well, last night you were very intoxicated. I need to make sure we have all the facts straight. Did you see anyone walking along the river, or on the nearby streets?"

The kids looked at each other and shook their heads.

"Any cars that looked like they didn't belong there?

Parked along the road, near the river, maybe?"

"Nope, we were the only ones out there. Just comin' home from a party and thought we'd take a little dip to cool off, ya know? Then we see this gross lookin' stiff, bobbin' up and down, tied to some funky little boat. Man, what a trip," the dark-haired, greasy kid remarked.

Maria looked at Freddie for confirmation.

"That's right, man. Not a soul out but us fuckin' night owls," he said, a pot-induced half-hysterical laugh escaping. He covered his mouth with both hands in an attempt to shut himself up.

"Okay," Maria said, putting her notepad away, realizing these two had told her all they were going to. "We may need to talk to you again, so don't leave town, okay?"

"We ain't goin' nowhere," the greasy kid said, and opened the door for her.

Once outside, she breathed deeply, relishing the fresh air after smelling the stink in the apartment.

Although glad to be out of there, she was apprehensive about her next visit. "This one won't be as easy," Maria said aloud, pulling the squad car out into the street.

Maria pulled up to the house and compared the address she had for the dead girl with the house number above the front door. This was where the grieving parents of Cheryl Roe resided.

It was a beautiful, two-story, Victorian-style home, overlooking Lake Harriet. Maria felt a sadness in her heart that the little girl who'd once laughed and played here, now lay in the morgue.

She rang the doorbell, and a man in his mid-thirties, dressed in a Brooks Brother's suit and tie, opened the door.

She showed her gold shield. "Detective Sanchez."

"Yes, come in. They told us someone would be coming over," he softly replied. "I'm afraid my wife is heavily sedated and finally asleep. I'd rather not disturb her."

"That's fine. If you could just answer a few questions for me, I won't take much of your time. I'm very sorry about your daughter. I know how difficult this must be for you." She followed him through the lavishly decorated living room.

They sat at the dining table as Maria listed off the facts she had about the girl's disappearance to once again make sure they were correct. Cheryl Roe had been playing outside in the backyard all morning. But when her mother called her in for lunch, she was nowhere to be found. There was no sign of a struggle.

When Mr. and Mrs. Roe reported her missing there wasn't the usual twenty-four hour waiting period, because every cop in the Twin Cities was alerted to the potential danger of waiting. With a child-murderer on the loose, virtually all street cops and civilians alike had been searching in vain for the last several days—until this morning when her body was discovered.

"I know from the police report that you've already answered these questions, but maybe you remember something new. Did you see any strange cars, or people, hanging around your neighborhood on the day, or days preceding your daughter's disappearance?"

He thought for a moment before answering. "I'm sorry, no. Nothing out of the ordinary. Nothing at all."

"Well, if you think of anything, even if it seems insignificant to you, please contact us," Maria said, handing him her card. "You have our deepest sympathy Mr. Roe. If there's anything you need—anything at all—please don't hesitate to call. We're here to help."

He looked at the card with a dazed, blank expression and nodded.

Maria thanked him and told him she could find her own way out. As she walked through the living room to the front door, she glanced back and saw Mr. Roe staring out the kitchen window at the swing-set in the backyard. The two swings gently moved back and forth in the summer breeze, while tears ran down his haggard face.

She quickly walked to her car, trying to get the man's haunted expression out of her mind.

By the time she arrived at the Bureau of Criminal Apprehension in St. Paul, it was 12:40. It had taken her forty-five minutes to get through downtown traffic because of the noon-hour rush. After picking up the file and conferring with the lab technicians, she drove back to Minneapolis, dodging traffic the best she could.

Half an hour later, she double-parked in front of the Hennepin County Medical Center, a huge, glass and brick building that spanned several city blocks.

The medical examiner's office was on the lower level. His secretary informed Maria he'd left for lunch about ten minutes ago, but had finished the autopsy on the Roe girl. She handed Maria the folder containing the report and told her to go ahead and take it with her.

"Dr. Lang said he'd be over at City Hall around 3:30 this afternoon if you need to talk to him about those findings," she said, nodding toward the manila folder tucked under Maria's arm.

Maria thanked her and left, impatient to read the latest information.

The air hung thick with humidity, and when she reached her car, she rolled down the windows, both front and back. She settled back with a can of Coke, warm from sitting in the hot car, and opened the autopsy report folder.

The autopsy report read almost identical to the other two victims. The liver temperature indicated the victim had died around 12:30 AM—roughly two to three hours before being discovered.

However, as she went over the information from the crime lab, she found something that piqued her interest. Traces of an artificial fiber had been found between the boards of the raft this time. According to the lab, they appeared to be a type of synthetic blue carpet fiber.

Maria put all the papers in order and stuck them into the folder, then drove over to where Joe was conducting the search on the riverbank.

Seeing the police barricade from the road along the west bank of the Mississippi River, she pulled in between Joe's old Chevy and the white van from the BCA.

As she climbed down the muddy riverbank, she spotted two forensic technicians combing the area about a half-mile down from where she stood.

She turned and looked in the other direction. Maria spotted Joe, stooped over a hollow log, peering in one end in the midst of heavy brush. She made her way over to him, mud squishing around her shoes, trying to suck them off her feet.

"Find anything?" she called from about ten feet behind him.

He jumped, then flushed a deep red upon seeing Maria approach. "Yeah, I think so."

Joe made his way out of the thick brush, into the little clearing where Maria stood. He held up a baggie, along with a piece of rubber tubing wrapped around a syringe. "Looks like someone was shooting a little dope down here. If it's the killer—and we're damn lucky—maybe we'll get a clean set of prints off this stuff," he said, pulling a folded up paper bag out of his back pocket and opening it. He deposited the tubing, syringe, and small baggie inside, then pulled off the latex gloves he was wearing and stuffed them into his front trouser pocket.

Joe produced a pack of cigarettes, offering one to Maria, and then lit both, inhaling deeply.

Maria had been trying to quit, but the stress and unease of this latest case foiled her half-hearted attempt.

They sat on a rock looking out over the river, and Maria told Joe about the synthetic carpet fibers. This, along with the drug paraphernalia just found were the first and only clues they had. With a little luck, prints would show up on the latter.

Maria looked at her watch. "It's already quarter to three. We'd better get back to City Hall. Dr. Lang is supposed to come by around 3:30. Why don't you ride back with me? That way you can look at the autopsy and lab reports. Just have one of them drive your car back," she said, nodding toward the two technicians helping search.

"Yeah, okay. They'll be happy to have something to work with." Joe laughed, holding up the bag containing the evidence. "They might even give it a wash and wax. I'll meet you at the top," he said, getting up and jogging over to the technicians, looking spry and handsome—his well muscled body resembling that of a much younger man—for his forty-two years of age.

Driving back to City Hall, they remained silent. Maria thinking about her daughter and wondering how she was doing, while Joe sat engrossed in the reports from the medical examiner and crime lab.

* * *

Dr. Kenneth Lang was waiting for them when they returned. He was a tall, handsome, Nordic-looking man who loved himself much more than anyone else ever would. With his blond hair and blue eyes—not to mention his everlasting suntan—he was known as quite the ladies' man.

Maria considered him a fine M.E., but that was as far as her interest went. She knew him to be a womanizer, and also knew he'd had more than a couple of female lab assistants fired for refusing his advances over the last few years.

After discussing the findings from the Roe girl's autopsy, they all filed into Chief McCollough's office to go over the results.

"I don't even want to see you people unless you've got good news for me! Find anything?" The chief frowned, looking at Dr. Lang, his dislike for the man apparent on his face.

Maria placed the folder containing the reports on his desk, then told him about the possible evidence Joe found in the hollow log along the riverbank.

He grunted his acknowledgment without even looking up. When he finished reading the autopsy and crime lab reports, he gave them his attention. "We'll only give the media the information we have on the drug paraphernalia. I want to hold off telling them anything about these fibers until we know more, understand?"

"Yes, sir," they said in unison.

"Lang, you can say for sure that all three kids bought it from the same lunatic, right?"

"Yes, I think that's obvious, isn't it?" the doctor replied.

Chief McCollough ignored his sarcasm and continued. "Sanchez, Morgan, check with the lab on your way home. See if those boys had any luck lifting those prints.

"I want you all to be fresh and alert tomorrow morning for the press conference. You look like death warmed over," he said, nodding at Maria, noticing for the first time the dark circles under her eyes.

"Why, thank you, sir," Maria replied. "I could say the same about you."

The chief smiled. "That's all for now. I'll see you all in the morning. Close the door on your way out."

While Maria got the files out of her desk that Liebert and Mackelroy would need, she noticed Lang out of the corner of her eye. He was standing off to one side of Joe's desk, watching her intently. She chose to ignore him, hoping he'd fade away into the woodwork.

Joe offered to stop by the lab since the BCA was on his way home.

Maria uttered a tired, "Thanks" and left, exhausted from the long day and previous sleepless night. She decided to take the stairs down the three flights, because at 5:00 PM the elevators would be jammed with tired employees trying to beat the traffic rush home. She was halfway down the stairs, between second and first floor when she heard the stairwell door bang shut.

Thinking about the day's events, Maria was startled when Dr. Lang grabbed her elbow.

"Hello, Maria," he said, exuding false charm. "You ran away before I could ask for your gracious company at dinner this evening."

"Don't ever do that again," she hissed, putting her hand to her pounding chest. "You shouldn't sneak up on people." She felt foolish at being startled so easily.

Sensing her vulnerability, he leaned close, his minty breath warm on her cheek. "Well?"

"Listen, I'm really beat. The only thing I want to do is go home, soak in a hot tub, and climb into bed," she replied, pulling her arm free from his grasp and meeting his gaze. She realized that her choice of words was not wise by the shifty look in his eyes.

"My, now that conjures up a lovely image—you soaking in a hot tub. Maybe you'd like some company?" he asked, pressing her up against the cold cement wall of the stairwell.

She could feel his male hardness and was appalled, along with being somewhat frightened. "You know me better than that, Doctor. As I've told you before, *no*," she said, shoving him backward—hard enough to make him stumble—then briskly walking down the steps.

Lang kept pace with her. "We'd be great together, Maria. Why don't you give us a chance? I guarantee I'd make you happy." He smiled seductively. "I've never had any complaints."

She stopped her rapid descent and glared at him. "Your inflated ego wouldn't know a complaint if it slapped you across the face, which is exactly what I'm going to do if you don't leave me the hell alone. I have no interest in you and *never* will. Got it?"

He examined her with cool blue eyes, a smug smile dancing on his too full lips.

Only an inch or two shorter than the doctor, she leaned close, as if to kiss him. "Oh, one more thing," she whispered.

He looked at her expectantly, thinking she was only playing hard to get, like so many others he'd conquered in the past.

"Next time you get the urge to hit on me? Go fuck yourself, you egotistical, self-centered prick, and save us both a lot of trouble!" She left him with his mouth hanging open as she ran out into the steamy heat of the parking lot.

2

Maria was still shaken from her confrontation with Lang when she got home. She'd just unlocked the door when the phone started ringing.

"Hello," she answered, short of breath.

"Hi, it's me, Joe." I just wanted to make sure you made it home okay. I saw that asshole, Lang, hanging around and—"

"I'm fine, Joe, but you're right. He accosted me in the stairwell—of City Hall no less," she said with a tired laugh.

"That prick. I don't know why he keeps pestering you when you've made it crystal clear how you feel about him. Are you sure you're okay?"

"Yes, I'm sure, but thanks for worrying. Did the lab turn up anything, yet?" she asked, wanting to change the subject.

"They're still working on it. Connely told me to leave him the fuck alone so he could do his damn job. Guy's got an attitude problem."

"Well, that's Connely for ya. Did you tell him the chief was the voice behind your actions?"

"Yeah, he didn't want to hear it."

"Nothing new there. Hey, what are you doing for dinner tonight?" She knew he'd just open a can of soup or a TV dinner, like he did every night, and she worried about him, too, living alone with no one to look after him.

"Not a thing, just gonna open a can of soup or something.

Nothing special."

Maria laughed. "Well, how about coming over around 7:30 and I'll make some of my world-famous spaghetti?"

"That sounds great; if you're sure you're up to it. I know how tired you must be."

"Just be here at 7:30 and bring the wine. I'll supply the rest."

Maria filled the bathtub to the top and slowly lowered her tired, aching body into the hot, steamy water. She sipped a glass of red wine and tried to relax, closing her eyes.

Just recently, she realized the reason she liked Joe's company so much—she felt safe with him. She never had to worry about Joe making a pass at her. He was her closest and dearest friend. She felt a tug at her heart when she thought of him—his prematurely gray hair and those piercing blue eyes, his stumble-bumpkin way of always saying what she needed to hear, not to mention his constantly disheveled, messy appearance.

They'd have fun tonight, but it was too bad Tess wasn't here to enjoy it as well. Maria felt a profound emptiness without her daughter. Thank God she'd be home by the end of next week. She was tempted to call the camp, but had promised Tess she wouldn't check up on her; that she'd call *only* in an emergency. Loneliness was not an emergency—at least not yet.

Maria sat up with a start. She must have dozed off, because the bath water was barely warm. She'd been dreaming of Jack, her deceased husband. It seemed so real. She put her hands to her face and found it wet with tears...but *not* from missing him. No, she was glad he was dead. While alive, he'd made her and Theresa's life a living hell with all the drugs and physical abuse. His death was a welcome friend.

She'd left him after Theresa was born, when the abuse became unbearable. But he had tracked them down within hours and promised to kill them both if she ever tried to leave again.

About two years ago, she stopped having the terrifying nightmares. She shuddered, thinking of him, and drained her wine glass. The fight that took place on the day she eventually escaped was their worst ever. Maria knew he would have killed Theresa on that fateful day if she hadn't stopped him at the last moment. She would never forget the look of murderous hate in his eyes.

Joe and her brother, Carlos, were the only two people in the world who knew her true feelings about Jack.

Tess was only two and a half when he died and couldn't remember him at all. Maria hadn't seen the point in telling her the horrible truth when she was younger, in fact, she felt blessed the girl had no recollection.

Jack had vowed to get revenge on Maria for having another man's baby, but it was paranoia from the drugs that was doing all his thinking. He used to threaten to carve his initials in her face, so no other man would want to look at her, let alone sleep with her. He wanted to teach her a lesson she'd never forget, that lesson being, *remember who you belong to.* She had a one-inch scar on her left cheek where he tried to do just that, but their next-door neighbor had intervened just in time and threatened to call the cops. That stopped him—that time.

Maria had never been unfaithful to Jack. Theresa *was* his daughter, but that was something he went to his grave never knowing. He didn't deserve her anyway.

She had a special relationship with Tess. Since there was only the two of them, over the years they'd developed a unique bond, which made them best friends as well as mother and daughter. There was no deeper love in the world than that between mother and child.

Maria thought back to the time when she and Jack were first married. They were happy then—for a little while anyway—until Jack started using. With Jack it was all or nothing. He got into the heavy stuff right away and began dealing within a matter of weeks. Maria couldn't reason with him. She couldn't even talk to him when he was high, and he was *always* high. She realized later how naïve and foolish she'd been to marry a man she barely knew. Maybe if her mother and father had still been alive they could have helped her to see what a terrible mistake she was making. Carlos had tried, but she refused to listen.

Maria now knew that she'd never loved Jack. It was more pity than love. He was abandoned as an infant by his mother and raised in an orphanage. He was sickly as a child, and never felt needed or wanted. The only way to get attention was to be *bad*; therefore, that's what he became very good at. Maria thought she could change him by giving him the love he so desperately needed. She was wrong.

In a strange way she owed a lot to Jack, because if it weren't for him, she wouldn't be a cop, and would never have come to the Twin Cities on her own. They came here when they were first married, so Jack could work in the construction business, which was booming in the Cities at that time.

After Jack died, she sold the little house and bought a condominium on Marquette Avenue. That's when she decided to be a cop. She wanted to make a difference and help those who couldn't help themselves. Maria could relate to the victims of abuse who felt they had nowhere to turn. She remembered feeling the same vulnerability as a young mother in her early twenties.

Now at thirty-one, she'd done what many people didn't believe she could do. Even Carlos thought she was crazy to want to be a cop. He'd begged her to stay in Chicago, but Maria knew she would become too dependent on him if she did. He had his own life to live, and she needed to make a separate life for her daughter, and somehow find her own identity in the process. Carlos feared she would be killed or end up in the hospital the first year on the streets, but Maria had proven him, and all those who'd doubted her, wrong. She was a good cop right from the start and loved her job. Her dedication had paid off. Now she was considered one of the best homicide detectives in the city of Minneapolis. Last year she'd received an award from the mayor stating just that. She had also helped open two new shelters for abused and battered women—one in Minneapolis and one in St. Paul.

But now there was a crazy man running loose—raping and killing children. The media had dubbed him the River Rat, because his victims were always found in the Mississippi. He was one sadistic son of a bitch, but also smart because he'd evaded the police thus far.

Maria *knew* she would get him—felt it in her heart and soul—but they only had thirty days to do it. *One way or another,* she thought to herself, *I'll bring this crazy son of a bitch down. I may die trying, but so help me God, I'll do it!*

Startled by the doorbell, she sat up. "Coming," she yelled, hopping out of the tub, which was now ice-cold, and slipping into her bathrobe.

She looked through the peephole, surprised to see Joe

standing there. "It can't be 7:30," she muttered, opening the door to let him in. "Hi, Joe, I'm afraid I lost track of time. Is it 7:30 already?"

Joe checked his watch. "In fact it's 7:35." He brought the other hand from behind his back and produced a large bottle of white zinfandel and a bouquet of yellow roses, clutched together. "These are for you," he said, clearing his throat and averting his gaze, feeling uncomfortable. *God, she is gorgeous.* He hoped she wouldn't be wearing that robe through dinner. He wouldn't be able to eat. He'd choke on his spaghetti for sure. He could see every curve and contour of her long, slender body. He wanted to kiss her, hold her in his arms and—

"These are lovely." Maria interrupted his thoughts, holding up the roses and inhaling the scent. "Thanks. Why don't you have a seat on the sofa while I put these in water and stick the wine in the fridge," she said, already in the kitchen, hunting for a vase under the sink. "Sorry, I haven't even started dinner yet. I'm afraid I must've fallen asleep in the tub."

"I've been thinking," Joe said from the kitchen doorway, watching her arrange the flowers in a vase. "I'm really in the mood for pizza—large, with everything on it! How does that sound?"

Maria looked at him, a smile spreading across her face. "But I invited you over for a home-cooked meal. I would feel terribly guilty."

"How about a rain-check on the world-famous spaghetti? Like I said, I'm really in the mood for pizza," he persisted, picking up the phone and dialing.

Maria shrugged her narrow shoulders and laughed. "Okay, pizza it is. And we'll have that spaghetti dinner when Tess comes home next week."

"Wonderful," he said with a wink, then proceeded to give the girl his order for a large pizza with everything on it while Maria went into the bedroom to change into something less comfortable.

"Jeez, I probably gained ten pounds," Maria laughed, leaning back in her chair and patting her stomach.

Joe lifted the empty bottle of wine. "Polished this off, too. Hope we don't feel its after-effects at the press conference tomorrow morning."

"God, I'll be glad when that damn press conference is over," Maria said, standing up to clear away the dirty dishes and pizza carton.

"Yeah, I know what you mean," Joe said, joining Maria. "I'm sure the mayor will let it be known to the public he's given us thirty days to get this creep or else. Hey, kiddo, you look wiped out. I'm gonna go and let you hit the sack."

"Okay, thanks for the pizza, Joe. You're the best. Remember, I owe you a spaghetti dinner. Next Friday for Tess' homecoming?"

"Sounds great! See you tomorrow bright and early." He leaned over and kissed her cheek.

Joe hurried out the door and home to a cold shower.

3

Cameras flashed as Maria walked into the room where the press conference was being held at the Hennepin County Government Center. Reporters from the *Star Tribune* and *Pioneer Press*, as well as from several local television stations, hovered close by.

Maria took her seat between Chief McCollough and Joe, with the mayor and his assistant seated on the other side of the chief and Dr. Lang seated next to Joe. A couple of agents from the BCA were also at the back of the room, away from the cameras and out of the direct line of fire. She spotted the district attorney leaning against the far wall, playing the strong, silent type.

The mayor's assistant stood and cleared her throat. "First, I'd like to thank everyone for attending this conference. These are difficult times for the city of Minneapolis, and I know you all have busy schedules to adhere to." She then read a prepared statement, focusing mainly on the efforts that would be undertaken by the department and all those involved to bring the perpetrator to justice, giving the floor to the media when she finished.

The barrage of questions started.

The first question was from Dianna Herold, Channel Seven—Cities 7 News. "Chief McCollough, any leads on the killer, the so-called River Rat?"

The chief stood, his large frame dwarfing the reporter to the point of being comical. "I'll be more than happy to answer your questions, but first, if I may, I'd like to take this opportunity to address the public."

"By all means, sir. Go ahead."

"Thank you. I would just like to say that the Minneapolis Police Department is doing their best job possible. To reiterate what the mayor's assistant has previously stated, our city is in a crisis situation right now, and we're doing everything we can to remedy that. Extra officers have been put out on the streets, and we are working closely with the FBI and the BCA on this case. We have our two finest, most successful homicide investigators working exclusively on this case, and as you all know, Detectives Sanchez and Morgan have brought forth quick results in the innumerable cases they've worked on in the past.

"Now that I've gotten all that off my chest. In answer to your first question, Ms. Herold, *yes*, we do have one or two leads on the case. Yesterday afternoon, Detective Morgan here discovered some drug paraphernalia down by the river where the latest victim was found. There appears to be a clear set of prints on it, and we'll be working on matching them up to a suspect as soon as we get the final results from the lab."

"You said you had a couple of leads, Chief. What's the other one?"

The chief laughed. "I said one *or* two. For investigative purposes, I'm not at liberty to discuss anything else, but you'll be the first to know when we're ready to release any new information," he said, giving her his most charming smile.

"Dr. Lang, could you tell us your thoughts on this case. Are there many similarities in the victims and the way they were killed?"

Kenneth Lang leaned back in his chair, appearing confident as always. "Yes, indeed. They're all relatively the same age, and all victims were sexually abused and beaten, sustaining lacerations and mutilation by a sharp instrument. The autopsies show that they were abused, literally tortured, over a period of several days before being killed—strangled. Since the victims have been both male and female, gender doesn't seem to be a factor, and as you all know, the victims were discovered in the Mississippi River in Hennepin County." He paused dramatically, looking directly into the camera. "I think the River Rat is someone who could never deal with relationships and therefore looks to children which he can overpower and take control of."

"That sounds like pop psychology to me—better stick to cadavers, Doc," the chief muttered, pissed that Dr. Lang had decided on his own accord to divulge so much information without consulting the department first.

There were a few nervous laughs, and Lang shot the chief a look that said, *Go to hell.*

A dark-haired reporter from Channel Four stood up. "Mayor Johnson, it's been rumored that you've given Chief McCollough and his detectives thirty days to find the killer or you'll send in a special investigations team to take over the case. Is this true?"

"Yes, it certainly is. We can't have our city living on the edge of panic. This has gone on long enough, and I think one month is a sufficient amount of time to bring this child-murderer in and have justice finally served. We owe it to the people of Minneapolis to get results and get them fast."

"Thank you, sir. Detective Sanchez, how do you feel about this? Do *you* think you can find the killer in one month's time?"

"I have confidence in our police department and, yes, I think chances are very good we'll bring the perpetrator in soon. We're a very dedicated group here, and there will be many a sleepless night until the killer is brought to justice," Maria boldly stated.

The press conference lasted several hours, with the news media attacking the police department, insisting *more* had to be done to protect the children of the Twin Cities.

By that time, everyone, especially the chief, was getting irritable. He stood and announced in a booming voice that they *all* had their work cut out for them; therefore they had damn well better get busy instead of sitting on their asses. That little remark was the highlight of the evening news.

Maria and Joe spent the entire afternoon trying to match the fingerprints found on the evidence. It was a long and tedious procedure, because they'd found several sets of prints on the syringe, tubing and small baggie. Comparing the prints to the FBI's VICAP database proved unsuccessful—another perp that fell through the cracks of the system perhaps, or maybe the crimes weren't violent enough to rank with these heinous criminals. They hit pay dirt around 5:30 PM, finding a match in Minnesota's Mentally Disturbed Sex Offenders files.

His name was Lenny Milano and he had an extensive record, including several drug busts and four sexual assaults on small children several years back. He was currently on parole.

Maria went into the chief's office with the latest information.

"Good work, Sanchez. Now what? Bring him in for questioning? There were traces of heroin in that baggie, but we can't prove it was his. Even though his prints are all over the stuff, we can't make the drug charges stick unless it was found on him."

"Yeah, I know. And I don't think we should let him know just yet that we're on to him. If he *is* the killer that would be just enough to scare him into hiding until things cooled off and then he'd start killing again. If not in Minneapolis, somewhere else. No, I think we should put a tail on him and see what happens. For a couple of days at least."

"You're probably right. If we want to catch this son of a bitch, we don't want him to know we suspect him of *anything*. I just don't want him to butcher any more kids."

"Well, we've got his last address. I'll have it checked out, and if he's still there we'll set up surveillance. He won't make a move without us knowing about it first."

Maria left the chief's office, and five minutes later had verified Lenny Milano's current place of residence.

He was in his element now. Soon, night would cover the city, and once darkness was upon him it would be time for the fun to begin. He looked at the little girl lying in a crumpled heap on the floor of his shabby, run-down apartment. She appeared dead, but he knew it was only the dope he'd given her. In about three hours, she would be lively game.

Her parents probably haven't even missed her yet, he mused. It was surprising how easy it was for him to get them. *Didn't their mothers warn them to stay away from strangers?*

He laughed a shrill, uncontrollable cackle, spittle running down his chin, which he wiped off with the back of his hand.

All it took was a puppy. *God, how fucking simple*, he thought, still on the verge of uncontrollable glee. And when the little snots came over to pet it, they were his for keeps, or rather, for as long as they were useful.

He laid out another line to keep his buzz going. Coke mixed great with the crystal meth he mainlined about twenty minutes ago. He was flying high now.

Remembering the intense surge of power coursing through his body after he wasted the last chosen one made him smile. She was a rich little bitch who lived in one of those big, fancy houses on the lake. He couldn't remember which lake. For that matter he couldn't even recall what the little snot looked like. But he *did* remember her screams, and the way she begged him to stop when he pulled out the knife and started cutting into her fresh, pink flesh with the care of a skilled surgeon. And the fear in her eyes—that was what he thrived on—*FEAR*. He was getting an erection just thinking about it.

And to think I'm having this much fun and getting paid for it, too, he thought gleefully. *Money makes the whole fucking world go round.* Thanks to *them*, his creators, he had money for his many needs and his daily habit. Big bucks were paid for his films, and he enjoyed the creativity. Enjoyed it almost as much as he enjoyed killing the chosen ones when their duties were fulfilled. But the key word was *control*. Once he took out the knife, he had to keep reminding himself to use it sparingly. He didn't want them dead too soon. He needed them for his videos, and besides that, he wanted them to suffer first…before he'd give them the privilege of dying.

The killing was for his purpose only. When he felt his hands around their little throats, squeezing the life out of their young bodies and watching the light go out of their eyes, it was the ultimate orgasm for him. It was as if he absorbed their youthful energy at the moment their young lives ceased to exist. Shuddering with pleasure, he thought about what was to come.

His creators never questioned him about the kids. As far as they were concerned, it was his business where he got them and what he did with them afterward.

Standing up, he felt blackness creep into his line of vision. Holding onto the edge of the table, he waited until the darkness lifted, then walked over to the video equipment in the corner of the room. Since this was his livelihood, he had to make sure everything was in working order.

He removed the tarp covering the expensive equipment and lights. They supplied the camera, through their black market of stolen goods. It was similar to those used by TV reporters and could be set up so no one had to operate it—you just focused it on the subjects and it basically ran itself. The results were top-quality, too.

Once he was assured everything would work properly for tonight, he walked into the bathroom to shower and shave.

After undressing, he stood in front of the mirror, admiring his naked self. He was handsome—tall and very muscular, with wavy, coal-black hair and deep-set green eyes.

But even *he* noticed the strangeness in his eyes. That's why he wore dark sunglasses wherever he went, day or night. Because looking into those eyes, and seeing the unleashed madness lurking within, made ordinary people fear for their lives.

4

The surveillance van was set up on First Avenue, across the street from Lenny Milano's apartment.

From the outside, any passerby would think it was some kid's rusty piece of junk. It was an '89 Ford that had been light blue at one time, but now the predominant color was rust. That was from the outside.

On the inside sat two veteran cops with high-tech equipment.

Harris and Peterson had instructions to watch Lenny Milano and not let him out of their sight. Harris held the high-powered binoculars up to his face and let out a long whistle. "Man, he's got a hot number tonight. Take a look at this one, Larry." He handed the binoculars to his partner who took his turn looking at the peep show.

"Jesus, look at them go at it. You'd think they were a couple of goddamn dogs," he said, letting out a bark of laughter.

Maria and Joe parked a block away in her Ford Mustang and walked the short distance to the van.

They knocked twice and went in through the back door. Once inside, their eyes had to adjust to the darkness. The smoky-black window that ran along one side of the van was one-way glass—they could see out, but no one could see in.

Harris and Peterson had been there about forty minutes. As soon as Maria had verified where Milano lived, they'd cruised over to find a spot where they could watch his apartment for the evening. They'd change location tomorrow so they wouldn't look suspicious.

"Anything interesting?" Joe asked.

"Yeah, you could say that," Harris snickered. "See for yourself." Grinning at his partner, he handed the binoculars to Joe.

Joe looked and flushed several shades of red, but kept looking.

Maria grabbed the binoculars, not quite anticipating the scene unfolding before her eyes. "My God," she exclaimed. "They look like a couple of goddamn dogs."

They all burst out laughing.

Handing the binoculars back to Peterson, she said, "Let me know immediately if anything *serious* happens up there. I mean, concerning the case," she added, reading his twinkling eyes.

He gave her a salute, "Yes, ma'am. Sure will."

When Maria got home that evening there was a letter from Tess in the mail. She wrote about winning first place in the canoe race and the excitement of receiving a blue ribbon. She told of horseback riding and hiking on woodsy trails, ending her letter by admitting she was getting more than a little homesick and was glad she'd be home in a week.

Maria kicked off her shoes and collapsed on the sofa, exhausted.

She missed not having her daughter to come home to after a long day's work.

Tess was growing up so fast; she'd be ten years old

already, October first. She'd been asking Maria a lot of questions lately about her father, and Maria hated to lie to the girl. When Tess came back from summer camp, Maria decided she would tell her the truth about Jack. She was old enough to understand a little better now. Maria sighed heavily. How could she expect a little girl to understand what even she couldn't? All she could do was try. Maria prayed that Tess would forgive her for lying to her all these years and understand that she'd only wanted to save her the pain that knowing the truth would surely bring.

Maria closed her tired eyes, intending to rest for just a minute, but before long she was sound asleep.

When she awoke, it was 3:30 in the morning and a fierce thunderstorm raged outside. Rain pounded against the windows with the driving force of nails and the sky flickered with lightning. Thunder rumbled in the distance, native drums sounding a warning.

Maria sat up and stretched, her back stiff from sleeping on the sofa. "Well, no news from Harris and Peterson," she mumbled to herself, walking into the bedroom. Her stomach growled from lack of food, because instead of eating dinner, she'd slept the evening away. This was getting to be a bad habit, she realized, getting undressed. She climbed between the cool sheets and closed her eyes. But sleep eluded her, and even though her body needed the rest, her brain was now wide awake.

She started thinking about the case and would lay odds on it that Milano wasn't the killer. It was more of a gut feeling than anything else, but she'd learned from experience that in this line of work, more often than not, gut feelings were right.

Give it a couple more days, she thought. Through their initial investigation, they had discovered Milano went to work at a downtown deli at 10:00 AM each day. Her mind went back to the blue carpet fibers that were found between the boards of the raft the Roe girl was tied to. She started thinking they should go in and have a look around his apartment after he left for work in the morning, but without a search warrant, they would be breaking and entering.

Even though dawn wouldn't break for several more hours, she called the chief, apologizing excessively for waking him.

"Goddamnit, Sanchez. Couldn't this wait until morning?"

"Sorry, Chief, but no. I've been thinking, maybe we should go have a look around Milano's apartment when he leaves for work; see if we can find—"

"Can't do, Sanchez. You know as well as I do, with Judge Hansen out of town, and both Judge Morris and Capstan out sick with the flu, it'll take the better part of a day to get a warrant—courthouse is like a zoo without a keeper."

"Bullshit," Maria said. "You've got connections."

"No, I don't. My 'connections' as you put it, are temporarily unavailable. I can have your search warrant by late afternoon—no earlier," he said, hanging up.

Maria set the phone back on the bedside table, thinking. Late afternoon—four o'clock, maybe even five, which meant they'd get to Milano's by six, considering it was rush hour. That was just too damn late. By then he might spot the surveillance van, being it was parked outside the deli where he worked all day—not to mention his apartment last night as well.

Not wanting to get Joe in trouble, she decided that if she went against her better judgment and checked out the apartment, she'd do it alone. After all, the warrant was pending, and they needed answers to some very important questions. They needed them *now*.

Maria got out of bed, wide-awake, and started making a huge breakfast for herself: scrambled eggs, bacon, waffles, and fresh squeezed orange juice.

She ate and reread Tess' letter, making a mental note to call her brother. She hoped he was still coming this weekend to keep her company while Tess was away.

The rain let up and the early morning sun tried to peek through the clouds. With luck, the day would show similar improvement and provide some new insight into the case.

Maria called Harris and Peterson on their mobile phone when she got in at 6:30. They were still watching Milano, but had nothing new to report. His lady friend had stayed until about midnight, and after that, all was quiet on the home front. They would keep their post until Milano left for work and then another surveillance team would relieve them and follow him over to the deli.

At 9:45 AM she left City Hall, telling Joe she was going over to the Government Center to do some research, and she'd be back around eleven.

Maria parked her Mustang across the street from Milano's apartment, in virtually the same spot the van had left just fifteen minutes ago.

An old man waited for the bus on the corner, and two teenage girls stepped out of the drugstore with ice cream cones, giggling. No suspicious looking characters appeared to be lurking around Milano's apartment building.

After wrestling with her decision, she got out of the car and locked the door, then strode across the street and into the building.

In the entryway were mailboxes with the tenants' names and apartment numbers on them. Milano lived on the first floor, apartment 101.

Maria opened the battered wooden door that led to the first floor landing and found herself standing outside the door to Lenny Milano's apartment. She knocked. Just as she expected, no answer.

Looking up and down the dark hallway, she jiggled the knob, then, producing a lock pick from her purse, went to work on the cheap door lock. *Milano should have a dead-bolt living in a neighborhood like this*, she thought, suppressing a laugh. Within a matter of seconds, she had the door opened and crept inside. Closing the door behind her, she relocked it.

The place stunk like dirty bodies and stale cigarette smoke. She walked around the small apartment looking into each dingy room, only to find no carpeting in any of them. Old, dirty rugs scattered here and there covered the bare wood floors.

She looked through the closets, hoping to find a clue of some kind—shipping crates, an old roll of blue carpeting maybe—but found nothing unusual.

Entering the bedroom, which she'd had a bird's eye view of last evening, brought back to mind the X-rated scene of Milano and his lady friend. She cringed at the thought of it. The sheets were balled up, crusted with come, and tossed to one corner of the bedroom. She opened the chest of drawers and found a fix kit—several syringes, spare needles, and rubber tubing—along with a couple of crack-smoking pipes, buried under his underwear and shoved way to the back. Checking the rest of the drawers and the old roll-top desk, she found no other incriminating evidence. She ran her hand under the mattress—one of the most obvious places to hide things—but it was clean also.

Then she explored the tiny kitchen, looking though all the

cabinets, then the refrigerator, finding only a 12-pack of beer and a package of stale bologna. The freezer contained a tray of ice cubes and nothing more. Milano didn't have an oven, only an electric hot plate.

Next, she went into the bathroom and searched the medicine cabinet and linen closet. Then on impulse, lifted up the heavy porcelain top to the toilet tank, and that's where she found it. Carefully wrapped in layers of cellophane to stay dry and taped with heavy masking tape to the underside of the porcelain lid, was the heroin.

It wasn't exactly what she was looking for, but it was more than enough to put Milano behind bars for a long, long time. "He's selling this shit. Son of a bitch," Maria whispered, looking at over five hundred thousand dollars' worth of the stuff.

She replaced the tank cover, then retraced her steps to make sure there was no sign of her intrusion, not wanting to alert Milano someone had been here if he came home early.

She went to the door and listened. All was quiet out in the hall. Checking to make sure the door was securely locked behind her, she quickly departed, running across the street to the safety of her car.

Once inside, she let out a sigh of relief and reached into the glove compartment, searching for a pack of cigarettes that had been there since last week. She lit one and inhaled deeply, not minding the stale taste, but feeling guilty at the same time for breaking down and having one.

She cruised slowly back to City Hall, not sure how she should go about explaining the heroin and her questionable entry.

By the time Maria pulled into the parking lot of City Hall, she'd decided to tell Chief McCollough everything—that she'd broken into Milano's apartment, looking for evidence to link him to the murders. For some reason, she felt it imperative she did it *now* instead of waiting for the warrant, while Milano was at work.

As she rode the elevator to third floor, she rehearsed in her head what she would say. The elevator door opened, and she ran smack into the chief who was on his way to lunch.

"Sanchez," he bellowed. "Why the hell don't you look where you're going? Give a guy a goddamn heart attack," he grumbled.

Startled and somewhat flustered, Maria blurted: "I need to talk to you. *Now!* It's important."

"Break in the case?"

"Yes…er, no…maybe…" she stammered.

"Let's go back to my office and discuss this privately," he said, looking sourly at a longhaired juvenile delinquent who was entering the elevator.

Maria followed the chief into his office, and then proceeded to tell him of the morning's events. "So, after Milano left for work this morning, I got into his apartment—"

"What do you mean, *got* into?"

"Well—I broke in—picked his lock," Maria boldly stated.

Chief McCollough looked sternly at Maria from under heavy, furrowed brows, then threw back his head and laughed. "I'll be damned. You got guts, kid, that's for sure. What did you find?"

Astonished by his reaction, Maria sat stupefied, at a momentary loss for words, then recovered and continued to tell him of the heroin she'd found.

She also mentioned the fact that there was no carpeting anywhere in the apartment, reminding him of the fibers found with the last victim—it was, after all, her reason for breaking into his apartment in the first place. "The way I see it is this guy is a real menace to society, and we can put him away for a long time on these drug charges. If he is the River Rat, we got him. If he's not, we got one less junkie on the streets selling his wares."

The chief picked up the telephone, pushed one of the in-house extensions, and a moment later was talking to Narcotics. He gave them Lenny Milano's address and the name of the deli where he worked, then told them where they'd find the goods. "But get a search warrant first—it's already in the works," he barked, giving Maria a look that would melt rock. "And read the asshole his rights. Do everything by the book! We don't want this guy getting off on a technicality."

He hung up the phone and looked long and hard at Maria. "Good work, Sanchez, but I hope you realize you broke departmental rules."

Maria looked at him, ready to be reprimanded.

"Don't worry," he said. "We'll keep this between you and me. *This* time. But don't *ever* let it happen again!"

5

When Narcotics brought Lenny Milano in, he was scared—crap your pants scared. He'd already admitted to the heroin being his, but now the cops were trying to pin this other shit on him.

Lenny sat in the interrogation room, sweating profusely under the intense heat of the lights. Unfortunately, he was *coming down* hard and needed a fix desperately—he'd do just about anything for a fix.

"I already told you, man, I didn't kill no little kids. I'm not into that kind of thing," Lenny said, his voice trembling.

"I don't believe you, Milano. We can place you at the scene of the crime where the last victim's body was found." Maria held up the bag that contained the syringe and rubber tubing with his prints on it. "Look familiar?"

"That could be anyone's, man. It's not like it's got my fuckin' name on it."

"You're wrong, Milano. It might as well have your fuckin' name on it, because it has your fingerprints all over it. We got you, asshole, and we know you like little kids. We got the facts right here." Maria tapped the file lying on the table between them. "Maybe I should refresh your memory," she said, flipping it open. "We have you categorized as a mentally disturbed sex offender, Lenny. Sexual assault on a six-year-old girl in July of 1989." Maria glared at him, then continued reading the file. "Sexual assault on a five-year-old boy in November of 1990. Attempted rape—"

"That was then, man—I've changed. And I never killed 'em. I don't know nothin'. Honest, man." He started shaking all over and put his head in his hands, moaning. He looked up at Maria, eyes bulging out of his face. "I swear to God, man, you gotta believe me. I never killed no little kids. Give me a fuckin' lie detector test, man. I'll prove it to you! I never killed 'em."

"Milano, the way you're starting to shiver and shake, coming down off that smack, a lie detector test wouldn't be reliable, and anyway, they aren't admissible in a court of law," Joe said. "Tell you what, after a few days in Detox maybe we'll *think* about letting you take the test. You have some rough times ahead of you, my man. You're going to be in prison a long, long time, even if you're *not* the killer, and that's a pretty big if."

Milano's blood-shot eyes filled with tears as he shook convulsively from head to toe.

"The way I see it, you must know *something*, due to the fact you're selling drugs to every junkie in the St. Paul/Minneapolis area," Joe continued. "Think about it, Lenny. You have nothing to lose. In fact, it's very possible you could get a lighter sentence on the drug charges if you cooperate. The state prison in Stillwater is no cake-walk."

Joe stood and took his time walking to the door, while Maria gathered up the files and followed suit. At the door, he stopped and looked long and hard at Milano. "Unless of course, we've already found our man. I'd really hate to see you take the rap for something you didn't do, though," Joe said, smiling.

* * *

When Maria and Joe were back at their desks and Milano was locked up tight in the Corrections Facility, she turned to Joe. "Don't ask me how I know—just a gut feeling, I guess—but I don't think he's our man. It's just too damn easy. You're probably right about one thing, though. He knows something, maybe even who the River Rat is, but he's scared shitless. Time is running out, Joe. We gotta get this maniac before he strikes again, if he hasn't already. For all we know he's already got his next victim, even as we speak."

"Well, no new missing-persons reports have come in. We'll get Milano to talk before that happens."

Maria was getting ready to leave for home when Joe pulled his chair up next to her desk. "Sit down, Maria. I think we need to talk."

She knew what was coming by the tone of his voice. He was pissed.

"I heard about your little escapade—breaking into Milano's apartment," he said between clenched teeth. "Next time, why not let your partner in on it? I still can't believe you did it behind my back. I thought we were partners, not to mention friends, for Christ's sake!"

"Joe, I'm sorry. I just didn't want to get you in trouble. I'm lucky I wasn't suspended. I never meant to do anything behind your back, and we *are* friends, good friends—best friends. Don't be mad! I won't ever do it again!"

"Promise?"

"I promise," Maria said, raising her right hand. "So help me, God."

"Okay, I guess I'll forgive you then," he said, cracking a smile.

When Maria got home that evening there was a message

on her answering machine from her brother, Carlos. He said he'd be in the Twin Cities by about noon tomorrow.

She was looking forward to seeing him again. It had been over three months since she last saw him. They were always close growing up, and when their parents died in an automobile accident when Maria was eighteen, they'd became inseparable, until she married. Then, after her trouble with Jack, Carlos became her best friend and protector from all evil.

She often remembered how helpful he'd been when she and Theresa had fled to the safety of his home in Chicago, seven years ago. And when she received the news several days later that Jack had been killed in a car crash, she remembered feeling guilty at the instant relief she felt.

"You foolish girl," Carlos had said. "Can't you see? God is watching out for you and has given you true freedom from that crazy man. Don't ever feel guilty. Feel happy and free, because you and your beautiful baby daughter have your lives and a fresh start. And don't *ever* forget, Maria, he would have killed both of you. He beat you half unconscious and would have killed your child if you hadn't found the strength to stop him."

Maria would never forget the look on his face when she showed up on his doorstep, limping and in bandages, carrying Tess in her arms. She recalled the gratitude and love she felt for him that fateful day. Unshed tears stood in his sparkling, brown eyes, so much like her own, as he carried her into the house. Over time, he'd helped heal her wounds, both physical and emotional.

We'll have long talks, and go for a picnic in the park, like we did when we were kids, Maria thought. But unfortunately, Tess wouldn't be home to see him. She loved Carlos very much, and it might ease the pain when she learned the awful truth about her father.

Maria went into the kitchen to make a grilled cheese sandwich. She didn't realize she was crying until she saw her reflection in the door of the microwave. "God, I'm not meant to be alone," she cried, grabbing a piece of paper towel and getting half the roll by doing so.

That incomplete feeling she tried so hard to ignore, washed over her—the feeling in the pit of her stomach when watching couples together—holding hands, whispering in each other's ear and laughing. She'd had several relationships with men she thought important in her life, but they never lasted more than a few months. She never *really* trusted any of them. Maria pushed these thoughts from her mind, which thankfully she was always able to do. She wasn't one to wallow in self-pity. *Well, maybe for a little while.*

Maria ate her sandwich and made out a grocery list. Listing all the ingredients she would need for a home-cooked spaghetti dinner, she found herself thinking of Joe, wondering what he was doing. She wanted to call, just to talk to him, but knew she wouldn't. Joe was becoming a very important part of her life; more so every day, she realized, and it wasn't their jobs bringing them closer. They'd always had a complete understanding about one another, but lately Maria felt things deep inside that were more than just friendship.

She didn't like feelings she couldn't control.

Maria changed into her jeans and was getting ready to go to the store when the phone rang. She almost dropped the receiver when she heard the news on the other end. It was an officer from Missing Persons, who informed her another child was reported missing about twenty minutes ago. She took down the information about the nine-year-old girl and got the parent's address, then dialed Joe's number.

"Shit!" Then after a pause, Joe added, "Maybe she just lost track of time. She's probably on her way home right now." He let out a long sigh. "Looks like your gut feelings about Milano were dead center. He's not our man. *Damn!* I'll swing by and pick you up in about ten minutes. Let's go have a talk with Milano when we're done. We gotta find out what that slimy, little bastard is holding back!"

"I'll be waiting." Maria set the receiver down. It rang again.

"I take it you heard the news?" the chief growled.

"Yeah, Missing Persons just phoned. Joe is on his way to pick me up. We should arrive at the kid's house in about twenty minutes."

The chief responded with a grunt and hung up.

BCA agents had already been and gone by the time Maria and Joe arrived at the McReedys' house.

As they pulled up on Thirty-First Street, a couple anxiously approached the car. Maria flashed her badge out the passenger window, before stepping out.

"Have you found her? Have you found my baby?" the woman asked Maria in a high-pitched, hysterical voice. It was obvious she'd been crying for a long time. Her eyes were red and swollen, and she clutched her husband's arm so tightly you could see the white marks her fingers left in his flesh.

"No, ma'am, there's no sign of your daughter yet, but hopefully she'll turn up soon. We have every available officer out on the streets looking for her."

"But if that sex murderer has her, she'll turn up *dead,*" she screamed at Maria. "Oh my baby, my poor, poor baby. What are we going to do?" she wailed, searching first Maria's then

Joe's face for an answer, with frantic, animal eyes.

"First we have to pull ourselves together if you want to help find your daughter, Mrs. McReedy," Joe said, putting an arm around the distraught woman's shoulders. "I know it's hard, but try to get hold of yourself. Your daughter's life may depend on it. Now, think back to when you last saw, Betsy. Was she playing in the front or back yard?"

Patsy McReedy stifled a sob with the back of her hand. "I think she was out front, looking for babies in the bird nest in that evergreen over there," she said, nodding toward the large tree. "She's always been such a nature lover. Oh my baby, my poor—"

"Was she alone or with friends?" Joe interrupted.

"Betsy was alone. She's shy and doesn't make friends easily. She's more mature than most girls her age and likes to keep to herself."

"Did you see anyone hanging around who was a stranger to the neighborhood? Any strange cars?"

Patsy McReedy shook her head, then paused, thinking. "Wait a minute. I did see a red car parked across the street, but I didn't think anything of it at the time. Since the park runs parallel with our house, sometimes people park there to go for walks."

"Did you happen to see the driver of the car?"

"No. When I noticed it, it was empty."

"How about the make, model, license plate? Anything you can remember about it may help."

"Well, all I can tell you is that it was small and red. Like I told you, I didn't pay much attention to it. And John was at work. He's the one who usually notices things like that," she said, looking at her husband. "Now I wish to God I had. Do you think that car might have something to do with my Betsy's disappearance?"

"Well, it's hard to say, ma'am, until we get more information," Maria said.

They spent another half-hour talking to the McReedys, then went through Betsy's things to get a better idea of what the girl was like. They found a couple of recent pictures the McReedys allowed them to take. Betsy was a beautiful little girl, with long blond hair and large, sparkling blue eyes.

"We'll be leaving now. We will let you folks know if we find out anything. You've been very helpful and if you think of anything else, please call this number," Joe said, handing them a card, which listed the phone numbers where they could be reached day or night.

Maria and Joe crossed the street, entering the park to have a look around.

Joe walked over to two boys playing catch.

"Do you boys live around here?"

"Yeah," they said in unison, then took a couple of steps backward, seeing Joe's gun.

Joe followed their gazes to his firearm and smiled. "Don't worry, I'm one of the good guys. I'm an officer of the law."

At that, their eyes opened wide, and they started asking all sorts of questions like: "Have you ever shot anybody?" and "Why aren't you wearing a policeman's uniform?"

"We're detectives."

"Way cool!" They looked at Maria with skeptical looks. "Her, too?" one of the boys asked, wrinkling his freckled nose.

"Yep, her too," Joe said, giving Maria a wink.

"Do you boys know Betsy McReedy?" Joe asked, showing them one of her pictures.

"Yeah, she goes to our school. Why?" the dark-haired boy asked.

"Well, she's been reported missing, and we were wondering if either of you boys saw her earlier today?"

They both shook their heads no.

Joe asked them about the red car, but they hadn't seen it.

"We were huntin' toads in the pond behind Jimmy's most of the day and didn't get to the park until a little while ago," the freckled-face boy said with a grin that showed several teeth missing. He produced a very large, brown toad from his pocket.

Joe laughed. "Looks like you got a monster toad there. I'm surprised he even fits in your pocket."

The toad let out a loud croak as if in response to this, and they all laughed.

"Well, you boys have a great summer and don't talk to strangers, okay?" Joe paused. "And don't go too far away from your parents."

"We won't. My sister came with, so you don't got to worry," the dark-haired boy responded, nodding toward the swings where a leggy teenager sat dangling her bare feet in the dirt.

"See ya, mister." They smiled shyly at Maria, then turned and raced over to the swings to join Jimmy's big sister.

Maria and Joe briefly questioned Jimmy's sister who reluctantly replied with one-word answers and knew nothing about anything. They then went door to door, visiting some of the McReedys' neighbors, but had no luck. Most of them worked during the day, and the ones who were home stayed busy gardening or doing other chores and hadn't noticed anything unusual.

When they climbed back into Joe's car, Maria lit a cigarette and turned to Joe. "Well, now I guess we just have to hope Milano can shed some light on the subject."

Joe grunted. "Don't count on it. He's still pretty strung-out from the drugs. I don't think he's seeing things too clearly yet."

"Well, we'll just have to *make* him then, won't we?" Maria said with a cutting edge to her voice.

They drove the rest of the way in silence, each thinking their own thoughts, but exactly the same. Their minds were focused as one on the killer and what he was doing to poor Betsy McReedy.

6

Betsy McReedy fainted. She tried to fight it, but the darkness came over her like a black shroud.

"Son of a bitch," he growled, getting up from the girl to turn off the camera. The little brat wasn't supposed to pass out in the middle of Act 1. Well, he'd make sure she paid for it. He walked into the kitchen and turned the cold water on, letting it run while he rummaged in a cupboard for a large pan. He filled it to the top and carried it back into the living room, splashing water on the floor as he went to where the little girl lay, motionless.

He stood over the naked girl, a twisted grin plastered on his face. "Rise and shine, sleeping beauty," he said, dumping the entire pan of water on her face.

Betsy McReedy's eyes fluttered open as she sat up, choking and coughing. Momentarily confused, she muttered, "Where am—" and then she saw him, and the horror of everything that was happening to her registered. She tried to crawl away, but he grabbed her ankle and slid her back.

"You can't get away, so you may as well just give up and be a good little girl like I told you. Understand?" he said, smiling sardonically, bringing the knife up to her face, and turning it so the bright camera lights reflected off its sharp, gleaming edge.

Her eyes were glued to the knife hypnotically as he

brought it down to her belly and drew a straight line from her navel to her breastbone, pressing ever so lightly with the tip of it. A thin, red ribbon of blood appeared, looking as if he'd painted it on.

"Now, I want you to do everything I tell you, and if you try to get away or pass out again, I'll have to hurt you real bad. Do you understand me, you little brat?"

Betsy whimpered and nodded her head, eyes wide and in shock.

He walked back to the camera and flipped the switch to *On*.

"We're going to finish where we left off, and you just lie there. Don't fight it, or I'll slit your throat from ear to ear," he said, getting on top of her and entering her.

She cried out in pain, then bit down hard on her lower lip to stifle her cries. Tears streamed down her face as she prayed to God this nightmare would end and she could go home to her mom and dad where she would be safe and warm. That's why she did as she was told and kept very still, trying desperately to think of a way to escape this terrible dream. She didn't want to die.

After what seemed like forever to Betsy, he withdrew from her and got up to turn off the camera and lighting equipment. He threw her a blanket and told her to crawl back to the corner of the room, which she did obediently, wrapping the blanket around herself and curling up into a ball.

"Tomorrow we're gonna have some more fun," he said, more to himself than to her. "Another day, another dollar. Maybe I'll invite Lenny along for the ride, since he enjoyed himself so much last time." He needed to replenish his dope supply anyway, and Lenny was supposed to be getting a shipment of dynamite smack from L.A. *Yeah, I'll give ol'*

Lenny a ride tomorrow, he thought to himself, laughing.

He laid out another line of coke even though it was getting late, and he was already wasted. He snorted it up and waited for the rush, which he got in a couple of seconds, then dumped the remaining coke in the vial on the mirror.

He looked over at the shivering girl, curled up in the corner of the room, and felt not the slightest bit of sympathy for her. He felt only hatred, and the desire to satisfy that need in him that demanded power over his victims and ultimately death.

He *needed* to kill them. He was doing the videos for drug money, and *them,* but he was killing them out of necessity.

He was pretty sure they knew, but didn't care. Being involved in so many other illicit deals, they didn't have the time, or see the need to baby-sit him. And even if they did object, that wouldn't stop him from doing what he *had* to do.

7

Exhaustion consumed Maria, leaving her miserably defeated. Joe was right about Lenny Milano. He had the heebie-jeebies so bad coming down off the heroin, he didn't make any sense when they tried talking to him. Maria even tried scare tactics, threatening everything from a lifetime prison term, to excessive bodily harm, but nothing she said or did made him open up. He'd sealed his lips tighter than King Tut's tomb, while his body shook with the need for a fix. Eventually, he ended up breaking down and crying like a small baby, saying over and over how he didn't want to die, and the walls were closing in on him.

Disgusted with the sight of him, they let the guard take him back to his cell, where he could freak alone.

After Joe dropped Maria off at her condo, she tried telephoning Carlos again. It was after ten in the evening, but he still didn't answer, so she left a short message on his answering machine to call her when he got in.

Even though tomorrow was Saturday, it would be a very busy day. They were all to meet at the Government Center in conference room 23B at 7:00 AM sharp to see what information they could put together on this case.

They needed to come up with some kind of lead. Milano was hiding something, but he just wasn't ready to talk. He was obviously terrified of something or someone. They had to make him spill his guts, even if it meant getting him off on a lesser charge and putting him back on the streets. No price was too high if he could help them catch the killer.

Maybe hotshot FBI agent Peter Slade could get through to Milano. The chief informed her and Joe that afternoon that Slade would be working with them until they solved the case. He was supposed to arrive in Minneapolis first thing Monday morning. The prospect less than thrilled Maria. She'd met him once before on a homicide investigation a couple of years back. He was a know-it-all Fed, who thought the world would stop spinning without him in it, and had a take-charge attitude that drove Maria nuts. He worked in the Behavioral Science Unit, so they'd talked on the phone several times already concerning this case. Their personalities had conflicted right from the start. Maria always got along with everyone, but not this guy for some reason. The chief thought it was because they were so much alike—both determined to be leaders, but not followers. Maria disagreed with this analogy, not appreciating being compared to an egomaniac like Slade.

Maria rubbed her tired eyes and lay down on the sofa. She'd just dozed off when the telephone rang. It was Carlos. She explained to him that she'd be working all weekend and wouldn't be able to see him. "Next weekend would be better, and Tess will be home by then. She'd love to see you and *I'm* really going to need your moral support, Carlos. I'm planning to tell Tess about her father. I think it's time she learned the truth, don't you?" Maria asked, her voice rising emotionally.

"Yeah, Sis, I do. If you're ready to tell her, I'll be there."

Maria let out the breath she'd been holding in. "Oh, Carlos, I don't know if I'll *ever* be ready to tell her. I know it will hurt her terribly, but I feel it's something that must be done. I've waited seven long years and can't bear to keep this dreadful secret any longer. I'm glad you're on my side, big brother. You've always been there for me."

"And I always will be. You'll see. Everything will turn out all right. I promise. Between the two of us, we'll make Tessy understand. Please don't worry, honey. I love you, and I'll see you next weekend."

"I love you, too. Bye." Maria hung up the phone and walked into her bedroom, somewhat relieved.

She sometimes envied Carlos, with his simple bachelor lifestyle in the windy city. He had few demands on his life— no wife or kids—setting his own hours in his own business.

They'd grown up in a run-down housing project in the inner city of Chicago, with very poor but very loving parents. Their father was Hispanic and their mother was French and English. Back then, in the early 1970's, they were considered a mixed couple and weren't accepted by either race, Hispanic or white. But they taught their children that love conquered all problems, big and small, and race didn't matter as long as you had respect for one another. So, what they lacked in material possessions, they more than made up for with the special bond they shared as a family. But Maria *had* felt the racial tension growing up, even though her parents had tried to shelter her from it—it was everywhere. Looking back now, she realized that it had played a factor in her eagerness to start a life with Jack. He was part Hispanic also, and she'd felt a special link, a commonality that would bring acceptance from those who had offered none to her parents.

When Maria met Jack, she'd hoped to have the same kind of devoted family as she and Carlos had experienced, with the exception of living in poverty. She couldn't wait to get out of the big, dirty city after they were married. She'd begged Carlos to go with them, but he wouldn't even consider leaving.

Everything had changed dramatically since then—some things for the better and some for the worse. They both had successful professional careers. Carlos owned his own furniture refinishing business in the Loop, and Maria made a difference in this crazy world with her career as a cop in Minneapolis. It was too bad their parents weren't alive to see how far they'd come, even though their personal lives told a different story.

Carlos seemed happy, although he once told Maria he'd never marry again when his first marriage failed miserably after only six months. Maybe they were both destined to be alone the rest of their lives.

At least she had Tess. Carlos always said that the only thing he missed was not having kids, but he loved Tess like his own.

Maria stripped down to her panties and climbed under the cool, crisp sheets, checking the alarm clock once more to make sure it was set for 6:00 AM. She turned off the lamp on the bedside table and fell asleep.

It was not a peaceful sleep, though. She tossed and turned, the sheets twisting around her legs. The recurring nightmare of Jack beating her and then going for Theresa with murderous rage, plagued her sleep. Only this time Theresa wasn't a baby. She was the same age as now.

In the dream, Maria tried to rescue Theresa from her father, but no matter how hard she tried, she couldn't move. Her feet seemed cemented to the floor, while her daughter cried out to her for help. The knife in Jack's upraised hand would strike Theresa at any moment and she could only watch.

Maria opened her mouth to scream, but no sound came out. She tried again and again to go to her daughter's aid, but her feet wouldn't move! Every part of her body, inside and out, was frozen and immobile. Tears of anguish coursed down her fevered face, not knowing how to help the one person she loved more dearly than anything else on earth.

She woke with a start, sitting straight up in bed, screaming, and in a cold sweat. It took a couple of seconds for her to realize it was her own voice she heard screaming.

Maria ran a shaky hand through her sweat-drenched hair. "It was only a dream. Oh, God, only a dream," she said aloud, getting out of bed and stumbling to the bathroom to get a drink of water. She cupped her hand under the cool water and drank deeply, feeling somewhat better in the bright light. She looked at her tear-streaked face in the mirror and was startled by the haunted woman who stared back at her. "You'll never be rid of that son of a bitch," she said to her reflection.

The nightmare seemed to be coming more and more frequently. Maybe she should start seeing a shrink. It probably had a lot to do with the case, she told herself. The disappearing children and the day-to-day stress of her job, life, everything!

"I've gotta get this guy before I go crazy," Maria said, grabbing her robe off the hook in the bathroom and slipping it on. She padded into the kitchen and started the coffee maker, then went back into the bathroom to take a long shower. Exhausted from chasing phantoms in her sleep, she hoped the strong, hot spray of the shower would cleanse her mind as well as body, giving her a clear head for the meeting that was to take place in less than two hours.

8

They sat around the long table in conference room 23B, sipping strong coffee, self-absorbed in their notes. There were six of them—Chief McCollough, Dr. Lang, BCA agent Bill Foley, FBI agent Peter Slade, Joe, and Maria.

Maria looked over the top of her clipboard at Peter, who wasn't supposed to even be there for two more days. They made eye contact and she immediately looked away.

Chief McCollough cleared his throat. "I think everyone here has met Mr. Slade prior to this case, with the exception of Agent Foley here," he said, nodding toward the BCA agent who'd been on the job only eight months.

Agent Bill Foley nodded curtly, the florescent lights gleaming off his bald head. He'd sized up the FBI agent when he first entered the room, trying to determine who would win at arm wrestling. Slade was taller, but that was about it. It would be no contest, he decided—the FBI guy looked like a wimp, with his skinny arms and 'mama's boy' curly brown hair. He probably didn't even work out.

"Peter caught an early flight out from D.C. so he could attend this meeting," Chief McCollough continued. "As you all know, he's been working with us long distance in the FBI's Behavioral Science Unit, now referred to as the Investigative Support Unit for those of you who may not be aware of this, and has agreed to help us out here."

Looking at Maria the chief added, "I want to make it understood that Slade is just helping us out. You and Morgan are still running the show, Sanchez, so nobody's pride needs to be hurt. Is that clear?" he asked, frowning at the FBI agent, seeing that he and Maria were already shooting daggers with their eyes.

"Perfectly," Slade replied coolly.

Maria smiled.

"Good. Okay, what do we have so far?" Chief McCollough questioned, standing up and walking over to the large blackboard that covered most of the wall opposite the table. He drew a line down the middle of the board and wrote the word 'VICTIMS' on one side and 'SUSPECTS' on the other.

Under 'VICTIMS' he wrote the following information:

Children between ages of 8-10 (4 victims...)

Male and female — Caucasian.

All reside in Minneapolis area.

Upper class, Middle class (no preference?)

No common characteristics or features.

Attended different schools: Public—Jefferson, Four Winds, and Martin Luther King. Private—Lutheran Christian Academy.

"Even though school is out for the summer, it's important to establish that they all attended different schools. So we know it isn't some psychotic teacher determined to cut down on class size for the upcoming school year, or something equally disturbing," the chief explained as he wrote.

"I never thought of that," Maria commented.

"It's happened before—nothing surprises me anymore," the chief grumbled.

Then under 'SUSPECTS', he wrote the following information:

"River Rat" - male

Drug User

Pornography involved

Red sports car??

Victim's bodies disposed in Mississippi River (Hennepin County).

Victims sexually/physically abused several days before killed.

Rafts built out of shipping crates, standard rope.

Blue carpet fibers.

"Okay, what else do we have?" the chief asked. Wiping sweat from his brow, he glared at each of them.

Maria stood up and walked over to the chalkboard, all eyes on her. Next to 'Drug User' on the 'SUSPECT' side she wrote 'Milano possible supplier?' and at the bottom she added, 'Uses knife on victims—severed fingers, rapes and ultimately strangles.' She set the chalk on the tray and returned to her seat between Joe and the medical examiner.

Dr. Lang cleared his throat. "Let's see, the time of death always seems to be in the early morning hours," he said, making no move to get up.

The chief picked up the chalk and added this to the list.

"And on one of the victims two different seminal fluids were found, indicating we have more than one suspect involved here. At least in the sexual part of one of the crimes," the M.E. added.

Peter Slade stood up to his full 6'2" height. "I think we're missing the obvious here."

"And what's that?" Joe asked, not liking Slade much more than Maria did.

"A pornography ring. This guy is getting kids for kiddy porno flicks."

Chief McCollough leaned back in his chair and winked at Maria. "I'm impressed, Slade, but Sanchez, as well as the rest of us, have already thought of it. We already know of one video, and where there's one there's probably more. But if it *is* a pornography ring, why kill them right away? That's money in the bank to those assholes. There has to be more to it than that. You don't kill the goose that lays the golden egg, do you? At least not in that short of time."

"I guess you're right, and since the boy wasn't killed on film—If it wasn't a snuff film, it must've been a thrill-kill—for his own gratification."

"Exactly," Maria said. "These kids have been killed relatively quickly, only a few days after they'd been abducted, and that just isn't the norm. We definitely have a mixture of deadly forces at work here—a serial killer and a pedophile to name a couple—so even though pornography *is* involved, it's not the main issue. In this case it's much more dangerous because we don't have the usual time factor on our side."

"It's possible organized crime is involved, considering the video showed up where it did. Our guy must have the right connections," Slade offered.

"Yes, very possible," the chief said, adding that to the list.

With a look that said *I'm bored* and a monotone that matched, BCA agent Foley muttered, "La Cosa Nostra." As way of an explanation he said, "Means 'Our Thing' to the mob."

They all sat in silence for several minutes thinking Foley was a fool and made less sense every time he opened his mouth, and mulling over what little information they had.

Maria turned to Joe, an exasperated sigh escaping her lips. "Let's try talking to Milano again when we're finished here. Maybe he's ready to talk now after spending a couple of nights going 'cold turkey'."

Joe nodded. "Yeah, I hope so. I'm afraid Betsy McReedy's young life may be coming to an abrupt end if we don't find some goddamn answers, and fast."

"You guys go ahead," the chief said, lighting his pipe and filling the small room with thick, choking smoke. "Go ahead and tag along with 'em, Slade. Maybe you can do some good."

"Yes, sir," Peter Slade responded.

"You, too, Foley," the chief added.

"Sorry, can't do," Bill Foley said, rising. "Already wasted the whole damn morning."

The chief ignored the remark, not willing to stoop to the level of pulling rank and going head to head with the BCA, which he'd done in the past and lived to regret. Turning to Maria and Joe, he said, "If this Milano creep knows anything, hang the fucker by his balls till he talks!"

Lenny Milano relieved himself, then lay back down on the cot in his cell, thinking. He'd already decided he was gonna spill his guts the next time those two detectives came around. He just hadn't decided how much he was gonna tell them. He knew enough to bring down a whole kingdom. And he also knew the walls had ears in this place, but *they* couldn't get to him in here.

He closed his eyes tightly, wishing the pain in his guts would go away, and his jaw would unclench. He was still going through withdrawals, but nothing like a couple of days ago when he'd seen snakes slithering in one corner of his cell and blood dripping down the walls. *Now that was heavy shit, man.*

He started to doze off when he heard a noise coming from the other end of his cell, but he was so very tired—too damn tired to open his eyes. He figured it was just one of the other inmates back from free time and screwin' around, which was often the case.

The last things Lenny Milano remembered were a rope being pulled tight around his neck, choking, eyes bulging, feet kicking in midair...then blackness.

By the time they reached the Hennepin County Jail they were already forty-five minutes too late. Apparently, someone did hang Milano up, but not by his balls.

"The warden has been trying to reach the chief for close to an hour, but couldn't locate him," the flustered assistant warden replied to Joe's rapid-fire interrogation.

"What the hell are you people running here, a jail or a goddamn three ring circus? He was our *only* lead in this case, if even that! And how the hell did someone get to him in here? Or did he hang himself?" Joe fixed the young man with his piercing gaze.

"We really don't know yet, sir. It could be a suicide, or it's possible someone had a contract out for him in-house. We're dusting for prints in his cell, so we'll know more soon. I'm sorry, sir, I can assure you this type of thing only happens once in a blue moon."

Joe gave the assistant warden an exasperated look. "Once in a blue moon, huh. That's just our luck. In this case it's one fuckin' time too many." He glanced at Slade, who was watching Maria. "Let us know right away what you find—and call the chief for Christ's sake!" he demanded, thrusting his card in the man's sweaty hand and storming out the door with Maria and Slade following close behind.

Once outside, Joe turned to Maria. "Damn, the chief is sure gonna be pissed about this major screw-up. Where the hell do we go from here?" he asked, looking into Maria's distraught eyes.

Maria shrugged her narrow shoulders, returning his gaze. "I don't know."

Peter jingled the keys in his pocket, one of his many nervous habits. "I know Milano's place has already been searched, but maybe something was missed. Why don't we cruise over there, have a look around and see what the three of us can turn up?" he asked, looking from Joe to Maria.

"Well, I suppose, considering we were planning on giving it another once-over anyway," Joe replied.

"Yeah, I didn't have enough time to do a thorough search when I found the heroin. Narcotics went over everything with a fine-tooth comb, but you know what they say, 'third time's a charm'. You may as well tag along," Maria said to Slade with a sigh, getting in the front seat next to Joe, leaving Peter the back once again.

There was still police tape across the door of apartment 101. They stood outside the door to Milano's apartment in the dark hallway.

"We don't have a key," Peter whispered. "We'll need to find the landlord."

Joe laughed. "That never stopped Maria before. And by the way, Slade, you don't need to whisper, we're the good guys, remember?"

Maria was standing between the two men and heard the "Fuck-you," Peter said under his breath, even if Joe didn't, or pretended not to.

Maria had the locked door open in less than a minute. The apartment was sweltering hot, and the stink was horrendous. "Phew! Let's open some windows," she said, putting one hand over her nose and mouth.

"Do you know what it smells like in here?" Peter asked, sniffing the air.

Maria looked at him over a raised eyebrow. "Do tell."

"A wet dog. When I was a kid I used to go swimming with my dog, and I'd come home smelling just like this."

Maria laughed in spite of herself. "Memories can be painful sometimes, can't they? God, what a smell! It's probably because Narcotics had their dogs in here sniffing out dope, and the place has been shut up since then."

"What do you say we start looking and stop reminiscing," Joe said, flipping through a stack of albums.

They had been searching the apartment for close to two hours and everyone was getting hot and irritable.

Maria was going through the old roll-top desk for the third time and Joe was searching the bathroom, when Slade gave a shout from the kitchen area. She walked the few feet to the entryway, several papers from the desk still in her hand.

"Lookit here," Peter said, as he opened an old cookbook in the middle and showed them how a square, approximately four-by-two, had been cut out. Placed snugly inside was a small black book. Slade pried the little book out with his pocketknife and opened it to reveal lines of code that appeared to be Greek, or something equally confusing.

"*Hmm*, looks like some sort of address book." Maria snatched the little book from Peter's hand and examined it. "I'll bet this contains the addresses to Milano's drug contacts. But what the hell is this, some kind of secret code?"

"Some of it looks like hieroglyphics," Joe said from behind Maria, peering over her shoulder and pointing at a symbol.

"Well, it's something isn't it? It sure as hell is *something*," she said, more to herself than anyone else. "Good job, Slade." She slipped the little book into her purse and walked toward the door. "Oh, shut the windows—looks like rain," Maria added, going out the door. She heard the word 'bitch' come from the other room and smiled at Joe. "I don't think he likes me."

By the time they left Milano's apartment it was after five o'clock, so they dropped Slade off at his hotel, then went back to City Hall.

The chief had just received all the details from the warden, and wasn't too happy with the findings. He looked long and hard at Maria and Joe before speaking. "Apparently there were too many prints in Milano's cell to get anything identifiable from whoever hung him up. It was definitely no suicide. I'd bet my own life on it. Milano was scared to talk for a reason. *Son of a bitch*!" he bellowed, red-faced, slamming his fist so hard the stack of files teetering on the edge of his desk toppled to the floor. "Back to square one, with absolutely nothing to show for it," he said through clenched teeth. He bent down to gather the files scattered at his feet.

"Well, we may have something," Maria said, producing the little black book from her purse and sliding it across the desk to him.

"What the hell is this?"

"It appears to be an address book in some kind of secret code. We found it, or I should say Slade found it, inside an old cookbook in Milano's apartment."

"I'll be damned," the chief said, looking through the little book. "Although, fat lotta good it'll do us. What the fuck kind of language is it in? Chink?"

"Joe thought part of it looked like hieroglyphics."

"We'll see if we can get started deciphering it first thing in the morning," Joe said. "I'm sure Professor Littleton at the U of M can help."

"Hopefully it will give us something to work with here, considering we are now up shit-creek without a paddle," the chief said, as he opened his bottom desk drawer and produced a fifth of Jack Daniel's. He nodded at Maria and Joe. "Drink?" He then proceeded to pour two fingers of whiskey into three Styrofoam cups.

He finished his whiskey in one gulp and poured himself another. "God, when the mayor hears about this, I may as well put my own balls in a vise and save him the trouble," the chief said, looking into his cup.

"Well, it sure as hell isn't your fault, unless of course *you* put the contract out on the little creep," Maria said, setting her empty cup on his desk and looking at him with mock suspicion in her large brown eyes.

He laughed. "I hope you know, Sanchez, only you can get away with talking to me like that," he said, filling her cup and grinning. "You're right though, goddamnit. It isn't anyone's fault, except maybe the warden's and believe me, I'm gonna make that little cocksucker wish he'd never been born. He knew our case was riding solely on Milano and he should have kept a closer watch on him. Yeah, he's gonna be one sorry son of a bitch."

The three of them sat and drank JD and talked about everything from the weather to the Minnesota Twins, trying to get their minds off the setback, if only for a little while. They decided it was time to call it a day when the weekend janitor knocked on the door at 10:00 PM and said he needed to clean up in there so he could make it home in time to watch 'America's Most Wanted'. This struck all of them as funny, and the chief laughed so hard he nearly fell off his chair, which made them laugh all the harder.

After a lot of fumbling around and cussing, Joe somehow managed to make a pot of very strong coffee and brought it into the chief's office. When the pot was empty, they had sobered up enough to remember why they'd gotten drunk in the first place—the fact that Milano was dead hit home hard.

"Somehow I don't think I'm gonna sleep much tonight," the chief muttered, head in hands. "No, not enough booze in the world could get me to sleep tonight."

"I'll call a cab," Maria said, sliding the phone on the chief's desk in front of her and dialing.

The three of them rode in the back of the cab in silence, stone-cold sober, thinking about the nine-year-old girl whose life was hanging by a very thin thread.

9

Betsy woke from a fitful sleep, feeling sick to her stomach and disoriented. She lay in the darkness holding her belly and listening to the night. It was very quiet. A cool breeze drifted in through the open window across the room, and moonlight shone an eerie beam along the bare wood floor she lay on with only a single, threadbare blanket for cover.

She slowly got to her feet, very unsteady, a wave of dizziness washing over her. Reaching out, she leaned against the wall for support until the dizziness subsided. The door to her left was his bedroom, and a bar of glowing bluish light—she guessed from a TV—was visible beneath it. She tiptoed to the closed door and listened, hearing static from the television and heavy snoring. Turning the knob, she silently opened the door an inch to peek in. He was sprawled naked on the bed, a half-empty bottle of liquor sitting on the bedside table. She shoved a fist in her mouth to stifle the scream that wanted to let loose at the sight of him.

Betsy closed the bedroom door, not making the slightest sound, and walked to the front door that led outside to safety.

She grasped the doorknob, her heart trip-hammering, and turned it, but found it wouldn't move. Then she saw the dead-bolt lock. It was high up on the door. Standing on tiptoe, she discovered it had a keyhole on the inside and was locked to prevent her escape. The key was probably in the pocket of his pants, which lay on the bedroom floor. She thought about this and realized she couldn't bring herself to go in there. The risk of him waking up and catching her was just too great. She fought back the tears that threatened to overcome, trying to think of another way out.

Betsy walked over to the open window in the living room and peered out. It was two stories up and a straight drop down to the street below, with no ledge to grab hold of and nothing to break her fall. *Well, maybe it wouldn't be so bad—at least the hurt would stop*, she thought.

"No," she whispered, a single tear sliding down her flushed face. "I don't want to die." Betsy crossed the living room on tiptoe so as not to make the old floorboards creak and opened the bathroom door. She heard something move from under the sink and her heart leapt into her throat.

Then she heard a whine and a steady thump-thump-thump where the puppy's tail hit the floor, ecstatic to see a friendly face. She bent down and scratched the pup behind the ears while his tail drummed the floor in a steady beat.

"*Shh,*" she whispered, holding his head in both hands, and looking into his trusting brown eyes. He licked her hand and thumped his tail again, gazing at her adoringly, head cocked to one side. The puppy's leash was so short he couldn't move more than a couple of inches one way or the other, and he had no food or water.

"Poor little thing," Betsy murmured, realizing for the first time this little puppy was somewhat responsible for her predicament. The man had seemed nice enough at first— asking if she knew anyone who wanted a free puppy because his new apartment didn't allow pets. When she bent over to pet the dog, she felt something sharp go into her arm, then darkness was all she remembered. She didn't wake until in his domain, just like the others he'd tricked.

She knew there had been others because he told her so. He also told her they were dead, and soon she would be joining them. She wiped the tears from her face with the back of her hand, missing her mom and dad so much. Would she ever see them again? *Maybe not.*

After letting the puppy drink water from her cupped hands, she stroked behind his ears while looking around the tiny bathroom. *No windows in here*, she thought, disheartened.

The puppy whined and looked at the linen closet with his big brown puppy eyes. Betsy opened the closet, and sitting on the floor was a large bag of Purina Puppy Chow.

"Hungry, huh? What a smart dog."

The puppy whined in response.

Dragging the big bag out of the closet, she poured some of the dog food on the floor.

The dog practically inhaled it he was so starved. He chewed while periodically glancing at the girl with simple adoration and a thump of his tail between bites.

Struggling to get the bag back inside the closet, her good deed done, she noticed a small rectangular door. She opened it and peered inside. It was a laundry chute, like the one her grandma used to have. A light seemed to turn on in her anguished mind amidst the dark despair.

Betsy remembered how she was cautioned to stay away from the small door when she was little. Grandma McReedy used to tell her she'd get stuck or worse—hit the hard basement floor and break her neck.

She stuck her head inside and peered into the inky blackness. She was pretty sure she'd fit. The big question was where did it lead to, if anywhere? Maybe it was blocked off at the end and she'd be trapped like a rat if she tried to go down.

This was an old house after all, she thought, looking at the peeling wallpaper on the bathroom wall. Probably no one had used this laundry chute for years. Her grandma had sealed hers up several years ago, before she got sick and sold her house to move to the old folk's home.

Betsy bent down and picked up a few nuggets of the puppy food, then dropped them down the chute, sticking her head inside to see if she could hear them drop at the other end. It was hard to tell. She picked up a handful of the chunks and tried again. This time she heard them hit something, but it sounded kind of funny, like a *boing* sound.

It's probably blocked off, she thought, chewing on her lower lip, trying to decide what to do. She looked at the puppy, then at the laundry chute, then back at the puppy. "Then again what choice do I really have?" she asked the dog, who cocked his head to one side and whined as if understanding her situation.

Betsy wrapped the blanket tightly around her torso and tucked one end under, and then proceeded to climb into the laundry chute, feet first. She looked at the puppy one last time, and he let out a worried whine as she worked the rest of her small body into the narrow space.

Now, all she had to do was let go and she'd be on her way to only God knew where. *But anywhere has to be better than this, doesn't it?* She panicked at the last minute, wanting to get back out into the open space of the bathroom, but then she thought of what lay in store for her. More of the same awful stuff he did to her last night and maybe worse, then eventually death.

With that last thought she closed her eyes tight and let go. The blanket made her slide easy enough, but it seemed an eternity before her feet struck the wire mesh that was nailed on at the bottom. *That* was the '*boing*' sound she heard when she dropped the dog food down. Her worst fear had come true—she was trapped! She felt the panic start to surge through her once again, and bit down hard on her lower lip to keep her wits about her.

It was so dark inside the chute and the basement beyond, she couldn't see anything but total blackness. Crouching way down, she crossed her arms above her head, palms flat against the cool metal wall of the chute, bracing her from moving upward. Pushing against the wire mesh with all the strength her legs had in them, she heard a splintering noise—nails pulling out of rotten wood—and the covering gave a little bit. She tried again, and then again, each time feeling it loosen a bit more. The third time the wire mesh gave way entirely, hanging on by only one nail.

Betsy fell several feet onto the hard concrete floor of the basement, which now served as storage for the upstairs tenants.

Stunned, she couldn't move for several minutes.

She sat up and rubbed the back of her head where it hit the rock-hard floor and felt a large goose egg rising. Pulling the blanket over her nakedness, she stood up and looked around the filthy basement, her eyes now adjusted to the darkness. There were boxes piled everywhere and shipping crates were stacked six feet high in one corner, along with rolls and rolls of ugly, old blue carpeting.

Betsy slowly climbed to the top of the basement stairs, feeling all at once the unbelievable hell she'd been through. Her legs threatened to buckle and send her sprawling several times. When she reached the door at the top she was out of breath and had a painful stitch in her side.

Grabbing the doorknob, she said a silent prayer and turned it.

The knob turned easy enough, but the door wouldn't budge. She pushed on it again and again to no avail. It was either blocked or locked from the other side.

Realizing she was now locked inside a dark, dirty basement with no way out and no hope, she sat down hard on the small landing. Dropping her head to her knees, she sobbed, her long blond hair brushing the dirty stair below.

After a while no more tears would come. The well had gone dry.

Taking a deep, shaky breath, she finally stood up and walked back down the basement stairs, noticing for the first time several small windows set high up in the basement wall. With the dirt and grime so thick on them it was no wonder she hadn't noticed them before.

Betsy moved several of the crates over to a window and stacked them one on top of the other, then climbed up. Wiping a spot clear with her blanket, she gazed into the nighttime world. Standing on tiptoe, she was eye-level with the ground that a nearby street lamp helped make visible. The ray of hope she felt earlier seemed to shine a little brighter, as her wobbly legs brought her back down to the floor.

She rummaged through a pile of junk in one corner of the basement until she found something she could use to break a window. She found an old, brass lamp lying in a box amidst a lot of other stuff with the name Nelson printed on the side of it.

Armed with the heavy lamp, she scrambled back up to the top of the crates, perched precariously with each foot on opposite sides of the top crate to distribute her balance.

Shielding her face with the blanket, she hurled the lamp as hard as she could into the window. It shattered, raining glass down on top of her and the ground outside. Betsy knocked out the few sharp pieces that remained with the base of the lamp.

On each side, at the top of the window frame, a large rusty nail protruded, which was likely used to hang some type of window covering in the past. Hooking her blanket on one of the nails, she tested it to see if it would hold her slight weight—it did.

Using the blanket as a kind of makeshift rope, Betsy pulled herself up, hand over hand, bare feet flat against the cool cement block. She emerged out of the small opening into the darkened world.

She didn't even feel the glass cut her feet as she stood up outside, free at last. Reaching in and grabbing her blanket off the nail, she wrapped it around her thin body one last time.

Then she took off running as fast as her trembling legs would carry her into the night, tears streaming down her dirt-streaked little face.

10

The temperature was well past the 90-degree mark and it was only 11:00 in the morning. It was supposed to reach a whopping 102 by late afternoon, and Tess was coming home from summer camp today. Earlier in the morning, Maria had baked a double-layer chocolate cake, decorated with pink frosting and large, red hearts.

She was taking a vacation day in order to get ready for the party and pick Tess up, but she'd already called Joe twice, and stopped in around 9:30 to check on any new developments with the case.

Joe sent her home and promised he'd call if something came up.

Joe was coming over after work, and Carlos said he'd be in the Twin Cities by 6:00 this evening at the latest.

Maria climbed into her heat-trap on wheels—cursing the fact she never had the air conditioner fixed when it went out two years ago—and rolled down the windows, relishing the slight breeze coming through.

The camp bus was supposed to drop the kids off at the local YMCA at 11:30.

Maria's mind wandered over the past few days as she drove, thinking about the little McReedy girl lying in Minneapolis Children's Hospital. There hadn't been any improvement in her condition when she and Joe went to see her last night. The past few nights Betsy's parents kept a vigil by her bedside—not leaving her alone for even a moment—telling her over and over how much they loved her and how everything would be okay.

But everything was not okay.

A taxicab driver who was making his rounds near First Avenue found Betsy early Tuesday morning. She was conscious but incoherent, not even knowing her own name. The girl was in shock and bleeding internally as well as cut up pretty bad on the soles of her feet.

The hospital called the police station after she was brought into the emergency room, and when her description matched the missing-persons report, Patsy and John McReedy were brought in to identify their daughter.

Betsy had stared blankly at her mother and father, not recognizing them at all. Then late Tuesday evening, she slipped into a coma, shutting down all bodily functions.

An extensive search was conducted in the surrounding area where Betsy was discovered by the cabby, but nothing had turned up so far. Several plainclothes police officers were still patrolling, looking for anyone suspicious in nature. They would stay posted to that area until they were told otherwise, even though many surmised the McReedy girl had traveled a good distance before being discovered.

Was it coincidence that she ended up only several blocks from Milano's apartment? Maria wondered. Well, Milano was dead now, so he couldn't help them figure this one out.

They hadn't had much luck with Milano's address book yet, either. Both Professor Littleton and a colleague, who were well known for their work at deciphering codes and foreign language, were working on it. According to the professor, it was written in a combination of several different languages, hieroglyphics being only a very small part of the intricate coding.

Maria pulled into the YMCA parking lot, trying to push everything except Tess's homecoming from her mind.

She walked across the lush green lawn to wait for the bus with the other anxious parents already gathered there. Spotting Nancy Turow in the crowd, she went to greet the other woman. Their daughters were best friends, like sisters they were so close. Since both were only children and from single-parent families, they found they had a lot in common and had been best buddies since kindergarten. In turn, the two women had become good friends, also.

"Gosh, I've missed Jenny terribly," Nancy confided to Maria. She leaned over to take a closer look at her friend. "You don't look so hot. Are you feeling all right?" She looked into Maria's eyes with a worried expression.

"Oh, I'm fine." Maria forced a little laugh. "Just worried about the kid, I guess. I'll be glad when she's under her own roof. I've missed her an awful lot, too."

"Ya know, I had second thoughts after I sent Jennifer to camp, what with that crazy man running around—"

"I know, but they're probably safer at camp than in their own backyards. I'll tell you one thing, though—I've never appreciated my daughter more."

"God, how do you do it, Maria? Dealing with crazies all day long. No wonder you look like hell."

Maria just smiled.

The bus pulled into the parking lot at that moment, saving her from talking about her police work. She wanted, no *needed* to focus on Tess right now and nothing else, especially not her job.

The bus started unloading its hot, sweaty passengers, the camp counselors checking off each name on a sheet of paper as they disembarked.

Tess and Jenny were almost the last ones to get off, looking tired, dirty, and irritable. Tess's face lit up when she saw Maria. Throwing her backpack to the ground, she ran to her mother, giving her a tremendous bear hug.

"Oh, Mom, I've never missed anything so much as I missed you. Well, except maybe our bathtub," she said, looking down at her crumpled, dirty clothes and wrinkling her nose.

"I missed you too, honey. I had to practically cut the telephone cord to keep from calling you." Maria smiled at her beautiful daughter. "What do you say we get you home?"

"Sounds wonderful," Tess exclaimed, slinging her backpack over one shoulder and taking her mother's hand. "Let's go! Bye, Jen, call me tomorrow," she yelled to her friend.

Jenny waved, already running ahead of her own mother to their car.

"Boy, it's sure great to be home," Tess said, kicking off her sneakers and collapsing on the sofa in the air-conditioned comfort of their condo. "I've realized I took a lot of things for granted—like hot baths and going to the bathroom in a real toilet."

Maria laughed. "That bad, huh? I take it there were outhouses, or did you have to pick a favorite bush?"

"Oh, there were outhouses all right, but you had to hold your breath from the minute you stepped in until you stepped outside again, or else risk the possibility of passing out in there and probably dying of asphyxiation. It was totally gross."

Maria smiled to herself. Asphyxiation. Tess was going through a stage where she was trying to use one new word a day—Webster's Dictionary was her constant companion. "Well, you're home now. I missed you terribly and worried about you constantly," she said, leaning over to give her daughter a hug, tears threatening to spoil her composure.

"Mom, what's wrong?"

"Nothing, honey, now that you're home." Tess had a questioning look on her upturned face and Maria hurried on. "Now, I suggest you go take a long, hot bath and put on your prettiest dress, unless of course you don't *mind* looking like that for the party?"

"Party?"

"Well, just a little get-together really. Uncle Carlos is coming up from Chicago, and Joe said he'd drop by after work."

Tess's entire face lit up as she jumped off the sofa. "I haven't seen Uncle Carlos in ages! I've missed him terribly." Her large brown eyes softened. "And Joe, too. He's a real sweetie," she added, skipping to the bathroom, humming a tune as she went.

The party was a huge success. Tess squealed with delight upon seeing the beautiful cake Maria had baked for the occasion, and everyone, especially Joe, raved about the delicious spaghetti dinner.

Maria and Carlos decided the next day would be a good time to tell Tess the truth about her father. They'd go for a picnic at Como Park, and then go through the zoo that was located there. The orangutans were hilarious and always made Tess laugh. Ever since she was a little girl, Maria had taken her there on special outings, just the two of them. It had become a Saturday ritual for them during the long, hot summer months.

But tomorrow would be different, in that it would change the rest of Theresa's life—in more ways than one.

11

That evening Carlos and Tess went to the movies, while Maria and Joe drove to the hospital to check on Betsy McReedy's condition.

They arrived at Minneapolis Children's Hospital and went up to the second floor, where a police officer was stationed in the hall outside Betsy's room. Patsy McReedy was in the hallway also, crying hysterically.

"Has something happened?" Maria asked, putting her hand on Mrs. McReedy's fleshy shoulder. The woman just kept sobbing, oblivious to Maria and Joe standing next to her. John McReedy emerged from the hospital room, wiping his tears away.

"What's wrong?" Maria asked, a note of alarm creeping into her voice.

"Betsy is out of her coma."

"I—I don't understand. Why are you both so upset then?"

"She's what they call catatonic, and according to the doctors—" He let out a heart-wrenching sob, leaning on the wall for support. "At least she's alive—thank God for that—but our beautiful baby girl may never be the same. The doctors say she may never come out of it."

"But there's a chance she will! You both *must* have faith," Maria offered. "I've seen cases such as this before; victims in severe trauma and shock like Betsy has had have recovered completely, sometimes in as little as two weeks—"

"Or two years, or twenty, or maybe never," Patsy McReedy interrupted. "I blame you people. If you had done your jobs, none of this would have happened and my baby would be home safe and sound, all in one piece—not some vegetable lying in a hospital bed!"

"Patsy! For God's sake, stop it. What good does it do to blame them? It's not *their* fault; it's the maniac who took her. They're only trying to help," John McReedy said, giving them an apologetic look as he led his hysterical wife down the hall toward the elevators.

When John and Patsy McReedy left the floor, so consumed with grief they had to support one another, Maria and Joe went in to see Betsy.

The little girl lay on her back, propped up by pillows, staring blankly out the window. The respirator had been removed. Betsy was breathing on her own.

Maria sat down on the bed next to Betsy's small form and picked up her pale, lifeless hand, rubbing it gently. "Betsy? I know you can hear me, honey. I want to help you, but you have to help me first before I can. You have to get better, Betsy. We want to catch the man who did this to you, but we really need your help. Your mom and dad really miss you, honey. Especially your mom. I have a little girl about your age, so I know how they must feel. I think you'd like Tess.

"Maybe I'll bring her by to visit you once you get back home. Would you like that? You'll be going home soon—the doctors say in a few days. I know you're going to get better because you love life too much not to. Your mom told me you're good with little animals—squirrels eat right out of your hand. And she said you want to be a veterinarian when you grow up, so you can help sick animals get well. She told me you once nursed a baby robin back to health that had fallen out of its nest.

"Betsy? That's why you escaped, isn't it? To live again! Not in a shell of your former self—you want to live every minute of life to the fullest. You can't give up now, Betsy, you've come this far."

There was the briefest flicker in the girl's eyes, as if she knew exactly what Maria meant, but it was so brief, Maria thought she might have imagined it. She talked softly to the little girl, holding and rubbing her small, lifeless hand the entire time, for another half an hour or more.

When Maria finally stood up, she felt drained and out of sorts.

Joe put his arm around her shoulders and led her out of the hospital into the parking lot where his old Chevy sat like a dinosaur amidst all the newer models. "You are an amazing woman, Maria," he said, looking into her large, liquid brown eyes.

"Now, why in God's name would you say that?"

"I think you got through to the girl. I saw a slight change in her eyes, a movement, when you were talking to her."

Maria reached out and put a hand on Joe's shoulder. "You did? I thought I might have imagined it."

Joe shook his head. "No, you didn't imagine it. It was there—if only for a moment—it was there."

When they got back to the condo, Carlos and Tess still weren't back from the movie-theater.

"Have a seat, Joe. How about a brandy?"

"Sounds great," he said, flopping on the sofa.

Maria poured the brandy and turned on the stereo before

joining Joe. She sat down next to him and curled her legs up underneath her. The brandy felt warm and delicious going down, and she started feeling better immediately.

Maria smiled to herself. "Why is it I feel so damn comfortable and safe when I'm with you?"

Joe looked at her, surprised by her sudden confession. "I don't know, why don't you tell me?"

Their eyes locked and try as she might Maria wasn't able to look away from his piercing blue gaze. At that moment, she could see all the love he felt for her behind those clear blue eyes and felt her own heart start beating a faster rhythm. "Joe," she whispered, and then she was in his arms. When their lips met, she felt a hot fire surge through her, building into an all-consuming passion that ran deep within her. She was so caught up in the moment she didn't hear the door open.

Joe stood up so fast Maria nearly fell to the floor.

The look of surprise on Tess's face was comical, with eyes wide and mouth hanging open in a perfect 'O'. Then a sly smile spread across her features as she said, "Jeez, I guess we should have knocked first."

Carlos was grinning right along with her.

Both Joe and Maria were visibly flustered.

Joe cleared his throat and looked at his watch. "Man, look at the time. I gotta be going," He said, literally breaking into a run for the door.

"See you Monday, Joe," Maria said. Their eyes met and she felt heat go into her face as he turned and went out the door. *What has gotten into me?* Maria thought, trying to regain her composure.

Both Carlos and Tess were still grinning.

"Well, I'm bushed," Maria announced, looking sternly at Theresa.

She took her mother's cue. "Me, too. I think I'll hit the sack. Goodnight, Mom. Goodnight, Uncle Carlos, thanks for the movie," she said, giving them each a kiss on the cheek.

As Maria was pulling the bed out of the sofa sleeper, with Carlos's help, he said, "I never knew you and Joe had that kind of relationship, Sis."

"We don't, Carlos. I can't explain what happened here tonight. I don't know. But it won't happen again—I can promise you that. Joe and I are just friends, that's all."

"Yeah, right."

"Goodnight, Carlos," she said with a resigned sigh. "See you in the morning."

"Goodnight, Sis. Sweet dreams," he said with a smile still playing on his lips.

12

He wasn't mad anymore. So the little bitch got away—there were plenty more just like her. He'd been furious when he woke up and found she'd escaped.

But after he took his anger out on the puppy he felt somewhat better. He broke its skinny little neck when he threw it against the wall. Now he had a mess to clean up as well. He picked the pup's limp body off the floor and deposited it into a plastic garbage bag, then disposed of it in the Dumpster out back in the alley.

There was no way the little brat could tell the cops where he lived since she was passed out when he brought her here, and the taxi driver found her on First Avenue, which was almost ten blocks away. Anyway, according to the news reports she wasn't doing much talking. Just the same, he'd have to eliminate her to be on the safe side.

He climbed into his sports car and opened the glove compartment, removing the stash he'd squirreled away. He took a couple of good-sized snorts in each nostril and laid his head back on the car seat, feeling the coke permeate his brain and making him feel superior to the rest of the human race.

"Fuck," he said, thinking aloud. Now he wouldn't be able to finish the film, which meant less money; and worse, he missed out on the best part, killing the little bitch. Oh, well, he'd just have to find another one all the sooner. Maybe he'd go hang out at the park for a while and smoke a few joints, try to get his thoughts together—that was getting harder and harder these days. But first, he needed to pay someone a courtesy visit.

He realized to play it safe, they would need to get him another car, not to mention find someone else to be the go-between—to get his dope and deliver the goods. Oh well, his creators would take care of everything—always had—that was no problem. It was just a pain to deal with someone new again, especially after Lenny, who jumped at command, no questions asked.

Too bad for Lenny and his loose lips. Unfortunately, he'd had to be taken care of. It was easy enough. Because of *them* and their contacts everywhere, Milano was taken out nice and neat. They even made it look like a possible suicide. "Dumb fuck," he mumbled, starting his car. "You can run but you can't hide!" he said laughing, his tires squealing on the macadam.

The morning sun woke Tess up about 7:00 AM, which was late compared to 5:30, when the camp counselors woke everyone up. She yawned and stretched, then rolled over on her other side with her back to the streaming sunshine, trying to find sleep again. She lay there another fifteen minutes before finally giving in to the fact that she was up for the day.

The birds were singing their morning song and all was right in the world, now that she was home again. Tess looked around her cozy bedroom and couldn't help but smile to herself. The sheer pink ruffled curtains on the window matched the pink bedspread and canopy over her bed. A large, Victorian-style chair with an overstuffed pink velvet cushion sat in one corner of the room, and perched on the chair were all her dolls—a dark-haired Cabbage Patch Kid, Raggedy Ann and

Andy, various stuffed bears, dogs, and other critters. On the wall opposite her bed hung a poster of her favorite rock group, along with several other posters, one of which was 'Paris in springtime'. That one was her favorite, because whenever she looked at it, she felt she was right there in Paris, and the young couple holding hands looked so much in love.

Tess found herself thinking of Tyler, a boy she liked at school, and how they had held hands on the last day of school. She was thinking of boys more and more these days. It seemed that was all she and Jenny ever talked about.

There was a soft knock on the door and Maria poked her head in. "Mornin', sunshine. I thought you'd still be sleeping after waking up at the crack of dawn these past two weeks." She sat down on her daughter's bed and leaned over to kiss her forehead.

"No, I've been up for a while, just thinking about how great it is be home and wake up in my own bed. I've been thinking a lot about school, too. I guess I'm ready to go back. It's been a great summer, but I'm looking forward to meeting my new teachers and seeing the other kids and stuff."

Tess had told Maria about Tyler and she smiled thinking about it now. "I bet you're especially looking forward to seeing a certain boy?"

Tess blushed. "I hope he still likes me," she blurted out. "I've been thinking about boys a lot these days. Too much! Is that normal? I *never* used to."

Maria laughed. "You're growing up, honey. It's perfectly normal. I remember when I was your age; I had such a crush on Carlos' best friend. I would think about him morning, noon, and night. But then, when he'd come over to the house, I'd be so tongue-tied I couldn't say two words to him."

They both laughed and hugged each other. "I'm so lucky

to have a mom who is my best friend, too. When I grow up and have kids, I'm going to be just like you."

"Well sweetie, you make it easy—most of the time, anyway," she added as an afterthought, tickling ribs. "Now enough of this mushy stuff. What do you say we get dressed and you can help me make the potato salad? We have a full day of fun and excitement waiting for us, not to mention the orangutans," Maria said, trying to forget, temporarily, what the day *really* held in store for all of them.

13

Maria listened to nature's serene symphony—birds singing and insects buzzing—as she lay back, deep in thought, gazing up at the cloudless, blue sky.

They had stuffed themselves with cold fried chicken, potato salad, homemade biscuits, and lemonade. Tess and Carlos decided to go for a walk to the Ice Cream Pavilion for cones while Maria lay sprawled under a big oak tree, feeling so full she felt she might burst.

Her mind went over in startling detail her life with Jack, and she wondered how she would ever go about explaining it all to Tess. *Where to begin...there are so many lies.*

She heard Tess laughing and sat up, shielding her eyes from the bright midday sun. Tess and Carlos were holding hands and each was carrying a triple-dip ice cream cone. Maria smiled and waved, shaking her head and holding her stomach.

Tess plopped down on the blanket next to her mother and began devouring her cone. "Want a bite, Mom?"

"Oh, no thanks, honey." Maria laughed. "Where on earth do you find room for ice cream after the huge picnic lunch we just ate?"

"*Mmm*, always room for ice cream," Tess said between mouthfuls.

After Carlos and Tess finished their cones, they all walked

back to the car to deposit the picnic basket and blanket in the back seat, and then set out for the Como Park Zoo.

Upon arrival at the zoo entrance, they could hear the ruckus the orangutans were making.

Tess laughed. "They must know we're coming," she said, patting her purse, which contained several ripe bananas.

Walking through the zoo, they saw a family of adorable prairie dogs who made their homes in mounds of dirt. Next-door, three skinny coyotes paced back and forth in their cage—bored, pink tongues hanging out. Further along, a couple of ill-tempered badgers peeked out of their cave, looking as if they'd just as soon take a bite out of their hides as lay eyes on them.

They watched the peacocks ruffle their feathers, and then spread them out in a beautiful multi-colored fan.

They approached the orangutan cage—it housed a mama and two babies. The mama had an old dirty scarf tied on her head and was jumping up and down, scolding one of her youngsters.

"Boy, *that* sure looks familiar," Tess said with mock sincerity.

"Gee, thanks a lot. Are you telling me I look like a stinky old monkey?" Maria asked, hands on hips.

Tess giggled. "Well, if the scarf fits."

They all laughed.

Tess walked up to the cage. "Hi there, Big Mama." That was the orangutan's name, and the moniker was a perfect match.

The large primate stopped its tirade and looked at Tess with intelligent brown eyes, cocking its large, shaggy head.

"Are you hungry?" the girl asked.

Big Mama shook her head up and down and both babies followed suit, shaking their heads in unison.

Tess laughed and fished out three bananas. She ceremoniously tossed them each a banana then sat back on her haunches watching them peel back the skin, plopping the entire piece of fruit into their mouths.

Smacking their lips they started jumping up and down, making the entire cage tremble in their demand for more.

"Okay, okay, take it easy. This is it," Tess said, giving them each one more banana.

They devoured the fruit and tossed the peels over their shoulders. Then Big Mama clapped her hands and did a backward flip into the air, making an Olympic-worthy landing.

Tess clapped her own hands and laughed until tears rolled down her cheeks.

Maria leaned her head on Carlos' shoulder, smiling. "I'm so glad we came here today. This place has always been so special for her."

Carlos nodded, watching Tess. "She's a great kid. I hope this makes it easier, considering what she's about to learn."

"We don't have to tell her, you know?" Maria whispered, looking up into Carlos' deep brown eyes.

"I think she's old enough now, Sis. There's no point in prolonging the inevitable." He looked down at his little sister and could read the pain in her eyes. "I know it's hard, but you have to tell her sooner or later, and it's driving you crazy keeping all this bottled up inside."

Tess walked toward them. "I wish I had more bananas. Hey, what do you guys look so serious about?"

"Let's go for a hike and walk off some of that ice-cream. What do ya say, kiddo?" Carlos said, putting an arm around her shoulder. Tess grinned up at her uncle and put her own arm around him.

They walked on one of the many hiking trails, enjoying

the peaceful surrounding woodland, and eventually came upon a clearing with a lovely waterfall. They stopped for a moment to enjoy the scenery, watching the water cascade down in a rush, then flow gently over the mossy rocks in the little stream that babbled at their feet.

"I'd forgotten how beautiful it is here," Maria said, taking Tess's hand.

"I was just thinking the same thing," Tess said, smiling at her mother. "Thanks for today. It's been totally awesome."

"I'm glad you've enjoyed it, honey—so have Carlos and I."

They continued walking deeper into the woods, where only an occasional bird twittered in the woodsy silence, and acorns crunched underfoot.

A little bench had been placed along the path, and Maria suggested they sit for a while. They chatted about various subjects: the impending doom of school starting soon, Tess's stay at summer camp, the mosquitoes...

After several minutes of silence, Maria mustered up all the courage she could find and spoke.

"Tess, honey, there's something we need to talk about. It's going to be difficult for you to understand at first, but I want you to listen, and then I'll answer all your questions, okay?"

Tess looked alarmed. "What's wrong? Are you sick or dying or something?"

"No, no, nothing like that. This is about...your father."

"My father? But he's dead."

"I know, honey, but there are some things concerning your father that I think you're old enough to know now. I don't expect you to understand everything I'm about to tell you, because even I don't. But I think I've kept the truth from you long enough."

"Okay," Tess said in a monotone that scared Maria.

Looking to Carlos for encouragement, which he gave with a nod of his head and compassion in his eyes, Maria began...

By the time Maria finished, she felt drained. And the shocked look on Theresa's face told Maria her daughter felt the same way.

Theresa stared straight ahead, as if in a trance. Then she slowly shook her head, tears standing in her large brown eyes. "I don't believe you." She looked at her mother, confused. "You're lying! I don't know why, but you're lying," she cried, getting up and running off into the woods.

Maria started after her, but Carlos caught her arm. "Let her alone, Sis. She needs to sort this out by herself for now. She'll come back on her own, just leave her be for a little while."

A sob escaped from deep within Maria.

"Oh God, what have I done?" Maria moaned, leaning on Carlos. "I shouldn't have told her any of this. She just wasn't ready." She buried her face in her hands and let the tears come, while Carlos held her in his arms, rocking her back and forth. "It's not safe out there, Carlos, she shouldn't be by herself."

"*Shh*, Maria. It's okay. We'll just give her a couple minutes, and then I'll go after her. You did the right thing telling her the truth. Don't worry, Sis," he whispered, wiping the tears from her face with a handkerchief. Sitting together, they looked more like father and child than brother and sister as Carlos tried to soothe Maria's frazzled nerves.

"Carlos, *please* bring back my baby. Right now. I can't stand this a minute longer.

"Maria—"

There's a murderer on the loose. You haven't seen what can happen to a young child. I have first-hand knowledge—

and I'm *not* going to let Tess become another statistic." Tears flowed freely from Maria's eyes as she pictured every horrendous thing imaginable happening to her young daughter.

"Okay, okay. Calm down, Maria. I'll go find her." He instructed Maria to stay put while he went searching for his niece.

Afternoon soon faded away into early evening and still no sign of Tess. Maria was starting to reach panic-mode.

14

Tess couldn't believe her mother had lied to her all these years. Her own mother, for God's sake. She'd called her mom her best friend just this morning. What a pathetic joke. She cried so hard and so long there were no tears left. She felt tired and achy from walking and running. Running mostly. Running away from the terrible truth of having a father who was a drug user that hated her so much he'd tried to end her young life. And the fact that her mother would lie to her—life just didn't make sense sometimes.

Back on the walking path, Tess stumbled along and followed it through the thick, fragrant lilac bushes that lined either side. She heard a rustling sound coming from behind one of the bushes.

"Who's there?" she cried, startled by her own high-pitched voice in the stillness.

There was no answer, but she *knew* someone was there. Not only did she have a strange feeling of being watched; she could see part of a white T-shirt showing from behind a bush several feet away. Someone was following her!

Tess was scared and disoriented, not sure which direction was the right way back to her mother and uncle. She'd taken so many turns in her desperate flight; she was now confused. Leaving the path, afraid she would be too easy to trail if she stayed on it, Tess ran blindly in the opposite direction as fast as she could, not wanting to see the face of the man who was following her. *It's a monster's face*, she thought—*bloody and distorted, with bone jutting out through greenish skin, one eyeball hanging by a bloody stalk, teeth rotting and stinking, falling out of his head as he calls 'Thereeesssaaaa' over and over.* These morbid thoughts made her run all the faster until she heard a familiar sound. Up ahead was the waterfall. It was probably safe to stop and rest a while to rethink her strategy for escaping the monster. She'd always had an overactive imagination, and it was times like this she wished she could just turn it off like a light switch.

Carlos had been searching for close to an hour and still there was no sign of Tess. Upon coming back full circle to the waterfall, he happened to catch a glimpse of her flowered shirt. He'd almost missed her. She was crouched down in a squatting position *underneath* the waterfall. He stood there for a full minute, watching her. She was shivering now that the sun was going down, and her hair and clothes were soaking wet.

Treading carefully on the shiny, wet rocks to where the little stream met the cascading water, Carlos hunkered down so he was eye level with the girl. She was looking at him, but didn't move a muscle until he held out his arms to her.

Then she stood and made her way toward him on the slippery stones, nearly falling a couple of times. An anguished cry escaped her shaking body as he enfolded her in his big, strong arms and stroked her long, wet hair. "It's all right, honey. Let it out if it makes you feel better."

"Oh, Carlos…how could she lie to me all these years?" she wailed.

Carlos took her by the shoulders and leaned back so he could look her in the eye. "Tess, I want you to put yourself in your mother's shoes for a minute. Think how she must have felt. What was the point in hurting her precious little girl if she didn't have to? Think about it, Theresa! My God, child, she loves you more than life itself. That's why she saved your life years ago and spared you the pain by *not* telling you until now. Can't you see what it has done to her? She never wanted to lie to you, Tessy, but she knew how much the truth would hurt."

Tess looked at her uncle—with eyes blazing and passion in his voice for the love of his sister—and felt ashamed for being a selfish little girl with no regard for anyone but herself. She stood up. "Let's go find Mom, Carlos. I want to go home."

They walked hand in hand along the winding path, back to where Maria sat waiting for them.

When Maria saw them approaching, she stood up, brushing dirt from the seat of her shorts.

Tess ran into her arms, nearly knocking her over. "I'm sorry, Mom. I love you so much," she cried, burying her face in her mother's bosom.

As grateful tears coursed down her face, Maria looked over her daughter's head at Carlos and mouthed the words 'thank you' at her remarkable big brother.

Carlos drove while Maria and Tess sat in the back, holding hands and talking. The girl had many questions and her mother was finally able to answer *all* of them. Maria explained how after Jack died, she had sold their house and bought the condo they now lived in, wanting to be rid of all memories of him.

Everything seemed to make sense now that Tess knew the truth—like why there weren't any pictures of her father around the house. She remembered how upset Maria had become one day when she was about six or seven years old and was rummaging through her mother's closet. She came across her mother and father's wedding picture. Maria had tried to hide the dreadful fear that crawled through her belly upon seeing his face, but Tess knew *something* was wrong. She still remembered the straight-faced, dark-haired man that looked at the camera with contempt in his hazel eyes.

Tess asked her why she'd stayed with a man like that, and Maria explained how her life had been controlled by fear. She told her daughter, for the first time, the truth behind the scar on her left cheek that would remind her of Jack for the rest of her life.

Tess felt a newfound respect for her mother, realizing the strength it must have taken to endure all that pain and despair.

Carlos sat silently up front, driving and listening to the exchange between mother and daughter, until all questions were answered and they both felt a sense of closure.

15

When they got home that evening, there was a message from Joe on the answering machine that said it was urgent Maria get in touch with him as soon as possible. She called him at home but there was no answer, so she called Homicide. He answered on the first ring.

"Detective Morgan."

"Joe, it's me. What's up?"

"You're not gonna like this, Maria, so brace yourself."

"What now?"

"An attempt was made on the McReedy girl's life about two hours ago."

"Oh, no! Is she okay? You got the guy in custody, right, so at least we—"

"She's okay," Joe interrupted. "No change, still catatonic. Her neck is a little bruised, though. Her attacker tried to strangle her. He would have killed her if a nurse hadn't come in at exactly the right moment. And in answer to your other question, *no*. He got away."

"*What?* Shit!"

"Knocked the nurse out with a blow to the head and ran like hell. Nobody got a good look at him. Tall is all I got."

"Damn! There was supposed to be a cop posted outside her door at all times. What happened?"

"There *was* a cop there. This guy was dressed as an

orderly. We found the orderly he knocked out in a supply closet; bound, gagged, and naked as the day he was born. The cop on duty thought the guy was just another hospital worker making his rounds, and decided to take a quick leak, not realizing what was happening. He's been reprimanded. Anyway, we moved her to a different room and now have an officer inside *and* outside her room. It won't happen again."

"The poor kid. As if she hasn't been through enough already."

"I know. Hey, I heard from the professor about an hour ago. Can you get away for a while? I'd like to touch base on some things."

"Sure. Sounds like you've had a busy day. Why don't we meet at the coffee shop on Seventh? That's about halfway. In about twenty minutes?"

"Sounds great. See you then."

Tess and Carlos were so busy playing Scrabble, they barely mumbled their acknowledgment that she was leaving.

Maria saw Joe through the large window that covered the front of the little coffee shop, sitting in a booth near the back, drinking coffee, and ripping a napkin to shreds. As she opened the door a bell dinged, and the few customers gazed her way to see who'd entered their late night domain.

She slid into the booth opposite Joe. "Hey, partner, what's up?"

Joe shoved the bits of napkin into a small pile behind the menu holder, then reached into his front shirt pocket and pulled out a card, sliding it face down across the table to Maria.

She picked it up and looked. It was one of Joe's business cards with a number written in ink in the upper right hand corner.

Before Maria could ask, Joe said, "The McReedy girl's new room number."

She slipped it into her purse as the waitress approached. "Just coffee, thanks," Maria said, turning her cup right side up and watching Joe as the waitress filled her cup.

When the waitress left, Joe continued. "Professor Littleton called. He thinks they've cracked the code to the little black book. He and a colleague will be working through the night until it's completely deciphered. We're to pick up Slade and meet the professor at the University tomorrow morning at 8:00 sharp."

"That's terrific, but why drag Slade along? He doesn't need to be there."

"Not my idea—chief's orders." Joe shrugged his broad shoulders and took a gulp of coffee. "How was the picnic? Did you tell Tess about her father? We need to talk about last night, Maria."

"Whoa, slow down. You sure are covering a lot of ground fast. The picnic was great. Tess took the news about Jack hard, but I think she's already learning to accept it, difficult as it is." She paused, taking a sip of coffee and contemplating what to say next. "As for last night, well, I think we should just forget it—"

"Forget it?" He looked at her, hurt and confusion written all over his face; then shook his head as if to clear it. "Whatever you say. I'll pick you up around 7:30 tomorrow morning to go to the University." Laying a couple of bucks down to pay for the coffee, he made a quick retreat for the door.

"Joe, wait!" Scrambling to follow, she spilled her coffee in the process, drawing stares from several patrons in the cafe. She threw several napkins on the puddle of coffee and hurried out the door, taking refuge in the starry night, where she abruptly collided with Joe.

He wrapped his strong arms around her and looked deeply into her liquid brown eyes. "Forget it, huh? No way, lady," he whispered, lowering his mouth onto hers and drinking in her sweetness.

Maria's entire body was immobile. The only thing that mattered in life was this kiss. She felt a yearning deep in her center and moaned, responding to him unlike any other man before.

All of a sudden, the spell was broken as the door to the coffee shop opened and expelled an elderly, pot-bellied gentleman.

Maria put her hand on Joe's chest and halfheartedly pushed him away.

They stood there, breathless, just looking at each other for several moments, before either spoke.

Maria ran a shaky hand through her wind-swept hair. "God, Joe, we can't do this, it isn't right."

"Why, Maria? Why isn't it right?"

In a daze, heart pounding and too confused to think straight, she was speechless. Instead, she turned and ran like a child trying to escape the bogeyman, to her car parked a block away.

She broke the speed limit getting home, but once there, sat in her car for close to an hour, thinking about one thing—that unforgettable kiss.

16

When Joe picked Maria up at 7:30 the following morning, she thought they would both be uncomfortable, but much to her surprise he was the same easy-going guy as always.

Following Maria out to the parking lot—watching her hips sway—Joe felt his desperation even if he didn't show it. *Man, life really sucks sometimes. Why do the simplest things have to be so damn hard? You would think loving someone would be easy, but Maria is so damn bull-headed sometimes.* He let out a sigh as they approached the car, and Maria darted a furtive glance in his direction, then looked away.

Spotting Slade in the back seat, Maria had to smile to herself. *Did Joe and Peter hate each other so much they couldn't even ride in the front seat together?*

"What's so funny?" Joe asked defensively.

"Did he ride in the back all the way over here?"

"Oh, that," Joe said, looking relieved. "Yeah, I guess he's a little pissed off at me. I told him to let us do the talking when we meet with the professor. He's not used to taking orders, only giving them."

"I'm surprised a certain little someone from the BCA didn't tag along."

Joe laughed. "Foley? Guy's an egomaniac if ever there was one. I talked to the chief this morning. He said he didn't want to waste any more of Foley's time—I think he wants to keep him at a distance. Don't worry though, he promised to *personally* keep the 'powers that be' at the BCA informed."

"We're just one big happy family," Maria said, opening the passenger door, giving Slade a perfunctory glance, and sliding into the front seat.

They drove to the University of Minnesota in silence, each wondering what the other was thinking.

Professor Littleton's office wasn't much bigger than a broom closet, but the awards and diplomas that lined the walls were impressive.

The man himself was in his late fifties; short and stout, with a beard, thick glasses, and a slight English accent, he was the perfect stereotype for his academic profession. The desk he sat behind was a mahogany monster that took up three-quarters of the office space and dwarfed even further the small, mousy man that sat off to one side of the professor in a high-back chair.

The professor motioned for them to sit down. Since there were only two fold-up chairs available, Slade remained standing.

"You're five minutes late," he said, frowning, peering over the top of his glasses at them. "I have another engagement in twenty-five minutes, so let's not waste anymore time on formalities than is necessary. This is Dr. Phillips." He gestured toward the excessively thin man, who nodded toward them with an equally thin smile. "He has helped me immensely in solving the mystery of decoding this little book," he said, waving the black address book in the air.

Professor Littleton laid the book down and reverently opened it to the strange symbols and coding, then pulled some papers out of his top desk drawer. "And here we have the fruits of our labor," he said, patting the papers.

They listened to the professor explain the phenomenal detail that went into the decoding and how they came up with the end results. The intricate coding was comprised of Japanese and Greek lettering, along with a series of dots and dashes similar to Morse code. Hieroglyphics were also used to separate the entries. Dr. Phillips, being the expert in cryptography and a professor in foreign languages, explained how they translated each letter and symbol into the English version.

In the end, what they had on paper was a list of simply three names—two of which were accompanied by address and phone number. Both of these were well-known Mafia crime bosses in the Los Angeles area—Roberto Santini and Nicholas Freyhoff. The last name was J.R. Franco. No address or phone number, just the initials and last name, which no one had heard of.

"I know you gentleman are the experts, but are you absolutely certain *every* letter is correct here?" Maria looked from the professor to Dr. Phillips. "I mean, considering all the coding that was in that little book, it seems strange to say the least that all we're left with is a list of three names."

The professor sat up ramrod straight. "I can assure you, Detective Sanchez, each and every letter is indeed correct. We've checked and double-checked." He appeared to be slightly offended that she questioned his practices. "You must understand, the plan of whomever we are dealing with was to fool even the most professional eye," he stated, as if speaking to a small child.

Dr. Phillips responded with a curt nod and a thin smile.

"I'd say we have our work cut out for us," Maria said to Joe. "Franco is a fairly common name."

"Well, maybe we'll get lucky. If we can tie him to Santini

in any way, shape or form, we got him," Joe responded.

"Yeah, *If*," Slade offered, skeptically.

Joe stood and looked at Slade with equal measure, then returned his gaze to Maria. "I think we know why Milano was hanging out with these guys, considering the mass quantity of heroin he was dealing. But one thing is for sure, he certainly didn't do the coding in that little book. The man didn't have enough brains to fill a thimble, let alone something as involved as this." He picked up the black book, inspecting it, then slipped it into his front shirt pocket.

Professor Littleton stood, barely reaching Joe's chest. "Whoever devised that coding was indeed very intelligent," he said, nodding toward Joe's shirt pocket where one corner of the book was visible. "And they went to great lengths to hide its contents if it should fall into the wrong hands."

Maria rose, reaching out to shake first the professor's hand, then Dr. Phillips, who remained seated. "We want to thank you both very much. This has been very enlightening and hopefully something will turn up when we run a check on J.R. Franco. As for the other two, we know they're into everything from drug smuggling to prostitution. I think they're in even deeper than they realize, though. Well, good-bye, gentlemen. Have a nice day."

Joe and Peter mumbled *thanks* and they all filed out of the cramped, stuffy office and into the bright morning sunshine, squinting while their eyes adjusted.

The car was like an oven. It was going to be another hot, sticky August day, just like the previous week. As if on cue, they all rolled down their windows and sighed as the slight breeze made the heat *almost* bearable.

Walking down the cool corridors of City Hall was a

welcome relief from the sweltering outdoors.

Maria sat down at her desk and powered up her PC, with Joe and Peter seated on either side, waiting with anticipation. She keyed in the access code and put out a search for all Francos with prior arrests in the United States. The NCIC—National Crime Information Center—was a criminal justice network that supplied pertinent data to police officers in all fifty states. However, unless the perpetrator was arrested for a serious offense or had an outstanding warrant, he wouldn't be found in the system. The computer paused, cursor blinking, then beeped, and spit out a list of fourteen names. All of these with the exception of three had the wrong first name. Out of the three, one was female and the other two were already incarcerated, but Maria printed the list to go over again later.

"*Hmm,*" Maria said thoughtfully, hands flying over the keyboard again, eyes now scanning the DMV menu for the proper statewide licensing information.

They waited, watching the computer screen as if it were a god they were all worshipping. This time after the beep, a list of seventy-one names appeared, followed by license and registration information.

"Take your pick," Maria exclaimed. "I'll print this off and then narrow down the search to only the ones with a first name that start with 'J'."

The next list that filled the screen showed twelve names. Out of these twelve only five resided in the Twin Cities area. And of these five only two were male. "Look at this one," Maria said, pointing to the third name from the bottom.

The screen showed a Jake Franco, who resided on Chestnut Avenue, in the city of Minneapolis.

Maria gave a grunt of disbelief. "Oh Jeez! Take a closer look—check out the birth date. The guy was born in 1913.

That would make him how old?"

Peter laughed. "Ninety, if my math is right. *Hmm*, a ninety-year-old serial killer, that's a first. Hey, here's another one," he said, pointing out a Jim Franco, who lived in St. Paul and was closer to the right age. He was forty-two years old.

This time it was Joe who burst their bubble of hope. "Afraid not. Look. He's a paraplegic," he said, pointing at the little wheelchair symbol and reading the guy's driving restrictions.

"Shit," Maria said. "Why can't we get a goddamn break here already?"

She printed out this information then proceeded to investigate the remaining forty-nine states, putting out a search first for any and all Francos, then for only the ones with a first name beginning with a 'J' who were male. "This is going to take a while."

About twenty minutes later they had the results.

They found a grand total of 2,847 Francos in the United States who had valid driving permits, 236 of them males with a first name that began with the letter 'J'.

"I think we may have a better chance of winning the lottery," Maria said, sending these two lists to the printer.

"Slade, see if you can pull some strings and have some of your men put the heat on those two kingpins in L.A.—see what they can get out of 'em."

Maria turned to Joe. "Let's run these over to the Government Center and have them cross-referenced with Social Security and any other state and government records they can find. Hopefully we can tie one of them in with Santini," she said, taking the stack of printouts from the printer output tray. "Not that Roberto Santini ever did *anything* by the book, but we know he has several legit companies to cover his other scams, so who knows? Maybe we'll get lucky. We probably won't get the results back until at least Monday afternoon, but we can check out the two Francos in the Twin Cities, even if they don't fit the mold for deranged killer. Maybe the paraplegic is faking us out, or another scenario could be the old guy has a son, Jake Jr. let's say, who for one reason or another didn't show up on our computer. They're not infallible. What do you think, Joe?"

"Lots of maybes, but it's worth a shot. At this point I don't think we can pick and choose." Joe looked at his watch. "But it's getting late. I don't know if we can hit both of them today."

"I can do one when I'm done here," Slade volunteered. "Unless of course you want them both. I don't want to step on anyone's toes." He held up his hands, surrendering, and smiled crookedly.

"No, be my guest. Which one do you want?" Maria asked, feeling herself bristle at his smart-ass attitude.

"Ladies first," Slade said with a sneer.

"Fine. Let's go see what Jake Franco has to say for himself." Maria spoke directly to Joe, but noticed Slade nod as he pulled the telephone on the desk closer to make his calls.

Maria shut down her PC, then scribbled a quick note and slid it under Peter's nose just as he was starting to get angry at whoever was on the other end of the line. The note stated they were to meet at Finnian's Pub at 6:00 to discuss their findings, if any. Peter Slade glanced at the note and smiled at Maria.

"Let's go, Joe."

Maria handed the printouts to Tom Thompson, who was in charge of Operations in the Government Center's data processing department, which operated 24/7, explaining the order in which they should be done.

"Chief McCollough wants the results no later than tomorrow afternoon. Top priority," she said, knowing that's exactly what he would want when she informed him.

"Tomorrow afternoon?" he asked. He flipped through the stack that contained the names of all the Francos in the United States. "Whoa! There has to be close to three-thousand names here."

"Good guess, Tommy. There are 2,847 to be exact. But don't do any shortcuts. We need a thorough check run on each and every one, starting with the 'J's, first in Minnesota, then California and so on, like we discussed. I know with your mainframe, you've got access to almost every computer in the country, so use your resources to their maximum potential."

Tommy looked at her and frowned.

"Did I forget to say please? Sorry. *Please*?"

Tommy Thompson shoved his hands in his faded blue-jeans pockets and looked at Maria with a mixture of loyalty and trepidation. "I'll do my best Maria, but I'll need ear-plugs when I tell my staff they'll have to pull an all-niter...and on a Sunday," he said with resignation, shaking his head. "Let's see—double workload calls for double manpower—dayshift is supposed to get off at 7:00 PM, but maybe I can bribe them with pizza to help out the night crew. Man, I can hear the moans and groans already." He smiled, which made his thick glasses slide down his freckled nose, then ran his fingers through his short-cropped, blond hair. "Tell the chief I'll have the results by Monday afternoon, hopefully."

"Thanks, Tommy. I knew I could count on you," Maria said, talking to his already retreating figure.

Maria hurried out the door to where Joe waited double-parked in front of the Government Center, anxious to discover what the remaining afternoon held in store for them.

17

The ramshackle old house was rather large, with tall weeds overtaking the narrow stone walkway that led up to the front door. Unfortunately, this was the norm for many of the houses that lined the street in this neighborhood. Above the front door hung an old, weather-beaten sign that read 'Home, Sweet Home'. It had definitely seen better days.

Joe rang the doorbell while Maria walked over to the large double garage that stood between this house and the huge, dilapidated old mansion next-door. She peered in one of the small, grimy windows and saw two cars: one appeared to be an old model Chevy similar to Joe's and the other was a small, black, foreign job. It was too dark inside to make out the license plates, and the door located at the side was either stuck or locked. The main door operated by remote control only.

She walked back to where Joe was waiting. "Pretty snazzy car for an old fart," she said, nodding toward the garage.

Before Joe could reply an elderly, white-haired woman who smiled cautiously, opened the front door. "Yes?"

"Hi," Joe said with a smile. "We're sorry to bother you, ma'am. We're looking for a gentleman by the name of Jake Franco."

"That would be my late husband," she replied with a questioning look on her wrinkled face. "He's been gone almost three months now. It seems like yesterday..." She paused, looking off into space. "It seems like just yesterday he was sitting at the kitchen table drinking coffee and reading the newspaper."

Maria and Joe looked at each other, dumfounded.

Maria was the first to respond. "We're sorry, ma'am. We didn't know he'd passed away. Do you think we could still ask you a few questions?" She showed the old woman her badge, explaining they were police detectives.

"Oh, my! Why yes, I suppose, come in. I'll put on the coffee pot."

"Now don't go to any trouble on our account," Joe said.

"Oh, it's no trouble at all. Been so long since I've had company. Now you just sit right down and I'll be with you in a minute," she said, hurrying off to the kitchen. Maria and Joe took a seat at the dining room table.

The dining room was charming despite its peeling wallpaper and threadbare carpet. The woman obviously went to great lengths to keep everything immaculate. The deep brown, solid oak table had a shine that came from hours of polishing, and there were vases of fresh flowers scattered throughout the room.

The old woman entered the dining room with a tray of cookies balancing on one hand and the coffeepot in the other.

"Let me help you," Maria said getting up and taking the tray.

"Would you be a dear and fetch the cups?" Mrs. Franco asked Joe. "They're on the counter."

"Yes, ma'am."

"Please, call me Martha," she said, smiling at Maria. "I am just tickled pink to have houseguests. But I know you young people came here for a reason, didn't you?"

Joe returned with the cups and took his seat next to Maria.

"Yes, ma'am, I mean Martha, we did. Like we already said, we're police detectives and—"

"Oh, my, detectives!" she declared, having already forgotten that fact. "My Jake never made trouble for anybody," she said almost defensively.

"Oh, it's nothing like that," Maria explained. "See, the name Franco showed up in an address book we found while investigating a case, and your husband—having the same name—was only one of a large group of people we need to check out."

"Well, like I said before, he passed away three months ago, after a long nasty battle with Parkinson's Disease. He didn't get sick until he was eighty-three, so I guess we were lucky to have as much time as we did together. Parkinson's took its time to grab hold...he was bed-ridden for the last year and a half."

"I'm so sorry," Maria said. "Do you have children?"

"No, I couldn't give Jake children...but we had a peaceful, lovely life together."

"You're very lucky for that," Maria said. "What about relatives—brothers, sisters?"

"Yes, one younger brother, Dave. If I recall, much younger, by about twenty years or so. According to Jake, he was an accident that happened one night when his daddy came home drunk.

"Anyway, Dave lives in Hawaii I believe. He and Jake never had much to do with each other, being so far apart in age. Why, Jake had already moved out of the house by the time Dave was born. In fact, Dave never even came to his own brother's funeral. What do you make of that?" She didn't wait for a reply, just kept right on talking.

"Since Jake died I've been on my own, with no help from

hardly anyone." Martha got a wistful look in her eye, then cleared her throat, and smoothed the front of her simple housedress with her wrinkled hands.

"Yes, I think my Jake would be proud of me. I've managed to keep my head above water. With one less Social Security check, it certainly hasn't been easy...but I manage. I've started cooking meals for old Mr. Meyer and his boarders, next-door. Poor, old man; deaf as a stump he is. He gives me fifty dollars a week for doing what I enjoy most in the world, and another fifteen for the use of my half of the garage. He needed the extra space—I suppose for the tenant's cars. I have no use for it, now that my Jake is gone. I sold the car after he died—never did learn to drive. What with traffic so busy nowadays, I wouldn't dream of risking my life out on those streets! The bus runs right by the house, so I always manage to get where I need to go, and I usually make my weekly trip to the grocers with old Mr. Meyer. He's become a good friend since my Jake passed on. Us old poops need to stick together I always say." The sweet old lady beamed broadly at Joe and Maria, her blue eyes sparkling with unbridled mischief.

That explained the sports car in the garage, Maria thought, biting into a date-filled pecan cookie. "Wow, these are absolutely delicious, Martha. Did you bake them?"

"Yes dear, thank you. I'll send some with you when you go if you'd like." Her weathered hands clenched together as she smiled tentatively. "Would you care to see the quilt I'm working on?"

Maria smiled. "We'd love to."

Martha hurried to retrieve her prize possession.

When she left the room, Maria leaned toward Joe and whispered, "I think it's safe to assume we've reached a dead-end here."

Joe nodded his agreement, unable to speak around a mouthful of Martha's cookies.

Back to square one.

One hour later, they walked out of Martha Franco's, armed with date-filled pecan cookies and nothing else.

18

Finnian's Pub was packed on this Sunday evening, but Slade had managed to grab a table near the back in a corner. He was sitting alone, nursing a beer when Maria and Joe came in. He looked up with hooded eyes, slightly drunk, as they approached his table.

Maria sat down next to Slade, while Joe ordered a pitcher of beer from the bar. "Any luck with those two assholes in La-La land?"

"I've got a couple of agents working on it. They'll get back to me as soon as they find out something. Hopefully, by tomorrow, maybe sooner. Oh, and as for Jim Franco," Peter said as an after-thought, shaking his head in dismay. "We can rule him out as a suspect. The guy is paralyzed from the waist down and I'm *definitely* sure he wasn't faking it. Man, I wouldn't wish that on my worst enemy." He downed his remaining beer in one long swallow. "How about you guys? Is the old man our serial killer?" His eyes twinkled as he waited for her response.

"Not unless he's doing it from six feet under—he died three months ago. We had a nice long chat with his widow, though, a sweet old lady who is terribly lonely and bakes wonderful cookies."

Joe returned with a pitcher of beer and two glasses, sitting down next to Maria. "What's up?" he asked, giving Slade a sideways glance.

"Not much," Maria said. "Peter has a couple of men working on those two thugs in L.A. Jim Franco is out of the picture. We have nothing so far. But I'll bet something will turn up with Tommy over at the Government Center. He's helped us out before—I'm positive he will again."

"Well, I would bet my agents come up with something first," Slade stated, with a mischievous twinkle in his eye. "Do we have a wager, Sanchez?" he teased.

"So you're a gamblin' man, are ya? Well, let's see here...I need a new pair of shoes," she said, looking at her worn-out tennis shoe. "How 'bout a hundred bucks?"

"You're on!" Peter extended his hand and they shook on it, while Joe looked on disapprovingly.

Maria put her feet up on the empty chair next to Slade. "Man, I don't know about you guys, but I'm so tired I feel like the walking dead."

"I think this case is hitting all of us hard," Joe said. "I haven't gotten a decent night's sleep since the whole damn mess started."

"Well, maybe this will help," Peter said, filling their glasses.

"Couldn't hurt," Maria stated.

"This has gotta be my first and last." Joe rubbed his temples. "I've got a bitch of a headache and a little league game I promised my nephew I'd be at in fifteen minutes." He moaned, looking at his watch. "Oh, Jeez, make that ten." Downing his beer in three large gulps, he stood up to leave. Looking at Maria he said, "You coming?"

"I think I'll stay a while and drown my sorrows, or at least try to."

"Suit yourself," Joe said, not liking the idea at all.

Glowering at Slade he asked, "You'll make sure she gets home all right?"

"Sure, no problem. I have my rental car. As long as Maria doesn't mind my driving—I tend to have a heavy foot sometimes."

"I'll manage," Maria said, looking at Joe and winking. "Hey, partner, don't worry so much. I'm a big girl."

"Okay, okay. See ya tomorrow," Joe said, turning on his heel and heading toward the door, getting several long looks from lonely ladies at the bar.

"After the week I've spent in your fair city I think I need something stronger than beer," Peter declared, pulling out a small flask of bourbon. "Boilermaker, anyone?" He grinned broadly at Maria.

"Oh, God, after a couple of those I won't know my own name."

"That's the whole point, my dear—guaranteed to chase away the bogeyman."

"Unfortunately, not the real bogeyman, only the one in our minds," Maria added, taking the flask he offered. "Ugh! Who can drink this stuff straight?" She grabbed her beer, draining half of it to wash away the bitter taste of bourbon, but feeling its warmth all the way down to her toes.

They passed the flask back and forth several more times and Maria found the taste wasn't so bad after about the third time. In fact, she was starting to feel pretty damn good about life in general. It was a relief not to be fixated on the case—all the unanswered questions and possible scenarios.

She really didn't give a shit about *anything* at the moment. Slade had been talking about his life growing up in California, and she wondered how she could've misjudged him so. He was actually a nice guy, and she told him so.

Peter laughed. "Maria, honey, you're drunker than a skunk—*that's* why you think I'm such a nice guy. Believe me, tomorrow when you're sober you'll hate my guts just as much as you did before."

"No, I don't think so. Maybe it was *me* all along. Who knows, some sort of penis envy possibly?"

Peter laughed so hard he cried, and Maria started laughing too, seeing the tears roll down his face.

"I've never seen a grown man cry," she exclaimed. They both laughed until it hurt.

"Thanks, Slade," Maria said, when she could speak again without fits of laughter threatening to take over.

"For what?"

"I really needed that. I can't remember the last time I laughed like that."

"God, me either," Peter said, wiping his eyes. "Well, you know what they say."

"No, but I'm sure you'll tell me." She smiled expectantly.

"Laughter is the best medicine. People have actually died from not laughing enough."

"Yeah, right."

"It's true. Don't believe me if you don't want to, but it's in all the medical journals."

Maria noticed for the first time that Peter Slade was handsome. With his wavy, brown hair and deep-set brown eyes hiding behind wire-rim glasses, he had a college-boy sort of charm. Maria figured he was about her own age, considering the high position he held in the FBI, even though he looked much younger. His tweed jacket with the leather patch elbows helped contribute to his schoolboy persona.

At the same time Maria was observing him, Peter Slade was thinking relatively the same thing about her, only in a more sensual light. The way her large brown eyes sparkled and her wind-swept hair framed her beautiful face was very appealing. Her long legs seemed to go on forever, and he could see the outline of firm uplifted breasts through the thin silk shirt she wore. And that deep, sexy laugh would send any man into a tailspin. He found himself attracted to her, despite their many differences in the past.

A cocktail waitress approached to see if they wanted another pitcher of beer. They ordered coffee instead and were also able to get a couple of burgers before the grill closed.

The food sobered them up, and after a couple more cups of coffee, Peter drove Maria home.

He managed to keep the car at only five miles over the speed limit all the way, but it was tough.

Maria threatened to take the wheel if he didn't behave. She'd never told Slade about her parents both dying in an automobile accident, but he seemed sensitive to her needs without knowing the reason why.

He pulled into the parking lot of her condo and cut the motor.

"Well, thanks for a great evening," Maria said, opening the car door.

"Wait a minute, Maria."

Much to her surprise Peter leaned over. Wrapping his arms around her narrow shoulders, he kissed her. His heart was pounding so hard she could feel it against her own chest.

Maria gently pulled away from his embrace. "I'm sorry, Peter—"

"Why? Or do I even have to ask. It's Joe, right?" Reading her expression before she even answered, he said, "I knew it! *I'm* the one who's sorry."

"Ya know, I've been denying it for so long I'm surprised

I'm finally admitting it—not only to myself, but to you of all people. Yes, it's Joe," she whispered in the dark car. "I love him and I have for a long time. But this can't go any further than this car. Do you hear me, Slade?" Her voice rose and her large brown eyes glistened with unshed tears.

Peter put his arm around her. "I hear you, Sanchez. Man, you've got it bad. I don't know why you're fighting it. It's obvious he feels the same about you."

"I don't want to talk about it anymore."

"Okay, okay, but if you ever do, I've got a good ear for listening, and *I promise* I won't make another pass at you.

Maria laughed. "You're the best, Slade. I'm glad we're finally friends. After all of our hostility toward each other, who would've ever thought?"

"The world works in mysterious ways."

"Man, you're just full of clichés tonight, but you're right about that one. It sure does." Maria leaned over and kissed his cheek.

Then she was gone, running toward the lighted entrance of her condo.

Carlos had left the door unlocked for her, and was snoring on the sofa. Maria covered him up and kissed his cheek. Then, turning out the lights, she tiptoed to her own bed.

Peter watched to make sure she made it safely inside, then reluctantly drove back to his hotel, not looking forward to the cold, empty bed that awaited his return.

19

They were in a meeting when Slade joined them a few minutes late. He winked at Maria when he came in, and unfortunately, Joe saw it.

Joe bristled when Peter asked him who won the ballgame Sunday night. "Mind your own goddamn business," he replied.

"Man, someone sure woke up on the wrong side of the bed this morning," Peter responded, not in the least bit offended.

"Okay, boys, enough idle chit-chat. Let's get down to brass tacks," Chief McCollough said. "What have you got for us, Slade? Anything? Or is your pretty face supposed to be enough to keep us happy?"

"Well, I've been in touch with our agents in Los Angeles assigned to question those two Mafia bosses. The assholes claim to have never heard of J.R. Franco, but I really didn't expect them to admit it."

Slade looked at Maria and grinned. "But, they did find out something else rather interesting. It turns out Roberto Santini has a half sister—a Stephanie Franco. Does the last name ring a bell?" Slade paused for effect, but instead was reprimanded by the chief.

"For Christ's sake, cut the theatrics, Slade and get on with it!" the chief bellowed.

Maria held back a laugh that wanted to come bursting forth at this most inopportune moment.

Slade continued, undaunted by the chief. "Ms. Franco, or should I say *Mrs.*," he said, noting their expressions change at this one word. "Mrs. Franco lives in Ventura, California which is only a stone's throw away from L.A.—about sixty miles actually, more or less. She is married to a Jonathan Franco, who if my guess is right has the middle initial 'R'. But that's purely speculation on my part. Santini had to know we'd find out about this, but he probably didn't think we'd do it this soon."

"How did your agents find all this out in a matter of hours?" Joe asked with a note of hostility still in his voice.

"I can't reveal my sources, Morgan," Peter said. "But I *can* tell you the FBI has contacts everywhere—from the very high up to the bottom of the barrel." Slade shifted his attention back to Maria. "I took the liberty of calling your Tommy Thompson at the Government Center. It was after three in the morning, but believe it or not the guy was still there pounding away, trying to beat your deadline, Sanchez. I would have called you, but I know how you need your beauty sleep." He offered her a winning smile.

The chief shifted uncomfortably in his chair and glared at Slade, screaming at him to get on with the story without even saying a word.

Slade got the message and hurried on. "Well, to make a long story short, Tommy hadn't reached the 'S's in the golden state yet, so I had him plug Stephanie Franco's name into the computer. The system showed no ties to Santini, personally or financially, but it did show a marriage license with the name Jonathan Franco listed as spouse. Her maiden name was Weber for the record. Now the bad news. When Tommy ran a check on her husband, Roberto Santini's brother-in-law, Mr. Jonathan Franco, he came up with nothing. Nada. Zip. A big, fat zero.

"Tommy tried as many back doors as he could find in his computer, but it appears Stephanie's husband is not available for comment. He has no Social Security number, no birth certificate, no death certificate, nothing. It appears Mr. Jonathan Franco of Ventura, California doesn't exist, at least not in any computer we have access to."

"But that doesn't necessarily mean anything," Joe interjected. "A man like Santini can easily have things like records, or people, eliminated. And he's *known* for always being one step ahead of the authorities."

"Exactly," Maria agreed. "Unfortunately, *anyone* who has the know-how can get into almost any system and do irreparable damage."

"Well, Tommy told me to tell you, he'll keep plugging along and get back to you when he's done," Slade said, winking again at Maria and then adding, "By the way, I'll take my hundred in twenties, thank you very much.

"Oh, one more thing." Slade couldn't help but enjoy the pained expression on Joe Morgan's face. "I made a phone call to check out Stephanie herself as well as confirm her place of residence. I'm not sure what I would've said if she'd answered—probably, 'Sorry, wrong number'—but as it turned out no one was home. According to the answering machine, they're out of town on vacation, due back the middle of this week." Slade shrugged his shoulders and looked at the chief. "That's it, sir."

"Interesting, very interesting," the chief said, chewing on the stem of his unlit pipe. He got up and paced the length of the conference room. "I think we better get on top of this before it gets away from us, like everything else in this damn case." He scratched his unshaven chin, thinking. "Morgan, I want you in Ventura tomorrow morning to pay the Francos a little visit when they return home from vacation. If we're lucky, you'll arrive before they do—an element of surprise is our best bet."

"Yes, sir," Joe replied, taken slightly aback at being chosen over Slade.

"I know California used to be your home turf, Slade, but I want you and Sanchez to put your heads together and work on the killer's psychological profile. I hope you understand, Peter, nothing personal, but I want one of my own over there.

"Sanchez, I need you here to help me deal with things from this end. And since you have a kid to think about, I think Morgan here is the best man for the job, so to speak... It could take considerable time to find something of use to us, and it could be dangerous depending on what we find. Understand?" Chief McCollough asked, looking at each of them.

They each nodded in turn.

The chief looked over his spectacles at Maria. "If you get a chance, take Slade to see the McReedy girl. Maybe she can shed some new light." He glanced at his watch and took a last gulp of coffee. "Gotta run."

The three of them sat and looked at each other in uncomfortable silence for several minutes, and then they all spoke at once.

"Your brother, Carlos still in town?" Joe asked Maria.

"How was the little league game last night?" Maria asked Joe.

"More coffee, anyone?" Slade asked, filling his own cup.

They all laughed nervously.

Peter left the coffeepot on the conference room table and took himself and his cup of coffee to the outer office, sensing three was a crowd.

In the quiet conference room, Joe and Maria just looked at each other for several minutes, each waiting for the other to speak.

Joe broke the silence. "So, what happened after I left the bar last night?" He narrowed his eyes suspiciously.

"What happened?"

"Between you and Slade."

"Nothing. What makes you think something happened?" Maria responded, defensive.

"You're both acting different toward each other, like you're best of friends or *something*."

"Well, I don't think I'd go that far. He's not such a bad guy, though. We had a little too much to drink and did a lot of talking—"

"*Talking*?" Joe interrupted. "Is that *all* you did?"

A spark of anger lit Maria's dark eyes. "What is this, the fucking Spanish Inquisition? What *exactly* are you saying?"

"I think you know, don't you? I'm not as dumb as I look, Maria. A little too much to drink and who knows what can happen."

"How dare you! What do you think I am, some confused teenager who got a little tipsy and lost her virginity? You must be as dumb as you look, Joe 'cause you are dead wrong!"

Picking up her briefcase and spinning on her heel, she stormed out of the conference room, slamming the door so hard the pictures on the wall shook.

"Ouch," Joe said to the empty room.

20

"Mary had a little lamb, little lamb, little lamb. Mary had a little lamb whose fleece was white as snow. He followed her to school one day. Everywhere that Mary went that lamb was sure to go."

Everything was almost ready—ready to set his plan in motion. With school soon to start, he would be able to take his pick of the litter, and then he'd follow his chosen one until the time was right. Just like Mary's little lamb.

He got an erection just thinking about his hands around some little brat's throat, and the pleas for mercy that were music to his ears—he could hear it now. *Soon, very soon.*

He was set up with a different car now, along with phony license and registration, which changed with each new place of residence, but in this particular situation, was simply an extra precaution due to his last failed attempt. He had a new drug supplier too—Rocky, Ricky, something like that—but they were nervous and told him to lay low for a while. They said the Feds were asking too many questions, nosing around where it was none of their goddamn business.

Time to move on again, but he needed to do one more job here since the last one went awry. Every few months he relocated, always with the help of *them*. He stayed in small, out of the way rental units—hotels and boarding houses mainly—depending on the privacy they provided. He *had* to have his privacy. Sometimes he rented an apartment but only if it was on a month-to-month lease.

The most important factor was that he had to be certain there was no way his victims could ever escape—again. Yesterday he nailed the fuckin' laundry chute shut, so the little shits couldn't use that avenue any longer.

In the quarters he lived in now, he'd installed his own locks that could be locked both inside and out. The owner had agreed, said it was time to change the locks anyway—for safety reasons. *What a joke.* The landlord didn't know about the *other* remodeling jobs, though. He was so goddamn old he wouldn't know if a new window was cut out of the wall in the fuckin' dump. *That* was another factor that was considered before he took up residence—the landlords were usually old farts, or else didn't give a shit about anything but the money he paid them up front.

All rent and necessities were always paid for in cash so no questions were asked, and since he wasn't a very sociable kind of guy, no one bothered him about much of anything.

He had no friends to speak of, but that suited him just fine. His creators certainly were not his friends. Even though they pretended to be, always calling him 'Son', reminding him that without *them* he would be nothing.

They had trained him well. He'd done many different jobs for *them* in the past— everything from drug smuggling to being their personal hit man. They owed him—not the other way around!

He vaguely remembered being married once, many years ago. It was all fuzzy when he tried to think about it. His defunct mind told him he'd been running drugs across the Mexican border when he met her, but *something* buried deep inside told him different—perhaps it was *before* he was running drugs that he met her. In fact wasn't she the reason for all his hatred?

He couldn't remember her name…or anything else about their marriage, but he did remember her long, dark hair. That was as far as his abused memory would let him go.

His head started to ache, as it always did whenever he tried too hard to think about the past. It started out as a slow, throbbing pain and built momentum.

It was best forgotten as they so often said. He knew they *made* him forget things. But he didn't care—as long as he had his fondest memories…of killing. The drugs helped him not to care about anything anymore—except killing and not being caught, which was one thing he was very good at. *Nothing* was more important to him.

He always stayed one step ahead of the cops. Doing something different with the disposal of the bodies was the key. Sometimes they were left in Dumpsters with their throat cut, like he'd left a few in Detroit. He remembered how he'd disposed of several in New York by stuffing an apple in their mouth and setting them on fire. Very similar to a pig-roast, only the smell was different. He also recalled leaving mutilated corpses hanging from street lamps, although he couldn't remember what city or state that was in, somewhere down south maybe? Florida? Georgia? There were so many of them it was hard to keep track.

Nowadays the river was his friend. Different strokes for different folks. That way the cops didn't associate one group of killings in one part of the country with the others. The only constant for him in all the craziness was *them*. They were always there to help him with whatever he needed, whether it was drugs or something else. That was because he'd always been a loyal subject—exemplary in fact.

But he trusted no one—not even *them*. He knew they wouldn't hesitate to kill him if it suited their organization. That would never happen though... He was more powerful than even his creators knew. He would kill *them* while they slept if they turned renegade on him.

He walked to the small wooden cabinet above the compact refrigerator where he kept various odds and ends.

Rummaging through his belongings he finally found what he was looking for and pulled out a large, clear Mason jar. Holding it up to the bright light he examined the contents floating inside. "*Ahh*, tokens of their appreciation," he whispered, mesmerized. Inside were various body parts—eyes, fingers, toes, even an ear floated in the greenish liquid. He liked to shake it up and watch the contents dance like some gory snow-globe scene. He'd begun his collection about two years ago. Before that, he merely killed them and was left with nothing to remember their existence by. It made him sad to think of all the prizes he left behind. Pretty soon he'd have another item to add to his collection—maybe a nose this time.

He spent the entire day yesterday in Como Park, playing 'I Spy' and had spotted several potential candidates. A red-haired little boy was left alone to play on the swings while his mother went back to the car for some forgotten item. He could have whisked him away in a matter of minutes.

But he needed to wait.

He'd also followed a pretty, dark-haired girl on the wooded path while she cried and cried, mumbling nonsense to herself, obviously upset about something—another perfect specimen from what he could see, before she ran away.

But they said *wait*, so he would wait.

On the way back to his car that same afternoon he came across two dark-skinned girls who appeared to be twins, playing jacks in the parking lot with no adult anywhere nearby to interfere. *Twins would be fun...*

But he *must wait...* just a little longer.

Pressure was building in him and soon he would explode if he didn't fill his need—*but he must wait!*

Soon, very soon!

Children everywhere were anxious for the new school year to begin. So was he, because then the long wait would finally be over.

Once they gave him the green light, he would find the perfect time and place to make one of them his.

Forever!

21

The motion of the airplane, along with the previous sleepless night, put Joe fast asleep. He was dreaming of the woman he loved.

Clutching his pillow to his chest, he thought of Maria's warm, willing body. They were just about to make love in his dream when a voice said, "Excuse me, sir. Beef or chicken?"

He opened his eyes and glanced around the alien surroundings, surprised to see the lady in the seat next to him frowning. In the aisle, a cute, blonde flight attendant bent over him, smiling. In a singsong voice, she repeated her question.

"Beef or chicken for your dinner entrée, sir?"

"Huh? Oh, ah, beef will be fine," Joe stammered, still bewildered with the last vestiges of sleep and his dream of Maria hanging on to his subconscious.

Feeling the fool, he looked at the woman seated next to him who was still frowning, only now into a book. He quickly looked away and grabbed one of the magazines in the pocket of the seat in front of him.

The last conversation he had with Maria was not a pleasant one. The way her dark eyes flashed with anger and the sound of the door slamming reverberated in his mind.

God, she is so beautiful, even when she's really pissed off. He'd have to apologize to her the minute he got back. He had no right to accuse her of anything. He had no rights on her, period. Maria had made that crystal clear more than once. They were just partners, that was all.

Yeah, right.

He knew she felt something for him even if she was too damn stubborn to admit it.

After choking down his airline food—a beef and congealed gravy concoction over rice pilaf with a single spear of half-cooked broccoli—the pilot announced their descent into Los Angeles International Airport, and the seat belt signs blinked on.

Smog was a thick, gray layer across the city as they made their approach. The pilot informed them it usually lifted around noon.

Joe consulted his watch and reset it for the appropriate time zone—it was 11:15, L.A. time.

Jonathan and Stephanie Franco lived on Hacienda Boulevard in a modern, ranch-style house.

Joe was surprised to see a blue BMW parked in the driveway with the trunk open. A small boy struggled up the front steps with a large suitcase.

He parked his rental car in the street and walked up the palm-lined drive, stopping by the BMW.

A tall, dark-haired woman, clad in shorts and a midriff top, came bounding down the steps to get another load, when she spotted Joe and came to a halt.

"Who the hell are you?" she said, eyeing him suspiciously.

"So much for Californian hospitality. Detective Joe Morgan," he said, showing his badge. "Are you Stephanie Franco?"

Her eyes darted from her car to the house to Joe, like she was maybe thinking about running, but knew it was hopeless.

"Maybe…"

"I'd like to ask you and your husband a few questions."

"I'm kinda busy," she said uneasily.

"Here, let me help you," Joe said, grabbing another huge suitcase out of the trunk. Stephanie grabbed half a dozen bags out of the back seat then led the way back to the house.

"Go unpack your suitcase, honey," the woman told the little boy who obediently did as he was told.

"Have a seat," she said to Joe, sitting down at the kitchen table.

"We're trying to locate your husband, ma'am. Do you know where he is?" Joe questioned, taking note of the nervousness the woman exuded.

"My husband?"

"Yes. Jonathan Franco. He *is* your husband, isn't he?"

"*Was* my husband. I haven't seen him for more than five years, since before Tony was born. Why? Is he in trouble?"

"Yeah, you could say that. He's a murder suspect."

"Oh." Stephanie Franco stood and walked on trembling legs to the sink for a glass of water. "Can I get you something? Ice tea, maybe? Water?"

"No thanks," Joe said. "Just some answers."

She returned to the kitchen table with her water. "Look, detective, like I told you, I haven't seen him in years…we're estranged. We were married only a couple of months and then he took off shortly after I became pregnant."

"Not the fatherly type?"

"I'm afraid I can't help you."

"I think maybe you're just *afraid*." Joe had the distinct feeling this woman was holding something back. He watched her while she nervously inspected her fingernails, then looked at her watch. That's when he saw the needle tracks on the underside of her left arm. She quickly folded her arms, fear in her large, green eyes apparent.

"Do you know Roberto Santini?" Joe asked.

Stephanie Franco was so startled by the question her hand seemed to fly out of nowhere and knock the glass of water to the floor. "Oh God, look what I've done," she said, tears springing to her eyes. "What a klutz I am. Good thing it was plastic, or I'd be cleaning up glass as well." She grabbed a rag to wipe up the spill.

While she was down on her hands and knees wiping up the water, Joe asked again if she knew Roberto Santini.

"No, why would I?" she said, putting the empty glass back on the table and flinging her black, glossy hair over one shoulder.

"Let's just call it a sixth sense. There's something else I know, too."

The woman just looked at him.

"You're a user, Stephanie. I saw the tracks before you could hide them. Look, either you can talk to me here, or I can take you down to the local police station. I bet if I looked into that purse of yours," he said, nodding toward her handbag sitting on the counter, "I'd find whatever it is you're shooting into your veins."

"But, my boy, I *can't* tell you. You don't know what they're capable of," she stammered, fear written all over her face.

"I'll protect you and your little boy. You can come back to Minnesota with me—far away from the people you're so afraid of, where you'll both be safe. We *can* help you, Stephanie—with your drug problem, too," Joe offered.

"Really? I can't tell you how good that sounds—too good to be true."

"It *is* true, Stephanie. I promise you on my life it is."

They looked at each other for several moments, evaluating one another.

Finally, Stephanie let out a shaky sigh. "Well, okay, just let me check on Tony first and make sure he's all right."

She came back five minutes later and sat down across from Joe. "Where do I begin?" She looked like a lost little girl.

"How about at the beginning," Joe said.

"Okay, at the beginning. I was fifteen years old when I was admitted into a mental institution for the first time, and for the next three years, I was in and out probably a dozen times. My mother hated me and wasn't afraid to show it. I had the bruises to prove it. I was a very mixed up teenager.

"I never knew who my father was until I turned eighteen. When my mother was dying of cancer, she finally told me—he was Mafia boss Antonio Santini. She told me this, thinking—probably praying—it would drive me over the edge, but it had the opposite effect. I finally knew who I was. A year later, when I was about nineteen, I met him for the first time along with his only son, my half brother Roberto, who is about ten years my senior."

She paused and took a sip of water from the glass she'd refilled, looking at Joe uneasily.

Joe nodded his encouragement. "Go on." At least she appeared to be telling the truth—everything matched with what they had learned so far. He'd been briefed late last night on Stephanie's past. Whatever information could be discovered in cyberspace, Tommy Thompson from the Government Center had found it.

"They accepted me into the family readily enough," Stephanie continued. "Antonio had been a widower for about six months by then and figured he could bring me into his home without too much strife—although no one else knew I was his daughter besides him and Roberto. I was told to say I was a *friend* of the family, nothing more. That was okay with me. I was happy to be with my father, even if I had to keep it a secret. I lived with him for one blissful year, until he died of a massive coronary one night in his sleep.

"It was then that I started using heroin. Roberto helped me. But you must believe me when I tell you he meant me no harm. He really was only trying to help. You see, I was having *trouble* again and would've had to go into another institution, but the heroin was like a magic drug. It helped me to cope with my loss and my 'doomsday prophecy'.

"Roberto *has* been good to me—most of the time. He bought this house and found me a husband. My husband was not a nice man, though.

"Jonathan Franco was crazy, but Roberto thought we would be perfect for each other, considering we were *both* unstable. Jonathan was a user too, which was another thing we had in common, but that is where it ended. Jonathan was smuggling drugs from Mexico for Roberto when I first met him.

"Shortly after we were married, I became pregnant. I was thrilled. So were my husband and half brother, but for different reasons. You see, they had planned on my pregnancy all along. I was to become a big part of the family business finally. I would make my father's spirit proud, Roberto told me, by making babies for them to sell on the black market. We would bring in tens of thousands of dollars.

"Well, needless to say, I was totally appalled and refused to cooperate—just flatly refused. Both Roberto and Jonathan were furious. Their plans were ruined, but I stuck by my decision. Two weeks later Jonathan Franco left me. We all decided it was for the best. I'm sure I would have been killed right then and there if I was not family—my bloodline saved my life. That was more than five years ago. I haven't seen or heard from my husband since."

She stood, paced the floor several times, then wiped off the counter with a piece of paper towel where a couple drops of water lay. Returning to her seat at the table, she clasped her hands tightly together and looked Joe in the eye.

"Roberto has relinquished all social ties since that fateful day, but still supplies my drugs and enough money for Tony and me to get by."

Joe was so consumed by her story he was temporarily speechless. "Wow," was all he could manage at the moment. This woman was stronger than she looked—to have persevered through so much immorality and pain without losing faith was a testament to that. "Do you think Jonathan Franco still works for Roberto?"

"Probably, but I couldn't say for sure. Like I said, Roberto and I don't speak anymore."

"What about Nicholas Freyhoff, have you ever heard of him?"

"Yes, he was Roberto's right-hand man and best friend."

"Stephanie, I know this is a lot to ask, but would you be willing to testify against your half brother?"

She looked long and hard at Joe before answering. "If you meant what you said, about protecting me and my boy, *yes*."

"I meant it," Joe said, reaching over and squeezing her hand. "You're doing the right thing, for both you and your son."

"I know. I feel like a weight has been lifted off my shoulders. I'll be free, and most important, Tony will be free to be his own man when he grows up. He won't be under the thumb of an uncle that has no morals or scruples. Thank you." Tears stood in her large green eyes.

"No, thank *you*. With this leverage, we have enough to bargain with Santini and hopefully find out where your husband is hiding."

"It won't be easy to find him. He was not a sane man when I knew him."

"Well, I have a feeling he's even less sane now—over the edge. Is Jonathan's middle initial 'R' by any chance?"

"I have no idea. You have to remember I didn't really know the man, I was only married to him," she said, smiling thinly.

"Well," Joe said, looking at his watch. "We've been talking for close to an hour. Why don't you get your things together and come back to my hotel with me."

Stephanie glanced nervously at her own watch. "Can you come back and get us in a few hours? I'm expecting someone shortly."

"Your supplier?"

She blushed and looked away. "One last time. *I promise*."

"What do you do with the kid when you're doing that?" *Is this going to work?* Joe wondered. Would Stephanie be strong enough to withstand the pressure that would soon be building all around her?

"I usually send him next-door to play with his friend. And since we'll be leaving for good, he'll want to say good-bye."

"Okay, I guess I can look the other way this once, but you're not bringing *anything* back with us. Is that understood?"

"Understood."

Joe felt uneasy about the whole mess, but the supplier was

already on his way. "It won't be easy, you know, getting off the horse."

"I know...but I've been riding far too long—I'm ready. For my own sake as well as Tony's."

"I'll be back around 6:00 this evening to pick you both up," Joe said, standing up to leave. "It's at least an hour drive to the airport and there's a flight to Minneapolis that departs at 8:45."

"Okay, we'll be ready. Thanks," she said, hugging Joe. "We needed a knight in shining armor, but I thought he'd never come."

"I'm no savior, Stephanie...you have to save yourself in this world." Joe smiled at her. "But, you're very welcome. I'm glad I can help you. Remember, 6:00 sharp."

Joe walked out the door to his rental car, which sat baking in the hot California sunshine.

Stephanie gave her little boy milk and cookies, then explained in child-like detail the great adventure they would soon be embarking on. Tony was very excited. She then kissed and hugged him, sending him off to play at the neighbor's house, while she waited for her fix to arrive.

Stephanie Franco had hope in her heart for the first time in her life. Unfortunately, that hope—along with her dreams of a new beginning—would be very short-lived.

22

Maria and Peter spent the entire morning at Minneapolis Children's Hospital, first talking to Betsy's doctors at great length about her prognosis, then attempting to talk to the girl herself. Betsy was still unresponsive, and would be for an indeterminable amount of time according to her doctors.

They also talked to the nurse who'd been knocked out when an attempt was made on Betsy's life a couple of days ago. She told them exactly what she told Joe at the time of the incident—the man was tall and muscular. That was all she could remember. She thought he might have had dark hair, too, but she wasn't sure because everything had happened so fast.

Back in the car, Maria turned to Slade. "Well, what do you think? Do we have enough information to add anything new to your existing profile on the killer?"

Peter laughed. "Well, to be perfectly honest...*no*. But once we hear from Morgan and know more about our prime suspect one way or the other, we'll have something more definite to add. In the meantime, when we get back let's go over the files on the previous victims with a fine-tooth comb, and start from scratch. Hopefully by the end of the day we'll have something new to show the chief."

Spotting a McDonalds, they went through the drive-thru and ordered burgers and coffee, deciding to take a working lunch while they put together the information needed for the profile.

When they got back to City Hall, Maria pulled the necessary files on the previous victims and they began the tedious project of going through each and every detail. They perused crime lab results and autopsy reports, studying pictures and analyzing the similarities and differences in each of the cases.

Slade made a list of everything they knew about the serial killer:

Suspects: River Rat - J.R. Franco (age—mid-thirties)??
Tall/muscular
Dark hair?
Pedophile/Psychopath - victims abused both sexually and physically before strangulation.
Collects trophies (body parts—fingers...)
Pornography
Drug user?
Ties to L.A. mob / Milano?

Maria noticed her message light blinking. Being so involved in what they were doing, she hadn't noticed it before. She picked up the phone and punched in the code to listen to her message. It was received at 1:05. She listened to Joe excitedly tell of the progress he'd made, and he mentioned she should talk to the chief for further details. He had faxed Chief McCollough a detailed report from the Ventura Police Department. He also said he was sorry for being such a jerk yesterday and wondered if she would check on his cat, Mr. Peanut, on her way home from work today. Maria hung up with a smile on her face.

"Good news?" Peter asked.

"Yeah, I think so. That was Joe. It appears he has a lead. I'll be right back," Maria said, getting up and going to the chief's door, knocking once and entering.

"Why didn't you tell me right when we returned about the latest information Joe sent in?"

"I left you a copy of the fax in your In-box, Sanchez," he said, looking over his spectacles. "What do want me to do? Read the damn thing to you? I'm busy!"

"I'm sorry. I didn't check my In-box. I just got the message Joe left me and I—never mind." she said, talking to the chief's back, as he was turned around looking for something in his file cabinet. She slipped out and softly shut the door, not wanting to disturb him further.

Back at her desk, she rummaged through the contents of her In-box and found the fax near the bottom. Reading it, she could hardly believe her eyes. This was a major break-through. Now they had something to bargain with—or rather someone.

Stephanie Franco would blow the top off the neat little box Santini had closed himself into.

"Before you do anything else, read this," Maria said, handing Slade the fax Joe had sent.

By the time Slade finished reading it, he had a smile plastered on his face as big as Maria's. "Man, I bet the chief is happy. This is just what we needed."

Maria had a puzzled look on her face. "You know, I would think he'd be thrilled. But he's not. He's in a foul mood and would barely talk to me when I went in to see him. I wonder what's going on. Must be something he doesn't want me to know about."

Peter read the fax again, deleting most of the question marks they had just put in the profile they were recreating, and then adding the new information:

> *Estranged wife: Stephanie Franco—Roberto's half sister—married approx. two months.*
> *Son: Tony (unknown to suspect)*
> *Employer for past five years (?): Roberto Santini (Mafia)*
> *Apparent dislike for children.*
> *Suspect previously resided in Ventura, California.*

"Wow!" Maria said. "What a tangled web we weave, huh?"

"Yeah, you got that right. Now, let's see what we can put together on this guy's psyche. He's a classic textbook example of a psychopath. In fact, you could probably pick up any medical journal or Merck manual and find virtually the same information as I'm about to describe."

Peter's hands flew over the keyboard as he read what he was typing to Maria.

> *"Suspect, J.R. Franco, appears to have anti-social (psychopathic) personality. Psychopathic individuals characteristically act out their conflicts and cannot conform to social rules. They are amoral, irresponsible, and impulsive. Suspect demonstrates these aforementioned traits, along with the following psychopathic traits disclosed:*
> > *"*Cannot form close relationship with others—but charm and plausibility may be skillfully used for own needs.*
> > *"*Tolerates frustration poorly, and opposition elicits aggression and/or serious violence.*
> > *"*Behavior is not associated with guilt or remorse,*

since individuals with this disorder tend to rationalize and blame their behavior on others.

"In conclusion, this personality type is often associated with a history of drug addiction, alcoholism, sexual deviation (as in the suspect—pedophile), promiscuity, failure to hold an occupation, etc."

Peter leaned back in his chair, hands behind his head. "Well, what do you think so far?"

"You're good, Slade. It's a lot more detailed than the original profile you faxed us. I'm sure you'll get another big, fat 'atta-boy' from the chief."

"Thank you, Sanchez. Your words warm my heart. But seriously, if it weren't for Morgan we'd still be sitting at ground zero. He's the one who deserves the pat on the back. I may have discovered the goose, but he got her to lay the golden egg—I think the chief said something similar about a week ago, didn't he?"

Maria laughed. "He said: 'You don't kill the goose that lays the golden egg', referring to your suggestion of a pornography ring. But now, with Santini involved, anything is possible." Maria shook her head. "Where were we? Oh yeah, who deserves the pat on the back... Well, I think Stephanie Franco should get some of the credit, because without her cooperation and testimony, we would have nothing. It must have taken a lot of guts to go against *'The Family'*. I'm sure we'll accumulate tons more information to add to that profile once we talk to her more extensively."

Maria looked at her watch. It was already 5:30. "Why don't you print that off and put on the finishing touches later."

"Yeah, okay. I brought my laptop. I'll work on it tonight in my hotel room. What are you doing for dinner tonight,

Sanchez? Or will your boyfriend disapprove?"

Maria laughed, even though she felt like punching him. "My boyfriend? Do you mean Joe?"

Slade nodded, a smug smile dancing on his lips.

This time Maria did punch him, and hard.

Peter rubbed his arm. "Man, you sure throw a mean punch. That hurt," he whined.

"Oh, don't be such a big baby. It serves you right. And if you want to come over to my house and bring the pizza and beer, I'll help you eat it."

"Man, what a deal."

"Well, your other alternative is sitting alone in your hotel room with your laptop computer for company."

"Yeah, I guess you're a little better than that. What time?"

"How about 7:30?"

"Okay, see you then," Peter said, still rubbing his arm.

23

Maria pulled up to Joe's house on Hamline Avenue in St. Paul and got out of the car, thinking about her partner in California.

She checked under the welcome mat and found the key Joe had left there. *You would think, being a detective, he would know this wasn't a safe place to put his house key. Everyone knows that's the first place a burglar looks when he's casing a house for an easy break-in.* She chuckled to herself.

Mr. Peanut was snoozing on the couch, sunbathing. He looked up lazily and yawned when Maria approached.

"Hi, puss, how ya doin'?" Maria asked, sitting down next to the huge tan cat, who really was shaped like a peanut.

The cat stood up and stretched then sauntered over to Maria's lap, kneading her stomach like bread dough and purring.

"Oh my, you are a big, old, lazy puss, aren't you?" she chided, scratching the cat behind his ears. "You miss Joe I bet, don't you? You know what? So do I...but don't tell him I told you, okay?"

The cat responded by letting out a funny sounding meow, because it was mixed with his intense purring.

Maria laughed, stroking the big, lovable cat and crooning to him. She was in no hurry to get home, because she knew Tess wouldn't be there. She was spending the day over at

Jennifer's house and would likely call after supper requesting to spend the night too, since school would be starting in a matter of days and sleepovers would soon dwindle to just weekends. Maria had given her daughter permission and enough money to put several things on layaway for the big back-to-school shopping trip Nancy was taking the girls on today. Nancy promised she'd watch what Tess bought and make sure it wasn't too outrageous—in price *or* style.

Maria walked into the kitchen with Mr. Peanut following close behind. She gave him fresh crunchies, even though he still had some left in his bowl, and filled his water dish with fresh water. For a treat, she gave him a small saucer of milk, which Joe said he sometimes liked.

Seeing the dirty dishes piled in the sink, Maria figured this was what every bachelor's house in America looked like. Filling the sink with hot soapy water, she left the dishes to soak and went in search of a vacuum cleaner, with the cat following her every move, trying to trip her with his insistent rubbing on her legs.

By the time she left, Joe's house looked like a different place from the one she'd entered only sixty minutes ago. Mr. Peanut seemed to like it, too—he was sprawled on the freshly vacuumed carpet, preening, and giving himself a thorough grooming.

By the time Maria got home, it was almost 7:00, and her own house looked like a small tornado had swept through it. She went into her bedroom and slipped on a pair of shorts and an old T-shirt, then set about straightening up before Slade arrived with the pizza.

Carlos had gone back to Chicago early in the morning. He'd stayed longer than originally planned, but they still hated to see him go. All three of them had tears in their eyes when he left, but he promised he'd be up again before the holidays. He and Tess had spent some much-needed quality-time together while Maria was at work, and they had developed a deep friendship that would last a lifetime. They spent a lot of time talking about the past, which was important to Tess since learning about her father.

Maria noticed the message light blinking on her answering machine and pushed the play button, listening to Tess's excited voice tell of their successful shopping trip and pleading to spend the night at Jennifer's. Maria laughed. The girl was so predictable.

She'd just returned Tess's call and had no more than hung up the phone when the doorbell rang. She peered through the peephole and saw Slade with a large pizza balancing on one hand and a 12-pack of beer in the other.

He put his eyeball to the outside peephole and grinned. "Pizza delivery, ma'am."

Maria opened the door. "Come on in, Peter." She laughed. "*Mmm*, that sure smells good. I'm starved. Right this way please, if you want a tip," she said, leading the way to the kitchen.

They sat together like old friends, devouring pizza and guzzling beer, keeping conversation to a minimum while they stuffed their faces.

24

It was 5:45 PM when Joe left the hotel to pick up Stephanie and her son. He made reservations for the return trip to Minneapolis on Northwest Airlines for the three of them. The flight left at 8:45 from L.A. International, so they didn't have a lot of time to spare, considering it would take at least one hour, maybe more, to get to the airport from Stephanie's house. He hoped she would be ready to go when he got there. He also hoped she wasn't so wasted that she didn't remember the deal they'd made.

As he drove, he recalled his phone call to Chief McCollough. The chief was upset with him. If this fell through it could possibly mean his job—he'd said as much... The chief didn't like the idea of Joe leaving Stephanie alone, especially for the sake of getting one last fix. Joe knew he'd used poor judgment, but at the time he didn't see any other way. This last fix seemed symbolic to her—and the dope deal was already in the works. If she wasn't there it would cause unwanted suspicion on the part of Santini before they even got out of town. Joe tried to explain this to Chief McCollough, but he wanted to hear none of it. He said at the very least, Joe should have stayed hidden in another room while the deal went down. Looking back now, he realized the chief was right, but he needed to get back to his hotel to pick up his things and arrange for the flight. He also had to fax all the information he'd gleaned from Stephanie from the fax machine located at the Ventura Police Department to the chief and Maria back in Minneapolis.

Joe didn't think Stephanie was a flight risk, considering she was so desperate for help, but like the chief said, *'You can never trust a junkie.'* Oh well, hindsight was always 20/20—it was too late to change anything now.

Traffic was bumper to bumper, so it took him about twenty minutes longer than expected to reach Stephanie Franco's house.

Pulling into her driveway, he noticed the front door standing ajar. Hopefully, Stephanie would be ready to go with bags packed. She was probably anxiously awaiting his arrival, considering he was more than twenty minutes late.

Joe checked the time—it was 6:24 PM according to his digital watch.

He walked up to the open door and knocked, sticking his head inside.

"Stephanie?"

No answer—that was odd.

Joe stepped inside, and the strong, coppery odor of blood, mixed with the smell of gunfire, assailed his nostrils. There was no mistaking it—he knew only too well what he was about to discover.

He pulled the Glock nine-millimeter from his shoulder holster, then proceeded into the living room with caution.

Bright red blood splattered the white living room wall in a pattern of violence, and Stephanie Franco lay sprawled beneath it, her body riddled with bullet holes.

Joe knelt down next to the body, feeling for a pulse even though he knew she must be dead. Her body was still warm—

blood oozed from the bullet holes in her head—she couldn't have been dead very long. "I'm sorry," he whispered as he closed her eyes and covered her ravaged body with the quilt that lay draped over one end of the couch.

He gradually stood up, feeling as if everything was moving in slow motion.

The boy—where was the boy? Would he find him dead, too—perhaps lying in the kitchen, the life gone out of his large green eyes—his body looking like Swiss cheese from all the bullet holes, much like his mother?

As he made his way into the kitchen, he felt something crunch underfoot. Bending over to get a closer look at the broken syringe, Joe wondered if Stephanie got her fix before she was murdered. *Probably not,* he thought. The animal who did this was more than likely the one who delivered the drugs, with orders to take her out at the same time. And it was possible the guy was still in the house—somewhere—considering the smell of gunfire was so strong when he first came in, and Stephanie's body was still warm. He picked up the telephone hanging on the kitchen wall, intending to call for backup, but the line was dead and his cell phone was back in the car.

Joe realized now the place could very well be bugged. They could've heard Stephanie confessing everything to him and realized they had to move fast before he could get her out of town and out of their reach.

Checking the kitchen, he expected to find the little boy's body, but found nothing. He quickly looked in the cupboards and anywhere else a little boy—or a killer—might hide.

He then went into the downstairs bathroom that was just off the kitchen, but found nothing there either.

Backtracking his way through the living room to the

staircase leading upstairs, he glanced at where Stephanie now lay dead—nothing but a lump under a blanket—and knew he would never forgive himself for letting her down. She had trusted him, and in turn, he'd promised her and the boy safekeeping for helping him. He was just starting up the stairs, when he heard a soft thump come from the closet by the front door.

Joe stopped, not taking a single breath as he stood with one foot frozen on the carpeted stairway...listening. He turned and slowly moved toward the closet, not making a sound, anticipating Stephanie's killer rushing him at any moment.

With his gun aimed at the closed closet door, he reached for the handle and grasped it. His hands were slippery with sweat and he could feel the slick knob try to slip through his fingers. Joe tightened his grip, heart pounding out a staccato beat as he flung the door open wide.

Little Tony Franco huddled in one corner, eyes wide and terrified in his small, pale face.

Joe lowered his gun, relief washing over him. He took the boy into his arms and held him, patting his back. "It's okay, son, everything's going to be all right," he whispered.

He steered the child out the front door onto the steps, then knelt down so they were eye level. "Now I want you to listen to me very carefully, Tony."

The boy looked dazedly past Joe, through the front door and into the living room in the direction of his dead mother.

Joe gently turned the boy's face toward him. "Your mom would want you to listen to me, Tony. Did she tell you I was going to help you?"

Tony nodded, his large, green eyes that were so much like his mother's filling with tears.

"I want you to run next-door and have the lady call 911.

I'll come and get you when it's safe. Do you understand, Tony?" Joe could tell the boy was in shock, but he had to get him out of this house—and with Stephanie dead and the killer possibly still on the premises, there was a good possibility he might need backup.

The boy nodded, looking up at Joe with such vacant, sad eyes, he felt his heart ache.

Joe hugged the boy again. "Okay. You go on now. Have the lady call 911, and I'll come and get you as soon as I can. Run, Tony." He gave the boy a little push and watched him run next-door, glancing back at Joe once before running up the front steps of the adjacent house.

Less than a minute later, Joe saw a woman stick her head out the door and acknowledge him with the phone already up to her ear. She and the boy went back inside and Joe did the same, heading toward the staircase that led to the upstairs bedrooms. Backup would soon arrive, but the level of adrenaline pumping through his blood pushed him forward.

All the doors were closed, so if Stephanie's killer was up here it would be a guessing game—with Joe on the losing end. He went to the first closed door and with gun drawn turned the knob, then kicked the door wide open. This was Stephanie's bedroom. He scanned the room, checked under the bed and in the closet. No one was here.

The next room down the hall was the bathroom. It was so tiny; he didn't think it necessary to check every nook and cranny. He could see everything from where he stood; toilet, sink and shower stall. The larger bathroom was on the first floor, which he'd already checked.

Finally, he came to the last door, which was obviously the boy's room. Taking a deep breath, he kicked the door open, ready to fire at anything that moved.

Nothing.

He checked under the bed and in the closet, only to find the same—*nothing.*

"What the hell," he muttered under his breath. "Son of a bitch got away?"

Back in the hall, he looked at each of the three rooms, scratching his head. He could have sworn the killer was still here, not just from the fresh smell of gunpowder and Stephanie's recent demise—but he felt it in his gut and every fiber of his being.

He was walking past the little bathroom he'd felt no need to search earlier because of its tiny space, when he heard a noise.

Too late, he turned, catching only a glimpse of a large, black man, moving fast, before the bullets tore into him, bringing him down hard.

Stephanie's killer flew past him, and Joe squeezed off two shots before consciousness left him. He heard sirens in the distance quickly approaching. The last thing he thought of before darkness surrounded him was Maria, and how he never told her that he loved her.

25

It was 9:05 PM when Maria received the phone call from Chief McCollough. He'd been contacted by the Ventura Police Department and informed Joe Morgan had been shot.

"Oh my God! How bad is it? Is he going to die?" Maria asked, sitting down hard, feeling disbelief and dread wash over her.

"Calm down, Sanchez, he'll make it. But he was shot several times. He's damn lucky to be alive, that's for sure. Stephanie Franco wasn't so lucky, I'm afraid. She's dead."

"Dead? What about her little boy?"

"I don't know. I didn't get all the details yet. Nothing was said about the boy. I assume he's okay."

"I'm taking the next flight out," Maria said. "Do you have a problem with that? Peter can take care of things here for a day or two."

"I figured as much. Just be careful, Sanchez. And don't blow up at Santini when you talk to him. It definitely won't do you any good; he's a very dangerous man."

"What makes you think I'll even talk to him?"

"Because I know you, Sanchez, and your great desire to get answers no matter what the cost. But listen to me, damnit. *Be careful!*"

"I will."

Maria hung up and went into her bedroom, taking her

suitcase from under the bed and throwing clothes into it helter-skelter.

Peter stood in the doorway, firing questions at her back, which she answered to the best of her knowledge.

"I don't know any more, Slade. Leave me alone, goddamnit, so I can think for a minute. I'll call Tess and see if she can stay at her friend's for a couple of days. Can you drive me to the airport?"

"Yeah, no problem. When will you be back?"

"Soon. Probably two, three days at the most. Hopefully I'll be bringing Joe with me. God, I can't believe this has happened—Stephanie dead—Joe shot. What else can go wrong?"

"Plenty. You could end up dead, too. Be careful, Maria. Maybe I should go with you."

"Forget it, Slade. I can take care of myself and besides, the chief needs you here to help run the show until I get back."

"Okay, but keep in touch with me by phone, so I know what's going on. I want you to rely on me, Sanchez, do you understand? Like you rely on Joe. If I'm to help run the show here as you put it, I'll need to know everything that's going on in California. Let me know when you're going to do something *before* you do it."

"Yeah, yeah, don't worry. You sound like the chief. I'll be careful. I want to get back to Minneapolis in one piece, you know. I have a daughter that needs me. I would never do anything stupid to jeopardize that."

Maria called Nancy Turow and explained the situation.

Nancy was more than happy to have Tess stay for a couple of days, or however long it took.

Maria was grateful and told her so. "You're a good friend, Nancy. I owe you one."

"Don't be silly. Tess is like a second daughter to me and like a sister to Jenny. I know you would do the same for me."

"You're right. I would... Nancy, this is a weird question, but I feel I have to ask you."

"Go ahead."

"If something happens to me—I mean if the plane crashed or something—"

"You don't even need to ask. I'd take care of Theresa in a heartbeat! Like I said, she's like a daughter to me."

Maria let out her breath. "Thank you. Carlos and I have discussed it as well and he would raise Tess—it's in my will. But, it's good to know that you and Jenny would be a part of her life as well."

"That goes without saying."

"Well, I better say good-bye to Tess. Thanks again, Nancy."

"I'll get her. Hang on." Nancy covered the phone with her hand and called Tess to the phone. "She's coming. Have a good trip Maria, and *please* be careful."

Maria talked to her daughter briefly and told her how much she loved her and that she'd be back soon, without revealing too many details. Knowing how close the girl felt toward Joe, she didn't have the heart to tell her he'd been shot.

Ending the connection with her daughter, Maria called the airline and reserved a seat on the next flight out to Los Angeles.

26

Roberto Santini leaned forward in his leather desk chair, fingers steepled under his chin, eyes closed as he listened to Tyrone Spencer tell of his half sister's demise.

"Okay, you did well, Tyrone. There will be a little something extra with your paycheck. Have Carol check that shoulder. It's just a flesh wound, but you don't want infection to set in."

Carol Severson was Roberto's secretary but had been a registered nurse before she became his employee. She'd been caught stealing morphine at the hospital where she worked and was abruptly terminated. That was four years ago. Roberto had helped her get her feet back on the ground, and in turn, she became an invaluable asset to him. She was his mistress as well as employee, and he loved her as much as he could love anyone without getting too close.

When Tyrone left, Roberto looked over at Nicholas Freyhoff, who was gazing out the large window that looked out over the city of Los Angeles, some thirty-odd stories up. "Well, what is your take on the situation?"

Nicholas looked at his partner with raised eyebrows. "We should have taken care of Stephanie long ago, and then we wouldn't be in this mess. Stupid nigger, shot a cop for Christ's sake. I say the *something extra* he should get is a bullet through his thick skull," he offered.

"Calm down, everything is under control. We should be thankful he wasn't caught and spilled his guts. And as for the extra bonus I promised?" Roberto laughed. "I've already made arrangements for our friend, Mr. Spencer, to have a little accident."

"Good. But what do we do about the cop? There *will* be questions, you know."

"So? They have no proof. Nothing can be connected to us. All they have is speculation, and that will get them nowhere. With Stephanie dead, it's all merely hearsay. We have *nothing* to fear. Let them ask their questions," Roberto replied.

"What about our J.R.?"

"He's becoming more trouble than he's worth, isn't he?"

Nicholas turned to gaze back out the window. "Yes, I'm afraid we've created a monster—literally."

"Do you think he's a threat to *us*?" Roberto laughed.

"He's crazy, Roberto. More so than even we know, I'm afraid. We haven't kept close enough tabs on him. He does his own thing, and we go along with it, without question. I think he's beyond our control."

"You sound like a scared little girl," Roberto teased. "He's been conditioned. Of course we are in control." He thought for a moment. "And if you are right by some off chance? We'll simply destroy him."

"How?"

"He is still a man—flesh and blood like you and me. We know where he lives, for God's sake. We will have Rico keep an eye on him to see what he's up to at all times, okay?

"Don't get paranoid on me, Nicholas. Nobody is indispensable, you know."

Nicholas Freyhoff studied his long-time associate and realized—not for the first time—he could end up like Tyrone Spencer would end up later this evening—one more anchor lost at the bottom of the deep, blue sea.

27

Maria arrived at Community Memorial Hospital in Ventura, California at 3:55 AM.

The night-shift nurses had dwindled down to two in the ICU, softly laughing and drinking coffee, with the background music of electronic monitors and an eerie green glow surrounding them. Seeing Maria approach, they stopped talking. The older nurse smiled at Maria and gave the younger one orders to check on one of the patients.

"May I help you?" she asked, taking in Maria's disheveled appearance.

"I hope so. I'm looking for my partner—friend, uh—I'm sorry, I'm a little out of sorts today."

"I understand. You look like you could use some coffee," she said, pouring Maria a Styrofoam cup full of strong, black coffee. "Here, drink this and you'll feel better."

"Thank you," Maria said, wrapping her hands around the cup.

"Now, what's his name?"

"Joe, Joe Morgan. He was admitted several hours ago...ah...I guess it was last night," Maria said, looking at the clock and realizing she was in a different time zone.

"Oh yes, Mr. Morgan. And you are?"

"Maria Sanchez," Maria stated.

"I hate to ask you, but could I see some identification?

Orders from above, I'm afraid."

"Oh, of course. I'm glad they're taking precautions," Maria said, fishing her badge out of her purse.

The nurse inspected her badge and scribbled down the number—comparing it to a sheet she was given for authorized visitors—then returned it with a smile. "Well, everything looks as it should. Your partner and *friend*, Mr. Morgan, is doing just fine. Dr. Mettifield removed the bullets. He's one of the best surgeons at Memorial. Your friend was very lucky the bullets didn't damage any vital organs. He took one in the upper chest and a couple in his left arm. He's doing remarkably well for a multiple gunshot victim. We'll be moving him out of ICU later this morning. He'll probably be discharged in a couple of days if he continues improving and has no setbacks."

"Can I see him?"

"Well, he's heavily sedated and resting." The nurse looked at Maria's crestfallen face and gave in. "Okay, I'm sure he'll be glad to see you. I'll tell Laurie not to disturb you," she said with a conspiratorial wink. "But don't tire him out too much. He's been through a tremendous ordeal."

"I'll be gentle, I promise."

The nurse led Maria down the darkened corridor and pointed her toward Joe's room, then padded back to her workstation.

Maria quietly entered the Intensive Care Unit, not wanting to awaken Joe or the other patients. He looked so vulnerable lying in the hospital bed—not like the strong man she knew so well.

She sat down in the chair next to the bed and took his hand. He didn't move a muscle. Maria brought his rough hand up to her cheek and kissed it. "Oh, Joe," she whispered, a single tear falling on the back of his hand. "I missed you so, and I love you—more than you will ever know."

Joe groaned and stirred, then whispered her name. "Maria? Is that you?" he asked, turning his head, his gaze coming to rest on her face. "Is it really you, or am I in heaven and you're my angel of mercy?"

Maria leaned over the hospital bed and whispered. "I came as soon as I heard. How are you feeling?"

"Pretty good, now that you're here. I didn't think I'd ever see you again."

"*Shh*, don't talk too much. I promised the nurse I wouldn't tire you out," she said, laying her hand on his rough, unshaven cheek. "I'm so glad you're okay. You really had me worried. I thought I was going to have to find a new partner."

"You probably will," Joe whispered. "The chief told me as much."

"No, he didn't—"

"Yes, he *did*. I screwed up, Maria, *big time*. Stephanie's dead. She trusted me and I let her down," he said, looking away.

"Joe, listen to me," Maria said, whispering in his ear. "It wasn't your fault. It was a judgment call. We make them all the time. It's part of our job. The chief knows that. I'll tell you one thing—I wouldn't have done anything different than you did. Under the circumstances you had no choice."

"Do you honestly mean that?"

"Yes, you *know* I do. Since when do I say something I don't mean?"

Joe laughed weakly. "Since never."

He tried to sit up but found he didn't have the strength. "I promised Tony, Stephanie's son, that I'd come and get him when it was safe. I sent him next-door, and then I got shot.

One more broken promise," he said with a weary sigh.

"Don't worry. I'll check on him first thing in the morning and explain everything," Maria reassured him.

"What will happen to the poor kid now? Stephanie was the only family the boy had. Or the only one who would acknowledge his existence, anyway."

"I'll find out, I promise. Just try to put things out of your mind for now and concentrate on getting better. I need you, Joe."

Joe looked at Maria, unable to take his eyes off her beautiful face. "I have to tell you something, Maria."

"What?"

"I love you, Maria. The last thing I thought of before I went down was that I never told you how I felt. Well, I'm telling you now, I love you," he whispered.

"I—I love you, too."

They kissed, more a gentle brush of the lips than a kiss. Maria laid her head on the pillow next to him—holding hands; they resembled two young lovers reunited after a long separation.

28

The morning light showed promise. Joe looked more like his old self and was even flirting with the pretty young nurse who was giving him a sponge bath. Bright California sunshine streamed through the hospital window, promising another picture perfect day.

Dr. Mettifield came in, making his morning rounds. "So, how are you doing today, Mr. Morgan?" he said, checking Joe's chart.

"Pretty good, Doc. When can I blow this joint?"

The doctor laughed. "Well, considering I just dug a considerable amount of lead out of you last night, I'd say in at least a day or two." He checked Joe's bandaged chest and arm. "You *are* doing remarkably well, though. What's your secret? Or do I even need to ask?" he inquired, looking over at Maria.

"I'd like you to meet my partner, Doc," Joe said.

"My pleasure," Dr. Mettifield said, shaking Maria's hand. "Your partner's a very lucky man. The bullet in his chest missed his heart by about an inch and came damn close to puncturing a lung, but somehow managed to miss that, too. I'd say someone was looking out for him," he added, looking up.

"Thanks for taking such good care of him. I wasn't looking forward to training in a new partner," Maria said, giving Joe a wink.

"Just doing my job. We'll be moving you out of ICU later

this morning to a private room," he said to Joe. "Hopefully in a couple of days you can blow this joint, as you so eloquently put it."

The doctor returned Joe's chart back to the clipboard that hung from the rail at the foot of the hospital bed. "Nice to meet you, Maria. Keep an eye on this one for me...he's a little too rambunctious for his own good."

"I will, Dr. Mettifield, don't worry. He's my number one priority."

Maria stayed while Joe ate his breakfast, reading him the sports page in the local newspaper and keeping his spirits up by giving her own editorial comments after each segment she read.

"Well, you need your rest and I have some errands to run," Maria said, folding the newspaper and setting it on the bedside table. "I have Stephanie's address from the fax you sent the chief. Hacienda Boulevard, right?"

"Yeah. Talk to the lady who lives next-door. It's the light gray house on the right. Oh, and give this to the kid. Don't forget," he said, handing her something wrapped in Kleenex, which she put in her purse.

"Okay. I may be a while. I'll probably get settled into a hotel for the night. I can't sleep in that chair again or I'll be crippled for life," Maria said, stretching her back. "So, don't worry if I don't come back right away. You just get some rest, you hear?"

"Okay, but Maria? Promise me something."

"*Hmm*?" she said, rummaging through her purse for the rental car keys.

"Promise me you won't go see Santini."

Maria stopped what she was doing and looked at Joe. Try

as she might, she couldn't lie to him. "I'm sorry, Joe, I can't promise you that."

"Damnit, Maria, listen to me. It won't do any good to go see that asshole. All you're going to do is make—"

"Tell me something, Joe. If it was me lying in that hospital bed, tell me that *you* wouldn't go see Santini," Maria interrupted. "Go on, tell me."

Joe just looked at her with an exasperated expression on his face.

"See, you would. Don't worry, I'll be careful. Get some rest. I'll be back in a few hours," she said, leaning over and giving him a peck on the cheek, then hurrying out of the ICU.

Maria pulled up to the light gray house next-door to Stephanie Franco's and got out of the car. There were still a couple of squad cars parked in Franco's driveway and she saw two uniformed policeman searching the grounds, as well as a plainclothes detective smoking a cigarette on the front steps. Maria walked up to the front door, feeling the detective's eyes bore through her from his perch some twenty yards away, and rang the doorbell.

A young, red-haired woman answered the door with a harried expression on her face. Maria could hear a baby crying in the other room. "Yes?" the woman said, looking past Maria distractedly. "Can I help you?"

"Hi," Maria said. "I'm Detective Sanchez—"

"I've been talking to the police and detectives all morning and most of last night. They told me they wouldn't be bothering me anymore today," the woman cut her off.

"I'm not here to question you about the case—not officially, anyway. I wanted to check on Tony, Stephanie's boy. It was my partner who was shot last night."

181

"Oh, I'm sorry. Please forgive me. I'm Catherine O'Riley," she said, extending her hand. "I didn't mean to snap your head off. Come on in."

Maria shook the other woman's hand. "Maria Sanchez," she said. "I'm sorry to bother you. I know things must be really hectic right now."

"Oh, it's okay. How is he? I heard he was shot up pretty bad."

"He'll pull through. He's a strong man. He's more concerned about Stephanie's boy at the moment," Maria said. She saw two boys about the same age—one with red hair, the other dark—watching cartoons on the living room floor. A child of about the age of two sat in a playpen in the middle of the room.

"Tony, honey? Can you come here a minute?" Catherine called gently.

The dark-haired little boy got up and shuffled over to where the two women stood, hands in pockets and eyes downcast.

Maria knelt down so she was eye level with the boy. "Hi, Tony, my name's Maria. My friend, Joe, wanted me to check on you and make sure you were all right. He would have come himself, but he's getting better in the hospital."

"He's not dead?" the boy asked, wide-eyed.

"No, honey, he's not dead. He's hurt, but he'll be okay. He felt real bad that he couldn't keep his promise to come and get you last night, and he was worried you might be upset."

"I'm glad he's not dead. He was very nice to my mom and me. He was going to take us away on an adventure." The little boy looked lost for a moment and then seemed to come back. "My mommy's dead," he said. "So I guess the nice man won't be taking us."

Maria didn't know what to say.

"Joe gave me something he wanted you to have," Maria said, opening her purse and retrieving the item Joe had given her earlier.

It was wrapped in several Kleenex and the boy carefully unwrapped it, putting each tissue in his pocket as he did so. When he took away the last tissue, a gold pocket watch glittered in the boy's small hand.

Maria was as surprised as Tony. She knew the watch had belonged to Joe's father, who'd been dead for more than ten years now. It had always held special meaning for Joe.

"Wow! A gold watch," he said, opening it up. "I'll always keep it. Forever and ever. I'll never lose it. Tell him that, and tell him thanks. Not just for the watch, but for trying to help me and my mom."

Tony was unable to take his eyes off the beautiful gold watch. He walked slowly back to where the other boy sat on the floor and joined his friend, admiring his gift while Bugs Bunny blared in the background.

Maria could hardly believe this young man was only five years old. He seemed much older and wiser than any five-year-old she'd ever known. She hoped that in time, he would regain his childhood, but Maria had a feeling he wouldn't. Losing the only person in the world that mattered to him most at this young age would affect him for the rest of his life.

Maria followed Catherine into the kitchen, where the kids were out of earshot.

"A social worker is coming by around noon today to pick him up," she informed Maria. "I told them I could take care of him for a while, but they insisted it was best to get Tony used to new surroundings under the circumstances. I guess a foster family will be taking care of him starting the first part of next week. I'll let you know when I get all the details."

"Please do. Here's where I can be reached during the day, and my home number is on the back," Maria said, handing her a card. "We'll probably be going back to the Twin Cities tomorrow or the day after. I wonder if they'll let Joe see the boy before we leave."

"No, they won't. At least not yet. Tony has to go through a psychological evaluation and stuff. I don't know all the details, but the social worker said no one would be allowed to visit him for at least several days. I promise I'll call you when I know something more."

"Okay. Joe will feel terrible about not saying good-bye," Maria said with a resigned sigh. "Well, thank you for all you've done. You have been a Godsend. I'm sure Stephanie would appreciate everything you've done for her son." She shook the other woman's hand.

Catherine nodded. "Stephanie was a good friend and a good mother to Tony, despite her many problems. She had a heart of gold," she said, holding back tears.

Maria said good-bye to Tony and hugged him, then quickly departed, unable to withstand the devastated look in the boy's eyes at one more desertion.

29

By the time Maria walked next-door to Stephanie Franco's, only one squad car remained, but she still saw the same two officers searching the grounds.

She walked over and introduced herself, explaining that her partner was the man who was shot last night. After showing them her police identification, she asked if she might go in and have a look around.

"Well, everything that needed to be taken out as evidence was removed late last night. The crime scene unit finished their work around 4:00 this morning so I suppose it's okay. What do you think, Ralph?" the shorter man asked his partner.

Ralph, who was obviously in charge, looked Maria up and down for a moment, his eyes coming to rest on her breasts. "Yeah, I suppose. Chief Peters said we should cooperate— McCollough informed him late last night you were flying out."

"Jeez, why doesn't anyone ever tell me anything?" the shorter man whined.

"You're told what you need to know, Dave," Ralph said, hitching up his trousers.

Maria could sense the tension between the two men and felt uncomfortable—not to mention sorry for the cop named Dave.

"Just don't disturb anything in there, okay," Ralph ordered more than asked.

"I won't, don't worry. I just want to take a look around. I won't so much as touch anything."

"Okay, good. But I gotta warn you, it's not a pretty picture," Ralph said, smirking, seeming to take a perverse pleasure in telling her this.

"What can you tell me about what happened?" Maria asked.

"Well, it looks like Stephanie Franco was shot with a high powered weapon, probably an automatic assault rifle by the looks of it—a lot of holes if you know what I mean. It must have been equipped with a silencer because the neighbors heard nothing. Your friend was a little luckier. The Doc dug out three .38's. Either the killer used up his ammo on the woman and had to resort to a back-up weapon, or it's possible there was another shooter involved. We know a drug deal was going down, and thanks to your people, that Santini was definitely behind it; although he won't admit it."

"So some of your people have already talked to him?" Maria asked.

Ralph laughed. "Yeah, but it didn't do much good. He claims to know *nothing* about it and we can't prove anything—yet."

"I figured as much," Maria said with a sigh. "Have you talked to the boy?"

"Yeah, If you could call it that. He wasn't very talkative. From what I could gather, he walked into the carnage after his old lady was already whacked, then heard someone moving around upstairs and hid in the closet until your partner found him. Lucky for the kid it was your partner who found him first, otherwise—"

"He'd be dead along with his mother," Maria finished the sentence for him.

"We've got someone watching the house. " He nodded next-door. "Just in case they come back to finish the job, although it's highly unlikely. You can't be too careful when dealing with these types."

Maria noted the unmarked car parked across the street. "Good idea. Well, thanks for your help. I won't be long in there," she said, starting across the lawn toward the front door.

"No, I bet you won't," Ralph said with a snort, watching her walk away.

The body of Stephanie Franco was long gone—cold in the morgue for some time now—but from the blood that remained, it appeared a small battle had been waged here. It was splattered on one wall and even on the ceiling. A large, reddish-brown stain had soaked into the carpet, which was still sticky in spots, but she could see lighter spots where it was starting to dry. More than a dozen bullet holes marked the wall like some maniac's dot-to-dot picture.

Next, Maria walked up the stairs that led to the bedrooms. She stopped short, her heart pounding when she saw the large, dark stain that soaked the hallway carpet—it was Joe's blood. *He could have died in that very spot!* She couldn't shake the eerie feeling that destiny or fate, she wasn't sure which, had stepped in to spare him. It was a miracle, pure and simple that he wasn't dead.

Maria was not a religious person. In fact, she couldn't remember the last time she'd been in a church. Growing up, they had been devout Catholics, but after her parents died, she'd stopped attending services.

Now, she felt a re-evaluation might be in order. After seeing the carnage that was left downstairs, she felt certain it was an act of God that Joe was still alive.

* * *

Maria checked into a Best Western Hotel located several blocks from the hospital where Joe was staying.

She took a quick shower, then called Directory Assistance to get the phone number to Santini Realty in Los Angeles. It was a well-known front to Santini's covert operations—and where his main office was located. Even though he *did* dabble in real estate, his main market was the drug trade and prostitution, along with several other shady ventures, which included black market goods, pornography, fake ID's and illegal gambling houses, just to name a few. Maria knew she'd have to play the game right the first time, because there would be no second chance.

She called Santini Realty and spoke with his secretary. She was told she couldn't see Mr. Santini without an appointment and would need to make it several days in advance.

"But I'm only going to be in town till tomorrow morning. My daddy left me in charge of his finances when he died and I thought Mr. Santini could help me with some investments. I got his name from a friend of my daddy's who said Mr. Santini would be more than happy to help me. A Mr. Devereau?" Maria lied, knowing Devereau was an attorney who'd worked for Santini in the past. Maria had done her homework and it paid off.

"Well, I guess if Mr. Devereau sent you, maybe we could squeeze you in. Let's see, how about 1:15 this afternoon? Would that be suitable?"

"Oh yes, that would be perfect. Thank you so very much," Maria said, leaving the name Maria Sands with the secretary, and hanging up the phone. She smiled to herself, satisfied with her deception.

It was already 11:30 and the drive to L.A. would take the better part of an hour, so she figured she'd better get going.

Maria dressed in an ivory linen suit that set off her dark hair and skin, with silk stockings and matching pumps. Giving herself a last-minute appraisal in the bathroom mirror, she grabbed her purse and left the hotel room, soaking up the bright California sunshine as it hit her face.

Her thoughts turned to Joe, lying in the hospital and the man she was about to meet who'd put him there.

The drive into downtown Los Angeles was an experience Maria would never forget. She was used to city driving, but not on this large of scale. Cars flew past her on US Highway 101 like she was standing still, as she tried to look at her map and keep from being rear-ended at the same time. She was flipped the finger more than once from fellow commuters, but managed to keep her cool. She found the exit she wanted to take on the map about two seconds before she saw the sign and veered over into the right lane so she wouldn't miss it, cutting off a blue-haired old lady, who shook her fist at her and mouthed obscenities that would make a sailor blush.

Maria pulled into the parking lot of a huge office building that reached high into the sky and was made of glass that reflected its surroundings. The sign in front stated that it housed—among many others—the office of Santini Realty.

Maria leaned her head back and closed her eyes for a moment, trying to get her thoughts together before she met the man responsible for the destruction of so many lives.

Riding the elevator up to the thirty-fifth floor where Santini Realty was located, Maria realized she forgot to call Slade. Before she left for California, he'd made her promise to call him *before* she did anything like this. Oh well, no point in worrying about it now. She would call him when she got back to the hotel later. He would no doubt be mad as hell. Maria smiled to herself, thinking of his inflated ego and the way sarcasm seemed to be second nature to him.

30

Santini Realty was located in a small but elegant office. The reception area was decorated in cream and pale mauve, with plush carpeting that felt as if you were walking on pillows. Expensive-looking abstract paintings hung on the walls, and fresh cut flowers adorned the glass coffee table and the receptionist's desk, filling the small waiting room with an exotic aroma.

Maria approached the receptionist who eyed her critically.

"May I help you?" the blonde said in cool, clipped tones.

"Yes, I have a 1:15 appointment with Mr. Santini..." Maria said, meeting the other woman's gaze.

The pretty blonde scanned her appointment book with one long red fingernail. "Maria Sands. Here we are, a friend of Mr. Devereau?"

"Yes, that's right," Maria said, feeling uncomfortable at the lie.

"If you'll have a seat, Mr. Santini will be with you shortly."

Maria took a seat on the cream-colored leather couch and picked up a magazine, pretending to read it, while her heart thumped with apprehension. Now that she'd arranged to meet with him, she wasn't sure what she would say to Roberto Santini. She wanted to kill this man who made his living on other's misery. If only she could get him to admit his involvement—

"Mr. Santini will see you now," the secretary said, standing over Maria.

Maria jumped, startled. "Oh, I'm sorry, I guess I was doing a little wool-gathering," she offered as way of an explanation.

Maria followed the blonde down a long, dark hallway until they came to a set of double doors. The woman knocked once then opened the door, standing aside so Maria could enter first.

Roberto Santini was on the phone and he motioned for Maria to be seated, then covering the mouthpiece of the telephone, winked at his secretary and said, "Thanks, honey, that will be all."

The blonde smiled smugly at Maria and turned on her four-inch heel, leaving Maria and Roberto Santini alone.

Santini's office was larger than the entire reception area, with a spectacular view of the city of Los Angeles. The color tones in here were of a deeper, richer shade than the outer office, otherwise virtually the same, with soft supple leather furniture and gleaming glass coffee and end tables. Maria noticed another door, separate from the one she entered, and wondered what lay beyond.

She eyed the man she'd come to hate, who was laughing softly into the telephone. Roberto Santini was not a large man, but what he lacked in stature he made up for with dark, Italian good looks and impeccable dress—and as Maria was soon to find out, he could charm the skin off a snake.

He ended his telephone conversation and walked over to where Maria was seated on the couch, extending his hand. "Welcome to Los Angeles, Maria Sands."

"Thank you, Mr. Santini." Maria offered her hand, which

he took gallantly and kissed.

"Call me Roberto, please," he said, sitting down. "I am told your father was a friend of Mr. Devereau?" he asked, his eyes slowly traveling over her long legs, pausing at the curve of her hips, then casually assessing the swell of her bosom. His eyes danced with amusement, as Maria fidgeted, uncomfortable under his scrutiny.

Maria cleared her throat. "Yes, my late father was good friends with Mr. Devereau."

"Please accept my deepest sympathies at his passing. I know how hard it can be to lose someone so close. I lost my own father years ago and still miss him to this day."

"Was your father in the real estate business too, Mr. Santini—Roberto, I mean?"

Roberto smiled slyly. "Well, something like that. Now, what can I do for you? You are interested in investing I am told?"

"Yes, I'd like your advice on what would be the most lucrative. I was hoping you could help me find something that would pay off in about a year or less. I don't know much about it, but my daddy always said a good investment was better than money in the bank and a lot more fun because of the risk involved. I love taking risks."

"Well, that's refreshing to hear," he said, standing up and walking over to the wet bar. "Drink?"

"No, thank you."

He poured a splash of brandy into a glass and returned to the couch, sitting a little closer than before. He held the brandy up to the light and swirled the amber liquid around and around. The glass was a beautiful lead crystal with designs that resembled fish intricately etched into it.

"That's a beautiful piece of crystal," Maria remarked,

uncomfortable at his closeness.

"Yes, it is, isn't it? My sister gave them to me for my fortieth birthday...." He inspected the glass, his long slender fingers caressing the carvings. "Tell me something, Maria?"

"Yes?"

"Was your father a fisherman? Did he enjoy taking you with him on trips as my own father did?" He had a far away look in his eye and a slight smile played on his full lips as he reminisced about days gone by.

"Yes, my daddy used to take me on his yacht when I was just a little girl," Maria lied, never having stepped foot on a yacht. "He did some of his best thinking, he always said, with a fishing pole in his hand."

Roberto laughed. "Your daddy was a smart man. Probably smart enough to know better than to go on a fishing expedition without any bait," he said.

Maria looked at him, puzzled.

"Guess who I was talking to on the telephone when you entered my office earlier?"

"I—I—don't know," Maria said, realizing the game was over before it had even begun.

"Why, your good friend, Mr. Devereau. I'm afraid you have some explaining to do, my dear. You see, Mr. Devereau never heard of you or your daddy. So, why don't you tell me who the hell you are and what you want? *Right now*—before I call security and have you tossed out on your shapely little butt," he said through clenched teeth, trying to control his temper.

"Okay, Roberto, let's put our cards on the table shall we? I'll answer your questions if you'll answer mine," Maria said, meeting his gaze. "Stephanie Franco is dead because—"

"STOP! I want to hear no more," he shouted, putting his

hands on Maria's shoulders and squeezing hard. "Who are you and what do you want?"

"Get your fucking hands off me, you slimy, murderous bastard," Maria hissed.

Roberto responded as if he'd been slapped. *No one* spoke to him like that, especially not some hot little bitch. *Wait a minute!* Roberto threw back his head and laughed. "You're a cop aren't you?" he asked, walking over to his desk and pushing a button on his telephone.

Maria didn't answer. "We know you hired a hit on your sister, Santini, and we know—"

Just then, the door she'd wondered about earlier flew open and two jumbo-sized thugs entered.

"Please escort the young lady out, *now*," Roberto said calmly.

"I'm leaving," Maria said, heading for the door. She opened it and turned, gazing evenly at Roberto. "Your reign as king is coming to an *end*, asshole." She looked the two goons up and down who'd followed her to the door. "Touch me and I'll personally see you doing time for assault and battery."

She could hear Roberto's laughter all the way down the long hall and into the outer office, where she emerged both angry and frightened. She quickly left, jabbing the elevator button several times, anxious to get the hell out of there.

"I want the bitch followed. Find out who she is and what she knows." Roberto said into the telephone. Slamming the receiver down in anger, he poured himself another brandy and began his meditative breathing.

C. HYYTINEN

31

Maria was still feeling vulnerable and unsettled when she back got to her rental car. God, what a nightmare—she'd *never* forget her encounter with Roberto Santini. It was as if she were an unknowing participant in a well-rehearsed play, where Roberto knew his lines perfectly and she was a last minute stand-in.

Pulling out of the parking lot, Maria stepped on the accelerator, wanting to get as much distance between herself and Santini as soon as possible.

Braking slightly at the entrance ramp onto the freeway that would take her back toward Ventura, she noticed a black sedan in her rearview mirror. She realized it had probably pulled out of the parking lot behind her, but had paid it no attention in her hasty retreat. However, now she could see the driver—or at least an outline of a man in a large hat. When she accelerated, he did the same, attempting to stay a short distance back with only a couple of cars between them. He was trying not to be *too* suspicious—but she was on to him.

Maria took the next exit and pulled into a service station to gas up. She still had half a tank, but this seemed like a good time to fill it up and try to lose her unwelcome friend. Mr. Black Sedan followed, pulling into the convenience store parking lot across the street. She tried to read his license plate, but couldn't make it out because the glare from the sun bounced off the chrome and made it illegible. Keeping her eye on the car the entire time she gassed up, she saw that he never left his spot or got out of the car so she could get a better look at him.

She went to pay the cashier and when she returned, Mr. Black Sedan was gone. Letting out a sigh of relief, she convinced herself she was just being paranoid.

Maria got back on the freeway, trying to tune in a radio station—while glancing occasionally in her rearview mirror—when she noticed the car again several vehicles back. *Same car, same big hat.*

"Shit!" Maria said aloud. Pressing the gas pedal all the way to the floor, she weaved around those who blocked her way. She was going twenty miles over the posted speed limit and kept her foot on the accelerator, flying down the highway.

The black sedan was stuck behind two semi-trucks who were going neck and neck, so he couldn't pass.

Maria laughed, but her laughter died on her lips when she saw two flashing lights in the rearview mirror.

She pulled over onto the shoulder and stopped. Rolling down the window, she impatiently waited for the state trooper to approach.

"Good afternoon, officer," she said, seeing herself reflected in his mirrored sunglasses.

Mr. Black Sedan slowly passed and she caught his license, committing it to memory.

"Do you know how fast you were going, ma'am?" the cop asked.

"Yes, I do, but—"

"May I see your driver's license, please?"

Maria pulled out her driver's license along with her police identification. "Please listen to me so I won't have to repeat myself," she demanded. "Go ahead and take down my badge number and have me checked out—everything is legit. I'm working on a murder case and some goon in a 10-gallon hat has been following me for the past half hour. He is driving a black sedan, license number 555HFY. I want you to stop him for something—I don't care what—and detain him for a while so I can lose him. Can you do that for me, officer?" She flashed him a big smile.

The state trooper scribbled in his pad, then handed back her license and ID. "My pleasure, ma'am," he said, tipping his hat. "Always willing to help out a fellow cop." He waved her on and jogged back to his car.

Maria pulled back into traffic and sped up, coming alongside the black sedan, which had been going as slow as the law allowed in the right lane. She flipped up her middle finger and sped off, with him following in hot pursuit—until the state trooper came up behind him, lights flashing, and motioned him to pull over.

Maria laughed. "Who says there's never a cop around when you need one?" she said to herself, turning up the radio, feeling some of her anxiety subside…just a little.

Joe was propped up with several pillows, reading a fishing magazine, when Maria stuck her head in the door of his new, private room.

"Are you up for some company?" she asked.

"Maria! Come on in. I've been going crazy waiting for you to get back. How did everything go? Wow, you look great!" he said, taking in her sophisticated attire in one full sweep.

"Man, am I beat." She collapsed into the chair next to his hospital bed. "First things first. How are you feeling? You sure look better. Nice digs," she added, looking around the room.

"I'm doing *great*. The Doc says I'll probably be discharged sometime tomorrow afternoon. Now, don't keep me in suspense any longer. Let's hear it."

Maria picked up the notepad lying on Joe's bedside table. "Looks like you've been busy, too. I thought you were going to get some rest," she said, reading the information he'd gotten from the Ventura Police Department and Social Services. The latter concerned the Franco boy.

Joe snatched the notepad away from her. "Like I said, I was going nuts just sitting here like a bump on a log. I had to do something, and I was worried about the trouble you were getting yourself into, with no backup if something should go wrong. So, come on, spill it. What happened?"

"Okay, okay. Well, I guess you already heard about Tony Franco, judging from what I read. Oh, by the way he loved the gold watch you gave him. He was totally mesmerized. That was very kind of you, Joe."

"Yeah, well, it's the least I can do, considering the kid's life will never be the same again. I was hoping I'd get to see him when I got out of here, but Social Services told me that wasn't possible."

"I know. Sorry," Maria said, reading the guilt and anguish apparent in his clear, blue eyes.

"Doesn't matter," Joe lied. "Now, what about Santini?"

Maria shifted uncomfortably in her chair. "Santini...where the hell do I begin? Things didn't turn out exactly as I expected," she said with a sigh. She explained in detail her conversation with Roberto Santini and the way he'd duped her from the onset, ending with his accusing her of being a cop and calling security and then being followed. "I drastically underestimated the man. I thought I was pulling off this big deception, but the asshole was on to me the moment I entered his office—*before* I entered his office."

"I knew you shouldn't have gone alone. The man is crazy—has no morals! You should have at least been wearing a wire and had backup ready if something happened. You're damn lucky to be sitting here telling me about this."

"Oh, come on, Joe. I don't think I was in any immediate danger in the man's office, for God's sake. What do you think—he'd have me tied up and shot execution-style?"

Maria stood up. She removed her jacket, draping it over the chair, standing before him, clad only in a thin silk chemise. She turned around so her back was to him, revealing the small .38 snub-nose tucked neatly into a holster, clipped to her belt and hidden in the small of her back. "See, I did have backup. And I've also got my police-issue nine-millimeter in my purse, loaded and ready to put a bullet between the eyes of any low-life who so much as looks at me cross-eyed. And let's not forget the switchblade knife that's built into my shoe," she added.

"I should have known. You're a regular James Bond aren't you?" Joe said, looking at the beautiful woman who stood before him half-naked.

"Yes! And don't you forget it!" she said, slipping her jacket back on.

A nurse arrived with Joe's supper, setting the tray on his bedside table.

"I'm going to go back to the hotel, take a quick shower and grab a bite. I took a room at the Best Western, just a few blocks from here," Maria said, eyeing Joe's baked chicken. For hospital food, it sure looked and smelled delicious. She realized she'd forgotten to eat lunch and now was suddenly ravenous. "I'll be back in a couple of hours. Try to take a little nap after you eat your supper—you have dark circles under your eyes." Giving him a peck on the cheek, she left the room.

Maria realized she sounded like either Joe's mother or his wife—she wasn't sure which. She frowned, and then smiled to herself. For the first time in years, she wasn't appalled at the idea of being someone's wife. Now *that* was progress.

32

"What? I don't believe it. I pay you good money to get the job done right. If you can't do something as simple as tail a woman—" Roberto listened impatiently as the man tried to explain his situation. "Excuses! I don't need excuses, I need results. And if you can't get them, I'll find someone who can," Roberto said, slamming down the phone.

The bitch was proving to be more trouble minute by minute.

Thinking of the way she'd spoken to him earlier made him volatile. His anger seemed to increase steadily, feeding on thoughts of his encounter with her. He controlled this renewed surge by taking several deep, cleansing breaths, and meticulously planning sweet revenge in his calculating mind. No one spoke to Roberto Santini that way—*No one!*

He pressed the intercom button. "Carol, please come in here."

"Right away," a sultry female voice answered.

He pushed another button summoning his partner and friend, Nicholas Freyhoff.

Carol Severson checked her makeup and touched up her lipstick, then walked down the long hall and entered Roberto's office. Disappointment showed on her pretty face as Nicholas came through the inner office door at the same time.

PATTERN of VIOLENCE

"Carol, honey, mix us all a drink," Roberto said, sitting down behind his desk. Leaning back in his chair, fingers laced behind his head, he waited for Carol to finish her task behind the bar before beginning.

Once she was seated next to Nicholas on the couch, Roberto began. "I'm going to need your help—both of you—with something very important that has come up. It concerns the woman who was here earlier. I attempted to have her followed, but the moron lost her—or, I should say, *she* lost him. Maria Sands, as she calls herself, played another one of her games—it appears she has many up her sleeve. I have decided someone needs to teach this bitch a lesson she'll never forget, but first I need to find out *exactly* who she is. I'm pretty sure she's a cop—in fact, I'd go to the bank on it—but I need her *real* name. That's where you come in, Carol. She appeared on the scene shortly after that cop was shot by Tyrone—who, by the way is no longer employed by us," he said, winking at his partner.

Nicholas knew exactly what he meant.

"I think she's tied in with the cop somehow. He's in Ventura Memorial Hospital and I want you to use your connections, Carol. Find out who he is and what his condition is. Then, more importantly, find out if he has had any visitors, specifically female and beautiful. I need a name."

"But I don't have any connections over at Ventura Memorial, only L.A. County where I—"

"I don't care how you do it," Roberto snapped. "Just do it!

"Then once we have a name you can run a background check on her, Nicholas. I need results *today*, understand?" He didn't wait for a reply, but stood up and walked over to the large window that looked out over the city.

"Miss Maria Sands, or whatever the hell her name is, will

rue the day she ever tried to fuck with me," Roberto Santini promised aloud, a calculating smile spreading across his handsome face.

Several hours later, Nicholas knocked and entered the now dark office.

The sky beyond the large window was a deep purplish-black as the sun had disappeared close to an hour ago.

Nicholas cleared his throat. The man behind the desk was so quiet and still, Nicholas thought he might be asleep.

"Yes?"

Nicholas put the file on his desk, then walked over to the window, looking out on the darkened world.

Roberto turned on his desk lamp and studied the information before him, pleased with the results. The old saying, *It's a small world*, was definitely true in this case. It was almost inconceivable that this little morsel had fallen into his hands by accident—in fact, Roberto was convinced his dead father must've pulled some strings from *up above* to help out his son.

He summoned his friend to the bar and brought out his best cognac, pouring them each a generous drink, commending Nicholas on his fast and expert results. That was one reason Roberto had kept Nicholas with him as long as he had. The man was pure genius on the computer and could find, retrieve, or alter any information in the world of cyberspace. The reason he'd made him a partner, at least in the other man's mind, was a trust and loyalty issue that was required in order to have a successful business—but Roberto would always call the shots and did his best work solo.

"Pack your bags, my friend. You'll be taking a little trip soon," Roberto promised. The private jet would leave at midnight tonight and fly to Minneapolis. Once there, Nicholas would join Rico, who was hired to look after their mutual friend. Together they would go to work on J.R., filling him in on all the *details* so everything would happen according to plan.

Unlike Lenny Milano, their new go-between, Rico Smits, could be trusted with this most important job. He would go to his grave if necessary with his lips sealed. Rico was family after all, a distant cousin, but family just the same, and he'd worked with the Santini family for many years. Milano, on the other hand, had been an ex gang-banger—a loser who wanted one more chance—desperately needing a break after being in trouble all his pathetic life.

Roberto learned a valuable lesson after making the mistake of hiring Milano to work for him—never trust anyone *but* family. It could have cost him dearly if the stupid son of a bitch had decided to talk, but luckily he'd put a stop to it—or him—in the nick if time.

They spent the next hour and a half going over all the details, then Roberto dismissed Nicholas, suggesting he get some rest before the long flight.

Once alone in his office, Roberto Santini put his feet up on his desk and chuckled to himself. The chuckle turned into mad laughter that came bubbling up from the bottom of his evil soul. He threw back his head and let it roll out of him until tears streamed from his eyes and his belly hurt.

He wiped the tears from his face and spoke. "Oh, this is just too perfect. She even has a nine-year-old daughter. What more could we ask for?" He picked up the picture of his father who looked back at him with a proud smile of victory.

33

Maria arrived back at the hotel with a half-eaten bag of fast food and a six-pack of beer. She had planned to relax, have a beer, and eat dinner while watching the evening news in her hotel room, but found she was so hungry that the enticing smell of French fries and chicken were just too much. She'd nibbled on the drive back, only to find her food almost gone by the time she arrived at the hotel. After driving several miles *past* her lodgings to get the food and beer, she now felt disheartened at having foiled her plans at relaxation. Oh well, she'd soak in a hot bath instead.

Entering the hotel room, she tossed her purse and the bag of remaining food—along with the beer—on the queen-size bed, then went into the bathroom to fill the over-sized bathtub. Letting the water run, she checked the outside door to make sure it was locked and slipped the security chain into place. She then kicked off her shoes and took off her pantyhose—relishing the instant relief all women universally felt at this simple task—then proceeded to get undressed.

Sitting on the bed cross-legged, clad in only her bra and panties, she finished her food while waiting for the tub to fill.

Then bringing two beers with her, she popped the top on one, taking a long drink, and set the other on the edge of the bathtub.

Stepping into the hot, steamy bath, she lowered herself

until only her head was visible. The tub was huge—obviously meant for two—so for once, her knees were allowed to soak with the rest of her body. Taking another long pull on her beer, she let a long, weary sigh escape her lips. "Man, what a day."

Maria was looking forward to getting back home—she missed her daughter. She'd call Nancy tonight after she got back from the hospital to see how everything was going.

She closed her eyes and tried to push the awful day's events from her mind while her body melted as one with the hot, steamy water.

Roberto leaned toward her, knife raised in one hand while he held her face firm with the other. The face changed. It was now Jack who loomed over her, hatred burning in his glazed eyes. She watched the blade slowly descend, cutting into her face, blood dripping. An alarm clock was ringing somewhere in the distance. Roberto was laughing as he held her. Jack was teaching her a very important lesson.

Maria cried out and sat up with a start, touching her face and the blood that dripped steadily from it.

She looked at her fingers. *Nothing.*

It was sweat—not blood. She ran her fingers over the small scar that was noticeable to her, but imperceptible to others.

The telephone was ringing.

She wiped the beads of sweat from her face with a bath towel and stood up to go answer the phone, but it stopped at that moment.

She wet her hair and applied shampoo, working it into a deep lather. She'd just finished rinsing her hair when the telephone rang again. "Who the hell could that be?" she said aloud. No one knew she was here, except Joe, and she'd just left him an hour ago. Wrapping the bath towel around her, she hopped out of the tub, dripping all the way.

"Hello," she said, exasperated and still disoriented from the dream.

"Well, well, look who's finally back!"

She recognized the voice. "Slade! How did you know—"

"I called every damn hotel in Ventura, California, that's how! I thought we had a deal, Sanchez. You promised you'd keep me informed *before* you pulled any Rambo shit!"

"Slade, hold on a minute, I'm naked and dripping all over the carpet." She set down the phone and grabbed another towel for her hair, then rummaged through her suitcase, pulling out her terrycloth bathrobe and slipping it on.

Peter found himself grinning into the receiver like an adolescent, despite his anger.

"Okay, I'm back, and I didn't pull any Rambo shit. How did you know, anyway? And I did mean to call you first, but forgot, until it was too late."

"Morgan called the chief. I guess he was worried you were in over your head. Go figure."

"Well, I wish you guys would stop treating me like a child that needs a baby-sitter. I had things under control. Well, for the most part anyway."

"I'm afraid to ask," Peter said in a menacing voice. "Okay, tell me everything."

Maria told him all about Roberto and his tricks, then about the goon in the ten-gallon hat he had follow her.

Peter whistled into the phone. "Man, sounds like you had one hell of an interesting afternoon."

"Yeah, tell me about it. Too many more like these and I won't live to see my next birthday. Now, what about you? Any new developments in the case?" Maria asked.

"No, nothing, and let me tell you, it's no picnic being

under the microscope here. The press has been harassing the chief and he has no one to take it out on, but me. When are you coming back?"

Maria laughed. "Looks like Joe will be released tomorrow afternoon, so we'll try to catch a flight out early tomorrow evening."

"Good. So, Morgan's condition is a lot better, huh?"

"Yeah, he's doing great. The doctors can't believe it. I guess it's true what they say, *You can't keep a good man down.*"

"Gee, that sounds like something I'd say. Are things any better between the two of you? I know you had a little disagreement before he left for L.A."

"Man, there's nothing you don't know, is there?"

"Let's see, *no*, there isn't," he said after thinking a moment.

Maria laughed. "Things are pretty darn good on that front. But, hey, do me a favor?"

"Anything."

"Play down what happened to me at Santini's when you tell the chief—he'll go through the roof, and I'm already on his shit list."

"Sure. No problem."

"Thanks, well, I guess I'll see you when we get back."

"Okay. Call me when you get into the Twin Cities tomorrow. No matter how late."

"Okay, and thanks again. Bye, Peter."

Maria hung up the phone then went into the bathroom to drain the bathtub—and the rest of her half-empty beer. She combed her hair and dressed in a pair of khaki shorts, T-shirt and sandals, looking forward to spending a couple of hours with Joe.

34

Joe was watching television when Maria arrived. His eyes brightened when Maria came into the room. "Hey, you made it back!"

"Don't sound so surprised. I told you I would, and I brought you something."

"I hope it's got everything on it. You know how I like my pizza," Joe replied.

"Not pizza—but almost." Maria opened her large shoulder bag and Joe peered inside, finding a couple cans of beer and a large bag of peanuts. Maria laughed seeing Joe's face light up like a kid. She'd never seen the man drink a beer without a bag or bowl of peanuts close at hand, which was also the reasoning behind his feline's name—that and the fact he resembled the odd shape of a peanut.

The Minnesota Twins were playing against the Anaheim Angels at the Hubert H. Humphrey Metrodome in Minneapolis, so the game was being televised in California. Maria knew if Joe was home he'd be *at* the game, so this might make him feel better.

Maria had argued back and forth with the night nurse on duty and had convinced her no harm would come from a beer, peanuts and a ballgame. The nurse reluctantly agreed, but admonished that if they got caught by the doctor, Maria would have to take full responsibility and she would swear she knew nothing about it. Maria promised she'd take the blame if they were caught, knowing the doctor had more than likely left for the day, considering it was almost 7:00 PM and he started his final rounds at 5:00, according to Joe.

"So, what's the verdict?" Maria asked, nodding toward Joe's bandages.

"I'm good as new, or almost. The doc promised he'd have me out of here by noon tomorrow.

"Great! I think there's a flight to Minneapolis at 3:30. Should I reserve us a couple of seats on it, or would you rather wait until evening?"

"Yes!" Joe said. "The sooner I get home, the better. I wonder how the cat is?"

"He's fine. I had Slade check on him—he was given strict orders to feed him and change the litter box, which he wasn't too thrilled about. So, don't worry."

"I kind of miss the old tom," Joe said, channel surfing with the remote control until he found the ballgame. It was just starting and a young teenage boy was belting out the Star Spangled Banner with such gusto, it sent shivers up their spine.

Maria handed Joe a beer and took one for herself, then settled back in the chair next to Joe's hospital bed.

Joe moved over and patted the empty space on the bed next to him. "There's plenty of room here if you want to join me and share those peanuts you brought."

Maria laughed and kicked off her sandals, then grabbing the bag of peanuts, scrambled onto the bed next to Joe.

"We aren't going to get in trouble for this are we?" Joe asked grabbing a handful of peanuts.

"No, don't worry. I spoke with the nurse and convinced her it would be therapeutic. But maybe we better quickly finish these beers before she changes her mind."

Joe laughed. "Well, she made her rounds just before you got here, so we have about an hour before she comes back. I'm off the heavy pain meds—at my request—so I think I can handle a beer."

"I know, I was here when you told the day nurse and believe me, you wouldn't be drinking that beer if you weren't."

They lay side by side, swilling beer, munching peanuts and watching the Twins lose inning by inning against the Anaheim Angels.

"You know, I've been thinking about something. I don't know if you would want to do this—maybe not, but..." Maria faltered.

"What?" Joe asked, watching Maria fidget.

"Well, I was thinking you could stay with me at the condo—just until you're feeling one hundred percent of course—and I could make sure you get at least one home-cooked meal a day. What do ya say?"

"I appreciate the offer, Maria, but I don't want to put you out, and I'm getting better every day," Joe said, hoping she'd keep trying to convince him.

"You wouldn't be putting me out, Joe, and Tess would love it. I'd like to do this. After all, we're partners and best friends and..." She didn't finish the sentence.

"And...?" Joe prompted, looking into her deep brown eyes.

"And...maybe something more," she said, meeting his gaze.

Their lips met and they kissed, first gently exploring one another, then demanding more, feeling their bodies melt together as one.

Joe slowly moved his hand under her T-shirt and cupped a breast, feeling her nipple harden under his caress while kissing her long, slender neck, then her breasts, leaving a trail of hot kisses wherever his lips touched her skin.

Maria moaned and responded to the one man she trusted and loved more than anyone in this world. Having no control of her feelings now—deliriously ecstatic—she felt a yearning so deeply embedded in her soul, it frightened her. She had *never* felt this way before. It was as if a wildfire was burning out of control low in her belly, throbbing to be released.

What began as a gentle brush of the lips suddenly became an animal urgency. Clothing discarded haphazardly, they made love forcefully, almost brutally, with wild abandon, each feeling as if the world had stopped, except for them and this one burning moment in time.

Maria felt her body explode with pleasure time and time again, until she could stand no more, and Joe lay contentedly next to her, breathing heavily.

"Did I tell you the cat can stay, too," she whispered in his ear.

Joe laughed. "Well, that clinches it then. If the *cat* can stay, I will, too."

"Good."

"You sure know how to persuade a guy. Many more nights like this and they'll have to bury me instead of discharge me."

"Oh, God, are you okay? Did you bust anything open? Oh, Joe, I'm sorry," Maria said sitting up, the sheet falling below her breasts.

"*Shh*," Joe said, putting his finger to her lips, then tracing a line with his fingertips to the swell of her bared breast, encircling her nipple. "I'm fine. I was kidding."

Maria laid her head back on the pillow and turned to face Joe. "It really was *something* wasn't it?"

He looked at her and smiled. "Unbelievable. We make quite a team, Sanchez."

"Yeah, we do at that, don't we."

"I love you, Maria Sanchez."

"And I love you," Maria said, brushing a lock of hair away from his sweaty forehead. She kissed him then slid out of bed, dragging her clothing, which was scattered all over the room, into the bathroom.

When Maria emerged, she looked as fresh as when she'd arrived, with the exception of an earthy musk smell that surrounded her. She straightened the bed around Joe, helping him secure his hospital gown, and then put the empty beer cans in her shoulder bag to take back to the hotel.

"I have to go now. I'll see you in the morning," she said, kissing him goodbye.

"I wish you could spend the night," Joe said, holding her close.

"I know, so do I. Soon," Maria whispered, touching a finger to his lips and leaving the hospital room.

Joe snuggled deep down into the blankets with the smell of Maria surrounding him and slept a deep, dreamless sleep— realizing just before he went under, he had no idea what the final score of the game was, but found he didn't much care.

35

Nicholas Freyhoff sat back and relaxed with a drink in hand, as he waited for the pilot to announce take-off.

Santini's private jet had all the comforts of home, including a big screen TV and VCR, along with a bar fully stocked with only the finest labels.

Nicholas was checking off the list of things that needed to be done once he arrived in Minneapolis.

Roberto had arranged to have a car waiting for him at the Minneapolis/St. Paul International Airport, so he wouldn't have to worry about transportation once he got there.

He would most likely arrive in the Twin Cities before 3:00 AM, so he would have plenty of time to get everything ready for his therapy session with J.R. Nicholas needed to prepare himself mentally as well as physically, because a session always exhausted him, often draining him for a full day. And this one would prove to be even more difficult than the others, because this time *they* were choosing the victim, not J.R. At the very least, it would require more time and patience on his part—both of which he was short on these days.

Nicholas opened his briefcase, checking the contents once again to be certain he didn't forget anything. Along with a number of therapy tools were several vials of Metrazol, which would be used in the shock treatment. He counted the vials of Seconal that would be administered first, in order to produce

C. HYYTINEN

the desired hypnotic effect. It would also be used as a sedative
on the girl when she was initially abducted. He had four vials
and hoped that would be enough. He lifted the false bottom
and counted more than a dozen small white envelopes
containing enough methamphetamine to supply half of
Minneapolis—but would last their friend only a matter of days.
The drug was manufactured in-house and was top-quality.

Santini had his finger on the pulse of America's youth.
Along with the crystal meth—or crank, as it was commonly
called—he also manufactured various other types of
amphetamines and LSD.

Rico had been shipped a large supply of heroin and
cocaine, with strict orders to distribute it sparingly to their
friend over the past few days. They wanted him in a somewhat
needy situation. In fact, if Rico followed instructions, J.R.
would be climbing the walls right about now. He hadn't had a
fix in almost…six hours, Nicholas figured, looking at his Rolex
and smiling.

Over the years, Nicholas had done extensive research on
the workings of the mind and human behavior. Indeed, he had
more than enough knowledge to be a professional in the field
of psychology.

That is why a psychotic individual such as J.R. Franco
intrigued as much as frightened him—he was a dangerous man,
unpredictable and very intelligent, even given the quantity of
drugs that had no doubt altered his brain. J.R. was a loose
cannon, ready to go off at any given moment without warning.

The pilot announced they were ready to take off.

Nicholas closed his briefcase, satisfied he had everything
that was needed.

He buckled his seat belt then turned to the laptop
computer that was sitting on the small table next to him and

turned it on. He'd charged the battery prior to the trip so he would have two to three hours before it needed to be recharged.

He entered the access code that allowed him entrance into the data bank of information he'd compiled over the years, and brought up one of the files on Roberto Santini.

Nicholas had documented every transaction in detail—both legal and illegal—within the organization. It was his personal guarantee against Roberto Santini. He knew he would need to show this information only once to his longtime friend in order to get the desired results. But that would be a *last* resort—a life or death situation. Roberto had an idea of what Nicholas was doing—he was not stupid—but he didn't know the extent of it. If he did, they would never be friends again.

Roberto was unstable in his own right—Nicholas knew from experience—and wouldn't hesitate to end their relationship if it suited him. But Nicholas knew he was needed too much at present to worry about it unnecessarily. With his mind-bending skills as well as computer expertise, he was irreplaceable, for now. And perhaps his most important asset was the simple fact that he knew *too* much. But if something did inadvertently happen to him and foul play was involved in any way, shape, or form, all the information he'd gathered over the years against Santini would be made public and Roberto would go to jail.

Copies of all Roberto's indiscretions were squirreled away in a safety deposit box at a downtown bank in Los Angeles. Nicholas' younger brother, Stephen, carried the key with him at all times, knowing what needed to be done and when.

So for now, Nicholas was sitting pretty. He was second in command to Roberto, his so-called partner, and had no one to thank but himself, and his father, God rest his soul. If not for his father's dealings with Antonio Santini, Roberto's father, he might never have known the family up close and personal. He first met the Santinis when he was a boy of twelve, tagging along with his father one day nearly twenty years ago.

Samuel Freyhoff owed gambling debts totaling close to fifty-thousand dollars and Antonio Santini was willing to put up the money needed to pay them off, along with an extra twenty thousand for young Nicholas' education. Considering Samuel had saved Antonio's life in W.W.II and had never asked for anything in return, Antonio had figured it was the least he could do.

When Nicholas turned eighteen, he was accepted at the college of his choice and graduated with honors four years later. He then accepted the offer to join the organization for one year at his father's advice—and had been there ever since. Shortly after his father died, Roberto's father passed away also, which seemed to bring the two young men closer together. They had both been ruled by their fathers for so long, each with no mother present, they were lost without them—until they focused all their efforts on business and making money, which had brought them to the exceedingly rich wealth they shared today.

But Roberto was not like his father. He had a temper that ruled his mind as well as his heart and gave him an unhealthy outlook on the value of life. Others' lives meant nothing to Roberto Santini. He cared about one thing and one person only—money and himself.

Nicholas and Roberto were very different—in looks as well as personality. Nicholas's tall stature and cool blonde good looks offset Roberto's dark handsome Italian heritage. He was non-confrontational as well, while Roberto thrived on going head to head with anyone who was willing. Perhaps the most important difference was that Nicholas had a heart—

maybe it was slightly off-beat, but he had one, which was more than he could say for Roberto.

Nicholas freshened his drink and lit a cigarette. Looking out the small window at the ink-black heavens, he discovered the only thing he looked forward to was the flight back to L.A., after his obligations were fulfilled in Minneapolis. His next plan was to convince Roberto to take out J.R. The perfect opportunity would present itself after they used him this one last time. It was customary that they meet to decide their next move when the time came for J.R. to relocate. It would be just as easy to put a bullet in his skull. If Roberto refused, well, maybe Nicholas would have to take matters into his own hands. The task would not be an easy one, though, considering everything he knew about J.R. Franco. He was more than just a man, regardless of what Roberto believed. He was an animal that offered no mercy to his victims and would not succumb to death easily—of that Nicholas was certain.

For some reason Roberto had developed a kinship with their friend. He found he could relate to J.R. and his deranged mind. He also felt a certain pride—having an evil puppet that would do whatever his master desired. It was everything Roberto had ever asked for. He'd helped to mold the man and make him what he was today; therefore he felt a parental affection toward J.R.

Nicholas leaned his head back and closed his eyes, deep in thought. If he decided to go against Roberto's wishes and have J.R. eliminated, he'd have to relinquish Roberto's hold on life as well. But he knew—no matter what his safeguards—to defy Roberto Santini was to be a dead man.

36

Joe was discharged from Community Memorial Hospital by 11:00 AM the following day. He breathed deeply of the dry California air, tilting his face upward toward the warm sunshine beating down. "Man, it's good to be alive, isn't it?" he said, turning to Maria and taking her hand as they walked the short distance to where she'd parked the rental car.

Maria squeezed his hand. "Yes, it certainly is. Sometimes it takes a tragedy to realize just how good life is. I'm just glad to have you by my side again—even if you're still the walking wounded. Maybe we should have taken that wheelchair after all. I don't want you to overexert yourself," Maria said, looking worriedly at Joe.

His left arm was in a sling where he'd taken two bullets and his chest was still bandaged where the third one went in, lodging in a rib but doing remarkably little damage. The doctor gave him strict orders to get plenty of rest and reminded him to see his physician in the Twin Cities in one week.

"Don't worry. I feel like a new man," Joe stated, eyes twinkling.

Maria looked at him. "If you say so. You do look extremely happy. I bet you're glad to be going home."

"That's one of the reasons," Joe said, winking at her. He sighed. "To tell you the truth, I didn't think I'd ever get out of that damn hospital room. Seems like I've been laid up a month instead of just a few days. What day is it, anyway?"

"It's Friday and the start of Labor Day weekend. Summer is rapidly coming to an end and Tess starts school in a few days." Maria trailed off, a frown creasing her forehead.

"I'm sorry," Joe said.

"Sorry? For what?"

"For keeping you apart from your daughter. She just got back from summer camp, if I remember right, before all of this happened."

"There's nothing to be sorry about," Maria said punching Joe lightly on his good arm. "And besides, we've talked on the phone a lot. She's a great kid, ya know. She understands I had to be with you. We'll just have to make up for it when we get back. She'll be thrilled to have you staying with us. I haven't told her yet. I wasn't sure if you'd accept my offer until last night."

"Well, you can't say I didn't warn you—I'm a real slob. Being a bachelor hasn't exactly required neatness. And the only entertaining I do is for my cat."

"I know, I know," Maria said laughing.

They reached the rental car and Maria unlocked the passenger door first for Joe.

He opened the door and got in.

Letting out a loud grunt he got back out before Maria even had her door unlocked.

"Wait a minute, Maria. Someone left you a little surprise."

Maria peered in the side window, shielding her eyes against the glare of the bright sun, in order to see inside the car.

On the driver's seat lay a large, dead rat. Tacked to its hide was a bloody note—BITCH.

Maria looked over the top of the car at Joe, who looked

slightly green. "Santini," she said.

"Yeah," Joe managed. "It's starting to smell."

"In this heat, I'm not surprised," Maria calmly replied. "It couldn't have been here more than a few hours though." She'd arrived at the hospital around 8:00.

Maria opened her car door and rolled down the window, instructing Joe to do the same.

Joe picked up an old newspaper Maria had discarded in the back seat and walked around to where she stood. He then attempted to try to wrap the rat in the newspaper with his one good hand, without touching the disgusting thing despite her protests.

"Joe, let me—"

"No, no, I'll get it," he interrupted, finally getting the paper under the dead vermin then wrapping it up.

"There's a Dumpster," Maria said, pointing to the other side of the parking lot. "You don't look so hot. Lean against the car," she said, grabbing the rat package and sprinting across the parking lot to dispose of Santini's unsavory gift.

When she returned, Joe had the hood popped up and was inspecting the wiring. Satisfied, he shut it and looked at Maria. "Just wanted to make sure nothing else was tampered with...."

Maria looked at her watch. It was quickly approaching noon and she still had to check out of the hotel, and then drive them to L.A. International Airport. "If we want to catch that 3:30 flight we better get moving."

"Yeah, let's get the hell out of California. I'd just as soon forget I was ever here. Not too many fond memories I'm afraid," Joe said, getting into the car with a groan. "Well, I take that back. There's one very fond memory. Last night ranks at the top of my list."

Maria smiled, her heart trip-hammering at the sudden

closeness she felt with this man she'd grown to love and almost lost. She started the car and pulled out of the hospital parking lot. "Are you hungry? There's a row of fast food joints on the way to the hotel."

"Yeah, starved!"

"Well, holler when you see something you want and I'll pull over," Maria said, turning onto Main Street.

They ended up getting burgers and chocolate shakes, then headed back to the hotel where Maria had to pick up her suitcase and check out. She would have done it earlier, but wasn't sure when Joe would be released, knowing how hospitals could sometimes take hours longer than anticipated.

They approached the door to Maria's room with caution.

Joe felt exposed without his weapon, which was still being held by the Ventura Police Department as evidence. It was the only gun found on the Franco property, and even though they knew it was his and used to deter the assailant, they refused to release it. Maria had a spare—the small .38 snub-nose she carried when confronting Santini—but it was packed away in her suitcase, inside the hotel room. At least they had one weapon between them. Things could be worse.

With gun drawn, Maria unlocked the door, then pushed it open with her foot, scanning the interior. "All clear," she whispered to Joe who was by her side—almost in front of her, acting as her shield without realizing it.

"Let's hurry up and get the hell out of here. We don't want to be sitting ducks for another one of Santini's pranks," Joe said, checking under the bed and in the closet. "You got everything?"

"I packed earlier, but I always forget something," Maria said, checking the bathroom and finding her toothbrush. "See?" She brandished the toothbrush in midair, depositing it in the suitcase.

She rummaged through her things until she found the .38 and handed it to Joe. "Here, I know you must feel naked without a gun."

Joe smiled. "You got that right. Thanks."

Maria took another quick look around and was satisfied. Grabbing her suitcase, she closed the door to the hotel room and on this chapter of their life. "Let's go, partner."

They drove almost the same route Maria had taken yesterday when she was going to see Santini. This time, however, she was experiencing a much different feeling. They were going home, together. All those she loved would be under one roof and for once in her life, she felt complete—satisfied in all departments. But she couldn't account for the minuscule doubt at the back of her mind—an intuitive undercurrent—that something would happen to change it all.

37

Maria and Joe arrived at Los Angeles International Airport with no further encounters with Santini or his men.

They boarded the plane with trepidation, but once they got off the ground their unease seemed to disappear along with the dwindling California coastline.

"Well, we're finally going home," Maria said, sipping the bloody Mary the flight attendant just brought. "I called Slade from my cell phone while you were buying a newspaper. He'll pick us up so we don't have to worry about taking a taxi. Boy, he's relieved we're coming home."

"Yeah, I bet."

"Joe," Maria said, frowning. "He's relieved we're *both* coming home. I think the chief has been taking out his frustrations with the case on poor Peter."

"Poor Peter, my ass," Joe mumbled.

"Believe it or not, he doesn't have any designs on me. Maybe he sort of did…at one time…but he knows how we feel about one another, and he's all for it. Really," Maria said, reading his doubtful expression.

"If you say so," Joe said, shrugging his broad shoulders. "I was probably too hard on the guy. I don't know, he just rubs me the wrong way."

"Yeah, I know. I think that may be his goal in life, but he's not so bad sometimes. Enough talk about Slade, for God's sake. Let's talk about our plans for Labor Day weekend. I thought we could go for a picnic, the three of us. Maybe grill some steaks, have a couple of beers. How does that sound?"

"Great! And I can still throw a mean curve ball with my good arm if Tess wants to practice that swing she was having trouble with earlier."

"I think we'll hold off on the curve balls for a while," Maria replied.

"We'll see," Joe countered. "Hey, what's the status on the McReedy girl? Is she out of the hospital yet?"

"She got out Wednesday. Patsy McReedy decided it would be a good time to go and stay with her sister. She lives in St. Paul. The chief suggested she leave the Twin Cities, but since they had nowhere else to go, we put a couple of undercover officers in that area for their protection."

"Is she still catatonic?"

"Yes, for the most part anyway. Sometimes she seems to come out of it, but only for a couple of minutes, then she relapses. I hope in time she regains her former self. It tears me up inside to see a little kid suffer so."

"Yeah, me too," Joe said, looking into his drink for answers.

"You're thinking about the Franco boy again, aren't you?" Maria asked.

"Something about that kid seems to pull at my heart strings. I don't know why I should feel different about him— I've dealt with this kind of thing in the past and thought I had developed a thick skin—but there's just something about him."

"I know what you mean. He seems to have knowledge well beyond his years. And there's something in his eyes that almost looks…I don't know…familiar."

"Yeah, that's it! I couldn't put my finger on it, but that's it," Joe said, rubbing his chin thoughtfully.

"You look tired. Why don't you try and catch a few winks?"

Joe smiled. "I am tired. I guess this drink did me in," he said, leaning his head back. Soon he was softly snoring. His head lolled to the side and came to rest on Maria's shoulder.

Maria smiled to herself, thinking how uncomfortable the rest of the flight would be, but loving every minute of it just the same.

Peter Slade was waiting by the baggage claim area when they arrived at the airport.

"Looks like it may be bedtime for our patient, huh?" he said, looking at Joe's wrinkled shirt and messed up hair, then winking at Maria.

"I fell asleep on the plane, just woke up," Joe said, yawning. "You want to make something of it, Slade?"

"Here," Slade said thrusting a package in Joe's hand. "Before you punch me, take this expensive bottle of scotch I bought you. I wouldn't want it to break."

"Uh, I guess I'm kind of cranky. Sorry, and thanks."

"Anytime, my friend," Slade said amiably enough, taking both Maria's suitcase and Joe's duffel bag. "So, where to first? I imagine Joe wants to get home to see that *thing* he calls a pet."

"Joe will be staying with me, so maybe we could go pick up his things *and* his cat, if it's not too much trouble," Maria said.

Peter raised his eyebrows at Maria's revelation, but said nothing. He looked over at Joe and winked. "No trouble at all," he said with a grin.

* * *

The cat was ecstatic to have Joe home. He was a miniature, furry bulldozer, attempting to knock them over with his affectionate leg-rubs. He barked out meows in an attempt to get attention when Joe stopped petting him. Joe had to carry him over one shoulder so he could get his things together.

Peter helped Joe get his suitcase packed and Maria got together the cat's things, which included a litter box, cat litter, a large variety of cat food—both crunchy and soft—and a catnip mouse.

"Man, I hope you travel lighter than the cat, or there won't be room for us in the car," she said, as Joe and Peter emerged with suitcase in tow.

"Let's see. I think I've got everything; clothes, razor, toothbrush, cat," Joe said, petting the animal who was still riding on his shoulder.

"Don't forget your PJ's," Slade couldn't resist saying.

"Got 'em," Joe said, refusing to rise to the bait.

"Okay, let's go then, before I change my mind," Maria said, holding the litter-box at arms length.

"I wonder if I should take the Chevy—I've already left her sit for almost a week."

"Maybe you should," Slade muttered.

"No. We can pick it up later," Maria said. "Maybe Tuesday, on our way to work, or else on the way home, when your arm's a little better." She frowned, remembering the way Joe had held his arm earlier this morning in a grimace of pain, when he didn't think she was watching.

"Yeah, I suppose that would work," Joe said, giving a backward glance at the garage, then looking at Maria, reading the concern for him in her eyes.

Maria smiled and led the way to Slade's rental car.

"Your cat won't crap in my car, will he?" Peter asked,

eyeing the feline warily as he walked behind Joe.

"No, don't worry, Slade. He never craps in the car, but he does get car-sick unless he's sitting on the driver's lap," Joe added, chuckling at the expression of horror on Slade's face.

38

"What a sight for sore eyes, huh?" Rico grinned from ear to ear. "I had to threaten him with this," he said waving the pistol in the air.

"Put that damn thing away before you shoot someone, you idiot," Nicholas hissed, looking with disgust at the man Santini had chosen to replace Lenny Milano. God, how he hated stupid people, and Rico Smits was stupid, pure and simple.

He walked over to the half-naked man lying in a fetal position on the unmade bed. "Wake up! I come bearing gifts, my friend," Nicholas said, touching his shoulder.

"Get the fuck away from me," J.R. growled, turning over and curling into a ball once again.

Nicholas took the syringe out of his suit coat pocket and removed the cap. "This will help you relax. It's Seconal, and when we're done with our session, if you're a good patient, Rico will fix you the best speedball you've ever had. He's got the heroin, don't you, Smits?"

"Right here," Rico said, holding up the goods. "And some excellent coke, my man," he added, sniffing and doing a little dance.

"I brought a fresh batch of crank. It's even better than the last, so it's up to you, my friend. Cooperate and you'll get what you want."

J.R. rolled over and held out his arm while Nicholas tied

rubber tubing around his upper arm, then plunged the needle into a vein.

Nicholas watched J.R. start to relax. It was time to begin.

J.R. sat in a straight-back chair with rope wound around his ankles and wrists and across his chest, binding him to the chair.

The entire room was awash in darkness except for a bright circle of light from the lamp suspended over J.R.'s head. J.R. was now in a hypnotic state, eyes transfixed on the crystal object that dangled before his eyes as he listened to his hypnotist's monotonous repetition of words.

The stage had been set to have the girl taken and disposed of in J.R.'s usual manner. The only difference was, this time *they* were choosing the victim. Nicholas went over the details again and again until he was certain *everything* would work according to plan.

Now, he had filtered into another path of the patient's brain, and would begin his own version of electro-convulsive therapy. With the help of a small dose of Metrazol—which he held in his hand ready to go—and the electric cattle prod that lay at his feet fully charged, he began.

Nicholas went methodically over J.R.'s past, beginning two years earlier. He found it wasn't necessary to go back any further. He'd done his work well seven years ago, ingraining in J.R.'s brain the most important things. It was the hardest part of the entire process and had consumed many hours of time and patience. Now he only had to remind J.R. of where his loyalties ultimately lay and to whom—what was always referred to as the *rites of passage.* "Your creators will always be here for you, son. We have helped you from the beginning and will continue to do so, as long as you continue to cooperate."

He administered the shot of Metrazol, then looked into his patient's eyes. He almost stepped back from the pure hate that emanated from deep within, but knew that would be a big mistake. *Fear* was the main element the beast thrived on, and to show it would mean defeat. Instead, he picked up the cattle prod and met J.R.'s hateful gaze.

"You will remember only those directly related to your assigned task—the girl and Rico. When you wake up, you will remember nothing of this session. You will not recall my name or anything specific about the organization—we are known only as your creators. Is this understood?"

J.R. just looked at him with his malevolent stare.

"Do you understand?" Nicholas repeated, touching the electrified tool to the base of J.R.'s skull, eliciting a howl of pain in response. He waited twenty seconds, then applied the magic wand again, repeating vehemently, "Do you understand?" This time he got a much more desirable reaction.

J.R. Franco bucked against the ropes that bound him to the chair and nearly tipped it over. The current that went through his brain seemed to sear a white-hot path through his very soul. The pain was excruciating, but along with the pain seemed to come a revelation of sorts—he knew at *that* moment, his existence on this earth was not determined by his actions, but from a higher being. He *must* obey, but had to fight against the primal urge to kill this man who repeatedly tortured him. "I—I—understand!" he cried, glaring at his enemy through a blood-red veil of confusion and pain. He would obey, he would do as they ask, but when the job was complete, he would have a surprise for them. "Yes," he said aloud. He appeased the demon that dwelled within as he repeated his litany silently to himself—*he would kill them all— kill them all— kill them all—*

"That's more like it. I knew you would come to see it my way." Nicholas smiled. "Remember the dark-haired girl—no other will do. She must be your *only* choice. You may sleep now and when you awake, you will feel renewed and remember nothing of our visit." Nicholas snapped his fingers and J.R.'s head dropped to his chest.

"Untie him and get him into bed," he ordered Rico who appeared from the shadows. "He will sleep for thirty minutes. At that time give him a pop—have the speedball ready when he wakes up. I guarantee he will be more agreeable. I'm leaving pictures of the girl and a couple extra vials of Seconal." Nicholas handed him a large manila envelope.

It was pure luck that he'd found a picture, and so recent, too. The Minneapolis Police Department had held a picnic in early June and the local newspaper just happened to snap a picture of the pretty cop and her daughter. He'd cut off the part that pictured the cop, then had the second half with the girl, grinning, blown up. He managed to remove most of the graininess from the newspaper photo, so the resulting picture was very clear. Nicholas smiled to himself, thinking how everything seemed to be going his way.

He looked at Rico Smits and his smile vanished—this moron could fuck it all up if given half a chance. "We'll be in close contact with you over the next few days," Nicholas stated. "We will communicate twice daily—call the pager number I gave you before you visit our friend and then again when you return. Don't forget, your life may depend on it. We will telephone you after we receive your second pager message. Carry your cell phone and pager with you at *all* times. Do you understand?"

Rico nodded enthusiastically, touching the electronic devices that were already strapped to his belt.

"You will be held responsible if *anything* goes wrong," Nicholas continued. "And remember, J.R. must think *he* has made the choice of his next victim—you must reinforce everything that was accomplished here today in order for this to work. Roberto doesn't take kindly to fuck-ups, relatives included," Nicholas said, walking to the door. "Just remember, do as you're told and keep a close eye on our mutual friend."

Nicholas boarded the private jet feeling satisfied with the therapy session. He would have a good report for Roberto, and that would help him toward his ultimate goals—first, eliminating the beast they created, and second, becoming head of the organization, which was something he now realized he'd always wanted. He could even bring his younger brother, Stephen, into the organization. *What a beautiful plan!* He would have to kill Roberto to fulfill it, but he'd likely end up wasting him anyway over J.R.'s demise.

He sipped his scotch and leaned back on his pillow, thinking of Carol in his arms instead of Roberto's and smiled, feeling his pants tighten over his erection.

Power was a potent drug that required constant sustenance, and he thought he had it all.

He was mistaken.

39

They all slept late Saturday morning, then spent the rest of the day not doing much of anything—which was exactly what the doctor ordered. They rented a couple of movies and Maria made enough popcorn to feed several families. After that, they played a game of Monopoly, which Tess won without trouble.

Late in the afternoon, Joe took a nap while Maria and Tess went to the Mall of America to pick up the clothes put on layaway last week when Nancy had taken the girls shopping. Tess managed to talk her mother into another pair of black denim jeans, a new belt, and some last-minute school supplies as well. They left the mall two hours later, loaded down with packages, tired but happy.

After a late supper and a fashion show put on by Tess featuring her new clothes, they all went to bed early.

Around 2:00 AM, Maria awoke from a terrifying dream—but waking up seemed to banish it from her memory. Again, she felt a strong sense of foreboding. Something bad was going to happen—*but what?*

She climbed out of bed and padded to Tess's room, opening the door a crack to peek in at her sleeping child.

Tess was softly snoring, her arm wrapped protectively around her stuffed bear. The blankets lay in a twisted knot at the foot of the bed.

Maria crept into the room and covered her up, then kissed

her forehead, gazing down at her beautiful daughter. In sleep, she looked younger than her nine years. Maria could almost imagine she was five years old again, ready to start kindergarten.

A fragment of her nightmare seemed to flutter to the surface for a moment, revealing Jack, standing over Tess, a nine-year-old Tess. Something glittered in his upraised hand.

Maria sat down hard on the chair in Tess's room, trying to remember more of the dream, but no more would come. Maybe that was good, a blessing in disguise. She knew it was the same nightmare that had haunted her sleep for close to a month now—and the difference between these and the ones that had plagued her sleep years ago was that Tess was older, and the overwhelming feeling of dread that consumed her afterward was unlike anything she'd ever experienced before. Maria leaned forward and lightly touched her daughter's cheek, a single tear sliding down her own face.

They had been through so much together, from the very beginning.

Trouble had started with Jack before Tess was even born, and Maria remembered protecting her unborn baby from the abuse she'd had to endure. Then after Tess was brought into the world, she had the responsibility of protecting both of them, trying desperately to find a way out.

Maria still blamed herself for not being able to remove her daughter from danger immediately, but over the years she'd learned to accept it. There was a time, right after Jack died, when she hated herself for it. She would often wonder how she could have married a man like Jack, even though he was different when they were dating. What did that say about her? What was *wrong* with her? Those thoughts—combined with the fear of being controlled by someone, anyone, ever again—

had haunted her for years. It took a long time for her to get over those feelings of guilt and inadequacy. However, after a lot of healing and soul-searching she'd discovered she was as much a victim as her daughter—a victim of abuse who'd lived each day out of fear. Fear of being killed and leaving Tess without someone to protect her—always searching for a way out—but finding no way of escaping the frightening nightmare that had become her unfortunate life.

But *that* Maria—the scared, frightened young girl—was a different person than the strong, aggressive woman she was today.

"We've come a long way, baby," she whispered to her sleeping child, smoothing a long strand of dark, glossy hair away from her face. They'd had their share of troubles in the years since Jack died but nothing life-threatening—just the normal problems associated with single-parenthood and growing up.

Tess stirred and rolled over, knocking her stuffed bear off the bed, then resumed her deep sleep.

Maria stood up and retrieved the old, battered bear, remembering the Christmas five years ago when she gave it to Tess. The little girl had squealed with delight upon opening the gift, hugging the large, stuffed-bear to her chest, then declaring proudly its name would be Merry-Bear, in honor of Christmas. Then when Christmas was over, they could just call her Merry—or Mary, whichever suited them.

Tess always had a special quality for interpreting things more like an adult than a child. Maybe it was because she was an only child and around adults more often than other children. Maria remembered how the child would astonish anyone willing to listen when she would pick up a *Newsweek* and start reading aloud at the age of three and a half. But even though she had a special talent for learning and understanding things remarkably well, she still had the insecurities of a little girl. Merry-bear (or Mary) had been her constant nighttime companion since she was a small child.

Maria returned the bear to her daughter's side and kissed the top of her head, then crept out, closing the bedroom door behind her.

She paused in the hallway, wondering if Joe was sleeping as soundly as Tess. Just when she decided he was and started back to her own bed, she heard her name whispered. She walked into the living room and found Joe sitting up in bed.

The cat sat perched on Joe's shoulder, eyeing Maria suspiciously as she approached, ready to spring if necessary.

"I thought you were sleeping. I didn't mean to wake you," Maria whispered.

"You didn't...couldn't sleep," Joe said, removing the cat before his claws could dig in any further. The cat hopped down, giving them each a dirty look.

"Me, either," Maria said, sitting down on the edge of the sofa bed next to Joe. "I had another bad dream." She felt tears burn her eyes, but tried to hold them back, feeling like a fool for acting like a baby.

"Come here," Joe said, opening his arms.

Maria let herself be soothed by Joe's comforting words. She cried quietly for a time, her face buried in his chest, while he stroked her hair and whispered assurances in her ear. She felt nothing or no one could harm her while she was nestled in his arms.

They snuggled together for a long time, whispering in the darkness, revealing intimate secrets and feelings that had been awakened in each of them.

Maria told Joe—at his gentle prodding—the details of the

dreams that had been haunting her sleep and what little she could remember of the dream tonight. The overwhelming feeling she felt afterward was the most disturbing. "This is very unsettling; they're different than the nightmares I used to have after Jack died. Theresa is the same age she is now. Why? I can't explain it," she breathed shakily.

"It's the case, Maria. We've been wading in this crap for so long, we don't know when to turn it off. When you're asleep you're probably subconsciously playing a part somewhere between your past experiences with Jack and this case."

"You think so? I mean, you don't think there's some hidden meaning here. I can't describe the terror in the pit of my stomach when I wake up, it's so...enveloping."

They held each other in the darkness.

"It's just the case and my past," she repeated, trying to convince herself.

"What else could it be?" Joe said, brushing a hair from her eyes and kissing her on the forehead. "I know I've been having some pretty bizarre dreams lately, too—only in my dreams, I always miss getting shot by a fraction of an inch...then I take the son of a bitch down."

When they made love, it wasn't a demanding lust like it was the first time—this time it was a slow and gentle exploration. Each kiss and caress carried with it the unspoken love they had carried around for one another for so long, and now, after all this time, they could be together—both body and soul.

40

Maria and Tess brought Joe breakfast in bed Sunday morning. He was sleeping soundly on the sofa bed with the cat stretched out along the full length of his legs. Mr. Peanut looked up lazily as they approached the bed while Joe snored softly. Maria put her finger to her lips, motioning Tess to set the tray on the bedside table. Joe needed rest more than anything. She thought of last night and couldn't help but smile to herself. *Well, you sure took care of his rest last night, didn't you?* she thought, feeling a twinge of guilt.

The cat yawned, letting out a strangled meow, interrupting Joe's sleep. Maria scooped the fat feline up in her arms, ready to take him into the kitchen when Joe opened his eyes and smiled.

"Well, good morning," Maria said. "I meant to take your two-ton tom into the kitchen, so you could sleep."

"I was ready to get up anyway," Joe said, stretching. He looked at Tess holding a vase with a single red rose, then at the tray laden with pancakes, and smiled. "Man, I must have died and gone to heaven. Breakfast in bed served by two beautiful women. What more could a guy ask for?"

Tess grinned and hopped up on the bed next to him, thrusting the rose under his nose. "And a beautiful flower to smell while you eat! Mom and I made your favorites— pancakes and sausage," she said, leaning over Joe and lifting the cover off his plate with a flourish.

Maria noticed Joe grimace when Tess leaned over. "Honey, watch the arm," she admonished her daughter.

"Oh, sorry. Here, let me set this on your lap," Tess said, picking up the heavy tray and balancing it precariously over Joe's bed.

Joe quickly sat up, watching the steaming cup of coffee slide to one end of the tray.

Maria laughed. "Let me help," she said setting the cat back on the bed, and taking the tray. "We don't want to *kill* you with kindness." She set the tray on his lap and smiled into his clear blue eyes.

Joe touched her face with his fingertips and smiled, then looked at the little girl who'd hopped back on the bed with the huge cat cradled upside-down in her arms, and he knew why he'd never felt happier than he did right now.

Maria dropped Tess off at Jenny's house for a couple of hours, so she and Joe could catch up on any new developments with the case.

She spoke briefly with the chief when they got back on Friday, and he'd mentioned more extensive lab work was done on the synthetic carpet fibers that were found. Apparently, entwined with several of the fibers was a hair that was missed the first time. The lab was in the process of performing a mitochondrial DNA test, which took considerably longer than nuclear testing—when scientists extract DNA from the nucleus of cells in flesh or blood. The chief thought it was interesting that the hair in question was dyed black. It was determined the original color was a dark brown.

The fact that it was Sunday *and* Labor Day weekend likely

had something to do with City Hall being practically deserted. They had met only one other person on the first floor upon entering. The elevator looked foreign without the mob of people surrounding it, and Homicide had an echo-effect when they entered.

Maria approached her desk with trepidation, already seeing a mountain of paperwork stacked on one corner. "Man, you'd think I'd been gone for a month."

Joe laughed. "Yeah, I'm afraid mine doesn't look much better. I suppose I'd better clean it up for the new guy the chief has probably already hired to replace me."

"Oh, Joe, don't be ridiculous, the chief is *not* going to fire you—"

"I should, but I won't," Chief McCollough said from the doorway. "Welcome home, Morgan. Good to have you back." He shook his hand, smiling.

"Thanks...." Joe said, relief apparent in his voice.

"I realized I was probably a little too hard on you—"

"No, you weren't. I screwed up—big time screw-up. I never should have left Stephanie alone."

"Yeah, you're right, but it's possible it was the only thing *to* do. You were there, Morgan, not me. You came up with what you thought was a reasonable solution to a series of obstacles. Who's to say what was right and what was wrong? Forget it, Morgan—let it go. What's done is done, and there's no point in rehashing it. It won't change the outcome," the chief said, patting Joe on the back. He could see the tortured look in Joe's eyes when he spoke of Stephanie, and the chief felt partly to blame. He hadn't made matters any better by threatening to fire him—but goddamnit, they just couldn't afford to make mistakes.

"Did you send Slade home for the long weekend?" Maria

asked the chief, sensing a need to change the subject.

"Hell, no. He wanted me to, but I couldn't see any point in it. In fact, he's supposed to be coming in later this morning."

"Speak of the devil," Joe said as Peter strolled through the door, arrogant as usual.

Slade stopped in his tracks. "Well, what do we have here—a meeting of the minds? I felt my ears burning in the hallway. Were you talking about me?"

"Yes, we were, but now that you're here, we'll stop," Maria said, grinning.

"Did the chief tell you guys about the hair?" Slade inquired.

"Yeah, weird," Maria said.

"Things are starting to add up on our prime suspect, Mr. Jonathan Franco," Joe said. "Unfortunately, everything Stephanie knew—which was quite a lot—is dead, along with her. But it could be worse, right guys?" he asked with a note of sarcasm. "At least now we know we're looking for a large man with black hair." He shrugged his broad shoulders and walked away, turning to add "A bad dye job, no doubt."

"Yeah—tall, dark and handsome with a mind as deranged as a rabid coon," Slade said. "But you've accomplished more than you realize, Morgan. Now we have a definite ID on the River Rat. We know the facts, not just speculation. It might end there, but it's more than we had. Anyway, this guy is past due for a victim, maybe he's moved on."

"Yeah, right," Joe mumbled, shuffling papers on his desk.

"Wishful thinking," the chief grumbled. "He's still here, I'd bet on it."

"Hey, speaking of victims, how's Betsy McReedy doing?" Maria asked the chief. "Any improvement since the last time we spoke?"

"As a matter of fact, yes. I received a phone call from her mother, Patsy, yesterday afternoon. It seems she's lucid more times than not, now. Her doctors say she'll probably recover completely, .but it will take time, and patience."

"That's fantastic! I knew Betsy was a fighter or else she never would have made it as far as she did. How is she coping with what happened—or does she even realize?"

"She knows something *bad* happened, Sanchez. That's about the extent of it."

"I'm thinking of paying her a visit tomorrow—maybe bring Tess to meet her. They're around the same age and I thought seeing another kid might help. With school starting in a couple of days I figured this would be my last chance. And while I'm there I can *carefully* see if the girl remembers something, anything."

"I'll give you their address and phone number before you leave here," the chief said. "I'd call first, though. You never know how receptive the mother and father will be to seeing you."

"I know, but I honestly think it would do Betsy good to see Tess. I promised her in the hospital they would meet someday. And I'd bet Betsy hasn't seen another kid her own age for quite some time, considering she's been under protective watch since she got out of the hospital."

"Well, if anyone can get Mrs. McReedy to cooperate it's you, Sanchez. Good Luck," the chief said.

"So, tomorrow being Labor Day and all, what's everyone doing?" Slade asked.

"The wife wants me to go to a damn flea market. I told her to take her sister. God, how I hate them things," Chief McCollough said.

"Yeah, I guess I'll just hang out in the hotel bar," Slade

said with a note of resignation. "What about you guys?" he asked Joe and Maria.

Joe watched the scene unfold from a distance, knowing what was about to happen.

"We're going on a picnic," Maria said.

"A picnic, *hmm*, that sounds nice," the chief said. "Like I said, the wife's going to a flea market, so..." He looked at her expectantly.

"Well..." She glanced at Joe across the room. "You're welcome to join us—both of you," Maria said, somewhat reluctantly, knowing they wouldn't give up until they had finagled an invitation.

Joe groaned inwardly when they both accepted, then busied himself straightening his desk so Maria wouldn't see the disappointment written all over his face.

It took them the better part of an hour to get things orderly for when they returned to work Tuesday. Ready to leave, they said good-bye to the chief and Slade, reminding them to be at Maria's by 10:00 the following morning.

Walking down the hall, Maria turned to Joe. "Don't worry," she whispered.

"About what?"

"We'll have our *own* picnic tonight, just the two of us." She looked in both directions to make sure they were alone, then kissed him full on the lips. "When the rest of the world is sound asleep," she promised.

41

Theodore Wirth Park was a beautiful reserve, and today it was packed with families trying to have as much fun as possible on this last day of summer.

They found a spot with a grill and picnic table, then set about making themselves at home. Maria, Tess, and Peter unloaded the food and supplies, while Joe and the chief readied the grill for the steaks.

"Hard to believe summer is over," Joe said, thinking aloud as he watched Maria struggle with a large cooler while Slade carried a small bag and a blanket. He laughed at the sight, thinking what a total jerk Peter Slade was.

"Yeah, it went too damn fast, that's for sure, always does though. Pretty soon we'll have snow up to our butts and we'll all be *dreaming* about weather like this. Only good thing about winter in Minneapolis is less homicides," the chief grumbled. "Too cold even for the scum-bags."

Maria set the cooler down by the picnic table and turned her attention toward the chief and Joe. "How's it coming?" she asked, referring to the grill.

"Almost ready. I'm a firm believer in rare steaks, how 'bout you?" Chief McCollough said, retrieving the steaks from the cooler. "Have a beer, Sanchez. You look like you could use a cold one."

"Yeah, guess I could at that," Maria said, grabbing a beer.

"I'll take one of those and a root-beer for the young lady, please," Slade said, referring to Tess, who'd been talking non-stop about baseball.

"So, who's your favorite ball player, short-stop?" he asked, tugging at Tess's baseball cap.

Tess stood with one hand on her hip. "Well, let's see." She looked up at the sky, squinting. "It *used* to be Kirby Puckett, no contest, but he officially retired," she expertly stated. "Torii Hunter's pretty good at the bat. Koskie's pretty cool too." She grinned. "Tom Kelly, who used to be the manager for the Twins, took his team to the World Series *twice*—he was totally awesome."

"Never heard of any of 'em," Peter joked. Fact was, he was an avid baseball fan and knew of the ball players well. He was impressed as hell that a nine-year-old girl did, too. "I could probably show them a thing or two, though, I used to play semi-pro, ya know, almost made it to the big league."

"Yeah, right," Maria laughed. "Don't believe a word this guy says, sweetie. He's all talk, no action."

"Hey, I resent that. I'm a little bit of action. Not, much but a little," he said holding two fingers an inch apart, winking at Tess. "Wanna show me what you can do with that ball, slugger?" He nodded toward the baseball she'd been throwing up in the air since the moment they'd arrived.

"You bet!" she said excitedly, grabbing the bat.

"Holler when the steaks are done—I'm starved," Slade said, running to catch up with Tess.

Maria laughed. "She seems to have found a fast friend in Slade."

"Well, you should see his baseball card collection—seriously," the chief said. "If the kid's smart she'll hit him up for his most valuable player."

"Oh, I almost forgot, I got hold of Mrs. McReedy this morning," Maria told the chief.

"And?"

"And she's expecting us around 4:00 this afternoon," Maria said, grinning.

"You're kidding, right?"

"Nope. Dead serious."

"I'll be damned. Well, remember to find out—"

"I'll find out what I can. I don't want to jeopardize her health, for God's sake," Maria interrupted. "Some things are more important than answers—even to me."

"I know, I know. I just meant, do your best. Christ, you're touchy. What's the problem? This case finally getting to you?"

"No. No more than usual, anyway. I'm sorry. I didn't mean to bite your head off. I haven't been sleeping well lately," Maria said, yawning.

"Oh?" the chief said, looking at Joe over raised eyebrows.

"No, it's not what you're thinking." Maria couldn't help but laugh at the guilty expression on Joe's face. "If you must know I've been having nightmares—nothing I can't handle— just your average run-of-the-mill nightmares," she said, dismissing the subject by turning and walking away to ready the picnic table.

The chief looked at Joe. "Is that all it is, Morgan? Or is there something more to it?"

"I don't know," Joe said evasively. "You'll have to take that up with Maria."

The steaks were grilled to perfection, and the laughter and good feelings made the day fly by.

By quarter to four, Maria and Tess left, waving at the

three guys they left behind. The chief, Joe and Peter planned to usher out Labor Day with a bang, and Maria promised she'd be back in a couple of hours to be their designated driver since she'd kept her drinking to a minimum.

She was driving Chief McCollough's Ford Explorer, being it was the only vehicle big enough to transport all five of them along with all their stuff to the park.

"What's this, Mom?" Tess asked, holding up a gift-bag and peering inside. "Ooh, cool."

"That's for Betsy, honey. I thought she might like that. What do you think?"

"She'll love it. I love it," she said, hugging the stuffed puppy.

"I'm glad, 'cause I got you one, too." Maria couldn't resist telling her. "I was going to save it for your birthday, but since you're obviously infatuated, well, I'll give it to you when we get back. I didn't know if you'd want one, being you'll be a big ten-year-old soon, but after I heard the cute little bark, and saw those big, brown puppy eyes—"

"Bark? How does it bark?"

"Squeeze the right paw."

Tess did and was rewarded with a series of short, playful puppy barks. She laughed and did it again. And again.

"Don't wear out the battery, honey. Every kid in the store probably tried it out, too."

"Does the one you got me look just like this one?"

Maria nodded. "Exactly."

"Cool. Thanks, Mom."

"You're welcome, baby." Maria looked over at her daughter. Tess was growing up so fast. She would be ten years old October first. Already she was the tallest girl in her class—and the smartest. And, Maria thought, the prettiest.

Tess caught her mother watching her. "What?" she asked, smiling.

"Oh, nothing, I was just thinking what a charming young lady you've turned out to be. What a special kid you are, Tess. I hope you know that."

"Yeah, I guess."

"Well, you are. Just ask anybody," Maria said. "And what do you suppose a special kid would want for her tenth birthday?"

"Funny you should ask. There's this really cool pair of leather boots at The Boot Company—you know—the store about a block from school?"

Maria smiled. "Yeah, I know where it is. How much are the boots?"

"Well, a lot, two hundred fifty bucks," Tess managed to get out.

Maria let out a long whistle. "That's a lot of dough, kiddo. It takes me a long time to make that kind of money."

"I know. But Mom, they're so cool, and Jenny has a pair."

"Well, Jenny's mom makes about ten thousand more a year than me," Maria mumbled to herself, then glanced at Tess. "We'll see, honey."

Tess looked at her mother. "Don't worry, Mom. I can live without 'em—besides I don't know if I want boots just like Jenny's. Maybe we can find a cheaper pair."

Maria loved the way Tess seemed to understand things most kids wouldn't. "That's the spirit, kiddo. We'll shop around, see what we can find, okay?"

"Okay," Tess said, happy again. "I love you, Mom."

"I love you," Maria said, turning onto White Bear Avenue, where Patsy's sister lived.

42

Nicholas knocked once and entered Roberto's office. He was exhausted and wanted nothing more than to go home and sleep for about twelve hours straight. His session with J.R. was successful but draining. He felt as if he were the one who'd been stretched to his mental limits, instead of the other way around.

Roberto was on the telephone, obviously annoyed at whoever was on the other end. He rolled his eyes at the unseen caller and motioned for Nicholas to have a seat. "Okay, I know. We don't need to go over it again. Just monitor him, and remember to call us. Okay." Roberto hung up the phone and got up to join his friend.

"So, how did it go this time?" Roberto asked, taking in Nicholas's disheveled appearance with concern.

"Beautiful, no problems. I'm extremely tired though. I guess I'm getting old."

Roberto laughed. "Aren't we all? That was Smits on the phone."

"Rico?"

Roberto nodded.

"Problems?" Nicholas asked, the hairs at the nape of his neck standing to attention.

"Only with Smits—overly cautious, that's all."

"Why, what's up?"

"He said J.R. told him the girl looked familiar," Roberto responded, gauging his friend's reaction.

"But—there's no way he could possibly—"

"No. No way in hell. He saw her a couple of days ago it turns out, in Como Park. He was scoping out some potential prospects, I suppose—I don't know. It's really quite ironic though, isn't it? I mean, who knows, maybe he would have taken her without our interference if we would have left him to his own devices."

"I doubt it," Nicholas said shaking his head. "I'm sure he encountered many candidates that day. It's all a game to him— probably a one in fifty chance he would have actually ended up with her. Still, you're right, it's very interesting."

"Yes, indeed. Very interesting," Roberto said, smiling to himself, thinking how fate had played a hand in this little game. It was proving to be more fun by the minute. "Well, Smits is on the ball at least, huh? And you weren't sure about him. I told you he would do fine."

"Yeah, maybe you're right. As long as he checks on J.R. daily and makes sure everything is going according to plan, he'll do just fine."

"Well, my friend, time will tell, won't it—for all of us," he said watching Nicholas. "Rico Smits knows which side his bread is buttered on. I have no concerns about that."

Roberto stood up and walked over to the bar to pour himself a brandy, not offering one to his comrade. He sat back down in the large leather chair and put his feet up on the desk, never taking his eyes off Nicholas. "I've decided there will be some rather big changes in the organization when this little *fait accompli* is history," Roberto challenged, enjoying the effect he was having on his longtime associate.

"Oh, what kind of changes?" Nicholas pressed, not liking

the way Roberto was playing cat and mouse with him. Did he suspect him of treachery? If Santini knew even half of it, it would have been curtains for him long ago, so it was doubtful.

"You'll find out soon enough," Roberto said evasively. "When this is over—in one week, at most two—I'll tell you all about it. I take care of those who take care of me—in one way or another." He smiled.

Santini was so hard to read. Even after all their years together, Nicholas had no idea if he was going to be punished or praised. "Whatever," Nicholas said, standing up to leave. "I just wanted to stop by and let you know everything went well. I believe I'll sleep for the next two days."

Roberto escorted him to the door. "Thank you once again for a job well done," Roberto said, patting Nicholas on the back. "You're like a brother to me, Nicholas. You know that." It was a statement, not a question.

Nicholas Freyhoff looked at Roberto Santini and could see nothing but sincerity in his face. "And you to me," he said, walking out the door.

Nicholas walked slowly down the long, dark hallway, trying to figure out what had just happened. He entered the lobby and stopped at the receptionist's desk. Carol had gone home several hours ago. Dusk was rapidly approaching the Los Angeles skyline.

Nicholas sat down behind Carol's desk, embracing her smell, her sweet, seductive scent. He opened the top drawer to her desk where she kept a few personal items and rummaged through the contents. He found lipsticks, tampons, a compact mirror, but nothing worth taking to help ease the longing for his unrequited love. He opened the remaining drawers and found nothing until he reached the bottom drawer. Here he struck gold, for lying in the bottom drawer amidst spare boxes of staples and extra paper clips was a silk scarf. He picked it up, letting the soft, silky fabric run through his fingers, then bringing it up to his face, he deeply inhaled. "*Ahh,*" Nicholas breathed, her smell permeating his brain—it was like an elixir he couldn't get enough of. He shut the desk drawers and stuffed the scarf into his pocket, content at last. He smiled to himself, looking forward to only one thing at the moment—going home to bed for a long, sweet rest.

43

Maria pulled into the driveway of a large, yellow, two-story house, noting with satisfaction the unmarked police car parked across the street. Further down but on the same side of the street as Patsy's sister's house, she spotted another vehicle. "I think this is it." She checked the name on the mailbox. "Yup, Erickson. We made it, kiddo," she said, tugging her daughter's ponytail.

"And we're right on time!" Tess said, consulting her Mickey Mouse watch. "Can I give Betsy her present? It would probably mean a lot more, you know, coming from another kid."

Maria laughed at the serious tone in Tess's voice. "Sure, honey—that's a great idea."

Patsy McReedy answered the front door, all smiles. "Come in, come in. Betsy was so excited about having visitors, she could barely settle down long enough to take her nap today." She looked at Tess, frowning slightly. "Betsy has been very sick, so she takes little cat-naps in the afternoon. Her doctor said it's very important she stays quiet," she explained to the girl.

"I understand completely, Mrs. McReedy. Please, don't worry about anything. We won't be loud, or upset her," Tess promised, looking earnestly into the older woman's eyes.

Patsy smiled. "No, I'm sure you won't." She gave Tess a

quick little hug and smiled at Maria. "Betsy's upstairs, watching TV," she said, leading the way to the staircase. "First door on the right. You two go on up. I'll bring up some milk and cookies in a little bit." She hurried off to the kitchen.

Maria started up the long, winding staircase with Tess following close.

"Neat house," Tess whispered.

"Yes."

"Old, but neat—look at the carved balustrade."

"My, you have quite a vocabulary for a nine-year-old," Maria marveled.

"Almost ten remember. 'Balustrade: a railing held up by balusters'," Tess recited from the dictionary. She laughed at her mother's questioning look. "I looked it up after flipping through a magazine at the dentist's office last week. There were pictures of all these beautiful, old houses that were built a long time ago."

"A railing held up by balusters, *hmm*, and what are balusters?" Maria asked.

"Why, that's easy. It's these small posts that hold up the upper rail," Tess said, running her hand along several of the small, ornately carved posts as they made their ascent.

Maria smiled at her daughter. Tess was a lot like other kids her own age in many ways, but at the same time, she was different. She had a yearning for knowledge in many adult things and a compassion for others that even many grown-ups lacked. Everyday it seemed to be something different. The other day, Tess had surprised Maria by putting an assortment of goodies together for the elderly lady who lived across the hall. She'd decorated a small wicker basket with lavender ribbon left over from Maria's birthday in July and filled it with tea and small tea light candles, then added foil-wrapped toffees. It was stuff gathered from home, but was put together with such care, it made both Maria and Joe feel the warmth. And needless to say, Mrs. Williams from across the hall was so delighted she phoned Tess twice to thank her.

Helen Williams had watched Tess grow up. She took care of her for an hour and a half every afternoon between the time Tess got out of school and Maria arrived home from work, as well as in the summer months. Maria had offered to pay for her baby-sitting services, but Mrs. Williams would not hear of it. She said Tess brought such joy to her life it just wouldn't seem right to take money for it. Mrs. Williams had lost her husband more than ten years ago. She missed not having children of her own, she confided often to Maria, and looked at Maria and Tess as the daughter and granddaughter she never had.

But now that Tess was almost ten, she insisted she was old enough to take care of herself for the hour and a half before Maria got home. Jenny did, she complained, and she was much more mature than Jenny.

So, starting tomorrow, Tess would be on her own after school for a while. Maria wasn't crazy about the idea, but promised she'd at least give it a chance on a trial basis. Tess had strict instructions to lock the door as soon as she got home and call Maria at work. There was no using the stove or making excessive phone calls, and if a problem should arise, Helen Williams was only a holler away. Helen had promised she would keep an eye on the girl as well.

Tess was becoming her own person and quickly growing up; at an alarming rate, it seemed to Maria.

Tess clutched her mother's hand as they reached the upstairs landing and approached the door to Betsy's room. They could faintly hear the sound of Mickey Mouse's high-pitched voice, as they got closer to the bedroom.

The door was standing ajar, so Maria rapped softly and poked her head in. "Hi, Betsy."

The little girl was propped up with several pillows in a large double bed, watching a video on a small color TV. She looked much better than the last time Maria saw her. Her cheeks had a healthy glow and her flaxen hair hung in a long braid down her back. Her eyes twinkled at the mischief Pluto got into on television. "Oh! You're here!" Betsy said excitedly. "Come in, please."

Maria and Tess entered the bedroom. The two girls smiled shyly at one another. "This is my daughter, Tess," Maria said, sitting on the edge of the bed and gently taking Betsy's hand. "I don't know if you remember, honey, but I promised you in the hospital I'd bring Tess to visit when you were feeling better."

"I kind of remember. It's almost like a dream—kind of fuzzy, ya know?"

Maria nodded.

"I do know I'm lucky to be here. I almost died, didn't I?" she asked Maria, her large, blue eyes filling with tears.

"Well, almost doesn't count, because you're here now, healthy as a horse, right?" Maria said, tugging her braid.

Betsy laughed at the expression. "Yeah, healthy as a horse. I love horses. Someday I'm going to have one of my own."

"Are you now? Does your mom know?"

"Oh, yes, and she said maybe I could get a horse—let's see how did she put it again?" Betsy said, looking up at the ceiling, thinking. "When donkeys fly."

"Well, donkeys are a lot like horses, they're from the same family," Tess said, giggling.

"Oh, I like donkeys, too. They're so cute with their big ears. I guess I like all animals; cats, dogs…"

"Well, maybe we can help you in that department," Tess said, scrambling up on the bed in an instant and revealing the colorful gift-bag she'd been holding behind her back.

"A present! For me?" Betsy asked with wide eyes looking from Tess to Maria.

"Who else?" Tess said, grinning. "Of course it's for you. I think you'll like it. Mom got me one, too, for my birthday, but she said I could have it early since I liked yours so much—"

"You better hurry up and open it, honey, before Tess spills the beans," Maria teased Betsy.

Tess gave her mother an exasperated look. "I won't spill the beans," she said indignantly, then laughed. "At least not on purpose."

"That's exactly what I meant," Maria added.

Betsy opened the bag and took out the tissue paper on top, finding a large red sucker tucked inside it. "Ooh, cherry is my favorite."

She then reached into the bag and pulled out the stuffed puppy, looking into his large, brown eyes and remembered the puppy the bad man had. Betsy thought of how she'd petted the cute little thing and fed him, and how the pup had helped her find a way out of that bad place. Betsy started rocking back and forth, clutching the stuffed puppy as tears rolled down her face.

"Betsy? Honey, what's wrong? I better go get your mom," Maria said, starting to get up.

"No, no, I'm okay. Don't get Mom, she'll make you leave, and make me go back to sleep. She worries about me so much. I'm okay," she repeated. "I remembered something," she said, looking at Maria with haunted eyes.

"Calm down and take a deep breath, then slowly tell me," Maria said.

The little girl took a deep, shaky breath and closed her eyes. "Well, I remember a puppy, a really cute puppy. He looked kind of like this," she said, holding up the stuffed dog Maria brought. "He was hungry and—and thirsty. I let him drink water out of my cupped hand. He was tied on such a short leash. I remember he had big brown eyes, sad eyes. He was whining and looking at the closet. I went to the closet and opened it. The puppy was whining loud and I told him to be quiet so we wouldn't wake up the bad man. When I opened the closet I found a bag of dog food—and—and a way out—a laundry chute. I fed the dog, and then climbed into the chute. I remember it was dark and I was scared. But not as scared as I was of the bad man." Betsy took a long, ragged breath. "That's all—all I can remember."

"Do you remember what the bad man looked like, Betsy?" Maria asked, not wanting to upset the girl further, but wanting, *needing*, answers just the same.

"No—well, maybe a little. He was big—and—and strong. I think he might have had black hair. I don't know. It was dark most of the time." The little girl shuddered. "That's all. I—I—can't remember no more."

"It's okay, honey," Maria said, enveloping Betsy in a hug. "Everything is going to be all right now. I promise, everything is going to be okay."

"I just love my present. Thank you. I'll sleep with it every night," Betsy promised, hugging the stuffed animal to her chest.

"Hey, we almost forgot the best part," Tess said, leaning forward and squeezing the right paw.

The puppy barked three short, playful barks.

Betsy laughed with delight and proceeded to do what Tess had done in the car on the way over—she repeatedly squeezed the pup's paw, giggling at the resounding barks.

"I hope my ears are playing tricks on me. I could swear I heard a dog barking. Your Aunt will have a fit when she gets home if you've had a dog in here," Patsy admonished, rushing into the room with a tray of cookies.

"Oh, Mom," Betsy laughed. "It's not *real*," she said, holding up the toy.

"Oh, well, thank heavens for that. Now, how about a cookie break?" Mrs. McReedy asked. "I can tell she's getting better when she starts with the *'Oh Mom'* stuff." Patsy smiled at Maria. "Oh, I almost forgot." She left the room for no more than a minute, returning with another tray, which carried two large glasses of milk for the girls and coffee for them.

"The cookies are great, Mrs. McReedy," Tess said between mouthfuls.

"Thank you, dear. Now you girls be sure to drink up your milk—builds strong bones you know."

Maria caught the look the two girls exchanged and smiled. "Betsy seems to be doing remarkably well," Maria said to Patsy.

Patsy McReedy looked at her daughter who was busy showing her new friend her stamp collection and crossed her chest in the sign of a cross. "Thank God. He's the one we should thank, and her psychologist," she said as an afterthought. "Dr. Sarah Jorgenson has done wonders with the girl. She specializes in helping children deal with traumatic experiences, and Betsy is like a different girl from the one who entered her office a couple of weeks ago. Betsy just loves her—I'm sure *that* helps, too. She's been remembering more things about the incident, you know, it's scary to her but she seems to come out of it okay afterward."

Maria related what Betsy told her earlier, hoping the woman wouldn't be too upset with her, even though she *didn't* pry it out. "The stuffed puppy seemed to release the memories," Maria confessed.

"She mentioned the dog once before," Patsy whispered. "But not the laundry chute. That's interesting—and terrifying. Thank you for telling me—I'll be sure to tell Dr. Jorgenson about it." She smiled and patted Maria's hand. "Don't worry; remembering is what will make her well. At least that's what the experts tell us." She looked at her daughter with love in her eyes and a smile on her face.

"I didn't think I would ever find anything to smile about again," she said as her eyes moistened.

"I know," Maria said leaning over and patting the other woman's hand. "You've held up remarkably well yourself, you know."

"Oh, I don't know about that. Poor, John, I'm afraid I've been a little erratic lately. Thank heavens for that man. I could never have made it through this ordeal without him. I hope you'll stay until he gets home. I know he wanted to thank you. I—I want to thank you. I was kind of hard on you before—I do hope you'll forgive me."

"Oh, don't be silly. You acted no different than anyone else would have acted given the circumstances. As for staying—we'd love to, but I'm sorry, we can't. Maybe some other time?"

"Yes. We must get together again, soon," she said, watching the girls.

Maria and Tess said their good-byes and the girls exchanged phone numbers along with a promise to call each other at least once a day.

As they were pulling out of the driveway, a blue Buick was just turning in. Maria stopped the Explorer in the street and watched as a woman emerged who looked a lot like Patsy, only taller. "Patsy's sister," she said, letting out a sigh of relief.

"Who did you expect?" Tess asked.

Maria didn't hear the question. She was trying to focus on the probability that the *'bad man'* was going to strike again. Betsy was safe—she had no doubt about that, with the police outside their door. But someone new. Maria felt a shiver race up her spine as she put the Explorer in gear. In theory, he'd probably already picked his next victim.

44

Tess awoke at daybreak on the first day of school. She sat in bed for a good fifteen minutes, willing the butterflies in her stomach to settle down. Finally, she got up and padded barefoot over to her bedroom window. She gazed out upon the early morning world and wondered if her best friend, Jenny, was up, too. Since Jen got on the school bus first, she promised she would save the seat next to her for Tess.

But sometimes things just didn't work out, and if that happened she'd end up being stuck in the back, because by the time the bus arrived at her bus stop it was almost full. The back of the bus was okay, unless Carla Bennet was lurking around. Carla hated Tess for some unknown reason and used every chance she got to let her know it. Tess remembered last year—on the second day of school, Carla had put a big wad of freshly chewed bubble gum on the bus seat just before she sat down. Tess ended up wearing her jacket tied around her waist the entire day to cover the huge gooey spot on her butt. Jenny had helped her get most of the gum off, but enough remained to make it stick to her jacket as well.

Carla was at least one year older—in sixth grade—and a lot bigger than she was. Tess was taller, but much skinnier—which was another thing to be teased about by Carla. Tess had started kindergarten when she was four years old—she turned five a month later, being her birthday was October first. But she'd always resented the fact that *everyone* in her class was older, and she hated, more than anything in the world, having attention drawn to herself, especially if it was to ridicule. She always managed to look like a wimp and walk away instead of confront Carla. Tess wanted to punch her in the nose, but knew she could never do that. *Well, maybe in self-defense.* But hopefully it would never come to that. If she could get through this year, she would be home free. Carla would be in seventh grade next year, which meant she would be going to junior high—different school, different bus.

Tess let out a sigh, and turned around to find her mother standing in the doorway, smiling. "Mom, you scared me," she cried, putting her hand to her chest.

"I'm sorry, honey. You just looked so deep in thought, I didn't want to disturb you. Everything okay?" she asked.

"Yeah, I guess," Tess said uncertainly.

"What's wrong?" Maria asked, sensing that something heavy was weighing on the girl's mind.

Tess let out a sigh and plopped on her bed. "Oh, I don't know. Nothing...everything," she admitted, looking up at her mother, feeling the tears start to come. "What if Carla Bennett has some evil trick she's been waiting all summer to spring on me? Maybe this time it's something really gross—like dog poop or something."

"Oh, Tess. Maybe she's changed. She's had the whole summer. People—especially kids—can change a lot in three months," Maria said.

Tess shook her head. "I doubt that very much, Mom."

"Well, I could give you a ride to school."

"No, I promised Jen I'd sit by her, and anyway, I don't want Carla to scare me into doing anything," she said, sitting up and drying her eyes. "I guess I'll just have to fight fire with fire."

"Just don't end up getting yourself into trouble. That's what usually happens, you know," she warned over raised eyebrows.

"Don't worry, Mom. I'll avoid her at all costs, but if she should bother me, *hmm*, maybe I'll borrow a surprise from Mr. Peanut's litter box." She laughed seeing the look on her mother's face.

"Theresa Ann Sanchez, I hope you're kidding," Maria said sternly, trying to hide her smile. "Besides, can you imagine how your backpack would smell after carrying around cat poop in this heat?" Now she did smile, seeing Tess' nose crinkle in disgust.

"Mom! Gross!"

"Yeah, gross indeed."

They both laughed then hugged each other. "It'll all work out, honey. Don't worry," Maria said, smoothing her daughter's long, dark-brown hair.

"I love you, Mom."

"I love you, too, so very, very much," she said, giving Tess another hug. "Now, what do you want for breakfast?"

"Oh, I don't know, my tummy feels kind of icky. I don't want to puke."

"Well, how about just a piece of toast for starters, and apple juice?"

"Yeah, okay," Tess said, slipping on her bathrobe and following her mother into the kitchen.

Mr. Peanut sat stoically by his dish, letting out a long, loud meow upon seeing Maria approach.

"I suppose you're hungry, too?" she asked the cat.

He meowed again, then rubbed back and forth as she opened a can of liver and kidney cat-food. The smell was enough to make her gag, but she kept it to herself for Tess's sake. "Here ya go, puss. Chow time," she said, setting his dish down and watching him devour it more like a dog than a finicky feline. "I think you're part pig."

"Hey, are you picking on my cat?" Joe called from the living room.

"Joe's awake!" Tess said, getting up and running into the living room. "Let me know when my toast pops, Mom."

"Hey, darlin', how's our school girl doing?" Joe asked as Tess plopped on the sofa bed next to him.

Tess sighed. "Okay. I guess. I wish I could stay home with you and Mom, though."

Joe tousled her hair. "Oh, it'll be great to get back to school and see your old classmates, don't you think?"

"Yeah, I suppose, but I'll miss you guys."

"Well, your mom and I have to go to work today anyway. Hey, how about if I talk your mom into taking us out for pizza tonight? Considering this is your first day back to school and my first day back to work, I think we should celebrate. What do you think?"

"That would be great!" Tess said, giving him a hug.

"Well, consider it done," Joe said, grinning.

"Hey, what are you two cooking up?" Maria asked, watching them and smiling.

"Uh-oh, we're caught," Joe said. "You go eat your breakfast and I'll work on your mom." He winked conspiratorially at Tess.

Tess ran into the kitchen, her spirits lifted to new heights as she ate both pieces of toast and drank a large glass of apple juice.

Maria plopped down next to Joe. "You sure know how to work a kid," she said, giving him a kiss. "What did you promise her? A pony?"

Joe laughed. "No pony. Pizza."

"Oh," Maria said. "The old pizza trick."

"Works every time," Joe said, slipping his good arm around Maria and pulling her close. "I told her I'd talk you into taking us out for pizza—even if I have to resort to bribery." He left a trail of kisses down her neck, sending shivers through her body.

"Well, let's not forget who's in the next room," Maria whispered. "And I'll hold you to that bribe, tonight."

"Promises, promises," Joe said.

"I always keep my promises, Morgan."

"I know you do, Sanchez. But last night—"

"If I remember correctly, I had to put you to bed last night—a little too much to drink at our picnic yesterday, remember?"

"Yeah, yeah, I know. My head won't let me forget," he said, rubbing his throbbing temples.

"So, what do you want for breakfast, besides a couple of aspirin?" Maria asked, smiling.

"You."

"Joe, I'm serious—"

"So am I."

"How about scrambled eggs instead?"

"Well, if that's *all* you have to offer."

"We could have pancakes."

"That's not what I meant," Joe said.

"I know what you meant," Maria laughed.

"Well?" Tess said, flying into the living room and landing on the bed between them. "Are we going out for pizza tonight?"

"Oh, I think we could probably manage that—or I could

make spinach casserole," Maria offered.

"Yuck! Pizza, pizza, pizza," Tess chanted.

"Okay, okay, pizza," Maria agreed.

"Yes!" Tess declared, giving Joe a high five.

"You two make quite a team," Maria said.

"Yeah, we do, don't we?" Tess said, getting up and skipping to the bathroom.

"I have never seen that child happier," Maria said. "She really loves you, Joe. I think, almost as much as I do." She gave him a quick peck on the cheek, then hurried off to the kitchen to start the scrambled eggs.

45

Maria watched Tess climb aboard the school bus from the large living room window that looked out over the parking lot a couple of stories above. Joe stood behind her and together they waved, seeing Tess and Jenny's face at one of the small windows near the front of the bus.

"Well, that's a relief. At least she won't have to sit by Carla Bennett on the first day of school."

"Carla Bennett? I take it she's a bad-ass?"

Maria laughed at Joe's expression. "Well, as much of a bad-ass as a sixth grader can be, I guess."

"Is that clock right?" Joe asked, looking at the clock that stood on top of the television set.

"Shit, yeah. We told the chief we'd be in by eight and I still need to take a shower."

"Me, too," Joe said, grinning. "Should we save time *and* conserve the hot water supply? I need help washing, anyway." He nodded toward his bandages, trying to look helpless.

"Wipe that grin off your face, Morgan, and strip down. I'll go get a garbage bag."

"Ooh, kinky. Whatcha gonna do with the garbage bag?"

"Put it on your arm," she said, grinning right along with him. "You're not supposed to get your bandages wet, remember?"

"Oh. I forgot," he said.

"What did you think I was going to do, perform some bizarre sex act?"

"Yeah, something like that," Joe said, walking into the bathroom.

Maria returned with the garbage bags and disrobed. Joe was already waiting for her in the bathtub with the shower curtain closed.

"What, are you turning modest on me?" Maria asked, opening the curtain and climbing into the tub.

"Fat chance on that, my sweet," he said, grinning. "Just wanted to surprise you."

"Boy, did you," she said, looking at his lean, muscular body. She carefully removed his sling and tossed it on the toilet seat. Slipping one garbage bag over his arm, she secured it with a twist tie, then taking another larger garbage bag—a green lawn bag—she wrapped it around his chest like a toga, covering his chest bandage. "There, how's that?"

"I feel like a goddamn mummy," Joe said, smiling, and pulling Maria close. "It is kinda kinky, though—all this plastic."

Maria laughed. Turning on the water and adjusting the spray, she squirted shower gel into the palm of her hand and worked it into a rich lather. First, she washed Joe's back, then one broad shoulder, washing around the garbage bag across his chest, slowly moving down his taut stomach in small circular motions. She moved her slippery hands between his legs, washing him, then gently cupped his balls, looking into his eyes with a seductive smile playing on her lips.

Joe moaned and wrapped his free arm around her, drawing her close and thrusting his tongue into her mouth, exploring and tasting her sweetness. He reluctantly pulled away. "You're next," he said, holding out his only available hand so Maria

271

could squirt gel into it. He proceeded to do the same thing she'd done, only one-handed—first washing her back and shoulders. Then, turning her around with great care and tenderness, he washed her breasts, feeling her nipples harden under his caress. Working his way down her stomach with deliberate slowness, he rinsed off his hand and rubbed between her legs until she moaned with pleasure. He kissed her neck, lips, breasts, their wet bodies slick in the steamy heat, and wrapped one arm under her bottom, picking her up.

Maria wrapped her long legs around him, straddling him, burying her face in his neck as he entered her. With each thrust, she felt a hot wave of ecstasy course through her body until she thought she could stand it no longer. They moved as one to the rhythm of love, their minds focused only on satisfying the need their bodies demanded. With the final crashing wave, Joe shuddered and whispered her name, reaching climax the same time as she, kissing her face and neck.

They looked at each other, exhausted and spent, still wrapped together as one. "Wow, Morgan, you sure know how to sweep a lady off her feet," she whispered in his ear, softly laughing. "You doing okay? That was quite a workout."

"Not to worry, darlin'. It's workouts like this that let a man know he's still alive. I love you, Sanchez. More than anything on God's green earth."

"Me, too, Joe, me, too," she said, kissing him on the tip of his nose.

They took turns rinsing each other off with the hand-held showerhead, then toweled off and quickly got dressed, laughing.

They were only fifteen minutes late and had even

managed to pick up Joe's car in St. Paul. The old Chevy started right up after sitting idle for more than a week, and Joe followed Maria across the bridge into Minneapolis to City Hall.

The chief hardly noticed them when they walked into Homicide. He was busy giving orders to two detectives who were assigned to the murder of a seventy-two-year-old woman who was found this morning by her son. Even though the son was said to have found her, he was the prime suspect. Apparently, with the mother gone, the thirty-six-year-old son was due to cash in on a large insurance policy, which, as coincidence would have it, he'd just taken out two months prior. That, along with strong evidence of a staged burglary and other incriminating evidence against him, would suggest he'd need a damn good lawyer.

Maria offered to get Joe a cup of coffee, and as she was walking back to their desks ran into Slade who'd been hidden from view in the chief's office.

"Hey, watch where you're going," she said, not looking up, too intent on watching the hot coffee slosh over the sides of the cups and burn her fingers.

"What are you, Sanchez, his slave?" Slade said, grinning ear to ear. "Considering you were more than fifteen minutes late, and by the looks of things, maybe you're his slave in more ways than one."

"Slade! I should have known it was you," Maria said blushing, knowing what he meant.

"Well, by the shade of that blush, I'd say the answer is a big, fat yes. I wish I had a sex slave. Tell me what it's like?"

"God, Peter. You're incorrigible."

"That's my middle name."

"Yeah, well, let's get down to business," Maria said, trying to change the subject.

The chief came up behind her and startled her into almost spilling the coffee again. "Let's all go into my office," he announced in a loud voice.

"God, I wish people would stop doing that," she muttered, summoning Joe as they all walked into the chief's office and shut the door.

"So, how are you boys feeling today?" the chief asked Joe and Peter, looking over his spectacles.

Joe blushed, thinking of this morning and looked at Maria, who was blushing as well. "Fine, sir—other than a hangover, I'm doing great."

"Same here, a little foggy, but I'll pull through," Peter said, grinning.

"Good. I woke up feeling as if someone had stuffed my head with cotton. I'm afraid the wife wasn't too understanding."

"No, I bet she wasn't," Maria remarked, recalling Mrs. McCollough wearing her robe and fuzzy pink slippers, along with a nasty scowl, when Maria brought him home.

"Now let's talk about our prime suspect at large. How did your talk with the McReedy girl go yesterday? I realize I was a little, well, let's just say out of sorts, when you came back to the park. I know you did say she remembered what he looked like, right?"

Maria smiled to herself. *Out of sorts?* All three of them were drunker than skunks when she and Tess returned to the park last night. She'd driven Peter back to the motel in the chief's Explorer, then took the chief home and called a cab from his house to take her, Joe, and Tess back to the condo. "Well, I guess you could say that. She thought he was tall and had black hair. She said he was very strong, but let's remember, this is just a little girl we're talking about here.

274

She'd probably think any grown-up was tall and strong. But she remembered something else rather interesting. She remembered he had a puppy—that must be how he got her, used the puppy as bait. What little girl doesn't love a puppy, right?"

"Creep," Joe muttered.

"Exactly," Maria agreed, then continued. "Anyway, she made her escape when looking for food for the dog. Opening the linen closet in the bathroom, she found a bag of puppy chow, and a laundry chute."

"A laundry chute?" Chief McCollough asked. "You mean to tell me the girl escaped through a laundry chute?"

"Yes, that's exactly what she did."

"Wow," Slade said. "That must have taken a lot of guts—I mean, who knows what might be at the bottom and how far of a drop, not to mention the risk of getting stuck. I don't think I could've done it."

"You could if you were being tortured and only nine years old," Maria said.

"Okay, so we know *who* we're looking for—J.R. Franco. And we know *what* we're looking for—a serial killer that preys on children, who's tall with black hair," the chief said, rubbing his chin. "But the big question is *where* the hell is he?"

"Somewhere in Minneapolis," Joe said. "Probably getting ready for his next victim."

"Well, maybe he left town. This is the longest he's gone without a new victim," Peter added.

"Yeah, but don't count on it," the chief grumbled. "I don't think he's done with our fair city yet."

"So, where do we go from here?" Maria asked, looking from the chief to Peter to Joe.

"I really don't know, Sanchez. The only evidence we have

are blue carpet fibers and a strand of hair that was dyed black," the chief stated.

"The original color was dark brown, right?" Peter asked.

"Right. Doesn't make much sense does it?" Chief McCollough said, looking to the ceiling, or maybe God, for answers. "Nothing about this case makes much sense. Let's try talking to the girl's psychologist—Mrs. McReedy mentioned the name when I talked to her earlier and I looked up the address in the phonebook. Maybe she can tell us something we don't know. I doubt it, but it's worth a shot." He handed Maria a piece of paper with the doctor's name and St. Paul office location.

"Yeah, okay, Mrs. McReedy informed me yesterday Dr. Jorgenson has helped Betsy immensely," Maria said, getting up. "We'll let you know what we find."

"What about me?" Slade asked, sounding like a little boy who's been left out of the game.

"I want you here. Try to put something more into that profile of yours. We need something to give the news media— they've been hounding me like junkyard dogs after a chunk of meat. And the meat appears to be my butt," the chief added with a sardonic grin.

They climbed into Maria's Mustang, holding their breath against the already stifling humidity.

"Damn, I wish this heat would let up a little; it's like a steam bath in here. I'll never bitch about being too cold again," Maria said, putting the key into the ignition.

"I'll remind you of that this winter when it's forty below."

"Yeah, I bet you will." Maria smiled, wiping sweat off her forehead. She turned the key, welcomed by a faint click instead of the sound of the engine. "Oh, Christ! Now what?"

She tried again with the same result.

"Pop the hood," Joe said, getting out. He checked the connections and noticed the wires leading to the battery were corroded.

"What's the diagnosis—dead?" Maria asked, still sitting in the car with the door open.

"Well, let's clean up your battery first and see if that helps. I don't know; it could be your starter solenoid is going bad."

"Oh, great. Just what I need. Tess wants boots for her birthday and instead I'll have to sell her on a new starter solenoid. Hey, where are you going?"

"Be right back. I've got a box of baking soda in my car," he said walking to his old Chevy, which was parked several cars away.

Joe returned with a bottle of water, a small wire brush, and a box of baking soda, then set to work cleaning the battery connections one-handed on the Mustang.

"No one can ever say you don't come prepared." Maria laughed, helping him clean the corroded wires with baking soda and water.

"Well, when you drive an old rust-bucket like I do, you do whatever it takes to keep it running. Good thing we decided to pick the Chevy up this morning, or we'd have to call the garage, and I'm sure that would cost a small fortune. There, why don't you give it a shot now," Joe said.

Maria turned the key and the car started up. "God, Morgan, you're a miracle worker. Thanks!"

Joe shut the hood and climbed in the passenger side, tossing his supplies in the back seat. "Hey, no problem. But don't let this fool you. It could still be your starter. After all, this is an old car."

"Hey, its not that old," Maria said defensively, then

reconsidered. "It's an eighty-nine—I guess it is getting kinda old."

"Yeah, we'd better take it in and have it checked, before it leaves you somewhere."

"Okay, I will, one of these days. Maybe after Theresa's birthday," she said, pulling out into the street, bound for Dr. Sarah Jorgenson's office and hopefully, some answers.

46

Dr. Jorgenson was busy with a patient when they arrived, so they had to wait close to an hour before she could see them. The outer office was decorated in soft pastel tones and large overstuffed chairs. The walls were adorned with pictures of animals—horses, cats, dogs—and the end tables were strewn with children's books and magazines. In one corner of the room was a large table surrounded by brightly colored chairs. In the middle of the table sat a large basket filled with crayons, and on one corner a stack of coloring books threatened to topple to the floor. Stuffed animals were strategically placed around the room, giving it a feeling of warmth and security.

The door opened and a small boy emerged. A blonde woman in jeans and a Mickey Mouse T-shirt followed. "I'll see you next week, Jason. Take it easy, buddy," she said, ruffling the boy's curly brown hair.

The boy smiled up at her. "Bye, Sarah."

Maria and Joe approached the woman. "Dr. Sarah Jorgenson?"

"Yes?" The woman said, turning and smiling.

Maria and Joe introduced themselves and asked if they could have a moment of her time.

"Sure, follow me," she said leading them into her office and closing the door. "Now, how can I help you?"

"Well, this concerns a patient of yours," Maria stated,

looking around the office with a sense of childlike surprise.

The doctor's office made the reception area look pristine in comparison. The leather couch was covered in a giant panda throw and the only other chairs in the room were made to look like animals. One was a dog, complete with large, floppy brown ears at the sides; the eyes and large black nose covered the backrest; the body, located on the seat of the chair, even had a tail to play with for reassurance. The other was a panda bear, much like the throw on the couch—each arm of the chair resembled a large black paw, and rounded ears protruded from the top of the chair. One entire wall had a painted mural of friendly animals that appeared real. Stuffed animals of a much larger scale than what were in the outer office adorned each corner of the room. A six-foot panda bear sat in one corner, while two giant monkeys and an ostrich occupied the other three corners of the large office.

Maria couldn't help but smile. "I'm sorry, I seem to be a little preoccupied with your decor. I love it!" she exclaimed, feeling a little embarrassed at her childlike wonder.

"Yeah, it's really something," Joe said, engrossed in the painted wall mural.

"Believe it or not, I get the same reaction from almost every adult who enters my office. You see, we all love animals—it's a universal thing. No matter what our age we feel more at ease, happier, more in tune with the world around us when we're around animals," Sarah Jorgenson said with sincerity. "You're here about the McReedy girl, Betsy, aren't you?"

"Yes, we are," Maria said, looking into the other woman's clear, blue eyes and sensing a motherly concern for her patient's well-being.

"Betsy has improved by leaps and bounds. She's a very

special little girl."

"I couldn't agree more. My own daughter has become close to her as well. I am amazed at how quickly she has recovered."

Sarah Jorgenson smiled and nodded. "Ah, yes. The marvels of the young mind; sometimes they can endure much more than we can even imagine. I'm sorry if I can't go into any detail about our sessions. Doctor-patient confidentiality, you know." She smiled apologetically. "If you get the okay from Betsy and her mother, I'd be happy to tell you whatever you think may help."

"Well, that's fair enough. I'm sure that won't be a problem."

"No, probably not. Betsy has mentioned you in our sessions. I think you may have helped her without even realizing it," the doctor said to Maria.

Maria blushed. "I just told her to fight for her life. It's worth it."

"You sound like you've had first-hand experience," Sarah Jorgenson said with concern in her soft voice. Seeing Maria grow uncomfortable she added, "Well, I suppose in your line of work, you deal with life and death every day."

"Yes, ma'am, we sure do," Joe said, joining Maria's side.

"We'll call you after we've talked to the McReedys," Maria said, reaching out to shake the doctor's extended hand.

Joe shook her hand. "Nice to meet you, Doctor."

The doctor looked thoughtfully at them both; Joe's bandaged arm holding her attention. "Yes, it was a pleasure meeting you both as well. I look forward to our next visit," she said, leading them out of her jungle-office and into the tamer reception area.

Walking out to the parking lot, Maria said, "Cool lady. I'd

love to see what her house looks like."

Joe laughed. "Probably got live monkeys swinging from the ceiling beams."

"Something about shrinks always unnerves me, though. You notice how they seem to sense things about you other people don't?" Maria whispered, even though no one was around to hear. "They look into your soul."

"Man, that's insightful. I noticed you squirm."

"I didn't squirm," Maria argued, stopping to glare at Joe. "Well, yeah, maybe I did, a little," she said, resuming her pace. She checked her watch. Already two o'clock. Tess would be home by herself in a little more than an hour.

"Thinking about Tess?" Joe asked, reading her thoughts.

"How'd you guess? Hope she'll be okay on her own."

"Don't worry. It's only for a couple of hours—not even that. How much trouble can she get into at home, behind locked doors, with Helen Williams down the hall and your strict list of instructions," Joe said, bending down and kissing her cheek. "Maybe the chief will let us out early."

"Yeah, you're right. She *is* almost ten. Her friend Jenny has been a latchkey kid for more than two years. I worry too much. But maybe the chief *will* let us out early."

"You better hurry up, Tess," Jenny yelled from across the street. "You don't want to miss the bus."

Tess looked at the boots in the storefront window then at her friend across the street, and then back at the boots, which seemed to draw her attention like a magnet. *God, how I want those boots, and it's not just 'cause they're like Jenny's.* The fact of the matter was, *she* had seen them first, but it just so happened Jenny's mom made tons of money and as usual, Jenny always got whatever her heart desired. She put her forehead against the window and closed her eyes.

"C'mon, Theresa!"

"I'm coming!" Tess shouted, giving the boots one last glance as she started back across the street, not noticing the small, black car that had just parked several feet from where she was standing. She stood there waiting for a break in traffic so she could cross.

The man in the small, black car waited as well.

47

The chief let Maria and Joe off early since it was Joe's first day back and there was nothing new happening with the case anyway.

Maria phoned Patsy McReedy before they left. She gave them the okay to talk with Dr. Jorgenson in detail about Betsy's sessions, but the doctor had already left for the day when Maria tried to call her. She left a message on her answering machine.

Joe followed Maria in his Chevy and they arrived at Maria's condo shortly after four o'clock.

"I'm going to scold that girl for not calling me," Maria said, pulling out her keys as they got off the elevator and approached the door. She tried the door first. "Well, at least she locked it after she got in." She unlocked the door and opened it only to find the safety chain in place.

"Hey, open up, kiddo," Joe hollered through the crack. They heard the sound of running footsteps, then the door shut as Tess removed the chain and opened it again.

"Hey, what are you guys doing home so early?" Tess asked, smiling. Then a frown creased her smooth forehead. "What's the matter, didn't trust me, huh?"

"We trust you, sweetheart. The chief just let us out early, since it was Joe's first day back. But why didn't you call me? I thought we had a deal."

"Hey, I tried, but it went to your answering machine. You

must've been on the phone or something."

Maria kissed her daughter on the cheek. "Okay, but next time at least leave a message, so I know you're home, okay?"

"Okay, Mom. I promise. Boy, was it ever cool coming home all by myself. I didn't even miss you."

Maria laughed. "Well, thanks a lot. No problems then?"

"No, not at all. I can take care of myself, Mom. I'm not a baby, you know."

"No, I know you're not. You managed to get in all right I take it. Didn't lose your key or anything?"

"Mom," Tess said in exasperation. "How can I lose it? It's on a chain around my neck," she said pulling it out of her blouse. "And besides, you gave Helen one, too, remember?"

"Yes, I guess I did," she said, looking at Joe who was giving her a look that said, *I told you so.* "You didn't flash it around, did you? Other kids don't need to know you have it—"

"Mom, you worry too much. Everything went fine. I came home, locked the door, called you—even though I didn't get hold of you—and turned on the TV. I was just sitting down to an ice-cold Pepsi, a bag of chips, and a really good episode of *Animaniacs*, when you guys got here," she said, looking from her mother to Joe and back to her mother again with hands on hips and a scowl on her face.

Joe couldn't help but laugh. "So, how was your first day of school, kiddo?"

"Oh, it was great. Jenny's in my class, can you *believe* it? We had hot-dogs for lunch, and oh, I almost forgot the best part—Tyler Donaldson sat by me at lunch. He is so cute. And he even gave me half his dessert."

"Sounds like you had an interesting day," Joe said, winking at Maria. "Probably too tuckered out to go out for pizza then. Oh well, we'll just—"

"Not on your life! You promised me pizza and pizza you'll deliver!"

"Theresa Ann," Maria scolded. "You are a stinker, aren't you?"

"Yup, and proud of it," Tess said, flinging her dark hair over one shoulder. "Hey, you know what? My new teacher, Mr. Keal, is really cool. I didn't know if I'd like having a man teacher, but he's really nice. He said we're going to be doing lots of science experiments this year and now that I'm in fifth grade, I get to be in the Science Fair. Cool, huh?" She didn't wait for a response, just kept right on chattering. "I thought I'd do something really neat, like a volcano that erupts, or something really awesome. Jenny says she's going to do something with bugs. Yuck! I was thinking maybe you guys could help me." She looked from Maria to Joe.

"Sure, hey no problem," Joe said.

"You mean it? I, or should I say *we*, could really use a man around here, right, Mom? Are you gonna marry Mom?"

"Theresa!" Maria exclaimed, blushing. She had retreated to the bedroom to change into jeans but had one ear trained on their conversation.

Joe laughed. "Well, I'd marry her right this minute, but I doubt if she'd have me, what with my bum arm and all."

"I knew it was more than a working relationship. Cool," Tess said, exultant. "For what it's worth, I think you'd make a great dad."

"Well, darlin', for what it's worth I think you'd make a great daughter. In fact, I already think of you that way. We've known each other quite a long time haven't we?"

Tess ran up to Joe and hugged him. "Yup, we sure have. Hey, maybe you can talk Mom into getting me those boots! The store is just across the street from my bus stop at school.

It's called The Boot Company. Man, you should see all the boots, and mine are in the front window."

"Hey, I already did the pizza thing, what to you think I am, a magician?" Joe asked, shrugging helplessly.

"Okay, okay, just see if you can put in a good word," she said, hopping back to the sofa and the last fifteen minutes of *Animaniacs*.

They ordered a large pizza—half pepperoni, which was the only thing Tess would eat, and half with everything on it. They managed to devour the entire pizza between the three of them. Joe had to help eat some of Tess's half, but everyone was stuffed when they finished.

At Tess's persistence, they stopped at the park on their way home and goofed around on the swings and slide; then walked down to the little creek that ran through one end of the park, tossing pebbles into the water and laughing.

"My father once told me if you skip a stone three times in a row you're automatically granted a wish," Joe said, looking toward the heavens.

"Really?" Tess asked, picking up a handful of rocks and trying to do just that.

"You gotta toss 'em like a Frisbee in reverse, kind of like this," he said, stooping over and taking her small hand that held a rock, helping her get the wrist action right. The rock skipped three times to the girl's amazement.

"Hey, we did it! Now let's see if *I* can do it by *myself.*" Tess took another rock and crouched down a little, then tossed it how Joe had shown her. It skipped the top of the water two times before sinking. "Hey, that was pretty close, one more try," she said laughing. "Three skips and you're automatically granted a wish, huh?" She looked at Joe with one raised

287

eyebrow.

Joe laughed, winking at Maria. "That's right. Anything you want, within reason of course. I mean, you can't wish for something like never going to school again, or eating breakfast on the moon—get my drift?"

"I gotcha. Something that's realistic. *Hmm*, let's see," she pondered, picking out a nice, flat smooth stone for her final toss. With a big grin on her face, she hunkered down, eyeing the surface of the water like a pro and tossed the rock.

It skipped the water three times, coming close to making it all the way across to the other side of the small creek. Maria clapped and Joe whistled, while Tess closed her eyes and made a wish, then grinned broadly at them both.

"You know what I wished for?" Tess asked, taking her mom's hand.

"Oh! You can't tell. That's one of the rules," Joe said. "My dad always said that was part of the magic."

"Oh, okay," Tess said, frowning slightly but then smiling. "Cool." She ran ahead of them to the car while they walked hand in hand, laughing and whispering.

"Boy, I can hardly guess what she wished for, can you?" Maria laughed, her head against Joe's shoulder.

They looked at each other and said in unison, "Boots." They laughed together and then kissed, feeling the warmth and love surrounding the moment.

48

J.R. looked at the picture of the dark-haired little girl and smiled wickedly. "Soon, my little lamb," he promised, kissing the photograph. In fact, it would be sooner than *they* expected. He would take her today—this afternoon if everything went according to plan.

She was different from all the others he'd previously chosen. He'd never had a picture before. They had planted her seed in his brain for some reason.

But the ball was still in his court even if those who controlled his mind thought otherwise. He was supposed to wait two more days, until Friday—but that's all he'd done was wait, wait, WAIT! What they didn't know wouldn't hurt them.

He would kill this one sooner, too. He didn't want to risk the chance of something unforeseen happening like it did the last time. He desperately needed the gratification—*fulfillment.* The moment their young lives ceased to exist and his own body absorbed their youthful energy was the *ultimate fulfillment.* He shuddered with pleasure thinking of it. He could *not* wait any longer!

Maybe this was the same girl he'd spotted in the park, crying and walking in the woods. He traced around her eyes, nose, and then her lips in the photograph. It looked exactly like her. If so, it's possible she might have become his *chosen one* even if they hadn't intervened. *Yes*, he thought, *very possible.*

He couldn't think right now—*it hurt!* He put his hands to his head and squeezed tightly, trying to stop the pain.

His brains were so scrambled he was no longer sure of his own name. And the sessions—something *bad* happened inside his head after each one. He knew, because the pain was just a little more intolerable afterward. The drugs he injected daily played a part in it as well. He didn't know who—or what—he was anymore. Sometimes it felt as if his brain would explode in a thousand tiny fragments—gray matter, blood and bony skull splattering the walls and ceiling—when he tried to think about anything too long or hard. It hurt—because of *them!*

If there was one thing he *did* know for sure, it was trust not in those who control your mind. They will kill you in the end—or make you wish you were dead. He'd figured that one out long ago. He was well beyond their grasp, however, and had already planned for a little accident concerning those in question.

He was wasted. The crank mixed with H had him trippin'. Hopefully, he'd get it together long enough to grab the girl after school without her putting up too much of a fight. Oh well, that was more than eight hours away. He'd be in top form by then—just do a little more meth fifteen minutes before leaving. Anyway, he'd give her a good dose of dope—couldn't risk anything going wrong.

But sometimes *he* was the one who lost control, and when that happened, he had a hard time regaining it. Once he got started, it was very hard to slow down and make it last, because he got so excited—especially when he needed the thrill so bad—so bad it hurt. Drugs were his savior—without them, he wouldn't be able to control that chronic need—and drugs helped him manage the excruciating pain that emanated from his head from the moment he awoke in the morning until he crashed late at night.

His need to kill was so powerful, so all-consuming that he often had to take it out on the neighborhood pets. *Poor little bastards. Lots of incidents which resulted in broken necks,* he thought, laughing.

He readied two syringes of Seconal, putting in a little more than usual for good measure and capped them, then slipped one into the large envelope with the photograph and the other in his jacket pocket. "This one's not getting away, no way, no how," he said aloud, proud of the fact he wasn't too fucked-up to remember to bring a backup syringe, just in case. His hunting knife was secure on his belt and a 40-caliber Smith and Wesson lay tucked under the driver's seat. The black sports car was a two-seater, but had a large trunk that suited his needs. On the passenger seat lay a large, white laundry bag containing several feet of rope, an old sock and a roll of shipping tape—all for his little lamb, his chosen.

Already in the trunk, lay a makeshift raft constructed of old, wooden crates, ready to carry its next unfortunate passenger to death's door.

49

Maria braided Tess's hair into a long, glossy rope down her back. "There," she said, wrapping a white ribbon several times around the end of it and tying the bow in a double-knot so it would stay.

Tess smiled at her mother in the mirror. "Looks great, Mom," she said, turning her head to try to see the back of it. Maria held up a hand-mirror so she could see the back better. "Cool," Tess added, picking up her toothbrush and putting a giant glob on the end.

"Careful, Tess, so you're not wearing that to school." Maria nodded toward the precarious glob.

Tess giggled and leaned over the sink, imagining it dropping onto the new black denim jeans she wore. Now *that wouldn't be too cool.* She finished up and grabbed her backpack out of her bedroom, giving Mr. Peanut several kisses on top of his furry head, as he lay nestled in her unmade bed. "See ya later, lazy bum," she said, stroking him behind the ears until he purred loudly. Skipping into the living room, she kissed her mom and Joe good-bye, then went to wait for the bus with the group of kids that had already gathered at the bus stop.

A message from Dr. Sarah Jorgenson awaited them when they arrived at City Hall. Her morning was free, and she stated it would take several hours to go over the sessions on tape so the sooner they could come, the better.

Maria and Joe stopped in to see the chief, but he was on the phone and irritably waved them off when they told him where they were going.

Slade was nowhere to be found.

A couple of detectives were on the phone tracking down various sources, while several others gathered in one corner, discussing their cases and gulping down coffee to wake up; still others were out on the early morning streets, chasing perps down dark alleys in hopes of tying up loose ends.

Maria turned to Joe, shrugging her narrow shoulders. "Should we split this scene?"

"Good idea," Joe said, glancing sideways at one corner of the room where two detectives had started a heated debate. Across the room, someone slammed down a telephone, cussing loudly.

"Hopefully we'll gain new insight into this case after hearing those tapes," he said over his shoulder, heading for the quiet sanctity of the hallway.

"Yeah," Maria agreed, following. "Although I'm sure it won't be pleasant."

"No, probably not. But what is these days?"

"Hey, do I detect a note of defeat in that usually strong demeanor?" she asked, joining his side.

Joe held up his good hand and smiled. "Not me, no way. Just stating the obvious."

Maria put her arm around his waist as they walked down the stairs that led outside. "Yeah, I know, sometimes life really throws you a curve-ball, doesn't it?"

"Yeah, and you'd better catch it and run with it, 'cause if you drop it, you're *dead meat*."

* * *

Dr. Jorgenson was waiting for them in her office when they arrived. Her secretary told them to go right in.

Maria rapped softly and opened the door.

"Hello, I'm glad you could make it so soon." The doctor greeted them with a genuine smile that lit up her whole face. "I have everything ready, so please come in and sit down," she said, shaking their hands. She wore faded jeans and a light blue Michigan State sweatshirt that matched her eyes. Her blond, curly hair was pulled away from her face and clasped with a large, gold barrette. She looked no older than twenty, but was in reality more than a decade past that.

Maria and Joe sat on the couch, while Sarah Jorgenson pulled a chair up to a small table that was set up with a tape recorder; a stack of five or six tapes lay near the edge. "I have transcripts as well, if you'd like to take a copy with you when you leave," the doctor said, patting the pile of papers that took up half of the small table.

"I hope you like cappuccino. I've brewed a huge pot." Dr. Jorgenson motioned to the small, unobtrusive desk in the corner on which stood an immense machine with the most wonderful aroma coming from it. Blushing, she said in explanation, "My husband bought it for me as a birthday gift last spring, but I didn't have room for it at home in our tiny kitchen." She shrugged her shoulders and smiled. "*Hmm*, by the smell I'd say it's done." The doctor walked over to the machine and gathered three large cups from a desk drawer, filling them each to the top.

"Thanks," Maria said, taking the steaming mug. She inhaled the rich scent of vanilla and cinnamon before taking a sip. "Wow! It's fantastic."

"Thanks. Shall we get down to business?" Dr. Jorgenson

took her seat at the small table and inserted the first tape. "Betsy was hypnotized on our third visit to deal with her selective traumatic amnesia. I don't use hypnotic inducing drugs—just relaxation exercises. When you hear Betsy's voice under hypnosis, you'll notice she sounds sleepy. At times she slurs her speech or it comes across very faint, and it's hard to understand her. You may want to follow along with these," she said, handing them each a paper-clipped copy of the transcripts.

Dr. Jorgenson pushed the play button and what followed was an extraordinary experience for both Maria and Joe.

The tapes all started out the same—with the doctor talking in soothing, soft tones, telling Betsy to watch the gold ring and never take her eyes off it, to watch it move back and forth until she fell into a sleep-like state. Dr. Jorgenson then proceeded to delve into the girl's past, taking her back to the moment before she was abducted and slowly working forward.

"I remember playing out in the front yard," Betsy's voice stated, trailing off to no more than a whisper. "Oh, there's a bird's nest," she added.

"Are you alone?" the doctor's voice gently prodded.

"Yes, for a while, then..."

"Is someone else there? It's okay, Betsy."

"Well, there's a man—on the sidewalk. He has a puppy. Oh, it's such a cute puppy. Maybe I should go pet it. No, I better not. The man is talking."

"What is he saying, Betsy?"

"I don't know. I'll have to get closer. He says he's looking for someone to give his puppy to. His new apartment doesn't allow pets."

After a moments silence the doctor's voice came over the tape. "What are you doing now, Betsy?"

"I'm petting him. Oh, he's so cute with the biggest eyes

and long, brown floppy ears—Oh! *No! Ohh.*" The last part was a moan.

"What is it, Betsy?"

"My arm—I feel funny. He did something—a shot or—I can't move. Help…me." Her voice was barely audible.

"It's okay, Betsy. Betsy!"

Silence.

"On the count of three you will wake up. One-two-three!" A loud clap was heard, then the soft hissing of blank tape.

Sarah Jorgenson ejected the tape and put in the next one without even pausing, then pressed the play button.

They listened to Betsy relate with terror the atrocities that were done to her. Her cries for help were bone-wrenching as she relived the ordeal—him raping and beating her, threatening to kill her, *promising* to kill her. She cried and called to her mother—called to God—and finally fell silent.

By the time they got to the last tape, Maria felt numb from the sheer horror the girl had been through, and managed to survive. They listened to Betsy talk in monotone about escaping by way of the laundry chute, and ending with breaking the basement window with an old brass lamp on her way to freedom.

The doctor ejected the last tape and put it with the others. "Well, that's it. I have a couple of others, but they're more about how she's dealing with things now—ways of coping with all the bad memories as they come out. Betsy doesn't remember all of this when she's awake—only bits and pieces. But it's all eventually going to surface."

Maria nodded, recalling the scene with the stuffed puppy. "I think this may be enough for us to at least get an edge on this guy. We'll go over these transcripts again, and if luck is on our side..." she trailed off as her eyes fell on the wall clock above the couch. "That clock can't be right. It's not almost five o'clock, is it?"

Joe checked his watch. "Man, I guess we were so involved with the tapes we lost track of time. I hope we didn't keep you from your patients, Doctor."

"Oh, no. On Wednesdays, I see only two patients. One is sick today and the other isn't due for another half hour."

"Well, we'll get out of your way. Thanks so much," Maria said, extending her hand.

"Oh, you're very welcome. I just hope you can catch this man before he does any more damage."

"So do we, ma'am. Believe me, so do we," Joe said, shaking the young doctor's hand, and then following Maria, who was already in the lobby.

"Look at the damn time," Maria said again, glaring at Joe's watch as they hurried through the deserted parking lot. "Tess has been home for nearly two hours. And the chief, he'll be furious. We should have at least checked in."

"Don't worry. We're covered. He knew where we were going, and as for Tess, she'll be fine."

"Christ, we won't be home for another forty-five minutes with the traffic the way it is," Maria mumbled, feeling dread creep into the pit of her stomach for some unknown reason. "I don't know why I have this feeling, Joe, but something is terribly wrong. I just know it."

50

Tess had aced her spelling test—Mom would hang it on the fridge and brag about it big-time. She grinned to herself as she gathered her backpack and the books she would need tonight for her homework assignments, then followed the other kids out into the late afternoon sunshine to wait for the bus. Jenny had a dentist appointment at 2:30, so her mom came and picked her up a little after two. *Lucky-duck*, Tess thought and then reconsidered. Jenny had to have two cavities filled. School was probably the better of the two.

"Hi, Tess. Where's Jenny?"

"Oh, hi, Melissa. Jen's at the dentist, getting her teeth drilled."

"Ouch! Glad it ain't me," the little girl said, grinning, then hurried off to find her younger brother before he missed the bus. "See ya," she called over her shoulder as she ran back toward the school and the kindergarten room.

Tess waved and leaned against the building, looking across the street at The Boot Company. "I wonder if they're still in the front window," she mumbled to herself. *What if someone bought them!* She glanced at her Mickey Mouse watch. *Plenty of time to check it out.*

She started across the street, looking both ways. The other kids were just standing around talking or hanging out; no one seemed to notice her cross the street.

Tess set her heavy backpack down on the sidewalk by the storefront window, and put her face to the glass, shielding the glaring sun by cupping her hands around her face. *Whew! They're still here.*

The girl was so predictable. Something in that store window had her attention, it was exactly where he'd found her yesterday. She was so preoccupied she wouldn't even notice him sneaking up on her.

He opened the car door, surveying the kids across the street as a large yellow bus pulled in. *It was now or never,* he thought, getting out and softly closing the car door. He wore a jacket even though it was hot; his hand nestled in the pocket, wrapped protectively around a syringe of Seconal.

Tess saw the reflection of the school bus in the large storefront window. "Oh, crud, there's the bus," she whispered under her breath, gathering her heavy backpack off the sidewalk and struggling to get it on her back.

"Here, let me help you."

The voice came directly behind her. She spun around and saw herself reflected in the twin mirrors of his sunglasses.

The grin he possessed was evil—*pure evil.* That was the last thought she had before feeling a sharp stab of pain in her upper arm, then darkness.

51

"For Christ's sake, Maria, slow down! You're gonna either get a speeding ticket or roll the damn car if you take another corner like that," Joe admonished.

"Sorry, Joe." She let up a little on the accelerator, only to resume her speed within a couple of minutes. "Listen, I know you think I'm nuts, but I have this horrendous feeling of dread in the pit of my guts. Do me a favor and call home, see if Tess answers."

Joe opened the glove box and removed the cell phone. He punched in Maria's phone number and pressed the send button. It took a moment to connect, then rang four times until the answering machine picked up. He pressed end and closed the phone. "Machine picked up, which doesn't mean anything. She could be in the bathroom, or taking a nap," he said, watching Maria's face betray her feelings.

"Shit. I knew it. Try one more time, will ya?" she asked, desperation creeping into her voice.

"Okay. Then I'll check your phone-mail at work. After you chewed her out yesterday for not calling when she got home, I'm sure she left you a message."

"I did make it pretty clear to leave a message if she couldn't reach me. But, why isn't she answering the damn phone?"

"The kid's probably taking the world's biggest bubble

bath—I'm talkin' bubbles all over the bathroom floor," Joe said, trying to ease Maria's fears.

"God, I hope you're right," she said, glancing nervously at Joe as he tried the number again with no luck. She drummed her fingers against the steering wheel while he called the phone-mail system at City Hall.

"What's your password?"

"Twenty-one, thirty-four," Maria said, trying hard to focus on driving.

Joe punched in the numbers and hit the pound sign, then pressed three to listen to Maria's messages. "Got a message from Slade. He's sick with the flu. Sounds awful. Say's he'll try to make it in tomorrow. Message from Patsy McReedy—just calling to see how our visit with Dr. Jorgenson went today. That's it," he said, closing the phone and putting it back in the glove box, avoiding Maria's gaze. "Look, don't jump to conclusions. Just because you haven't—"

"Yeah, right."

"Just because you haven't heard from her doesn't mean she's disappeared," Joe continued. "There are so many scenarios that could play out here, even if, God forbid, she isn't home," he said, meeting Maria's horrified gaze, and continuing. "She could have missed the bus, or more likely, she got off at Jenny's stop and decided to hang-out a while."

"She knows better than that. Then again—she did it once last year. I remember Helen called me at work, frantic."

"See? I'm just saying don't let your brain get carried away. Not yet."

"Yeah, I know, but sometimes that's easier said than done. Anyway, we came to a thorough understanding the last time she went to Jenny's after school without telling me. She promised never to do it again," Maria said, looking into Joe's eyes and seeing uncertainty despite his attempt to conceal it.

"Well, we'll know soon enough," Joe said, trying hard to keep his mind from jumping to the same conclusion.

Everything was going as planned, well, almost. J.R. was starting to worry about one *little* thing—the girl was still out cold, and close to three hours had passed since he'd brought her home.

It was the *extra* dose of Seconal that was the culprit. He shouldn't have resorted to that, he now realized, but wanted to make sure she was completely out before hauling her into his living quarters in the white laundry bag. Once they had arrived at his dwelling, she started coming around, moaning, and thrashing about. It was broad daylight. He couldn't very well carry a writhing laundry bag, slung over one shoulder into the house, greeting his neighbors—or, as was more customary, averting his gaze and *not* greeting his neighbors—and not cause suspicion.

However, now he was unsure of the girl's condition. Maybe she'd overdosed, but he doubted it. He'd give her another hour or so, and then apply more drastic measures if necessary. J.R. grinned, knowing he'd find a way to bring her around. Just the act of preparing her for the video would probably revive her. But if not, once a little cocaine crept into her bloodstream, she'd be standing at attention. Or maybe a little H mixed with meth would do the trick.

J.R. was confident everything would go according to plan. *His* plan of course, not theirs. This time the video would be for his collection only—unlike the others that he'd traded for drugs and money. Since there would no longer be anymore *them* when all was said and done, he need not worry about anything further. They had always given him strict instructions to make only one copy of each tape, for safety purposes, and to send it directly to *them*. However, he couldn't resist and had made a duplicate of each and every tape. It was a cheap thrill to watch, but he didn't do it very often. The thing that turned him on the most was what happened off tape, after his chosen one's last act. *The sweet reward of death.* Knowing he now possessed an intrinsic part of each one of them by absorbing their young lives was what brought him back to the videos every so often. And on a more materialistic level he had his *special collection*.

He looked over at the unconscious girl, and smiled. This would be the end of an era. He would finally be free from *them*—from all the pain. He would live his life as he saw fit, killing when he wanted, where he wanted, and how he wanted. He would manage to exist—somehow—without *them*. The pain in his head returned with a vengeance and he pressed the heel of his hands against the pressure points at his temples.

He would kill them. A*ll* of them—his creators and anyone else who got in his way—and take everything he could—both inwardly and otherwise. Rico would be the first to go—tonight—when he brought the drugs over like he did every night. This time, J.R. would have a little surprise waiting. Then the girl—he'd take more time with her, focusing on her every pain and fear until she could bear it no longer. And then he'd wait. They'd come on Friday probably, which was D-day—when he was originally ordered to take the girl. He laughed at his own cleverness—being able to override their orders even to such a small degree would play to his advantage. Within two days, they'd all be dead. He would make the one who caused him so much pain suffer greatly. And the other one, too—the man responsible for the actions of everyone else—the *big boss*. Absorbing all their energies should prove quite rewarding.

Plans to leave the country on a boat docked in Miami departing for Cuba had already been made. J.R. had to be in Florida by Sunday night and with two to three days of steady driving, his time frame was short. Everything *had* to be accomplished within the next day or two. Then he'd set sail with an acquaintance made at a local nightclub a week ago, who promised to take him along if he supplied the drugs for the trip. They also talked in great length about going into their own drug-manufacturing operation once they arrived in Cuba.

The girl looked to be out of it for a while yet. J.R. sat back and popped a vein with the last of his heroin. As soon as the initial wave hit his brain, he felt the throbbing pain replaced by a short-lived euphoria. He picked up the joint he'd rolled earlier in the day and put it to his lips, fumbling for the lighter in his pants pocket. He vaguely remembered lacing it with something. Lighting it, he inhaled deeply, holding the harsh smoke in his lungs and reminding himself to finish packing the already half-filled suitcase hidden under the bed.

52

"Okay, so where is she?" Maria demanded, coming out of Tess's bedroom, the last room down the short hall of the condo. She felt the panic, barely hidden earlier, resurface—and knew without a doubt she might very well never see her daughter again.

"I'll go check with Helen," Joe said, stepping out the already open door and across the hall to Helen Williams' door, knocking loudly. He waited a full minute and knocked again.

Helen Williams came to the door, bleary-eyed and obviously sick. Probably the same bug that had taken its toll on Joe a couple of weeks ago.

"Hi, Joe. Is something wrong?" she asked, immediate concern coming into her tired eyes.

"Well, we don't know for sure. Theresa didn't come home after school today. You haven't seen her have you?"

"Oh, my." Helen put her hand to her mouth and shook her head. "No, and I'm usually on the look-out for her, too. But I was feelin' so darn lousy I thought I'd flop on the couch, and wouldn't you know it, I ended up taking a three-hour nap. She didn't call or leave a message?" she asked, recalling how happy-go-lucky Tess had appeared this morning on her way out to the bus stop. Helen had been on her way to the drug store, already feeling achy and out of sorts. "What about her little friend's house? Jenny?"

"She didn't leave any messages but I think Maria is checking with Jenny now," Joe said, glancing repeatedly into the open doorway across the hall. Maria was on the phone talking with someone; then with an air of defeat she replaced the receiver. "Look, if you hear anything—"

"I'll let you know right away," Helen finished for him. "You go on, Maria needs you," she said, looking worriedly across the hall.

"Yeah, okay," Joe said, crossing the hall in two broad steps and entering the living room where Maria stood motionless.

He shut the door and approached her. "Well, what did you find out?" he asked, putting an arm around her slender shoulders.

"Nothing. She's gone—for good," Maria said in a trembling voice, her composure threatening to crack as she looked into Joe's penetrating blue eyes.

"Now come on. Get a grip, Sanchez," he said, leading her over to the sofa and sitting down, his arm never leaving her shoulders.

"She—she didn't go to Jenny's house. Jenny had a dentist appointment and left school early," she said, meeting Joe's gaze again and feeling her eyes well up with unshed tears.

She would not cry like a helpless woman. Theresa needed her—she needed her mother to be strong and capable. Theresa's life depended on her ability as a detective as well as mother and protector. Maria took a deep unsteady breath and continued. "I called Missing Persons."

"Good. I was gonna say, that's our next step," Joe said, brushing a stray hair from Maria's distraught eyes.

"BCA's on its way."

"Great."

"Santini has won, and the River Rat, or J.R., or whoever the fuck he is."

"No, Maria. *No one has won.* Tess is still alive. We will find her. We know he hasn't killed her yet."

"*Yet!* Oh, God, Joe. How could I have let this happen? I mean, if I wouldn't have left her alone—"

"He still would have gotten her. He took her from school, most likely—*not* here."

"Yeah, yeah, you're right. But me and my stupid pride. *Ugh!*" she cried in exasperation, rising from the sofa and pacing the length of the living room.

"What are you talking about, Maria?"

"I should have known Roberto Santini would be out to get me after our little meeting in L.A. God, he was pissed. Then there was the dead rat. Remember the dead rat with the charming message? I didn't even mention that to the chief. Why?" she asked, looking to the ceiling, then dropping her head to her chest in dismay.

Joe stood. "Where are you going with this?"

"If I was smart, I would have taken Santini's words as more than just idle threats, maybe had a guard put on watch!" Maria cried, resuming her pacing.

"Oh, come on. If we had protective watch every time someone threatened us, we'd be under 24-hour surveillance, seven days a week."

"This time was different, though. At the very least, being a cop I certainly should have been able to look out for my own. I mean—"

"Stop it!" Joe knew exactly how she was feeling, but beating yourself up never did any good—he knew from experience.

The doorbell rang, and they looked at one another for

several seconds before Joe moved toward the door. "You okay?"

Maria ran her fingers through her hair and wiped the tears from her eyes with the bottom of her shirt. Taking a deep breath, she tried to gather her wits by thinking of only one thing—Tess, her only child, her only reason for living. "Yeah, go ahead."

Joe opened the door to BCA agents Bill Foley and Cal Jensen. Maria groaned inwardly upon seeing Foley look around her home, a smug expression on his too smooth baby-face. She couldn't believe they sent this dip-squat. On the other hand, Cal Jensen was a seasoned veteran and a good friend. He greeted Maria warmly, offering his sympathies along with a promise to find the bastards who were responsible.

Maria led them to the kitchen table, offering them coffee and trying to appear normal—when in reality she was screaming inside, desperately wanting to turn off the images racing in her mind. She stood by the cupboard, hand in mid-air as an image assaulted her thoughts—Theresa being raped, a stranger's hands around her slender throat, squeezing tighter and tighter until—

"Maria, you okay?" It was Joe, come to her rescue.

She cleared her throat and looked at Joe, then averted her gaze, trying to regain composure. "Yeah, fine," she lied, opening the cupboard and retrieving the cups. She mechanically poured coffee into each cup and carried two to the table while Joe grabbed the other two.

"I have a recent picture," Maria said, taking her purse off the back of a kitchen chair and rummaging through her wallet. She handed the picture to Cal. "It was taken a couple of weeks ago, just before her camping trip."

"Okay. Thanks. Anything you can tell us that we don't

already know?" Cal asked. "I know you've been working this case exclusively, but I gotta ask. Is this just a coincidence or—" He left the question hanging.

Maria looked at Joe, then into her coffee cup. "No, no coincidence, I'm afraid. The bastard knew exactly who he was going after this time." She told them about her meeting with Santini in L.A. when Joe was hospitalized. "I didn't take his warning seriously," she said, referring to the dead rat. "I mean, I knew he was pissed, but—"

"Well, I guess you should have," Foley responded. "After all, we are dealing with a crime boss here, Sanchez, not some petty thief. At the very least your superior should have been informed." He leaned back in the kitchen chair so only two back legs rested on the floor.

"He knew of the meeting, just not the rat," Maria said, watching him balance on the chair. She had a sudden urge to kick one of the back legs and topple the little asshole over, but resisted only because of Joe.

"Listen, Foley, I was there, too," Joe said, starting to get angry. "I saw nothing that would suggest Santini had future plans on siccing his dog on Maria's daughter, for Christ's sake. You know as well as I do, we deal with shit like this every day in our line of work."

"He's right," Cal said.

"Yeah, yeah, yeah, but this case is different. *Everything* should have been brought out in the open. We could've finally had a chance to catch the bastard, using her daughter as a decoy," Foley argued.

"Are you telling me, Foley, if Maria would have reported the dead rat found in her rental car in a hospital parking lot in Los Angeles, that would have been cause to set up a sting at her condo here in Minneapolis? Huh? Are you? 'Cause if you are, you're further gone than I thought. And who's to say Santini had anything to do with the rat? See, Foley, even though *we* know he did, no one could've proved it. You know that, right?" Cal asked, glaring at his partner.

"Believe me, I've been beating myself up about this. I agree with Foley for once," Maria responded, feeling the tension heat up the room. "But right now none of this is doing Theresa any good. Let's focus our efforts on finding my daughter—not on what I should have done to prevent it."

"Yeah, let's go over the basics; when, where, why, how, and go from there," Cal said, taking a long drink from his coffee.

"At the bus stop. She never got on the bus," Maria said. "I called the school and they gave me the bus driver's home phone number. Theresa wasn't on the bus. He didn't think anything of it, since Jenny wasn't either. Said he figured the girls got a ride by one of us."

"*Hmm.* Any shops around there? Store owners that might've seen something?" Foley asked.

"The Boot Company," Maria and Joe said in unison, looking at each other in surprise.

"My God, that's it! I bet she was looking at those damn boots. It's right across the street from school," Maria said, looking at each of them excitedly. "I know the lady who owns the shop. Let's see, what's her name? Amy Edwards, no, Amy Edwins, that's it!" She grabbed the phone book and turned to the E's. "Let's see, I know she lives in Edina. Here it is." She grabbed the phone and dialed the number. No one answered.

"Why don't you write down that number and address," Cal said. "Foley and I will track her down and have a talk."

Maria scribbled the number and address on an envelope that was lying on the table. "Joe and I will cruise over by the school. Maybe somebody else who owns a business near there saw something."

"Maybe you should remove yourself from the case. I mean, you're a little too close to it now aren't you?" Foley grilled Maria. "We can't have your emotions getting in the way of your better judgment."

"Just try and stop me," Maria threatened, glaring at Foley.

"That's what I figured you'd say." Chief McCollough's deep voice boomed from the doorway. "I knocked, but no one answered and the door was open," he said as way of an explanation.

"Chief! Come on in," Maria said uneasily, feeling as if everyone was ganging up on her.

"You know, as much as I hate to admit it, Foley has a point," the chief said, looking at Maria. "I can't imagine what this is doing to you. It would probably be best if we removed you from the case. But we won't."

Maria breathed an audible sigh of relief.

"The only reason being is that I know you'd go behind my back."

"You know me pretty well."

"*But* and it's a big but, if I think this is too much for you; if you appear at any time to be in distress to the point of break-down, I will take you off this case faster than you can turn around."

Maria nodded in agreement, then turned and walked to the living room window. Staring out at the parking lot, she wondered how things could've changed so drastically since this morning when she and Joe had stood in this very spot and watched Tess get on the bus, waving furiously as the bus pulled away.

"We'll find her, Sanchez," the chief said, joining her side.

"We have to. God, we have to."

"Well, we're gonna head out, go talk to Mrs. Edwins," Cal said. "Where should we contact you—here or City Hall?"

"Well, Joe and I are heading out for a while—thought we'd make a circuit around the school, see if anyone saw something..." Maria paused as a sudden, hopeful thought sprang to mind. "Someone should give the McReedys a call. Maybe Betsy can help."

"I'll stay here and man the phones," the chief said. "And Mrs. McReedy will surely cooperate as long as we get the doctor's okay. I'll see what I can arrange."

"Great. Hang in there, Maria," Cal said, extending his hand and grasping hers. Foley stood off to the side, an odd look on his face as he watched his coworker. They left, closing the door behind them.

"I'll be right back," Maria said, leaving the room and the two men alone.

"Okay. Let's see," Joe said, looking at his watch. "It's still early, Chief. We'll check back with you in about thirty minutes. We've got a cell phone if any new developments arise." He met the chief's penetrating gaze for the first time and read the uncertainty in his eyes. "Maria's tough, sir. She's handling things well."

"Are you sure? Maybe you're a little too close to tell."

"I'm sure. I'd stake my life it."

"You probably will."

"Yeah, well, I'm ready. I'll kill the son of a bitch if he's hurt Tess."

"Chances are, he already has," the chief said.

"Let's go," Joe called to Maria as she came out of Theresa's bedroom with pictures and a teddy bear.

"I'm ready," Maria said, looking stronger than she felt. "I

thought we should bring some pictures to leave around the neighborhood surrounding the school. And the bear," she said, hugging it to her chest, "is for when I find her." She straightened the pillows on the sofa, then brought the empty coffee cups to the sink, trying to find sanity in normalcy.

"Call the McReedys, and thanks," Maria said to the chief, looking like a lost child with her teddy bear as she followed Joe out the door.

53

The girl was still unconscious, and Rico was due to arrive any minute. J.R. had stashed her away in his bedroom closet. It was a tight squeeze but after bumping her head a few times he got her situated.

He waited impatiently on the threadbare couch, a switchblade knife stashed under the middle cushion, ready to disembowel his only drug source. Lately, Rico had been only doling out small quantities of the drugs—under direct orders from *them*, no doubt—but J.R. would bet money he had the mother-load hidden in his van. He slept in a rented room somewhere close by, but *lived* in his van. J.R. remembered the little fuck telling him that when they first met.

He got up abruptly and nearly blacked out, then steadied himself and walked down the short hall to the door for the third time in fifteen minutes. This time he was rewarded with the faint but steady tread of someone coming up the long, winding staircase that led to his second floor apartment. No one but Rico ever came to visit.

The boarders and the owner of the rundown boarding house were located on the first floor, all sharing a single bathroom and kitchen. They pretty much kept to themselves— it was like having their own little family, being they were all over sixty and living on a fixed income.

The upper floor was converted long ago into a small

apartment that was rented out by the month. A paneled wall had been built at the top of the stairs on the second floor landing with a large oak door centered in the middle.

J.R. had done his own remodeling. He'd removed the paneling on his side of the wall and inserted sheets of Styrofoam to fit snugly between the two-by-fours, then replaced the paneling so no one was the wiser. It provided somewhat of a sound barrier, maybe. In addition, the heavy wood door had new locks installed, on *both* sides of the door. The inside lock was located high on the doorframe and a key was needed to open it once it was locked—in other words, those inside his apartment would stay there, until he decided otherwise. The owner knew about the lock on the outside—he even agreed to let J.R. put a new lock on the first floor main entrance of the boarding house. Little did the stupid old man know it would prove to be his demise in the end.

A short hallway led from the solid oak door on the second floor, opening onto a small living room and kitchen area. It was all one room, but had an old couch at one end and a compact refrigerator along with a battered Formica table at the other. A badly chipped ceramic sink jutted out from one wall, the faucets caked with rust and grime. A small electric hotplate sat on one of the two chairs by the table and was the single source for heating food. The small bedroom contained a bed and TV. The bathroom was located off to the side of the main living room/kitchen area, where J.R. had resumed his place on the couch—waiting.

J.R. had extended his current lease by another week, giving the old-fart landlord a full month's rent to stay one extra week. He would rather have sliced the wrinkled old bastard's throat—and maybe still would—but had smiled and handed over the cash, amiably agreeing with the argument that no one wants to rent an apartment halfway into the month. Maybe he would kill the old man before he left for Florida. Or maybe he'd come back a year from now, entering with his own personal key in the early morning pre-dawn to kill all the old fucks while they slept, putting them all out of their ailing, old-age misery. He chuckled to himself, listening for the telltale click. Rico had his own key.

J.R. had the inside lock open so Rico could enter without assistance.

Hearing the loud click that disengaged the bolt, he removed the knife from under the middle cushion and tucked it under his right leg.

He was the hunter waiting for his prey.

"Hey, man. How's it hangin'? Goddamn, it's a hot mother-fucker out there, ain't it?" Rico asked good-naturedly, bouncing into the living room. His black, curly hair was so oily it shined, and his dark skin glistened with sweat. A soiled, red bandanna was tied around his head, wet with perspiration. "Got some more stuff for ya." He reached into the inside pocket of the sleeveless denim jacket, his hairy chest prominently displayed.

He tossed the stuff on the couch where J.R. sat. "Go ahead, take a look. I know you're dyin' to. I was a little more generous this time, but don't tell no one. Shit, I figured what could a little extra hurt?" he asked, sitting down at the opposite end of the couch, grinning at his charge.

J.R. smiled at Rico's choice of words. He saw an opportunity and went for it seconds after the little man sat down. The knife was out and buried up to the handle in Rico's belly before another foolish word could be uttered. The look of surprise on Rico's face was worth a million. J.R. felt the inviting warmth of fresh blood ooze onto his hand. He would have loved to take his sweet time, but common sense told him to finish the job quickly, so as not to make too much of a mess. By giving a quick jerk to the left and then another immediate right, followed by a quick upward slice through a lung to lodge in the heart, he was finished in about a minute.

A certain dawning seemed to appear in the eyes of Rico Smits at the last moment of life—a peaceful realization that more was to come perhaps. J.R. shuddered as he felt the small man's energies enter his body. This kind of kill wasn't as satisfying as strangling—having his hands around their throats and watching as well as feeling the life slowly drain from them and enter into him—a hands-on experience, so to speak. But carving was one of his specialties, too, and it always produced an immediate thrill whenever he used his knife. He preferred much younger victims because their energies were more easily absorbed, and the kill was much more rewarding because trauma and pain were foreign to them and in turn more terrifying. However, drastic times called for drastic measures.

He looked at his work and grinned, leaning close to the dead man as if to tell him a secret. Sticking his fingers into Rico's mouth and pulling out his tongue as far as possible, he sliced it with one swift stroke, getting as much of the spongy material as possible. Clutching it in his fist like a coveted prize, he muttered, "Talked too much anyway," feeling mad laughter start to erupt.

J.R. laughed until tears rolled down his face, gasping for breath. After several minutes, he got control of himself and looked at his former drug source.

Rico was dead. His guts would spill out if J.R. tipped him forward.

J.R. always planned in advance and had draped an old gray sheet over the couch for just this purpose. Now he gathered up the ends and wrapped the body of Rico Smits tightly, making sure to keep the body belly-up in order to reduce seepage. One small spot of blood was visible on the couch, and that had dripped from the knife after claiming his prize.

He walked to the small cabinet above the compact refrigerator and found the clear Mason jar that contained a little something from all those he loved—and some of those he didn't. Removing the lid, he dropped Rico's tongue into the jar and watched with fascination as it sank to the bottom. He put the lid back on and held it up to the light, viewing the gory objects floating within—eyes, an ear, several fingers and toes, and now a tongue. J.R. felt satisfied—truly happy. This was all that mattered—his own kind of fun—and no one to tell him when or how to have it. He returned the jar to its resting place in the cabinet then walked to the kitchen sink. Turning the hot water on full force, he rinsed off the knife, and then washed his hands thoroughly. Pouring a small amount of baking soda into the palm of one hand, he walked over to the couch where the spot of blood lay. He sprinkled it with soda and watched it turn pink. In a short time, the baking soda would absorb most of the stain and he could brush the residue away.

J.R. left the body of Rico where it lay on the floor, walking back to the bedroom to check on the girl.

She was right where he'd left her, and still passed out. He'd left her in the laundry bag when stuffing her into the closet, but had opened it so she could breathe easier.

Now he dragged her out, her long braid trailing the dirty wood floor, and threw her on the bed. No response at all.

He'd take care of Rico's body and find the drugs stashed in the van. Then he'd have to see what he could do to bring the girl around. It gave him something to look forward to. *More fun to come*, he thought looking at her sleeping peacefully. He touched her soft hair. It was so shiny, and the color of rich dark chocolate. "Long, dark hair," he murmured to himself, gently stroking the girl's head. He shook his head, trying to snap out of his reverie before the headaches started again. J.R. had a lot of work to do and time was not necessarily on his side. He didn't know when his nemeses would show up. Hopefully, not for a while yet. It depended on when they expected to hear from the little spic. If not until tomorrow, then he'd be doin' okay, but if sooner, he might have a problem. He wanted the girl taken care of *before* he had to deal with *them*. Either way though, he would be ready.

J.R. forgot to retrieve Rico's keys before wrapping him up in the sheet, so he had to unwrap the body and dig through the dead man's pockets. He pulled out a ring with several keys on it, one of which was a Chevrolet key and another, his own duplicate apartment key.

J.R. took his apartment key off the ring and pocketed it, then took the remaining keys and set them on the couch while he re-wrapped Rico in the sheet and dragged him into the bathroom. For now he'd stuff him into the linen closet until a more suitable idea came to mind.

After all, when everything was said and done there would be several bodies to dispose of—maybe he'd have a mass burial or perhaps a large bonfire. Whatever the outcome, the fun of what was to come lingered in his thoughts as he whistled a tune all the way down the long staircase to Rico's van and the stash within.

54

Maria and Joe had no luck cruising the neighborhood surrounding the school. No one had seen anything unusual, and more importantly, no one had seen Tess. Maria left a couple of pictures at the coffee shop located a couple of doors down from the boot store, and the waitress on duty promised to show them to every customer that walked in. But other than that, they had *nothing*.

Maria climbed into the car on the passenger side, slamming the door with an air of defeat. "Damn!"

"Yeah," Joe said, exhaling loudly and getting behind the wheel of the Mustang. He was glad Maria had agreed to let him drive. It would be somewhat tricky operating a stick shift with only one good arm, but Joe assured her he was capable.

He took his left arm out of the sling. It was still wrapped in bandages and didn't hurt too much when he moved it. At least it wasn't his right side—he'd have no trouble shifting gears, and could steer with his bad arm.

"Are you sure about this?"

Joe nodded and smiled. He knew Maria was only letting him drive because she was totally exhausted, both emotionally and physically. She'd been on the go since dawn when awakened by yet another nightmare, and now she was living it. It was taking its toll on her, he noticed, observing the dark circles under her eyes and the stooped shoulders, which carried the weight of the world.

"Let's give the chief a call. It's been almost half an hour." Maria had the phone out and was punching in her own number before Joe responded. She listened to the persistent busy signal. "That's a good sign, maybe." Waiting about five seconds, she tried again. "Shit, still busy."

"Where to now?" Joe asked, starting the Mustang. It rumbled a low, throaty growl, the five-liter engine sounding like a racecar. The muffler was shot, so that probably had something to do with it. He revved up the motor a little, careful not to blow a new rusty hole.

"Head toward the McReedys," Maria said, dialing home and crossing her fingers secretly at her side like a child. It rang through—once—twice—

"Chief! Yeah, it's me. Any news? Really? Great!" Maria looked at Joe and gave a thumbs up, listening intently to Chief McCollough on the other end of the line. "Yeah, uh huh, we're on our way. No, no luck on this end. Yeah, okay. Now. I will. Okay." She pressed the end button and closed the phone.

"What was that all about?"

"Patsy McReedy said we could come by and pick up Betsy, take her for a little drive. Dr. Jorgenson had to give the final say so, of course. The chief promised her we would keep it short. We'll just cruise around the area where Betsy was found by the cabby, and take it from there."

"That everything?"

Maria glanced at Joe, averting her gaze out the window. "No, he's worried about me, I guess. Sounds more like a doting father than a boss," she said, smiling slightly.

That was the first hint of a real smile Joe had seen since this ordeal began. At least now they had something to work with. With luck, Betsy would remember something when they returned to the area where she was found. Joe was somewhat surprised the doctor hadn't insisted on going along, considering this was Betsy's first trip away from home without her mother or doctor. Maria's muffled tears interrupted Joe's thoughts. He glanced in her direction and found her crying discreetly into the side window, her head practically buried in her armpit. *Hang in there, kid,* he silently vowed. *We're gonna get her back. And that's a promise I intend to keep.*

Betsy was waiting for them when they arrived at the house on White Bear Avenue where the McReedys were still staying. She was reserved in her demeanor, but smiled uncertainly as Maria and Joe entered the living room. "Hi, Maria. I—I—I'm sorry about Tess." the little girl stammered, a single tear trailing down her cheek.

Maria knelt down next to Betsy, wrapping her arms around the distraught child. "I know, honey...me, too," she whispered in a shaky voice. "Thank you for being Theresa's friend, for helping us now. You're a brave little girl."

Patsy McReedy looked apprehensive, her concern for Betsy written in the deep worry-lines on her face. Turning to Joe she whispered, "This is just awful. How is Maria holding up?"

"Well, she puts up a pretty good front, but she's torn up inside."

Sarah Jorgenson entered the living room from the kitchen area. She'd obviously been there for quite some time because the cup of coffee she carried was almost empty, Maria noticed with something that bordered on anger. "Dr. Jorgenson, what a surprise. I didn't know you would be here."

"I'll be riding along. We can't be sure of the effect this

may have on Betsy. It's best if I'm present. I hope this won't create a problem." She smiled disarmingly.

"No, of course not," Maria said, slightly flustered at the fact that the woman did indeed cause a problem—she didn't want her here, pulling her sympathetic doctor crap. Dr. Jorgenson was a child psychologist; maybe Betsy needed her in the recovery process, but Maria did not. The doctor could very well interfere with their progress in finding Tess by playing nursemaid when Maria was capable of knowing when to stop if Betsy became upset. That, and the fact that Maria was the mother as well as the detective on the case, would no doubt sound an alarm to the doctor that perhaps she was too distraught to do her job properly.

As if reading her thoughts, Sarah Jorgenson leaned close to Maria, resting one hand on her shoulder. "I'm sorry about Theresa. You must be sick with worry."

Despite Maria's ambivalence toward the woman, she responded to the kind words. "Yes, I am, literally," she said, taking a deep shaky breath and running her fingers through her short hair. "But we're going to find Tess."

"Yes, of course you are," the doctor said with conviction, although Maria read something else in her eyes—doubt, pity maybe, or possibly sympathy.

"We should get going before nightfall," Joe said, glancing at his watch and gazing out the large picture window at the rapidly sinking sun.

"I'm ready," Betsy said, rising from the couch and giving her mother a quick hug, then joining Maria's side, taking her offered hand.

Maria couldn't help but feel a twinge of satisfaction at the look of surprise on the doctor's face—especially when the little girl looked up at her and said in a soft voice, "Let's go find Tess."

* * *

Maria slowly maneuvered the car down First Avenue in the vicinity where the girl was found by the cab driver. Betsy sat in the front passenger seat while Joe and the doctor occupied the back.

"Look familiar?" Maria asked Betsy who sat quietly, staring wide-eyed out the side window. Maria's nerves were frazzled—thoughts of Tess occupied her mind. She wanted to scream, *Tell me where he lives! You must remember!* But outwardly she showed a relatively calm front—no clue to the storm surging in the pit of her guts.

"It's where I ended up, where the cab driver f-f-found me," she said, looking at Maria with large, liquid blue eyes.

"Yes, that's right," Maria said, offering a small smile, her heart going out to the child. She patted Betsy's leg reassuringly. "Let me know if you see something, anything at all, even if it's just a funny feeling. Can you do that, honey?"

"Yes," Betsy promised, returning her gaze out the window.

Maria cruised the area surrounding First Avenue, gradually expanding the search block by block. She was painfully aware of every minute that passed—it was another minute off the clock on Tess's life. *Theresa Ann Sanchez, where are you?* she silently pleaded. *Tell me, baby, are you dead, or alive?*

Joe tapped Maria's shoulder from behind and gestured toward Betsy.

The girl's back had stiffened; her narrow shoulders were starting to shake.

Maria pulled over to the curb, her eyes following the girl's line of vision.

Dr. Jorgenson leaned forward. "What is it, Betsy? Take a

deep breath and tell me what you remember."

"I wanna go home. I don't like it here. Please," she whimpered.

"Does that statue scare you, Betsy? It *is* very frightening. Does the bad man live here?" Maria whispered.

The little girl shook her head no.

"Do you remember running past here when you got away from the bad man?" she gently coaxed.

The child looked up at Maria, her eyes filling with tears. "Yes. I—I was running and running. I remember thinking I couldn't go another step, then I saw that—that—monster," she said, gesturing wildly toward the small stone gargoyle perched on an old wooden post. "I got scared, more scared than ever, so I ran even faster."

The house with the gargoyle statue was on the corner of a residential street. Several large weeping willow trees hid the split-level house. Maria looked for a street sign, but saw none. "Do you remember what direction you were running from?"

Betsy tried real hard to think, looking first one way, then the other. She wanted to help. Tess needed her, but she was so confused right now. She looked around uncertainly, feeling the confusion mount until she thought her head would burst. "*No!* I'm so sorry!" she wailed, breaking down and sobbing. "Can't remember." Her breath was coming in short gasps and she trembled from head to toe.

"Let's go home, *now*," the doctor said, in a voice that expected no argument.

Maria reluctantly put the car in gear and pulled out, glancing in the rearview mirror and meeting Joe's eyes. She saw approval and couldn't help but feel a small glimmer of hope, hope that they were heading in the right direction, hope that they would find Theresa safe and sound, unharmed in any way, shape or form.

Betsy had calmed down considerably by the time they returned home. It was a good thing too, because Patsy McReedy was waiting for them on the front steps. She approached them, hands on hips, as soon as they pulled into the driveway. "How did it go?" she inquired, opening the passenger door and embracing her daughter.

"I'm afraid I wasn't much help, Mom," Betsy said, her bottom lip quivering.

"You did just fine," Maria said, coming around from the other side of the car. "At least we know the general direction you came from. You were more help than you know. Thanks, honey." She bent down and gave the girl a quick hug.

"I hope you find Tess. I know what you're going through," Mrs. McReedy offered.

Maria looked into Patsy's eyes and saw the pain still fresh as if it had all happened yesterday. "Yes, you do, don't you? Thanks. We have to go. We'll be in touch," she said, fighting to keep her composure.

They were both silent for the first ten minutes of the ride back to Minneapolis. Joe broke the silence when Maria went the opposite direction of her condo.

"You headin' back to where Betsy freaked? The house with the gargoyle?"

Maria nodded, her eyes on the road, her mind on only one thing.

"We should check back with the chief."

"Use the cell phone."

"Can't. Battery's dead. I tried already—bleeped out on me halfway through your number, and mine's in the Chevy."

"Shit! The backup battery is at home," Maria said. "Well,

we're almost there. Let's just check out the house quick and then we'll head back."

"Sounds like a plan. I wonder if Cal has come up with anything yet."

"Well, if anyone can, Cal Jensen can."

By the time they pulled up to the house, daylight had faded considerably. The approaching darkness was a bad omen to Maria. She opened the car door. "Are you coming? You can wait here if you want. I'll only be a minute."

Joe opened his door. "No, I don't want to wait." He followed Maria through the drooping willow branches on the walkway and up the front steps.

They looked at each other.

"I don't know what we hope to find here," Maria said, hand poised above the doorbell.

"We're leaving no stone unturned, that's all," Joe said, gently putting his large hand over her delicate one and pressing the buzzer.

No answer.

Maria tried again, while Joe peeked in the large picture window.

"No lights on. It's starting to get pretty dark out," Joe said, looking at his watch.

Maria tried the doorknob, locked. "Shit. Once again— screwed."

"We'll check back later."

"Yeah, later," Maria said with a world-weary sigh.

The sky was a purplish-gray with shades of orange and pink in the west where the sun went down. Beautiful. Tess loved sunsets and had talked of becoming a famous painter and traveling around the world in search of the world's most beautiful sunset, along with a zillion other professions. Such big dreams for a little girl.

Maria felt her heart ache, because in all likelihood her daughter would never see another sunset again.

55

"Now what?" Roberto Santini looked at his colleague, Nicholas.

"It's your call. I don't know. More than likely Rico just spaced it out—probably out getting wasted somewhere or getting laid, or both."

"Yes, possibly, but he was told to wear his pager and phone at all times." Roberto rubbed his chin, thinking. "And if that's not the case—if we ignore this—"

"And it turns out we're dead-wrong," Nicholas added.

"*Dead* being the operative word here," Roberto said with a raised brow. "I'll arrange to have the jet ready in thirty minutes. Throw together whatever you'll need for a few days, and keep trying Rico."

J.R. removed the laundry bag, then the girl's clothes, tossing everything on the floor and covering her body with a threadbare blanket. He'd already set up the camera equipment in the other room, but the girl was more than just an unwilling participant, she was unconscious. A speedball lay ready on the bedside table. He had carefully prepared it, mixing a small dose of heroin with methamphetamine. It would be enough to wake her up but shouldn't kill her, hopefully.

Tess felt the weight lift off the bed and opened one eye a slit. His back was to her. She had the perfect opportunity to smash him over the head with something—anything—except she couldn't even lift her head, let alone find something to hit him with.

Hopeless. It was as if she was awake yet her body was still asleep. He turned back around and she closed her eye. She could smell his breath as he leaned close to her—it was totally gross, almost to the point of gagging her.

J.R. looked closely at the girl. Her breath seemed to be coming faster. She was coming out of it.

The phone rang.

This was the fourth time in an hour. Someone was definitely eager to talk with him, and since only two parties knew his phone number—and one was rolled up in a sheet in the linen closet—this was *not* good. Maybe he should answer and make up some story to buy a little more time. *But what?* He had to get his shit together. Man, he was so fucked-up, his head was throbbing and sweat was pouring off him. He needed something.

Walking over to the wooden crate where his sparse clothing was kept, J.R. rummaged under several T-shirts and pulled out a cigar box. It was Rico's cigar box—one of many things he'd just removed from the van. Opening it revealed an ounce of primo red-bud Colombian as well as several large rocks of cocaine nestled in one half. About twenty small baggies of crystal meth and half that much heroin occupied the other half of the box.

"A regular fuckin' drug store," J.R. muttered, sitting down in front of the crate. He rummaged through the box and found a small brown vial with a tiny golden spoon attached. Opening it, he put his finger over the top and shook it, then licked the round white circle on the tip of his finger. He grinned—it was a mixture of coke, crank, and H. A triple-dipper as Rico, God-rest-his-soul, used to call it. "Here's to you, *my man*." J.R. saluted toward the bathroom door. Then in rapid succession he snorted two spoonfuls up each nostril and waited for the buzz to hit. It didn't take long.

The phone rang again. One, two, three rings.

J.R. crawled on his hands and knees into the living room and reached for the phone. He was pumped now. "Hello," he said, out of breath.

"J.R.! Everything okay?" Nicholas asked from the other end, surprised that he even picked up. *Maybe everything was okay after all.*

He knew it—one of *them.* *Act the part...don't fuck-up...too much at stake...everything at stake.* "Yeah, yeah. Everything is fine. Just got back from the liquor store...out of tequila," J.R. said without missing a beat, which wasn't far from the truth. He'd made a quick booze run earlier after he had confiscated Rico's stash.

"Seen Rico recently?"

Now came the hard part. Yes or no? "Yeah, right before I left for a booze run. He looked pretty wasted, said something about a hot date."

"Figures, fuckin' spic," Nicholas muttered.

"Huh?"

"Nothing, nothing. Hang tight, J.R., and remember *the rites of passage.*"

J.R. felt the familiar throbbing pain return with a vengeance to his temples. "*The rites of passage,*" he repeated mechanically. A dial tone resounded in his ear, becoming louder and louder until he felt as if his head would burst.

He was out of the room. Now was her only chance to do something. It was now or never!

Tess closed her eyes tightly, trying to focus all of her efforts on moving. She lifted her arm; her hand floating at the end of it like a kite at the end of a string. She couldn't sit, could hardly lift her head, so she rolled. Ever so slowly, Tess rolled to the edge of the bed.

The small bedside table was eye level and she could see the contents—a large bottle with gold liquid in it, a shot glass balancing upside down over the top; a syringe; a roll of peppermint lifesavers, and a pair of dark sunglasses. Her outstretched hand brushed the top of the tequila bottle, threatening to send the shot glass toppling off onto the floor. She quickly righted it and felt along the table, still unable to lift her two-ton head off the bed.

A loud crash resounded from the living room, like something falling over, then silence.

Tess tightened her grip on what was under her hand and rolled again, feeling herself tumble off the bed onto the floor. The last thing she remembered before everything went black was the sound of the bad man, cursing and crashing around, his voice becoming louder and louder as he closed the distance between them.

56

Maria could smell the sweet cloying cherry smoke from the chief's pipe as soon as they entered the hallway that led to her condo. She looked at Joe with a hopefulness that belied all her fears and anxiety. Opening the door, she had never felt this kind of uncertainty before—a deep-seeded confusion mixed with anger and doubt, hope and fear. They needed information on Theresa's whereabouts, soon if they wanted to find her alive. As time went by, her chance of survival diminished.

The chief sat on the sofa with a smoking pipe clenched between his teeth, shuffling papers and glaring at the phone. He looked up when Maria and Joe walked in. "Sanchez, Morgan, what's up?"

Maria sat down next to the chief. "Absolutely nothing. I hope you've had better luck," she said, running her fingers through sweat-dampened hair. It was so hot and muggy outside, the condo felt like a walk-in freezer. "Damn, it's as cold as a friggin' morgue in—" She stopped herself, realizing with sudden dread the words that so nonchalantly spilled out of her mouth were awfully close to the truth.

She started to feel ill and walked into the hall to turn down the central air, but even more to get out of sight. She was shaking all over; every part of her body trembled. *God, what is happening to me?* "Can't lose it now," she muttered to herself, feeling a band of tension stretch so tight across her chest, she felt as if it might snap. Maybe she was having a heart attack, or maybe her heart was breaking in two. Where was Theresa, her baby, best friend, soul mate? What was that fucking monster doing to her right now? Maybe she was already dead.

Maria leaned heavily against the wall for support, then slid down to a sitting position and buried her head in her hands, sobbing and praying. A hand touched her shoulder. *Joe.*

"It's okay, Maria. Let it out. You need a good cry. You've kept it bottled up for too long. Let it out," he whispered, embracing her as best he could with one arm in a sling as she buried her head in his neck and cried until she couldn't cry anymore.

Only minutes had passed, but it seemed like hours to Maria. "God, I can't believe I'm wasting time with this shit," she said, taking the offered toilet paper Joe gave her and blowing her nose long and hard. She did feel better, though. The band around her chest was still there, but it was bearable. She ducked into the bathroom and splashed cold water on her face.

"What must the chief think?"

"That you're human," Joe said.

"Not very professional. If he thinks he's gonna pull me off the case—"

"He won't."

"Any news from the BCA?"

"Nothing we can use—not yet anyway. Cal talked to the owner of the boot store, but she was busy with several customers at the time and didn't notice Tess outside the window. He's checking out the customers now. Chief's waiting for a call." Joe didn't know what else to tell her. He wished he could say something positive. Something that would help allay her worst fears, but he couldn't.

They walked into the living room and found it deserted. The chief was in the kitchen refilling his coffee cup.

"I'm gonna head out before he gets back in here. I don't want to face him right now," Maria whispered, heading for the front door.

"Maria, wait. Where are you going? I'm going with—"

"No, no, you stay here. Help the chief, he needs you here. I'll just drive by that house we checked earlier. Maybe someone's home by now."

"I doubt it. They're probably out for the evening. I think we should wait—"

"No! I can't wait, damnit." She was pissed at the world, but still trying to keep her voice down. "And please don't tell me what to do. This is *my* daughter, *my* case, and *my* life—I'm calling the shots. You do as *I* say. Just stay the hell away from me," she cautioned, practically running for the door.

Putting the Mustang in gear, Maria tore out of the parking lot onto Marquette Avenue.

Poor Joe, she thought, after her temper cooled down a bit. *What a first-class bitch I am. Why did I blow up like that?* She'd never used her authority in that way before. They were always equals—partners. She was going crazy, and losing everyone she loved as well. She remembered feeling that things were too good to be true, that she was too happy. Well, now she would pay the ultimate price—watching the life she loved crumble before her eyes—and felt powerless to stop it.

57

They were less than an hour away from the Twin Cities.

Roberto was passing the time by getting pleasantly drunk. Not deliriously drunk, just pleasantly drunk. This was his fourth martini in an hour. The chef on board was serving filet mignon shortly, so that would absorb most of the alcohol he consumed, and leave him levelheaded for their confrontation with J.R.

Rico still wasn't answering his pager or cell phone, and even though Nicholas had talked to their boy, things were not always as they seemed. Roberto thought it best to pay their friend a little visit.

Nicholas was feigning sleep so he wouldn't have to communicate with Roberto. He could hardly contain himself and was afraid he might give something away, so he just kept his eyes closed. Soon all his dreams would come true. *He* would be in charge after tonight—no more J.R., no more Roberto. Life was going to take a turn for the better, after tonight.

Roberto prided himself in knowing when someone was faking him out. Soon it would be time for everyone to put their cards on the table. There would be no more lies or half-truths. *Are you friend or foe?* Roberto thought, watching Nicholas pretend to sleep. *Soon I will know for sure.*

Rico was probably dead, regardless of what J.R. said over

the phone. And if everything was as it should be? If J.R. was telling the truth, it wouldn't be a wasted trip. They would just stay for the festivities. Roberto couldn't wait to meet the pretty, dark-haired child who looked so much like her mother—the bitch who threatened him, who pretended to be interested in real estate, but was really a cop.

Roberto chuckled to himself, planning, scheming—the internal mechanisms forever churning in his brain. He'd make sure the girl knew she was suffering for her mother's actions. Then, after the fact, when the girl was dead, he'd meet with the bitch; tell her he had crucial information about her child. This time she would be begging for mercy, first for her child, who would already be dead, then for herself when she realized her own death was imminent. Then he'd let her meet J.R.—he'd already rehearsed introductions over and over in his mind and couldn't wait for 'show and tell'. Thinking of her glossy dark hair and dark flashing eyes, the way she moved in a skirt, her long legs and voluptuous curves—made him hard. Oh *yes*, he was going to have tons of fun with this one before he killed her. *She is in for quite a surprise.*

J.R. didn't know how long he was out. His head was pounding again—big-time. *The fuckers.* Why did they have that effect on him? *What did they say?* He tried to remember and his head pounded even harder. Sitting cross-legged on the floor, he held his head in his hands and squeezed, moaning in agony. After a good ten minutes the pounding subsided somewhat.

Very slowly, he got up on all fours and crawled back into the bedroom.

Maria pulled up next to the house with the weeping

willow trees and the gargoyle statue, in the exact spot she had parked earlier with Joe. The house was still dark inside—no activity whatsoever. Joe was right. She sat in the car for five minutes watching the drapes in the front window for movement.

Getting out of the car, she strolled up the front walk, observing everything about the house—well kept yard, a child's ball, a small, well-tended garden. She rang the doorbell and listened for any movement on the other side.

Nothing.

She tried again, this time moving off the front steps and into the shrubbery in front of the large picture window. She peered through the crack in the drapes, and saw a flash of white.

Someone was home after all.

A small, furry face peeked between the drapes. A Persian cat hopped up on the inside ledge of the picture window and walked the length of it, rubbing against the glass and looking at Maria as if to say, 'Come on in.'

She went around back and tried that door as well—jiggling the knob and checking under the welcome mat for a key—with no luck. Everything was locked up tight and nobody was home, except for the family cat.

Walking back to her car, Maria tried to picture in her mind's eye the night Betsy escaped. Which direction was she coming from?

She walked to the end of the sidewalk, which wasn't far since this was a corner lot, and looked down the street. Nearby, there were mostly businesses—warehouses and storage garages—but further down it looked like it turned residential again. She decided to check it out. If poor Betsy hadn't become distraught they would have done it earlier.

Excited and hopeful, Maria got back in the car, put in the clutch and cranked the ignition. She was welcomed by a faint click, then total silence. "Okay, okay, not now, *please* not now," she coaxed the old car, and tried again.

Nothing. Not even a click this time.

She popped the hood, though little good it would do her. She knew it was hopeless—cars were not one of the things she was *good* at.

Grabbing the flashlight in the glove box and getting out of the car, Maria noticed the moon for the first time this evening, beautiful. It was almost full and had an orange cast to it; hanging so low in the sky it seemed surreal—looking like a giant orange balloon that was slightly deflated and just out of reach. She wondered if Tess was looking at it, or if she would ever look at the moon again.

Maria tried to concentrate on the task at hand. She fiddled with the battery connections, then checked the other wires and hoses, but all seemed to be connected properly. The wires that led to the battery still looked clean. She shut the hood and, crossing her fingers, got back in the car.

"*Please,* God, let it start," she prayed out loud, thinking back to that ominous day she'd escaped with her child many years ago. God had helped her then... She turned the key.

Silence.

Maria rested her head on the steering wheel. *This can't be happening, not now.*

She tried repeatedly, finally realizing it was pointless.

"Son of a fucking bitch. I can't fuckin' believe it," she swore, hitting the dash with her fist—it resounded with a loud crack. Now her hand throbbed, replacing anger with pain. "*Ow, ow, ow,* goddamnit!"

She reached for the cell phone and stopped halfway,

realizing her stupid mistake in her hurry to leave. "Oh, Christ," she muttered, pulling out the phone and looking at the dimly lit battery low light. It beeped weakly when she pushed the power button, then died. Nothing. *Well, this is turning out to be a fine day,* Maria thought, throwing the phone back in the glove compartment with disgust.

"What now?" she asked the night, gazing out the window at the moon. Its appearance had already changed. It was higher in the sky now and seemed to become a deeper orange as the evening grew darker.

Maria reached into the open glove compartment and pulled out the stale pack of cigarettes that were still in there. Lighting up, she closed her eyes and tried to concentrate. Her thoughts went to Joe—*what is he doing right now?* She should have taken his advice and waited for him—her partner—instead of going it alone. At least she should have taken his car being hers was acting up lately *and* the Chevy was equipped with a CB radio. She wouldn't be in this predicament if she'd just used her head. She wasn't thinking like a cop—more like a distraught, frantic mother. "Get your shit together," she told herself, taking a deep breath and running her fingers through sweat soaked hair. It was still so goddamn hot outside.

With flashlight in hand, Maria got out of the car and started walking in the direction from which she thought Betsy had come on that fateful evening. Her cop instinct took over, as she scoured the area with her eyes, looking for—she wasn't sure what—a lead, a premonition, anything, and eventually a telephone.

The night was dark even with the strange glowing moon, and shadows seemed ominous as Maria walked through the empty streets of the warehouse district. She had no weapon—that was left at the condo as well, along with the cell phone battery, and the rest of her brain.

She watched the flashlight beam bounce off the concrete in front of her as an old pickup roared by, black smoke billowing out the rear. It reminded her *again* of the day she and Tess had escaped in Jack's old pickup. She remembered how she couldn't get it started, and the fear, the fear alone had almost immobilized her. The fear of Jack stumbling out of the house at any moment, killing them before they made their getaway.

Maria stopped walking for a moment and listened to the night. The sound of crickets filled her ears. Just ahead lay a residential street; a single phosphorescent street lamp dimly lit the area and large, looming shadows of houses darkened the landscape.

She crossed the street and stood under the street lamp for a moment, looking around. "Chestnut Avenue," she read aloud from the street sign on the corner. "Who do I know that lives on Chestnut?" She racked her brain, but couldn't quite get it; it was just out of reach.

Maria looked at her watch—9:52. At least she remembered to wear her watch...she remembered putting it on when she was so distraught and had splashed cold water on her face, right before she blew up at Joe. Why couldn't she have remembered to pick up the spare battery for the cell phone and her gun, too? *Because you were too pissed off and in a big hurry to leave,* she reminded herself.

Moving on down the street, it was now pitch black, except for the moon-glow, which seemed to be following her—or maybe it was the other way around.

It felt right. *As long as I look over my shoulder and see that big orange moon, Tess is all right.* It was stupid, she knew, but couldn't help what she felt in her heart.

A dog barked directly to her right, making her jump back. She brandished the flashlight, her only weapon.

A low throaty growl emitted from the animal as his large beastly shadow hunkered down low to the ground.

Oh God, is he gonna attack? she wondered, frantic, wanting to bolt like a rabbit, but knowing enough about dogs to realize that was the wrong thing to do. Her heart was stuck in the middle of her throat as she slowly took a step back.

Then the dog lunged for her, but stopped short, as the rope he was tied to pulled taut. Fido was tied up, and thoroughly agitated by it.

Maria nearly laughed, but decided against it, his ferocious growls making the humor die before it could reach her lips. *Maybe the rope wasn't all that sturdy.*

The street was lined with large trees on both sides that blocked out most of the moon so it was darker than before. Many of the houses were dark as well—their occupants probably in bed, but a couple of them had a porch light on. Maria shined her flashlight at the darkened ones and scrutinized the others before passing them by.

She was looking at one old, rather large run-down house where the outside light was on and suddenly she remembered...

Home, Sweet Home read the tattered wooden sign above the front door. "Martha Franco," she muttered. How could she not have remembered? The sweet little old lady with the high-gloss table and the delicious, date-filled pecan cookies.

Maria walked up the narrow stone walkway that led to the front door and rang the doorbell. The house looked dark inside, except for a small night-light by the front entrance. She waited, nervously fiddling with the flashlight.

The door opened and Martha appeared in her robe,

Reader's Digest in hand.

"Hi, Martha. I—I—don't know if you remember me. I'm very sorry to bother you so late," Maria began.

Martha Franco looked her up and down, confusion in her eyes, then sudden recognition. "Why, Detective Sanchez!"

"You remember! Oh, Martha—"

"Come on in now, you look a sight. Is everything all right? Where's that partner of yours? Jack, John, what's his name?" she asked, smiling and leading Maria over to the well-worn couch.

Maria's heart skipped a beat at the mention of Jack. "Uh, Joe," she said, a little rattled.

"Are you all right, child? You look a fright," she said, leaning toward Maria, a worried frown creasing her wrinkled brow even further.

"Well—I—I've had better days," Maria admitted, wanting to spill her guts to this wonderful motherly figure. But she didn't. Instead, she squared her shoulders, took a deep breath and asked, "Could I please use your telephone? I'm having car trouble."

"Oh, my. That may be a problem. I'm afraid I don't have a telephone."

Maria's disappointment must have shown on her face, because Martha hurried on, "But don't worry, dear. You can go next-door to Mr. Meyer's."

"Mr. Meyer's?"

"Oh, yes. I'm sure I told you about him before, didn't I?" she asked, beaming.

Maria racked her rattled brain, finally remembering old Mr. Meyer who ran the boarding house next-door—Martha cooked meals for him and his boarders and offered the use of her garage. "Oh, yeah. I remember. You're kinda sweet on him aren't you?"

Martha blushed. "Oh, I don't know about that. We're just two old folks who like to help each other out now and then. Although, he did tell me once I was the most important person in his life."

"Well, you can't get a better compliment than that, can you?"

Martha blushed again. "No, I don't suppose so. Well," she said, straightening the afghan on the couch, "you didn't come to talk about my social life."

Maria smiled tiredly at the older woman. "Believe me any other time I'd love to hear all about it, but—"

"You don't need to explain, dear. I can see you have something weighing real heavy on your mind—it's okay, I won't ask."

"You're special, Martha. And I promise I'll come back for a visit—a real visit, just to talk, okay?"

Martha Franco smiled. "I'd like that. You'll find the telephone in the front entryway. The door is always unlocked until midnight on Wednesdays and Fridays because Charlie Norton plays bingo at the VFW until eleven. But by the time they finish waggin' their tongues it's usually closer to one in the morning when he stumbles through the door."

"Thanks," Maria said, hugging the older woman.

Martha returned the embrace, petting Maria's hair in a motherly gesture. "You take care of yourself now. I'll be lookin' forward to your next visit." She let Maria out and locked up.

Climbing into bed, Martha glanced at the clock—10:26, an hour past her usual bedtime. She drifted off as soon as her head hit the pillow, only to be awakened less than an hour later by the sound of gunshot.

58

Joe led Peter Slade into the kitchen where Chief McCollough and BCA agents Foley and Jensen sat around the kitchen table.

"Man, I can't believe it," Slade whispered, looking paler than usual because of his battle with the flu. He still hadn't kicked it. It was still reigning terror over his body, but *nothing* was going to keep him away. Tess had made quite an impact on him at their Labor Day picnic. Up until now every time he thought of her, it brought a smile to his face. The cute kid with the baseball cap jammed on her head, her long, dark ponytail flying in the breeze. The cracker-jack Twins expert. It's what his own kid would be like if he had one, he just knew it. "Can't fuckin' believe it," he muttered again.

"You don't have to whisper, Peter. Maria's not here," Joe said. "Sit down, you look a little green. I'll get you a cup of coffee."

He looked at Joe closely. This was probably the first time he'd used his first name. The guy looked exhausted, but ready for a fight. The dark circles under his eyes only emphasized the fierce determination in them. Joe was on the edge, but putting up a damn good front. "Where is she? How's she handling all this?" Slade asked, pulling out a chair and sitting down next to the chief.

"You know Sanchez. She's a hard nut to crack," Chief

345

McCollough said. "But this, it's doing quite a number on her. I can see it," he said, holding out his cup for a refill. "However, we're gonna find the kid, goddamnit, we're gonna find her."

"Who are you trying to convince?" Slade said, rubbing his unshaven chin. "And I repeat, where is Maria?"

Joe responded defensively. "She's checking out a lead, sort of."

"*Sort of*?" Slade asked, with a look in his eye that said he wasn't satisfied.

"No one was home when we checked out the house where the McReedy girl freaked out, so Maria was planning on going back," Joe said, as way of an explanation.

"Okay. I'll buy that, but why didn't you go with her?"

"She wanted to go alone," he stated evenly, giving Slade a look that said *don't fuck with me.*

Peter got the message. "Anything new since I last talked to you?" he asked the chief.

"Well, Jensen and Foley here made contact with one of the customers from The Boot Company. Appears the woman saw a small black sports car parked near the store with a shady looking character getting out just as she was leaving. She only saw him from a side view, but it sounds like our guy—tall, dark, and creepy. She remembered seeing a young girl with a backpack just outside the store—had to be Tess. But that's it. She was in a hurry to get home and left without another glance back." The chief took a long drink from his coffee.

"It sounds like the River Rat—also known as J.R., Mr. Tall, Dark and Gruesome—but I thought we were looking for a *red* sports car."

"He must've got a different car is all," Joe said. Something didn't sit quite right in his mind. He couldn't put his finger on it, but it was there, stuck in his brain like a stubborn sliver. "Well, there's no point in all of us sittin' around here on a goddamn coffee break. I'm gonna cruise around, see what I can find out," he said, slamming down his coffee cup on the counter and storming out the door.

Roberto Santini stood up and stretched. The flight had seemed longer than it actually was. He had a sour stomach from the filet mignon and too much booze. Nicholas was in a quiet mood and Roberto felt...disturbed. It wasn't just the heartburn. Something was going to happen on this trip that would change all of their lives—he just felt it.

The airplane came to a complete stop and the doors opened.

Roberto was first to disembark. The humidity was the first thing he noticed. The air hung heavy with moisture, and anticipation. He looked over his shoulder at Nicholas lagging behind. "Let's get a move on," he said, eyeing the laptop that never left his good friend's side. What damning information did that computer hold on him? *Probably every fucking deal that went down.*

He led the way, walking quickly in order to be the first one to the car that waited in the hot parking lot.

Roberto started the car, putting the air conditioning on full blast.

Nicholas opened the passenger door and started putting the laptop and carry-on bags in the back seat.

"I can put those in the trunk. Get in the car so we don't let all the cool air out." Roberto removed the trunk key from the glove compartment, and smiled at his friend. Getting out of the car and shutting the door, he walked around to the passenger side to pick up the laptop computer case and carry-on bags then closed the passenger door. Opening the trunk, he placed the bags inside, and lifting the computer up, set it inside with much ceremony. The open trunk temporarily obscured his line of vision with Nicholas. Roberto's hand never left the handle of the laptop case; he removed it, positioned it under the left rear tire, and closed the trunk.

Roberto got back in the car, and took several deep, cleansing breaths. The air inside felt cool and delicious in his lungs compared to the sticky shit outside. "Well, are we ready to pay our respects to J.R.?"

Nicholas nodded wearily.

Roberto put the car in reverse and backed up, crushing the computer as he did so. Just clearing it, he put the car in drive and drove over it again. "What the hell!" he said, in good imitation of surprise, stopping the vehicle abruptly.

Nicholas sat ramrod straight. Turning around, his heart lurched down to his stomach as he saw the laptop computer case, its contents no doubt crushed beyond repair.

"Oh, dear. I must have forgotten to put it in the trunk. I got distracted for just a moment and—" Roberto threw his hands into the air in a gesture of helplessness; then came the mad laughter.

Through his red haze of anger, the laughter cut like a knife. Santini was a lunatic. Nicholas Freyhoff faced forward and smiled, obliging his nemesis. "It doesn't really matter anyway. Everything important is backed up on disk back at the office." His smile broadened, thinking about the safety deposit box and the key in the hands of the one person he could trust—his brother, Stephen. "Even someone as computer illiterate as you must know that," he said, eye to eye with the man whose life would be taken by tonight if everything went according to plan.

Roberto stared at the fool, the smile never leaving his face even though the laughter had long since died. *How dare he!* He challenged Nicholas with his eyes and as usual, his comrade was the first to look away.

"Let's go. I'm tired, and we have a long night ahead of us."

"Yes. You're right of course." Roberto tuned in a radio station and drove away. "And I'm truly sorry about your computer, my friend. I feel terrible. I'll buy you a better one as soon as we get back," he said with genuine feeling.

Nicholas glanced at his partner and boss, then quickly looked back out the window without saying a word. *Time would tell.*

59

Tess realized she must have fallen asleep again, because she was startled back into consciousness by a loud crash next to her head. It was the bottle of booze. He'd knocked it off the table, but it didn't break. The bad man was in the bedroom with her. She lay very still, barely breathing, hidden from view. At least she had wriggled under the bed before she passed out or he would have found her already.

J.R. sat heavily on the bed, swearing. "Goddamn little fuck! Where are you? I don't want to play this game anymore, and I'm gonna make you real sorry. Stupid little cunt." He leaned over to pick the bottle up, intent on polishing off at least a third of it, when he saw her.

"Peek-a-boo, I see you," he called, all the blood rushing to his head and threatening to topple him to the floor. He sat back up on the bed and uncapped the bottle, taking a long drink. "Come out, come out wherever you are," he sang. "Except now I know where you are, don't I, little lamb?"

Theresa had wet herself in her fright. There was something about his voice that seemed familiar, but how could that be? She'd never met this awful man before, she was sure of it. And another thing she was sure of—she wasn't coming out on her own accord. He would have to drag her out. She positioned herself further under the bed, against the wall, molding to it like part of the woodwork.

"I said come out. *Now!*" He jumped off the bed and got down on all fours, reaching for her. "Stupid little bitch, you'll pay for this." He couldn't quite reach her. J.R. stood up too quickly and had to sit down on the bed for a minute to prevent a blackout. The throbbing in his head was threatening to return, and it was all the little cunt's fault. He stood up again and grabbed the metal brackets at one side of the headboard. Taking a deep breath he heaved half the bed off the floor and pushed it so it lay diagonally, exposing the girl.

Tess sat up, covering herself, for she was naked and hadn't realized it until this moment. She started crying.

Maria entered the boarding house; following Martha's directions, she located the telephone just inside the entryway. The house was dark, all the boarders asleep, except for Charlie Norton of course who was playing bingo down at the VFW.

Maria picked up the telephone and started dialing her home number when she heard a loud thump above her. It sounded like a heavy piece of furniture was being moved, more like dropped. "What the hell," she said aloud, hanging up the phone and moving closer to the winding staircase. She listened for several minutes, but heard nothing else.

She picked up the phone again—but dreaded calling Joe. The chief was probably still there and he'd question where she left her brains, taking off so unprepared. He'd probably pull her off the case and put someone else on it, maybe Liebert or Mackelroy. Why not? He'd given them all their other cases so she and Joe could work solely on solving this one. If she wasn't capable, he'd find someone who was. She'd seen it happen before. It was possible he'd pull Joe, too, replacing them both with the special investigations team the mayor had promised the public at a previous press conference.

Maria put the phone back on the cradle without making her call, and headed for the door, intent on walking back to her car. Hopefully, the owners of the white cat and the gargoyle would now be home, and she could call Joe *after* questioning them. That would definitely look better than calling from the boarding house next to Martha Francos. She stopped, looked back at the telephone, then at the door, still uncertain. Why couldn't she seem to make even a simple decision anymore? "Screw it," she said, opting for the door.

Walking out into the heavy night air made her breath come short. It was still so humid, more like August than September, and the exhaustion from this awful day—the worst day in her life—had set in full-force.

She looked up into the dark night sky for her moon but couldn't seem to find it. *Must be hidden behind a cloud,* she thought, searching diligently. Her eyes fell on a dimly lit window on the second floor of the boarding house at the exact moment the moon peeked out from behind a cloud. She saw someone silhouetted at the window for only an instant.

The shadowy, fleeting image of the man burned into her brain and all the hairs stood to attention at the nape of her neck. *Did I imagine it? Is my mind playing evil tricks on me?* reverberated through her head.

Maria walked back into the boarding house, past the telephone—pausing briefly, knowing she should call Joe, but unable to stop for fear she'd lose her nerve—and up the winding staircase.

Tess backed into the far corner of the room as the bad man advanced toward her. She was going to die now. The look in his eyes told her that much. He'd almost reached her when she realized her hand was clenched tightly around something long and pointy on one end. She vaguely remembered the syringe she'd grabbed off the table when rolling off the bed.

"*Tsk, tsk, tsk*. What a naughty girl you are. I was going to have some fun with you first, but now, now, I think I have a better idea," J.R. said in a low whisper, coming toward her, feeling his rage build out of control as the pain in his head steadily worsened.

Reaching out and wrapping his hands around her slender throat, he slowly squeezed.

Roberto Santini drove like a madman, barely missing a parked car when he rounded the last corner. He wore a smirk on his handsome face.

Nicholas felt like he was riding with the devil. "For God's sake, slow down! What are you trying to do—get stopped by a cop, or just get us killed?"

"Calm down, my friend," Roberto replied, letting up on the accelerator a little. "We want to get there, no? We've come this far on a hunch, and now that we're here I feel it was definitely the right thing to do. I can *feel* it, can't you?"

"Yes, yes, I do. But let's get there in one piece. Please," Nicholas pleaded.

Roberto laughed. "Okay, okay. I'll obey all traffic laws. We're almost there anyway."

"Yes, it's the next residential street we come to," Nicholas said, looking out the passenger window at the darkened warehouses and empty loading docks.

They pulled up outside the boarding house less than five minutes later.

Maria reached the top of the stairs, approaching the large oak door that stood like an out of place giant in the center of the paneled wall on the second floor landing. She felt strange, light-headed. She pinched herself hard, to make sure she wasn't dreaming, that this was reality and truly happening. It was too much like her repeated nightmares of late.

Reaching out she put her hand on the doorknob. If it was locked, she was screwed, because it was a Schlage maximum-security dead-bolt. And the way her luck had been lately...

The knob turned, and she quietly entered. Maria was surrounded in darkness. It took a while for her eyes to adjust. She didn't want to stumble and alert—*who?* She didn't know.

Why am I here? she asked herself, looking down the narrow dark hallway and wondering what it was that had come over her so powerfully.

Then she heard it—a scream, unlike any other. And a scream she'd heard only once before—when Tess was six years old and had happened upon a hornet's nest in the hollow of an old oak tree.

Maria ran, tripping on a bunched up rug on the dirty wood floor. She landed hard on her face, stunned.

60

Tess couldn't breathe. His hands were squeezing tighter and tighter as his evil grin got bigger and bigger. She felt darkness creeping into her peripheral vision, his face fading out, and she almost welcomed it. *It would be so easy to just let go.*

No! She brought up the hand that held the syringe before her faculties were any more diminished and plunged it into the bad man's neck. He looked surprised, then weird, as his grip loosened around her throat. She took the only opportunity she had, and filling her lungs with air, let out a blood-curdling scream, pushing him backward with all her might.

J.R. stumbled, but did not fall down. *What the fuck is happening,* he thought, starting to feel the drugs that were now entering his system. He felt a wave of dizziness and had to take deep breaths to keep his wits about him.

Feeling a presence behind him, J.R. turned and saw the woman. She looked deranged—mouth bloody and eyes wild—as she approached them. *How the hell did she get in? Shit, must've forgotten to lock the door after goin' down to Rico's van.*

Maria was in a state of shock but was operating on pure adrenaline. Tess stood in the corner shaking, naked; the look of a captured animal haunted her young face. "It's okay now, baby. Mommy's here," she whispered softly to Tess, never

355

taking her eyes off the man as she approached them. She was face to face with the River Rat, AKA the bad man, AKA J.R. Franco, and looking into his insane eyes made her suddenly tremble with fear, for he wasn't just a crazed madman...

Jack? This can't be happening.

Maria felt her mind threaten to snap.

Joe pulled up behind Maria's car. The house in question was still dark, so where was Maria?

Getting out, he walked over to her car. The doors were locked. He felt the hood; it was barely warm so she'd been here for a while.

Joe scratched his head. She could've had car trouble again.

He walked past the gargoyle statue and up the path that led to the front door. Trying the doorknob, which he already knew was locked from their previous trip, he banged loud enough to wake the neighbors. He kept his finger on the doorbell for a good minute, pissing off the white cat who sat perched in the window, meowing loud enough for Joe to hear.

Locked and no one home, like he figured. Checking the back door and finding the same, he got back in the old Chevy.

Joe slowly drove the exact route Maria had walked less than an hour earlier. Studying the darkened landscape, he half expected to find her—walking along the street in a daze, or worse.

J.R. pulled out the hunting knife that was strapped to his belt, and quick as a flash he had Maria in a chokehold, knife to her face. "Who the fuck are you, and what are you doing here?" he demanded, piercing her cheek with the finely honed point of the knife.

"Well, well, well, what do we have here? A family reunion?" Roberto Santini said from the bedroom doorway. The light was so dim in the room, he stood almost entirely in shadow except for his face. His eyes mocked Maria as he came into the room with Nicholas following close behind.

"Stop," Nicholas commanded his subject.

J.R. looked at the man who caused him so much pain in the past and lowered his knife, smiling passively. But what lay behind the smile was something else completely. He held the knife to his side but pictured it field dressing the son of a bitch who stood before him—his guts spilling out for the world to see. And the look of surprise on his face, how fulfilling that would be. Just like Rico, who lay in the linen closet, the last vestiges of life now totally gone, but listening to all their nonsense.

Maria looked from Jack to the man who issued the command. *What the hell is going on here?*

As if reading her thoughts, Roberto Santini leaned toward her. "We have him well trained. Kind of like a dog; a mad dog if you will.

"Has everyone met?" he asked as if hosting a Tupperware party. "Theresa, meet your father. I know you thought he was dead, but alas, he is very much alive. And Maria, pretty Maria," he said, gently touching the fresh cut on her cheek. "I'm sure you're thrilled to be reunited with your long lost husband. Not every wife gets a second chance for wedded bliss with her dearly devoted, especially after such a tragic death." He thought about it all and threw back his head, mad laughter bubbling up and filling the small room.

Theresa started to cry and Maria moved to go to her, but was abruptly stopped by Roberto's arm across her chest. "Not so fast, you can look but don't touch—only *we* can do that," he said, smiling, watching anger spring to her beautiful dark eyes.

"Don't you dare touch her," Maria said vehemently.

"Or what? Do you think I'm scared of *you*?" Roberto laughed. "Anyway, I'm sure we're already too late for that—if I know our J.R."

Maria looked at Theresa and then at the River Rat, the bad man they called J.R., whose real name was Jack. She felt tears spring to her eyes, but would not give Santini the pleasure of seeing her cry.

"What's the matter? Fresh out of comebacks? You should learn to watch that pretty mouth of yours—it's what got you into this mess," Roberto whispered, brushing up against her, wanting her. He had desired her from the moment they'd met.

"Please, let Theresa go. I'll do anything, anything you want, if you'll just let her go," she offered, seeing a way out for her daughter.

Roberto looked up at the ceiling, eyes closed as if deep in thought. "Anything? Anything at all? No," he finally said. "I don't think so. It's just too much fun with the whole gang here, don't you think? We'll just improvise and see what happens. But I *will* promise you one thing." He looked deep into her eyes. "If you cooperate fully, I'll make things less painful for both of you. I promise. Understand?" He slipped his hand under her shirt and cupping a breast, leaned over, kissing her neck.

"Tell me about Jack, J.R., first," Maria said, trying to buy some time and a way to keep Roberto's filthy hands off her.

"Ah, of course. You're curious, being the detective and all. Well, I suppose there's no harm in telling you all the sordid details now. I mean it's not like you're going to be around to arrest me or anything," Roberto said, smiling.

Maria met his gaze and said nothing. He stood so close

she didn't have room to breathe.

"It's all quite simple really. You see, we knew Jack since he was seventeen. Well, I take that back—I have a small confession to make." Roberto Santini moved away from Maria to look out the window. "This is something even you don't know, my friend," he said, glancing at Nicholas, then returning his gaze out the window. "I knew *about* Jack from the time he was a small baby left on the steps of an orphanage more than thirty years ago. I myself was only a boy of nine or ten."

Nicholas couldn't believe this shit. What was this garbage he was dishing out now?

"My father," Roberto continued, gazing out the window, "was in the habit of helping out people in need. Sometimes, total strangers. He met a woman one night on a street corner outside one of his offices. She was desperate, and beautiful. She had a small baby who was very sick, possibly dying. He helped her that night and for many nights to come. I waited silently—because he would tolerate nothing less—in the back seat of the limousine, learning, listening, taking in everything.

"On his death-bed, my father asked me to find the boy. Just check up on him. Help him if need be. So I did my part. At seventeen, Jack was a small time dealer, and a user. He did a couple of odd jobs for us, nothing major—your typical petty hoodlum stuff. But he was always paid generously, even more than we paid our own people. Sometimes we wouldn't hear from him for weeks, but he always called eventually—when money ran out or he was in need of a fix. We didn't keep tabs on him, didn't care that much. I was simply fulfilling my father's wishes to check up on him periodically.

"Then, seven and a half years ago or so… Well, let's just say Jack needed to disappear for a while. He lost his job, was having trouble at home, and just couldn't function in the real world anymore—as you already know," he said to Maria. "We did one better—we killed him. The body found was that of a homeless bum. We gave Jack a new identity and a new life— you could say we reinvented him. Hell, eventually we even provided a new wife—my half sister, Stephanie. But J.R. wasn't quite right in the head, as you, my dear, have witnessed first hand." He walked back over to where Maria stood. She'd managed to worm her way closer to her daughter.

He put his arm around her. "Isn't that right?"

Maria nodded. She'd been watching Tess the entire time he spoke. The girl was in shock, staring at the floor. She was sitting with her knees pulled up to her chest and hadn't moved for a long time.

Roberto grabbed Maria by the face and jerked her head toward him. "Look at me when I'm speaking to you."

Maria's eyes focused in on Roberto.

"That's better. Now, as I was saying, he wasn't, or shall I say isn't, quite right in the head. Wouldn't you agree?"

Maria looked at Jack and remembered how quickly his temper flared out of control so many times. The first time she'd witnessed his anger was on their wedding night when he became upset at the hotel's front desk clerk for giving them the wrong room key. He had scared the guy so badly Maria wanted to leave for fear he'd call the cops, but then Jack threatened her as well. He didn't hit her *that* night, but came very close. It was the first of many times she'd asked herself the question, *'What is wrong with him?'* But even *that* man— the man she left lying on the kitchen floor seven and a half years ago—was nothing compared to the monstrosity that stood before her now. Evil exuded from him, and his eyes—she couldn't bear to look at them. This wasn't Jack Sanchez.

"Yes," was all she could say, facing Roberto again.

"The fact that he was so ill as an infant may have something to do with it," he continued with an air of authority. "And the drugs certainly didn't help. He was perfect for our new project. With the help of my friend," Roberto gestured toward Nicholas, "we created a finely tuned machine, controlled by drugs and several types of, *uh*, let's just say psychological therapy."

"You mean you've brainwashed him," Maria said, glancing back at the man who was once her husband. He was empty, hollowed out, with no real mind to speak of. She looked away, feeling tears sting her eyes.

"You catch on fast, sweet Maria. He remembers nothing of his life prior to being J.R, .and probably not much of that."

"How can you do that to another human being?" Maria asked.

"It was the only way to control him." It was the first time Nicholas Freyhoff spoke without being directly spoken to since they'd arrived. "We had to find some way to control him. He is dangerous, psychotic, and smart enough to elude even the most intelligent of us, right?" Nicholas asked, looking at Roberto.

"Yes, well, the game's almost over, isn't it?" Roberto Santini narrowed his eyes at Maria. "The name of the game is control. We created J.R. and used him to produce some of the finest kiddy porn on the black market. But, except for once, he was never *instructed* to kill his victims," he stated with sincerity. "That was always done without our knowledge."

"Oh, and that makes everything all right? Because you turned your back for a moment to give him his thrill, your hands are clean?" Maria asked, disgusted at his disregard for life.

Roberto continued as if she hadn't spoken. He would

make her beg on her knees later. "Jack's new alias was comprised of the letters of our names," he said, finding himself incredibly amusing. "'J.R.' being my first two initials—R.J—switched around. My middle name is Jonathan if you haven't yet guessed. 'FR' are the first two letters of Nicholas's last name, 'AN' are the second two letters of Jack's—and your—last name." He smiled at Maria. "And 'CO' was the initials of the woman I was fucking at the time. What was her name again?" he questioned his friend.

"Cynthia Olson," Nicholas Freyhoff replied without pause.

"Ah, yes, what a beauty she was—tall, blonde and willing to spread her legs at the drop of a hat. Unfortunately, she's now dead, but that's another story.

"And as for his altered appearance? Well, drugs and time took its toll on our friend, but black hair dye and green contact lenses helped as well. Now, have I satisfied your curiosity?"

Maria's head was reeling. Satisfy her curiosity? Not by a long shot, but he wouldn't be willing to talk all night. He was impatient, antsy. She didn't like the way he looked at her—it was a feral, hungry look. "What about Martha Franco?"

"Who?"

"Martha Franco, the woman who lives next-door."

"Never heard of her." He chuckled. "Coincidence. Fate plays its hand in the strangest way."

"Where do *we* fit into all this?" Maria asked, interrupting his daydream.

Roberto threw back his head and laughed that same maniacal laughter as before—it bounced off the walls in the small bedroom giving it an echo effect, which made it even more disturbing. "That's the best part. Again, a simple twist of fate, as my late, great father Antonio Santini would say.

"You fucked me over in my office, sweetheart. You

purposely deceived me, insulted me, threatened me. I simply won't tolerate that—not from anyone," he said with a penetrating gaze that made her blood run cold. "Then when I had you checked out I could hardly believe my luck. Maria Sanchez—brilliant, upstanding homicide detective, and most important, widow of the deceased Jack, our beloved J.R.! I decided then to make you pay with your daughter, knowing nothing on this earth would hurt you more, right? You with your morals and values. And you look like *her.*"

"Who? Theresa?" Maria asked, uncomfortable at the way he looked at her—more like devoured her with his eyes.

"No, no. My father's mistress. I was a small boy, but I vividly remember her dark flashing eyes and…her skin…." He stroked Maria's arm, then her long slender neck. "Enough talk. Do you want to see your daughter live another hour? Do you?" he demanded, grabbing the hair at the nape of her neck and jerking her head back.

"Y-yes, please don't hurt her. Don't hurt my baby," Maria whispered.

"Cooperate with me and she'll live…for now. It's the best I can offer you, sweet Maria. Now, let me taste your sweetness," he said, lowering his lips onto hers and thrusting his tongue deep into her mouth.

Maria struggled to get away, but his grip held her tight. *Was he going to rape her right here, in front of her own daughter?* It appeared that was exactly what he had planned. He was much stronger than he looked and the more she struggled the more it amused him. His grip grew tighter—his hands steel bands around her arms, cutting off her circulation until her own hands felt tingly.

"Don't fight me, sweet Maria. I know you want it as much as I do," he whispered in her ear, crushing her to his chest, one hand groping a breast under her shirt. He unzipped his pants.

363

61

A low rumble started from the other side of the small bedroom. It sounded animal-like and moved across the room lightning quick, knife out, ready to disembowel one of *them*. Thoughts were on nothing but death and the final demise of *his creators*. Nothing else mattered. Not the girl, not the woman, only *them*.

The knife glistened in the pale bedroom light as it made its arc of descent, but never reached its target.

J.R. went down hard and lay dead at Maria's feet, shot between the eyes, blood slowly seeping from the single bullet hole. The smoking gun, which Nicholas Freyhoff held, had a silencer attached. All that was heard before the bad man went down was a soft *pop*. Tess was still looking at the floor, oblivious to what had just happened.

Nicholas checked J.R.'s pulse. "Dead," he pronounced.

"Goddamnit! Why did you kill him? You could've just wounded him," Roberto Santini responded angrily.

Nicholas could hardly believe his hearing. "What?"

Roberto just looked at him, already planning to have him eliminated once they got back to Los Angeles.

"I just saved your life," Nicholas retorted, his anger escalating to the boiling point.

"All that work for nothing."

Nicholas raised the gun, and pointing it directly at

Roberto's chest, he fired three times in rapid succession—*pop, pop, pop.*

Roberto Santini crumpled to the floor. The look of surprise that was plastered on his face would be fixed into place for eternity.

Now two dead bodies lay at her feet. Maria looked at the man who now held all the cards. Nicholas Freyhoff's smooth, blonde good looks were starting to look a little strained. "Please, just let us go," she said, bargaining for their lives. "I'll give you a chance to get out of the country, I promise."

Nicholas shook his head, reluctant to believe her, knowing she would say or do anything at this point. He'd seen it so many times in his history with the mob he stopped counting. Besides, it wasn't an option he would even consider.

"No one will know you were even here. They'll find two bodies and won't question it any further. They will think Roberto and J.R. were involved. The police will never catch you. I can—"

"You can do nothing for me. N*othing*." He smoothed the front of his expensive suit jacket and looked at her uncomfortably. "I'm sorry, truly I am but there's no other way. You can't live."

"Okay, okay, I can understand that." Maria realized she was shit out of luck, but maybe she could still save her child. "I can't live, but Tess, she's so innocent in all of this. Look at her. She's in shock; she won't remember anything. At least let her go. *Please,"* Maria begged.

Nicholas Freyhoff looked over at the little girl—her eyes stared vacantly into space—the woman was right—harmless. He met Maria's terrified gaze. "Okay," he finally said, raising his gun. "I'll let Theresa live. I promise."

Maria looked at her daughter one last time. Theresa was

still huddled on the floor, her eyes transfixed to a spot behind Maria. "I love you," she whispered to her only child, closing her eyes tightly as Nicholas Freyhoff leveled the gun at her chest.

A single shot rang out.

Joe stood at the bedroom doorway, dwarfing the small room even further. "Drop it," he demanded, after firing a warning shot into the air.

Nicholas turned, aimed and fired several times in rapid succession, then fell to the ground.

Joe went down too, but not before putting two rounds into the chest of Nicholas Freyhoff. He was hurt, bleeding from his good arm.

"You've been hit," Maria said, checking on Tess then running to Joe.

Sirens sounded.

"Just grazed the skin," he mumbled, checking it out. "Good job of staying put, Tess." He looked at Maria and smiled. "She saw me coming and had the guts not to make a move when I motioned her to sit still. One helluva kid."

"I know." Maria wrapped a blanket she found around her daughter, then enveloped her in a huge hug. "You okay, baby?" she asked, gently rubbing her back and leading her to the bed. "Did he hurt you before—before we got here?"

Tess looked at her mother and knew what she meant. "No, he threatened me, but he—he was just going to k-k-kill me instead," she stammered, touching her neck where his hands had left purple marks as her eyes welled up with tears.

"It's okay, baby. Everything's okay now, *shh*, it's over, *shh*," Maria said, rocking back and forth, holding her sobbing child, much like she did on that fateful day so many years ago.

She looked around at the dead bodies scattered here and there—Jack, Roberto and Nicholas—and wondered once again how she could have been so naive to get involved with Jack in the first place. *Stop blaming yourself. It's finally really over,* she told herself.

Maria and Tess sat on the bed while Joe went downstairs to meet the police officers.

Joe had radioed for backup before he entered the boarding house this evening—when he put all the pieces of the puzzle together. Everything clicked into place when he pulled up outside of Martha Franco's. The boarding house held all the pieces—the small black sports car Maria had spotted in the garage the first time they came here, and the broken basement window they had learned about in the transcripts at the doctor's office that day. Santini had parked his car on the opposite side of the street, so Joe hadn't noticed it.

Chief Frank McCollough and Peter Slade showed up five minutes after the initial officers on the scene, with two of the BCA's best forensic technicians in tow. Shortly after, BCA agents Bill Foley and Cal Jensen arrived, along with Dr. Kenneth Lang, the M.E.

The chief sat on the chair next to the bed. "So tell me, Sanchez, how did you end up here in the first place?"

"You probably wouldn't believe me if I told you." Maria took Joe's hand as he joined her on the edge of the bed. Tess held one hand while Joe held the other. She had the two people that mattered most in the world on either side of her and she felt complete—and thankful—for the first time in what seemed like an eternity.

"Try me," the chief said, crossing his arms across his chest.

Maria explained everything in detail, beginning with her

car not starting and the dead battery in her cell phone, to her following the mysterious moon. Gaining momentum as she spoke, Maria left nothing unsaid, describing how she walked the same dark path along the warehouse district that she hoped Betsy had come that night only in reverse. And how she came upon Martha Franco's—not remembering at first who lived on Chestnut, but finally realizing after seeing the '*Home, Sweet Home*' tattered wood sign—and went in to use her phone only to be sent next-door to the boarding house. "I can't tell you what made me go back inside after I had decided to leave. It was the moon and the disquieting glimpse of a man's shadow at the upstairs window the exact moment its glowing orb reappeared. The feelings that came over me—it was as if I was no longer in control of myself. I was on a mission. I *knew* it was Jack, but yet I *didn't*. I mean, how could I?" she questioned, squeezing Joe's hand.

Joe kissed her forehead, not caring what the chief thought about their relationship at this point.

Tess spoke, her voice wavering slightly. "Right before Mom came into the room I had been hiding under the bed, with a needle full of *something* that I had gotten off the night-stand. When he came at me I—I stabbed him and pushed the plunger-thing, then I screamed and screamed."

"A real fighter, huh?" the chief said, smiling at both mother and daughter.

Maria just looked at Tess. *What an amazing, brave kid I have. A true fighter, just like her mother,* she thought with pride.

Taking a deep breath, Maria told them about *the project*, how Jack was *helped* with his death more than seven years ago, and the brainwashing and drugs that soon followed. She related almost word for word everything Roberto had said and done, taking her time so as not to forget any of the details. She felt Joe tense next to her when she told of Santini's sexual advances and impending rape. And finally, Nicholas Freyhoff saving Roberto's life, only to take it away minutes later. "And then my partner came to the rescue. I wouldn't be sitting here with my precious daughter next to me if it wasn't for Joe," she said, putting her head on his shoulder.

"Well, I don't know what to say. I mean, you went well beyond the call of duty—both of you. You caught the son of a—Sorry," the chief said, glancing at Tess, uncomfortable.

"No, go ahead and say it. It was a long time ago that he was my husband, and it's a long story. Sometime I'll tell you all about it, or Joe can." She looked at the man she loved. "Some things you never forget. A lot of abuse took place." Maria said haltingly. "It was a terrible thing they did to him, though. They destroyed him—he was insane, unlike anyone I have ever seen in my life, and I've seen some real wackos, believe me. In summary, Chief, his death was the best thing that could have happened—both then and now," Maria stated with a resigned sigh.

"I think I understand." Chief Frank McCollough leaned forward in his chair. "I'm glad it's over, for all of us. Good job," he said, shaking their hands.

Peter Slade came over and got down on one knee so he was eye level with Tess. "How ya doin', slugger?"

Tess shrugged her shoulders and smiled slightly, moving even closer to Maria. "I'm okay," she said softly.

"I'm glad," Peter said, smiling. "Everything's going to be all right now. I promise, sweetheart."

Tess nodded and turned away, burying her face in Maria's armpit.

Maria smoothed her daughter's long braid and whispered

words of encouragement. Cal Jensen gave her a thumbs up from across the room, but had the good sense not to come over with Agent Foley at his side. Maria appreciated his thoughtfulness and smiled.

A forensic technician walked over to the chief, talking in hushed tones, but still loud enough for Maria to hear—Rico Smits was in the linen closet, dead, apparently with a missing tongue. The body count was now up to four.

"Are we done here? I'd like to take these guys home," Joe said, glaring at the technician and glancing at Tess every so often to make sure she was all right.

"Yeah, go ahead. I can answer any questions they may have," the chief said, nodding toward the technicians, BCA agents and the medical examiner that were all busy processing the crime scene. "Get some rest. In fact, take a couple of days off. You both deserve it."

Maria had Dr. Lang check over Theresa before leaving, wanting to be certain there would be no residual effects from the sedative that had been injected into her system and the attempted strangulation. The doctor assured her everything was fine—the girl's pupils were back to normal, and the bruises on her neck would fade in time with no apparent internal damage to report.

"Man, what a night," Joe said, watching Maria cover her daughter with a quilt on the sofa bed. Tess didn't want to sleep alone in her bed, so had asked Maria to fix up the sofa for the two of them. Joe lost his bed, but he gladly gave it up. He would sleep on the floor right below Tess and her mother, so they could all be together. Maria had already brought out a sleeping bag.

"That's an understatement if I ever heard one. We

definitely earned our paycheck today." She brushed a strand of dark, glossy hair from Tess's face. "She's already asleep; didn't even finish her hot chocolate. I hope—never mind."

"She'll be okay," Joe said, reading her thoughts, which he'd learned to do so well lately.

"God, I hope so. This is pretty heavy stuff, a lot for a nine-year-old kid to have to deal with," she said, joining him on the floor.

"Almost ten," Joe corrected, just like Tess always did.

Maria laughed. "Yeah, yeah, almost ten." Her face turned serious again. "I called Dr. Jorgenson earlier, told her everything. She's stopping by first thing in the morning."

"Good. Don't worry. Together we'll make everything all right. We're certainly familiar enough with the proper channels to go through. She'll get only the best of care. We'll see to that."

"I know. You better have that arm looked at, too."

"What, this?" he said, holding up his good arm. "It's nothing, believe me. I'll just put a Band-Aid on it."

"A Band-Aid?" Maria asked, incredulously. "You're serious."

"Very," Joe replied, smiling.

"*I'll* put it on," Maria said, getting up and grabbing the peroxide, sterile pads, adhesive tape, and antibiotic ointment from a kitchen cupboard and returning within about sixty seconds.

"Man, you're fast," Joe said, watching the fizzing bubbles as she poured the peroxide on his arm. Their eyes locked. "I love you, Sanchez."

"I love you, too, Morgan," Maria said, her voice cracking with emotion. "And before I forget, thanks for saving our lives."

"I just wish I could have gotten there sooner," he said, touching the fresh cut on her face. "And I really hate the fact that Santini touched you."

"It could have been much worse. He would have raped me, Joe," Maria said, looking at him earnestly. "I have no doubt about that. But Jack—Jack saved me in a sense. I don't think it was a conscious effort on his part—he just wanted Santini dead. The look in his eyes when he charged—for a minute I thought he was going after me." She shuddered, involuntarily.

Joe wrapped his arm around her, pulling her close. "It's over now, darlin'. No more ghosts to chase. It's just you, me and the kid, together, forever. I don't ever want to lose you," he whispered, kissing her forehead.

"Together." Maria gazed at Tess, lightly snoring; a deep frown wrinkled her otherwise smooth brow. Mr. Peanut lay sprawled on the girl's legs, the tip of his tan tail moving contentedly. "Forever," she whispered, wrapping her arms around Joe and burying her face in his neck, letting go of all the past pain and heartache. She felt hot tears travel slowly down her face, charting a new course in her life. With the tears, there seemed to be a cleansing of sorts—both body and soul—and a certain feeling of ease seemed to settle in. Gone was the tight band across her chest that threatened to suffocate; replacing it was a feeling of contentment unlike any she'd ever known before.

Maria was finally at peace with the world. No nightmares would haunt her sleep tonight.

EPILOGUE

Stephen Freyhoff retrieved the contents from the safety deposit box after learning of his only brother's demise. There was so much information to absorb it was unfathomable—Nicholas had spent his entire adult life working for Roberto Santini and every unsavory deal that went down was recorded.

The ball was now in his court...and the sky was the limit. He had enough knowledge to take over *the business*. And who could stop him? The top dogs were all gone—stiff with rigor mortis and no doubt waiting at the gates of hell for a trip to eternal damnation.

Finally, it's my turn. Stephen Freyhoff will soon be a force to reckon with, he thought, smiling, looking remarkably like his big brother.

FBI agent Peter Slade was already back in Washington, DC, but had sent a birthday present for Tess. He already told Maria what it was—baseball cards. But not just any baseball cards... These cards included every player on the team the last time the Twins won the World Series in 1991—and also this year's players.

Carlos was driving to Minneapolis from Chicago and wouldn't be here until late tonight, but had promised he'd make up for missing the party. He had a big surprise for Tess—her own personal computer.

Maria looked around at the small group gathered at the kitchen table, and thought, *What a beautiful family.* After working this last case, even the simplest things seemed to bring her joy—she would never take anything for granted again.

The Minneapolis Police Department had linked J.R. Franco to at least eleven other murders in different states over the last two and a half years—the pornographic videos found were evidence of that. It was anyone's guess how many more he committed. The fact that he was previously Jack Sanchez—Maria's dead husband—thankfully didn't come out in the press. The chief had managed to keep that little tidbit under wraps—for the time being, anyway. Upon searching the boarding house, rolls of threadbare blue carpeting, along with old shipping crates, were discovered in the basement; and many different drugs and weapons were confiscated in J.R.'s apartment, in addition to a large Mason jar containing various body parts. The results from the DNA test on the hair found among the carpet fibers were conclusive as well.

But all that is in the past, thank God. Maria leaned over the table and lit all the candles on the birthday cake.

"Happy Birthday to you. Happy Birthday to you. Happy Birthday, Dear Theresa. Happy Birthday to you," everybody sang.

Tess looked at her mother, grinning. She closed her eyes and made a wish, blowing out all ten candles on the huge chocolate cake to the sound of applause.

"I wonder what she wished for?" Joe said, winking at Tony.

Tony Franco looked at Maria and grinned. He'd only been living with them for one week, but had already won all their hearts, especially Tess's. He would be adopted after the wedding, which would be held in two weeks—a semi-private ceremony with only immediate family and a few close friends. Joe planned to adopt Tess at that same time, too. They would all be Morgans by the time the leaves turned to fall colors.

"What did you wish for, honey?" Maria asked, giving her daughter a giant birthday hug.

"Oh, Mom. I love you, but I can't tell you what I wished for, 'cause if I do it won't come true." She gave her mother an award-winning ten-year-old grin. "But just know it wasn't for any material possession."

Maria had to smile at her grown-up choice of words. Almost a month had gone by since her abduction, and with therapy they were *both* learning to accept what had happened and move on. "Okay, then I'll just take this back," Maria said, removing the biggest present from the pile.

Tess laughed.

It sounded so good to hear her laugh; it made everyone else smile.

"Don't you dare!" Tess said. "Maybe I should open my presents now before they start disappearing...."

"Go ahead, sweetie. They're all yours," Maria said, piling them in front of her.

"All except for one," Tess said, running into the living room and fishing out a large, gaily wrapped present from behind the sofa. She returned to the kitchen table, setting it in front of Tony with a big grin.

His large green eyes got even bigger. "Wow, for me? How come? It's not my birthday," he said, so excited he could hardly stand it.

"Well, let's just say it's a welcome-to-the-family present. Go ahead, open it."

The little boy tore into his present after carefully removing the grape Tootsie-pop that was taped to the outside and setting it on the table. He pulled out a large brown bear with a plaid bow tie and gentle golden eyes. Hugging it tightly, he closed his eyes and smiled. "Thanks, sister," he said, running to Tess and throwing his arms around her neck.

"You're welcome, little brother," she said returning his hug, patting his back like Maria always did when Tess was younger.

Maria had to fight back tears at the gesture. Her emotions were running high today anyway, and this was going to put her right over the edge. Tess must have spent most of her allowance for the bear.

"You could name him Barry Bear—spelled 'Ba' or 'Be'— or Larry Bear, or Gary Bear or whatever you want," Tess said to her half brother.

"I like Barry Bear. Kinda like your Mary Bear, right?" The little boy held the big bear up in the air. "Hi, Barry Bear," he sang with delight.

Tess grinned. "Now that's the best birthday present I could get," she said, watching Tony make the bear do an air-dance.

"Your turn," Maria said, pushing the biggest box in front of her.

"*Hmm*, I wonder what this could be?" Tess asked, turning the box around and around, already hopeful of the contents. She tore into it and flung off the top of the boot box. "*Ahh*! My boots, thanks," she said with somewhat mixed emotions.

"Check in the toe of the top boot," Maria said, looking at Joe and grinning.

Tess laughed and reached her hand deep into the toe, pulling out a long gold chain with a carved gold heart locket dangling on the end. "Ohh, it's beautiful." She opened the small golden heart to reveal a picture of her mom on one side and Joe, her dad, on the other. Tears sprang to her eyes as she looked at each of them. "Thanks," she whispered.

Maria hugged her, then Joe, and soon Tony joined in. They cried, laughed, and sang happy birthday one more time, celebrating more than just Theresa's birthday. It was really all of their birthdays—the start of a new and wonderful life together.

The End

Meet the Author

C. Hyytinen grew up in La Crosse, Wisconsin. She currently resides in rural Minnesota where she's busy working on her second novel, in addition to planning a sequel to *Pattern of Violence*.

Visit her website at
www.chyytinen.com

or send an e-mail to
author@chyytinen.com

Kfir Luzzatto

Crossing the Meadow

A strange nightmare, a young woman in a foggy city and a body buried underneath a bathtub, all converge to force an ordinary man to investigate a dark, long forgotten past.

A little girl who can see her dead cat, an old blind woman and a beautiful girl who died too young, unknowingly play a role in a game in which humanity must survive the death of the flesh.

They don't know what awaits them beyond that meadow, but they are determined to find out...

CROSSING THE MEADOW guides you into the twilight zone where dead people brush silently past the living ones and, often without noticing, affect their fate.

Warning: Your perception of the space around you will never again be the same!

ISBN 1-59080-283-7

To order, visit our web catalog at
http://www.echelonpress.com/catalog/

Or ask your local bookseller!

SO YOUR MUSE HAS GONE AWOL?

Pamela Johnson and Lori Soard

"A must for every writer—new or established. Creativity has never been so much fun!"
--Alexis Hart, author of *Dark Shines my Love*

Like it or not, the muse has a will of her own at times. Usually when you least expect it, she takes off for a quick manicure or a lunch date with some Greek hunk--and what are you, the writer, supposed to do in the meantime?

Here is your guide to moments when your muse takes an unexpected vacation, and you find yourself alone at the wheel. No need to file a missing muse report, these tips from some of the industry's "well-traveled" authors will get you (and your muse) back on the road to writing success!

ISBN 1-59080-336-1

To order, visit our web catalog at
http://www.echelonpress.com/catalog/

Or ask your local bookseller!

JUDITH F. BULLOCK
BURY ME IN SOMEONE ELSE'S PAJAMAS
Reclaiming Creativity

In order to take back your own imagination, you must develop a relationship with your many creative selves, embrace the solitary nature of the creative life and learn to laugh again. Ours is a society that often gives second place to the very best part of you-- imagination--leaving you silenced and stultified.

Now there is a guerilla guide to taking back the creative life, showing through a series of stories that nothing can stand in your way; not people, not tragedy, not death itself.

This cosmic comedic experience with a philosopher's heart explores the relationship between creativity and love, teaches you to look at time in a fresh new way, and examines perception, identity, worm racing, and the wisdom of the foolish heart.

ISBN 1-59080-133-4

T.A. RIDGELL
WHEN
Opportunity
KNOCKS

Special Agent Joe Franconi wants only to avenge his father's death. He's poured all his energy into building a case against the mob boss responsible for leaving his mother a widow.

Megan O'Riley, knocking on doors in hopes of finally making a sale, unwittingly enters a reputed betting house and is mistakenly identified as a runner and prostitute by Joe. His mission--become her client, infiltrate the mob, and bring his father's killer to justice.

Once secure in his abilities, Joe's well-structured world is turned upside down when Megan comes crashing through the door. Will Joe sacrifice his assignment to keep the woman of his dreams or will the door slam in his face?

ISBN 1-59080-293-4

To order, visit our web catalog at
http://www.echelonpress.com/catalog/

Or ask your local bookseller!

CRUMBS IN THE KEYBOARD

Stories From Courageous Women Who Juggle Life & Writing

"This is wonderful!"
--Fern Michaels, New York Times best selling author

Eighty authors come together with words of wisdom, encouragement, humor, and true-life stories of what it is like to juggle the demands of a career and maintaining relationships with those around them. Each author is donating 100% of her royalties from the sale of Crumbs to The Center for Women and Families in Louisville, Kentucky. Echelon Press is matching those monies dollar for dollar. By purchasing Crumbs, you will help in the fight against domestic violence.

ISBN 1-59080-096-6

To order, visit our web catalog at
http://www.echelonpress.com/catalog/

Or ask your local bookseller!

Printed in the United States
58683LVS00001B/13-33